Books by Carla Laureano

MacDonald Family Trilogy
Five Days in Skye
London Tides
Under Scottish Stars

Supper Club Series
The Saturday Night Supper Club
Brunch at Bittersweet Cafe
The Solid Grounds Coffee Company

Discovered by Love Series
Jilted (novella)
Starstruck (novella)
Snowbound (novella)
Sunswept (novella)

Provenance

The Song of Seare Trilogy
Oath of the Brotherhood
Beneath the Forsaken City
The Sword and the Song

THE COMPLETE NOVELLA SERIES

DISCOVERED BY LOVE

CARLA LAUREANO

LAUREANO
CREATIVE MEDIA

Jilted

A Discovered by Love Novella

one

"Bridezilla! Incoming!"

The hissed words made Bethany Hall look up from her *mise en place* in alarm as her sous chef strode through the swinging kitchen door. Her wide-eyed expression told Bethany all she needed to know. Mariska never broke a sweat even through the most demanding event, and now her expression looked downright harried.

Bethany set down her knife and whisked off her apron. "ETA?"

"Three minutes, maybe less. Eduardo overheard her talking as she left the bungalow."

"God bless him," Bethany muttered. There were some advantages to having a staff of twelve on an eight-acre private island that served no more than twenty guests at a time. No one could sneeze without the concierge knowing about it and arriving twenty seconds later with a box of tissues. She hurriedly unbuttoned the placket of her double-breasted chef's jacket and fastened it up the opposite direction to cover the smear on its front. With a four-thousand-dollar-a-night price tag, guests didn't want to see any evidence of the work that went into their stay.

Bethany had just washed her hands and was tucking a stray lock of red hair back beneath her bandanna when the door swung open again, delivering a willowy, exotic-looking brunette into her kitchen. Dressed in a skimpy sundress and four-inch espadrilles with a full flawless face of makeup, the woman couldn't have looked more out of place had she tried.

"Ms. Elliston." Bethany put on the required pleasant smile. "What a lovely surprise! What can I help you with this afternoon?"

Anna Elliston held up a piece of pearlized cardstock. "This is a disaster! Look at this. Nothing but seafood, the whole thing."

"Yes," Bethany said slowly, her smile wavering. "Traditional with a Belizean twist, just as you requested. This was finalized months ago."

"But my new father-in-law is allergic!" With a furious scowl, the woman waved the card in Bethany's face again. "Do you expect my fiancé's father to eat *salad* at our wedding? And what about cross-contamination? He could go into … shock or something."

Bethany repressed the urge to explain the difference between shock and an anaphylactic reaction, even though her smile had frozen into something closer to a grimace throughout the tirade. Possible responses ran through her head.

You should have thought of this before I brought in a hundred pounds of spiny lobster and six dozen conch.

This is why we clearly state in the contract that all menu changes must be approved by the chef a minimum of two weeks before the event.

Your father-in-law's allergies are not my problem.

No, that one definitely couldn't leave her lips, not if she wanted to keep her job. She decided to try reason.

"Ms. Elliston … Anna … I understand that you're upset. But I can assure you that we have plenty of experience with food safety. I can easily make another dish for your father-in-law that will in no way be contaminated by seafood."

"That would be very much appreciated."

Bethany jerked her eyes away from the bride at the new voice in the conversation, and instantly every coherent thought fled, taking with it a good part of her righteous indignation.

A dark-haired man strode forward from where he'd been standing in the doorway and extended his hand. "Sorry, I guess I should introduce myself. I'm Derek Moretti."

"Uh … Bethany Hall. Your …"

"Chef, right. I figured that, whites and all." He favored her with a brilliant smile, which made it even more difficult to think, especially while his fingers were still wrapped around her hand.

When he finally released her, she managed to suck in a breath and a little bit of her gray matter decided to start working again. Unfortunately, it only seemed interested in processing the details: tall and handsome, light brown hair tousled by the salt breeze, green eyes that she could swear had been enhanced by some kind of real-life Photoshop. The whole package looked straight out of a magazine actually, from the tanned skin to the blinding smile and artfully mussed linen shirt hanging untucked over khaki shorts. She'd run into a lot of grooms on the island, but never had one looked quite so at home in his surroundings.

Groom. As in, getting married. To Bridezilla here.

The words pierced through the stupid fog that had overtaken Bethany's brain. Fortunately, a quick look around told her that her silence hadn't stretched for as long as it had seemed, and the only drooling she'd been doing had been mental. Thank God. She cleared her throat. "I can assure you that the utmost care will be taken with your father's meal, to be sure there are no adverse effects."

"I'm sure it will." Derek looked at his bride, who was still wearing a petulant expression, and lifted her hand to his lips. "Anna, sweetheart, why don't you go back to the bungalow? I don't want you to worry about this. After all, you're going to be walking down the aisle in four hours."

Anna softened a degree and stretched up on tiptoes to press a kiss to his lips. But Bethany distinctly heard her whisper, "Don't you dare wimp out on this one, Derek."

He smiled but as soon as Bridezilla huffed off from the kitchen, his eyes lifted upward as if praying for strength. Then he looked back to Bethany with a wry smile. "I'm sorry about that. Anna usually isn't this high strung, but she's been pretty stressed out about the wedding."

"I understand. Weddings are a big deal. We're here to make sure everything is perfect for your special day." It was practically verbatim from the brochure, and a few minutes ago, Bethany would have choked on the words. But at this moment, lost in those mesmerizing emerald eyes, they spilled out with ease.

"I appreciate that," Derek said. "But you should probably know that my father isn't allergic to shellfish."

"Excuse me?"

He sighed and ran a hand through his hair.

She followed the movement without conscious intent, then gave herself a stern mental shake.

"No. He simply said that he no longer ate animal products because they weren't good for him. An idea that I'm pretty sure came from his new girlfriend, who is a twenty-nine-year-old vegan supermodel."

"Ah." Bethany pressed down the laugh that threatened to bubble out. "I understand. Trust me, I've seen stranger things in my time here. I'm sure I can come up with something that is authentically Belizean, but will not offend his … newfound sensibilities."

"I really appreciate that, Chef Hall." Derek smiled at her, and once more the blinding warmth of the expression pushed out every last sensible thought. "I promise, we'll attempt not to be one of those wedding parties that you complain about over cocktails. At least from here on out."

A chuckle rose up in her. "Thanks. I appreciate that. Though of course, you might have cost me my free sympathy drinks."

He grinned. "A small price to pay, I'd think." He looked to Mariska and gave her a friendly nod, then offered the same to Bethany before retreating the way he had come.

The door had no sooner swung shut behind him than Mariska stepped in front of her. "What the heck was that?"

"What was what?" Bethany reached for her apron and wrapped the strings around her waist before tying them off in a tight bow.

"You were flirting!"

"I was not! He's a married man. Or will be in four hours. I was just being friendly."

"'You might have cost me my free sympathy drinks,'" Mariska mimicked in a singsong voice. "I never thought I'd ever see you, of all people, lose your mind over a guy."

"Oh, please. You know me better than that." Bethany went back to her chopping, then set her knife down just as quickly. "What should I do for the father of the groom? Vegan?"

"Don't worry about it. I've got it. I used to cook for one of those yoga retreats on Caye Caulker. I've got some go-to dishes that look much fancier than they are. Besides, I wouldn't want cooking to get in the way of your daydreaming."

Bethany rolled her eyes, even though Mariska's teasing had started a flush that she prayed was covered by the high collar of her jacket. She had been tongue-tied, no way of explaining it otherwise. Over a guest. It was the cardinal rule of hospitality, especially at a high-end retreat like Halcyon Caye. Be friendly, but invisible. And under no circumstances flirt with or even have any improper thoughts about a guest, let alone a member of a wedding party. Years ago, a personal concierge had been caught making out with a drunk bridesmaid, and now he was barred from ever working at any resort within the Destinations family. Considering that the corporation owned not only this private island but over three hundred luxury resorts and retreats worldwide, that took a pretty sharp chunk out of potential employment opportunities.

Funny how Halcyon Caye had felt like a last resort when she'd been fleeing personal humiliation in Florida three years ago, and now she would do almost anything to stay. She straightened her spine and vowed she would behave with strict professionalism from here on out. She already knew what happened when you mixed business and pleasure.

Mariska stayed silent for several moments, then shot Bethany a mischievous look. "You have to admit, though, he's pretty hot."

Bethany grinned. "Like the surface of the sun."

"If you like the tall, dark, rich, and handsome thing. What do you think? I'm voting actor."

Bethany shook her head. "I don't think so. Not quite arrogant enough. I say finance. Or real estate. He's got money. You can tell by the watch."

"It's uncanny how you do that. I guess when your dad's a jeweler, though, you notice things like that."

"Well, I noticed the fact that Derek seems much too nice to be marrying that woman. Despite the fact that he tried to cover for her. Can you believe she practically called him a wimp?"

"I don't understand why the nice, good-looking ones always go for the straight-up b—"

A throat cleared behind them and Bethany spun, the blood draining from her face as she found herself looking into a pair of very familiar green eyes. "Der—um, Mr. Moretti. What can I do for you?"

He seemed to be struggling to keep a straight face, but whether out of amusement or anger, she couldn't tell. Her stomach dropped even further and settled somewhere around her knees. This time it wasn't because of the sheer force of those good looks.

"I know this probably goes without saying, but we'll be needing two vegan meals. One for my father and one for his girlfriend. I just wanted to make sure …"

"Of course. Yes. I'm assuming you'd like vegan options for the duration of their stay?"

He nodded slowly, then stepped back. "That would be perfect. Thanks. And … I'm sorry again."

"No, not at all. It's our pleasure." Bethany maintained her smile until he left the kitchen, and then let it slide with a deep groan. If he complained to management about their loose lips, it was all over. Getting fired from a Destinations resort meant she'd be blackballed from the best restaurants in Belize, as well as their entire resort network. She wasn't going back to Miami, no matter what.

Suddenly, she wished that hotter-than-the-sun Derek Moretti had never appeared in her kitchen.

two

DEREK WALKED SLOWLY from the Grand Palapa where the island kitchen was located, feeling strangely subdued. It was natural to have jitters just hours before your wedding, wasn't it? After all, his older brother, George, had been needling him about cold feet since they'd arrived on the island this morning. Said Derek had used work as an excuse to delay his arrival until hours before he was supposed to tie the knot so he wouldn't chicken out.

That wasn't it, though. Derek wasn't a quitter, and he certainly wasn't going to leave Anna at the altar because of a few jitters. He'd known her nearly his entire life. Some part of him had probably believed they were destined to be together since the time she'd been nothing more than his awkward next-door neighbor. Sure, they'd both grown up and changed immensely, particularly her—because who would have known that the girl with glasses and braces and knobby knees would end up as the new face of Ralph Lauren?—but they had a shared history together that no second thoughts could replace.

And yet the way she'd torn into the island's chef over something she knew was patently untrue made him wonder if there were things about Anna he still didn't know.

Derek rejoined the weathered wooden boardwalk that wound back through the sand and over a bridge to the one-bedroom bungalow that would be their honeymoon suite. He scarcely noticed the turquoise waters lapping the shore just feet away or the steady salt breeze that ruffled his hair and clothes. He'd talked Anna out of her dreams of an immense wedding in their hometown of Los Angeles, which considering who their parents were, would have inevitably turned into a circus of epic proportions. Instead, he'd lured her to Belize with the promise of island sunshine and blue waters and uninterrupted romance. Surely that was the reason for her sudden fit of high-handedness. The only details she'd gotten to fret over were her wedding dress and bouquet.

He just couldn't forget the way Chef Hall had swallowed down her very obvious annoyance to placate Anna … and the clear fear in her eyes when he'd walked in on them talking about Anna's behavior. Derek might have once been ruthless when it came to business, but he knew better than to treat staff as second-class citizens just because he could drop thirty grand on a private island for the week.

He strolled through the open doors of the bungalow, where Anna was reclining in a chair, two manicurists hard at work on her fingers and toes.

"Did you take care of it?"

Derek paused by her side and bent to press a kiss to her lips. "I did. She will have a vegan meal for both Dad and Eliza at the wedding and will provide non-meat options for the duration of our stay."

Anna stared at him. "That's not what I asked. I want the menu changed."

"Anna, sweetheart, we're in Belize. Seafood is just food here. And besides, the reception is in five-and-a-half hours. It's not like they can just run to the supermarket."

"For the price we're paying, you'd think we could have what we want."

Derek pulled up a stool and settled beside her. "We agreed on the menu months ago. Why the sudden change of heart?" He narrowed his eyes. "Is this because of Eliza?"

Anna didn't look at him, which was the same as a confirmation. "It just seems tacky to serve food that would offend your father. And it's not at all environmentally responsible."

Derek closed his eyes and prayed for patience. It was bad enough that his dad had to be dating someone younger than his own son; even worse that he'd met her at one of Anna's runway shows and fell instantly, madly "in love." Somehow, the fact that the great Dante Moretti was involved with Eliza had given her more influence than she'd had when she was merely Anna's friend.

"This is my wedding too, and I like seafood. So considering it's too late to do anything about it, we are going to eat it and we are going to enjoy it, regardless of how environmentally unfriendly it might be. Eliza and Dad can have their rabbit food and everyone will be happy."

Anna frowned at him, but the quiver of her lips told him all was forgiven. He bent to give her one more quick kiss. "I'm going to get my bags and make sure I have everything I need for the ceremony. And then the next time I see you, you will be walking toward me down a sandy aisle, about to be my wife."

"Send Eliza over when you see her? We need to start getting ready soon. The makeup artist and hairstylist will be here in twenty minutes. No way am I going to be looking all pale and windswept in our wedding photos. You know how critical the media will be when they get out …"

"I will let her know you're expecting her." He gave his fiancée a little wink and turned down the short, tiled hallway to the master bedroom, sure that the jittery feeling in his middle would be going away any second now. Instead, it only got stronger.

All men feel this way. It's normal. It doesn't mean anything…ominous.

Just because Anna seemed more concerned about how she would look in their wedding photos than about actually marrying him didn't mean anything. In fact, it was a relief. He'd stood at the front of a church too many times, watching yet another glowing woman with dreams in her eyes walk down the aisle toward his beaming father. The first one he'd missed, of course—that had been his mother—but there had been four others since. Eliza would likely make Wife Number Six. And in each and every case, Dante Moretti had been madly in love with the woman, couldn't bear to be without her.

Sadly, the excitement rarely seemed to last more than a couple of years before he found someone else he couldn't live without.

That's why Derek was approaching this in a more sensible way. He and Anna were perfect for each other. She traveled for work, and now that he was self-employed, he could travel with her. They'd never experienced any of the ridiculous jealousy and mistrust that plagued so many of their friends' marriages. They simply shared a history and the same desires for their future. Devoid of the unrealistic expectations of true love, they might actually have a chance at a long and happy marriage.

"Are you ready?"

Derek looked into the full length mirror of George's room in the Big House, the four bedroom "bungalow" that lay on the main part of the island, far from the private retreat that he and Anna would share for the rest of the week. Rather than put him in a tuxedo or suit, given the hot and humid Caribbean weather, Anna had selected a crisp white shirt and tan slacks. He now had his sleeves rolled partway back in keeping with the informal feel of their oceanside wedding. None of it especially mattered to him, though his flip-flops felt somewhat less than respectful for what should be a sacred ceremony.

"Not having second thoughts, are you?" George asked when he didn't immediately answer. "I didn't mean to throw you off. I was just teasing. We've always known you and Anna would get married someday. It just took you longer to get around to it than any of us thought."

"No, it's not that." Derek reached into his pocket and drew out the box that held Anna's wedding band, then handed it to his best man without looking at it. "The whole wedding thing has been a little tainted for me."

"Yeah, I know." George made a face. "But you're not Dad. And you wouldn't be doing this if you weren't sure."

Would he? Derek had never been the sensible type. Working on Wall Street for ten years had been more of a kamikaze, adrenaline-junkie venture than the stable financial move that most of his family thought it was. The thrill of high stakes, the big rewards. All things that got him going in the morning. Until one day he'd awakened in blinding pain and dialed 911 for an ambulance.

Turned out that the adrenaline and his concurrent diet of take-out food and alcohol had led to a bunch of ulcers. Oddly enough, it hadn't been his then-girlfriend who'd rushed to his bedside, but his childhood friend Anna, who was living and working in New York as a model at the time.

"You're right," Derek said finally. It was just the pressure of the wedding that had gotten to both of them, driving a wedge into their relationship. When this was all over, things could go back to normal. "I'm ready."

Out in the living room of the main house, his father stood there in similar dress, his expression expectant. "Ready, son?" Dante clapped a heavy hand on Derek's shoulder, his Italian accent still recognizable after half a lifetime in America.

"As I'll ever be."

Flanked by his father and his brother, Derek moved from the house and onto the sandy beach, the earlier breeze having turned into a stiff wind that ruffled the tails of their shirts. Anna would be annoyed, no doubt. Ahead of them, just outside the Grand Palapa where the wedding reception would take place, thirty of their closest friends and family occupied a sea of chairs draped in white linen. A string quartet waited on a wooden platform beside a wedding arbor that framed the stunning turquoise waters of the lagoon beyond.

Derek walked down the center aisle, pausing to greet the guests and thank them for flying to Central America for the wedding. His heart hammered furiously in his chest the entire time. He felt like he was stepping into a boxing ring rather than getting ready to marry the woman of his dreams. George, his only attendant, took his place beside him, and almost immediately, the quartet began to play the processional.

"Last chance." George nudged him in the side with his elbow.

"Very funny."

From the direction of the bungalow, two figures in pale turquoise sundresses half-walked, half-ran in their direction—Eliza and his sister, Rebecca. His heart stopped for what felt like a full minute. This was not the measured stride of a bridal attendant, but the frantic rush of someone bringing bad news.

Rebecca stopped in front of him, her green eyes pained. "Anna isn't coming."

Derek stared at his sister. Surely this was someone's poor idea of a joke. "I don't understand."

"She's gone, Derek. She said she needed some time alone, and when we went back to look for her, we found this." Rebecca pressed a piece of paper into his hands.

Only faintly aware of the buzz of conversation beyond and the alarmed expressions of the guests, Derek opened the note. It was the island resort's stationery, Anna's unmistakable writing splashed across it in blue ink.

> *I'm sorry, Derek. I can't do this to us. I know I've been difficult the last few months, but that's because I've been trying to ignore what I've always known.*
>
> *We can't get married.*
>
> *I know you love me as much as you can, but it's not enough. I need romance. I need to know that I'm the most important person in the world to my husband, and while I know you would sacrifice anything for me, you would do it out of duty and not love.*
>
> *I'm on my way back to the mainland. I know I'm a coward for doing it this way, but I can't face all the people I'm disappointing. Least of all you. I'm so sorry.*
>
> *Anna*

Derek crumpled the paper into a ball, his jaw tight. He cleared his throat several times before he could force out his voice loud enough to carry. "Sorry, folks, but it looks like there's not going to be a wedding today. Enjoy the island."

He tossed the note to the sand at his feet and strode resolutely up the aisle, ignoring the stares and whispers as he passed. Conflicting emotions warred for the upper hand.

The first one he fully expected—humiliation. He'd been jilted, left at the altar by the woman he was supposed to marry. But the second one surprised him far more than perhaps it should have.

Relief.

three

"How's the cassava?" Bethany called over her shoulder as she began plating the first of the conch *ceviche* in the line of glasses before her.

"Almost there, Chef," Mariska said automatically. "Ready in ten."

"Good." Bethany cast a glance at the clock on the wall. The ceremony should have already started, and considering that beach weddings were far shorter than their church counterparts, hungry guests would be making their way to the thatched-roof dining area for drinks and appetizers any minute. Compared to a regular dinner service—or a proper catering kitchen that fed hundreds—the intimate weddings on the caye were easy to put together with only two of them. But both she and her sous had spent years in restaurants, and their habits were permanently ingrained by now.

The kitchen doors swung open, delivering a breathless, middle-aged Hispanic man wearing the white polo and khaki pants that were the island staff uniform.

"Talk to me, Eduardo," Bethany said, not pausing in her movements.

"The wedding is off."

Bethany lifted her head as Mariska's spoon clattered to the range top. "What? He dumped her?"

"No," the concierge said, wide-eyed. "*She* left him. At the altar. Apparently, she convinced Juan to take her back to the mainland and left a note for her bridesmaids."

Bethany's mouth opened and closed several times. Of all the wedding disasters she'd witnessed during her tenure at Halcyon Caye, this was the only one she hadn't yet experienced. "What now?"

"The elder Mr. Moretti says go ahead with the reception without the bride and groom."

She shoved away her shock and recalibrated her thoughts. So the wedding was off, but that didn't change her job today. She gave Eduardo a sharp nod. "Thanks for the heads-up. The guests are on their way over now?"

"Lined up at the bar."

Then the ceviche needed to be done immediately. "Ready in five. Send in the servers."

"You know what that means," Mariska said. "He's available …"

Bethany snorted. "Jilted at the altar is not available. That's like permanently damaged. Not that I'm interested."

"Sure you aren't."

She didn't have time to dwell on the revelation, focused on getting the food into the hands of the island's staff and out the door. First the ceviche, which would be eaten at the bar's high tables alongside cocktails and bottles of local beer. Then the formal meal: house-made ravioli in a lobster cream sauce, followed by whole salt-crusted red snapper and roasted lemon-dill potatoes, the herbs taken from the garden she cultivated here on the caye. A bit heavy for their island location, in her opinion, but the bride had vetoed her more traditional Belizean suggestions in favor of familiar flavors.

Despite the news, the reception ran smoothly, Bethany and Mariska working together as a practiced team. By the time the dirty plates came back and the guests had moved on to the wedding cake, their job was done. Bethany removed her apron and slumped against the counter while Mariska retrieved two dark bottles of local beer from the walk-in refrigerator.

"Cheers to a job well done," Mariska said, tipping the top of her Belikin to Bethany's.

"And to a man who has absolutely no idea the kind of bullet he just dodged."

"I'll drink to that." Mariska took a pull from her bottle. "You know, he's probably all depressed and could use a shoulder to cry on. Last time I checked, you had two of them."

Bethany snorted. "Not my style. Besides, you're the one who believes in love. The last thing he needs is a cynic trying to comfort him."

"Trust me, if I didn't already have too many men to deal with, I'd be all over that." Mariska hoisted herself up onto the counter, her legs swinging. She was American like Bethany, but she'd embraced the Central American country's Caribbean lifestyle with enthusiasm, her efficiency in the kitchen a stark contrast to her laid-back approach to almost everything else. "We're off the clock until five a.m. You want to go to San Pedro tonight? Juan said he'd take us."

"Thanks, but I think I'm going to stick around here. I'm exhausted." San Pedro was the center of nightlife in Northern Belize's islands, a bustling tourist trap on nearby Ambergris Caye, filled with bars, clubs, and restaurants that catered to visitors and the large expat community. A night out there meant she would be spending hours dragging Mariska out of bars and fending off drunk, rich frat boy types. Not exactly her idea of relaxation. But if Juan, the island's boat captain, was going to take her, it also meant he'd make sure she got home safely. Bethany didn't need to mention that Juan was hoping his vigilance would earn him a spot as Mariska's latest boyfriend.

"If you're sure." Mariska hopped off the counter and set her beer aside. "Let me help you clean up, and then I'll leave you to your boring night."

"Boring? I just got a new delivery of books."

"Like I said."

The two of them cleaned and cleared the kitchen, while the servers returned plates and put them through the dishwasher. By the time they finished, it was already dark, the stars beginning to peek out of the deep blue-black overhead.

"Go," Bethany said, nudging Mariska out the door. "Just be back in time for breakfast or I'm going to wake you with a bucket of ice water."

"Noted, Chef," Mariska said with a salute. "See you tomorrow."

Bethany's stomach rumbled as the other woman stepped out the back door. She'd barely eaten today, too distracted by work and the afternoon's interruptions. Now that she had the quiet kitchen to herself, she really did feel bad for Derek. She knew how it felt to have your dreams ripped out from under you in the most public and humiliating way possible. No doubt she had far more experience with heartbreak than a Roman god like Derek Moretti.

She pulled leftovers from the fridge and started a pot of water boiling on the range. Earlier today, she'd cut some of the fresh pasta sheets used for the ravioli into fettuccini and set aside extra lobster in the fridge. The oil was heating in a stainless skillet, waiting for the raw lobster meat, when she heard the back door open.

"You forget something, Mariska?" she called over her shoulder.

"Pardon me?"

She spun at the male voice, then exhaled when she recognized Derek. He was still wearing what she assumed were his wedding clothes, though they now looked thoroughly rumpled. A bottle of Belikin dangled from his fingers. Automatically, she scanned his face for any signs of inebriation, but the eyes that looked back at her were merely weary, not intoxicated.

"Can I do something for you, Mr. Moretti?" She was impressed that her voice came out so steady and impassive.

He approached her slowly, but stopped before he reached her, instead leaning against the counter. "What are you cooking?"

"My dinner. I can make you something if you're hungry."

"It's probably out of line for me to ask you that, isn't it? I know you're off the clock."

"Considering the day you've had, I guess I can make an exception." She sent him a tentative smile that she hoped seemed commiserating and not pitying. "Lobster fettuccini okay with you? I'm willing to share."

"That sounds great. Thank you." He was still watching her, as if he were sizing her up, but since he didn't seem inclined to speak, she turned back to the range.

She was most at home in the kitchen, but now she was aware of every movement as she started her cream sauce and then dropped the lobster into the pan to sear in hot oil. Derek's presence filled the empty space, making her jittery, uneasy.

Get a grip, Bethany. This is your world in here. You don't have anything to prove. And yet she felt his scrutiny all the same.

Only when she plated their meals with as much care as she'd used for the wedding reception did she look up at him. "Enjoy. I'm just going to take mine out back. You can leave your plate under the palapa and I'll get it later."

"Could I join you?" Uncertainty flooded his expression, tugging again at her sympathies. He jerked his head toward the doors that led to the outdoor dining area. "My dad and his girlfriend are still out there. I really don't think I can handle their pity."

Bethany licked her lips while she considered. Fraternizing with the guests was a cardinal sin on Halcyon Caye, but this was an exception, wasn't it? Derek was clearly asking her, and it was her job to make sure the guests were satisfied with their service. Even if his request had made her heart leap with a certain amount of inappropriate joy.

"All right," she said finally, giving herself a stern mental warning. "Follow me."

He made the chef jumpy. And honestly, Derek couldn't blame her, not when he'd barged into her kitchen with a beer bottle in hand and then demanded she make dinner for him. She'd probably thought he'd be hiding out in his bungalow, drowning his sorrows after his fiancée decided to flee the island without him. Probably the last thing she wanted to deal with on her own time was a self-pitying guest.

But she simply grabbed her own beer from the counter and led him out the back door to a little bistro table set up beyond a clutch of tropical shrubbery, out of sight of the main eating and socializing quarters. The moon was already out, bathing the area in enough light to see where they were going but casting the rest of the island in shadow. The soft buzz of voices drifted from the Grand Palapa, reminding him of what he was escaping. Automatically, he pulled out a wrought iron chair for her before taking the one opposite.

"Thank you," she said, obviously startled by the gesture. In the dark, the white of her teeth and her jacket were the only things that stood out—that and the strands of hair the wind pulled from beneath her black bandanna and blew across her face. She set their utensils and napkins down on the table. Away from her kitchen, she looked far younger and more vulnerable than he'd initially thought.

"So," she said, "How are you doing? Really?"

He stabbed his fork into a piece of lobster. "I'm fine."

She studied him carefully, though what she might read from his expression in the dark, he didn't know. "Are you really? It's okay if you aren't. Most men would be pretty angry right now."

"You're right," he said. "Most men would be. Which makes me wonder why all I feel is relief."

The words spilled out before he could consider them, but she didn't seem shocked. She simply nodded and twisted the strands of pasta around her fork, then placed them into her mouth with an oddly delicate motion. He followed suit and found himself murmuring in appreciation at the flavors. If this was something she'd just thrown together, he'd definitely missed out on his own wedding feast.

"You didn't love her," she said finally.

"No. Not as much as I should have, I guess. It's not like I made any secret of it. It just seems at the last minute she decided what I could offer wasn't enough after all." He threw her a wry look. "It would have been nice if she'd have figured that out before we came to Belize."

"At least she did the right thing before it was too late," Bethany said.

"I should be looking for the silver lining, you mean?" He softened his words with a smile. The last thing he wanted to do was alienate the single person who could speak to him without the tinge of pity he saw in his family and friends' faces. "You're not going to tell me that there's someone else out there who will make me realize what I was missing with Anna, are you?"

Bethany snorted. "No. Trust me, that's the last thing I'm going to tell you."

He cocked his head and studied her. "A fellow cynic, huh? I never would have thought."

"Not a cynic. A realist." She leaned forward over her plate, and a glint of light from the hurricane lamp caught her eyes. Blue, he recalled. "Falling in love, all those great feelings and emotions, they're all chemical. It's no more a mystery than why lighting a match creates a fire and then burns out. Eventually, all chemicals wear off. What you're left with is the real person beneath, and either you can stand to be with that person for the rest of your life or you can't. So why spend your whole life chasing the high?"

It was the exact argument he'd used to justify his relationship with Anna, and yet he hardly expected this pretty young woman to be parroting it back to him. "That's what I had. Or so I thought."

Bethany shook her head. "No. Anna strikes me as someone who's used to getting what she wants. She thought she could change you. She figured given enough time, you'd fall madly in love with her."

He felt his mouth drop open. Bethany had pegged the situation perfectly. "She should know that people don't change."

"No. They don't. Sooner or later, their true colors will show themselves." Bethany clinked her bottle to his. "To a fellow realist."

"May the hopeless romantics fall into Belize's Blue Hole."

Bethany gave him a crooked smile. "Cheers to that."

Derek leaned back in his chair and took a long pull of his beer. For a local brew, it wasn't half bad, even if it didn't exactly go with the high-end cooking. "Thanks, Bethany. This was exactly what I needed."

"I'm glad. I hope you're going to stick around for a while. It's a shame to let one little mishap ruin your entire island vacation."

"One little mishap. Right." He let out a humorless laugh. "I figured I would go back to the mainland with the rest of the guests tomorrow. I should be able to catch an afternoon flight from Belize City to Los Angeles."

"Are you sure? Your fees are non-refundable. You could be miserable and irritated at home in the middle of smog and traffic, or you could be slightly less miserable and irritated in paradise. If you don't want to hang around here, there's plenty to do on the mainland."

He started to say no, but there was a certain kind of logic to her idea. Why not? It wasn't as if he were really pining away over Anna. Yes, he was disappointed and humiliated. Yes, he felt like a complete fool. But Belize was gorgeous. He had a private island and an entire staff at his disposal. He would have to be an idiot to not take advantage of it. Unless of course the solitude made him mope and question his life choices all week. He might be bored and alone at home, but at least he had his work to distract him.

Then a wild, utterly insane idea occurred to him. "I might consider staying. On one condition."

"What's that?"

"You have to be my tour guide."

four

"You said what?" Mariska stared at Bethany from where she manned the flat top, cooking the first batch of eggs for their guests' breakfast.

"I told him I couldn't." Bethany concentrated on her whisk as if the consistency of her batter were the only thing holding the universe together. "First of all, it's completely against the rules—"

Mariska made a sound of dismissal.

"—and second of all, it's a terrible idea."

Mariska rolled her eyes. "I don't understand why playing tour guide to an ultra-hot, newly single man is a terrible idea."

"Let me break it down for you. Ultra-hot guys who date supermodels aren't interested in women like me. And if an ultra-hot guy *is* interested in an average girl, he's just slumming. Why would I do that to myself?"

"You overthink these things, you know that?"

"Hey, I'm just being practical. Besides, taking things at face value is what got me into this situation." Bethany retrieved a ladle and poured the first scoop of crepe batter in the hot pan, rolling it so it coated the bottom.

"So, this is penance?"

Bethany waited patiently for a minute, flipped the crepe, and then slid it onto a plate. "I don't know what you mean."

"Having to be surrounded by weddings and honeymooners and generally tripping over the blissfully-in-love for a living. You figure this is your punishment for daring to think you could be one of them."

Bethany paused in her crepe-making. That was ridiculous. Wasn't it?

She'd come here to get her head together after Alejándro, and she'd liked it so much she'd stayed. Tropical breezes, easy work, good pay … and no eligible bachelors within so much as a thirty-minute boat ride. Her own personal paradise.

"You know I'm right."

"So what if you are? Whatever you think it would accomplish, Derek is as much of a cynic about love as I am. That's why his fiancée dumped him."

"He told you that?"

Bethany nodded.

"Then you have nothing to worry about." Mariska slid the first batch of eggs to waiting plates, her movements automatic, unconscious. "Listen. If you feel guilty about it, make it into a culinary tour of Belize. You can do all the foodie stuff you were hired for. Take him for Orange Walk tacos and conch and proper stew chicken. Not the frou-frou stuff we do here."

She did make a good argument. And Bethany had spent much of her last three years seeking out the best, most traditional Belizean food, from the high-end restaurants of Ambergris Caye to the local stands in the seedy parts of Belize City.

"I'm pretty sure this goes against regulations."

"So don't tell anyone."

Mariska *would* say that. She viewed rules, regulations, minor little things like contract language, as mere suggestions. But Bethany was a rule-follower at heart. Even in the kitchen where she felt most free and creative, there were still boundaries: the confines of physics, the realities of culinary science.

Of course, look where her rule-following had gotten her: Twenty-seven and alone in paradise, too afraid to break out of her routine for a few days of innocent, platonic fun.

Besides, it wasn't as if Derek had shown any interest in her as a woman. He was mostly intrigued by the fact she shared his cynicism. So she was in zero danger from him, even if her temperature did seem to ratchet up several degrees in his presence.

But that was merely pheromones and other easily explained chemical phenomena. Unlike Mariska, who seemed to think every impulse demanded to be explored, she had no problem keeping things in proper perspective.

"I'll think about it," she said finally. "Assuming he even decides to stick around."

"Mmm-hmm," Mariska said.

Bethany didn't turn out with the rest of the staff to see the guests off on the island's private dock. Instead, she finished cleaning the kitchen and headed straight back to her tiny bungalow, one of several that served as accommodations for the staff. As soon as the afternoon sunshine touched her face, she rolled up her pant legs and kicked off her clogs so she could feel the sand between her toes. Much better. See? She could let loose, whatever Mariska might claim.

She wound around the big house, confident she wouldn't be seen by the departing guests, who were well on their way to the mainland, but she barely made it a dozen yards before someone called her name.

No, not someone. Derek. Calming her suddenly over-anxious heart, she turned and waited while he jogged toward her. Once more, he was dressed in island wear: white shorts and a pale green shirt that contrasted with his tanned skin.

"You decided to stay after all."

"I did. I decided you were right. It goes against my endlessly thrifty nature to let a private island go to waste."

Bethany laughed. "Right. Clearly you're one for the sensible choice."

"I guess I was hoping you might rethink your decision."

She studied him closely. He looked calmer today, more rested certainly, but was that a hint of uncertainty on his face? It was appealing on him, even more so than the entitled confidence he'd displayed the day before.

No, better not to study him so closely. She cleared her throat. "Why me?"

"Why not you?" When she didn't answer, he sighed and scrubbed his fingers through his hair. "Listen, the last thing I want to do is spend a week staring at the water and thinking about all the ways I've gone wrong with my life. You seem nice. You're clearly smart, and you know the country far better than I do. Plus, we share the same ... beliefs ... about certain things."

A quiver of a smile reached Bethany's lips. "You mean I'm not harboring secret fantasies of a romantic island fling that turns into happily ever after?"

His smile flashed, though his expression looked a little abashed. "Exactly. Maybe it sounds cold, but it would be refreshing to spend some time with another logical adult."

He did make a compelling case, and considering the financial benefit Mariska had pointed out, it seemed silly to resist. Clearly he had no ulterior motives. Calling a girl *logical* was hardly the first step in seduction. It was the ones who used words like *seductive* and *irresistible* that you had to watch out for.

"Okay, your tour of Belize starts tomorrow. But I can only leave the island for two days before someone gets suspicious and reports me."

His fingers closed around hers, his palm pressing hers firmly. She absolutely did not feel the heat of his hand singeing her skin. It was merely the capsaicin left over from the peppers she'd chopped this morning. It had to be. Before she could contemplate the alternatives, she extricated herself and said, "I'll go work up an itinerary and present it to you at dinner. Seven p.m., poolside."

"Yes, ma'am," Derek said, giving her a wink.

It absolutely did not make her heart do a little hop either. Because that would mean this was a bad, impulsive decision.

And she was done with those.

If you were going to be jilted, Belize wasn't a bad place for it to happen. Derek leaned back in the slatted lounge chair positioned at the edge of the bungalow's private dock and sipped the cocktail the server—Lois, according to her name tag—had brought him. His laptop called to him from inside, arguing that because he was no longer honeymooning, he had no good excuse for neglecting his accounts.

Or maybe it was just an attempt to get away from the thoughts that nagged him. All the cues that he should have picked up, indicating that Anna wasn't as satisfied with their arrangement as he was, all the doubts he'd written off as cold feet. Not to mention the questions he would have to face from friends and family when he got back to LA.

If he thought he could immerse himself in work and just ignore everything until it blew over, he would. But as demanding as his work could be, it wasn't the all-consuming distraction he needed right now. Ironically, that was the very reason he'd left the high pressure environment of his Manhattan brokerage firm in favor of its more relaxed cousin, day trading.

Not that he often admitted it aloud, preferring to simply say he worked in finance. Saying he was a day trader made him feel like a tool, even though it was the natural outgrowth of the career he'd had to downshift. It wasn't about the money. Never had been. It was about the challenge, the cultivated knowledge of the markets, the process of bringing that knowledge—and a healthy tolerance of risk—to bear on quick decisions.

But Bethany hadn't even asked, which was one reason he figured she would be the perfect companion. Her sarcastic little speech was another. He'd been all set to make sure she understood what he was actually asking, but she'd made her position abundantly clear before he'd opened his mouth. What had he been intending to say anyway? *You seem like a nice girl and all, but don't go falling in love with me because apparently I can't promise any woman lasting happiness?*

At best, he'd come off sounding like a character in a Nicholas Sparks movie. At worst, he'd look like an entitled, obnoxious narcissist. He'd been all of those things at various times in his life, but now he tried to limit himself to only one at any given time.

Recalling Bethany's earnestness brought his first real smile of the day. She'd taken on the job with the determination of a devoted student given a particularly challenging assignment. And she hadn't shown even a flicker of interest in him beyond making sure he was getting the vacation he'd paid for.

Like he'd said. Perfect.

He managed to kill the rest of the afternoon, first lounging on the dock and later borrowing one of the kayaks to explore the outer edge of the island, all the while resisting the urge to go back to his laptop to check his brokerage accounts. As the sun was beginning to dip in the sky, he returned to his bungalow to take a shower. This time he dressed slightly more formally in trousers and a loose cotton shirt, then returned to the shore-side plunge pool where a small table had already been set up. Tiki torches burned around the perimeter, while candles flickered in silvery hurricane lamps hanging from the pergola overhead. It was almost painfully romantic.

As soon as he approached, one of the casually-uniformed servers—Lois again, he noted—approached to take his drink order. She was back within minutes with his soft drink and an appetizer, which she informed him was conch fritters with sweet chili sauce.

"Lois, would you ask Chef Hall to come out here for a minute?"

Lois looked alarmed. "Is there something wrong, sir?"

"No, of course not. I'd like to give her my compliments. Will you ask her to bring me the main course herself?"

Lois looked taken aback, but she merely nodded and hustled away. Derek bit into one of the fritters. Perfect breading—more tempura-style than Caribbean—surrounded flaky tender conch. The sauce was a combination of sweet and hot that left a pleasant warmth on his tongue.

Lois came and went with practiced discretion, refilling his glass and taking away plates, until it was once again just him, an empty candlelit table, and the warm sea breeze. He was beginning to think Bethany was going to refuse his request until he glimpsed a figure coming toward him with a domed silver platter. Today, her bandanna was red.

"I'm told you'd like to speak with me, sir?"

He blinked, taken aback, until he noticed her eyes were twinkling with amusement.

"I would. Everything has been wonderful so far. Except for one thing."

"Oh?"

"I hate eating alone."

Her neutral expression shifted into uncertainty. "I couldn't possibly—"

"You're not telling me you only made one serving of this, are you?"

"Of course I did. You're the only guest."

That made him pause. "That seems like a waste. At least join me for a minute."

She bit her bottom lip, clearly conflicted. "If someone complained, I could get written up."

"Who's going to complain? I'm the only one left here."

She looked around, as if gauging the accuracy of the statement.

"Please?"

That seemed to do it. She gave a sigh, and then nodded. "Okay. I need to check on something first. You should start without me."

He nodded so she wouldn't refuse, careful not to examine why it was important to him that she agree. He really did hate eating alone. So much so, he spent nights Anna was out of town at the local sports bar or cafe. Even if he wasn't *with* someone, he liked being surrounded by people. Here, it was all too obvious that the solitude was supposed to be romantic, and it only made him feel pathetic.

A few minutes later, Bethany returned and slid into the seat across from him, clearly uncomfortable. That was something he hadn't really considered when he talked her into being his tour guide—that he might be putting her job in jeopardy. "How much trouble would you be in if someone talked to your boss about this whole plan of mine?"

"A lot," she said immediately. "Maybe fired. Then again, if someone were to complain to my boss that I didn't cater to their every whim, I'd be fired too. So …"

"I'm not going to do that to you. If you want to back out, I'm not going to hold you to your promise."

"I didn't say that." She waved toward his plate. "Eat. It's not nearly as good cold."

Derek sighed. He was putting her in a weird position, and she didn't understand he wasn't trying to make trouble for her. Why would she? She didn't know him at all. "Would it help if after I'm gone, I have my father write a letter to corporate? Tell them how appreciative he is that the staff catered to his brokenhearted son's unreasonable demands?"

Bethany perked up. "That would help. But … why your father?"

"You really don't know?"

"Know what?"

Derek chuckled. "My dad is Dante Moretti. The TV producer."

Still, she stared at him blankly.

"You know, all the teen shows …"

Recognition lit her face. "Oh! The ones with the vampires and zombies and ghosts and such?"

"Yes, those would be the ones." His father had mostly produced soap operas and small budget films until he had the idea that the paranormal young adult book market meant a huge untapped potential for similarly themed TV shows. Dante Moretti was almost single-handedly responsible for the fact you couldn't turn on a network channel these days without tripping over a ghost hunter or psychic or brooding teenage vampire. "I guess while we're getting it all out there, I should also ask if you had any idea who my intended was."

She shook her head. Derek pulled his phone from his pocket, found a saved photo, and passed it to her. It was Anna's newest magazine cover. He made a mental note to delete it later.

Bethany's eyes widened. "You were legitimately going to marry a supermodel. Wow."

"Not only that, but her dad is the producer responsible for all the television shows about angsty groups of teenagers with too much money and not enough supervision. As far as Hollywood was concerned, ours would have been a marriage of TV royalty."

"Apparently I've been living in a hole." Her eyes narrowed. "Wait. You're not some famous actor or director or something, too, are you?"

He chuckled. "Hardly. I am the son who went into finance to avoid the entertainment business. The black sheep."

"Ha! I was right then!"

He looked at her quizzically, and she blushed … actually blushed. How long had it been since he met someone with the capability of being embarrassed?

"Mariska—my sous chef—and I were making bets. Almost everyone who comes here is either in the entertainment business, finance, or real estate. She was betting on soap opera star."

Derek grinned. "But you thought otherwise."

"You have far more of the 'corporate raider trying to remember how to relax' look about you. I mean, don't get me wrong, you've got the looks—haven't you ever noticed that soap opera actors are almost too good-looking?—but you seem the type that gets by on brains and money instead of …" She trailed off, coloring crimson. "Sorry. I'm going to stop now.

She stared at her lap, looking completely mortified, so he turned to his meal and thought about how to flip the conversation. Food. Food was good. Compliment her work. "This is amazing, by the way. It's snapper, right?"

"Very good. Rather an underappreciated fish, but it's popular here. I have standing orders with local fishermen, so this is about as fresh as it gets."

"You sound like you've been here for a while."

"Three years. I'm originally from Florida. Miami, actually. But I fell in love with Belize. I can't imagine going back."

"Well, since you're obviously the perfect person to be my tour guide, why don't you tell me what you have in mind for the next couple of days?"

Bethany brightened. She reached into her jacket and came up with a folded sheet of paper. "If you like diving or snorkeling—"

"I don't."

"Oh. In that case …" She withdrew a pen from her pocket and crossed through several lines. "How do you feel about hiking? And river cruises?"

"Yes to both." He sat back and watched her in amusement. She really was taking this seriously. "But I want some time to relax, too."

"I figured. Well then, tomorrow I thought we could go to Orange Walk Town and cruise up the river to the Mayan ruins at Lamanai. We can come back here overnight and then take a boat to Ambergris Caye the next day. You'll still have two full days to do nothing on Halcyon before you have to go home."

"Whatever you think. I'm completely in your hands."

She gave him a puzzled little frown, but he just kept an easy smile. He hadn't planned on going farther than the perimeter of the island, so he hadn't done any research on the larger surrounding areas. The places she named might as well be on the moon for what little recognition they sparked.

"Okay. Be ready to leave by nine then." She rose to leave.

"Where are you going?"

"To finish your dessert. Because as much fun as this might be, it's still my job."

He took the gentle reproof with a nod, then watched Bethany disappear into the Grand Palapa, her white coat the last thing he could see in the darkness. She was much too uptight. There was humor and a fun-loving soul buried beneath all that scientific seriousness. It might have been her mission to make him relax and forget his problems, but now he was determined to return the favor.

five

BETHANY DIDN'T SLEEP THAT NIGHT. Not because she was nervous about playing tour guide to an attractive man she barely knew—which she was—but because his vehemence against snorkeling had sent her entire itinerary out the window. Who came to Belize but refused to snorkel? For the longest time, only divers even knew about this former British colony, wedged between Mexico and Guatemala and straddling the division between Central America and the Caribbean. His veto eliminated the first two suggestions on her list: diving the famous Blue Hole and exploring the world's second-largest barrier reef.

That meant moving up her plans for the Mayan ruins, which also required changing all the transportation arrangements she'd made for later in the week. There was nothing to do but enlist Eduardo's help. As soon as first light broke, she went to the bungalow next to hers and knocked.

The concierge looked surprised to see her, but he was already dressed for the day. "What's wrong?"

"I need your help."

To his credit, he didn't ask for details, merely opened the door and let her in.

Bethany laid out her plans for the next two days with Derek, and Eduardo's smile grew with each passing minute.

"What? Stop looking at me that way. It's not what you think!"

"Sure it isn't."

"It's not. In fact, he asked me to go with him because he's not at all attracted to me. He just didn't want to be bored and alone."

"He said that?"

"No, but—"

"Listen." Eduardo put one hand on her shoulder in a fatherly gesture, reminding her that he had three teenaged daughters at home. "You are an attractive young woman. Regardless of what he said, he'd have to be blind not to notice."

"So you think I shouldn't go?"

"I didn't say that. Just don't be naive." He patted her shoulder and turned her toward the door. "I'll take care of all the details. You need rooms on Ambergris?"

"Yes. Please."

"One or two?"

Bethany's mouth dropped open, and Eduardo grinned. "Just checking. I'll email you the confirmation."

"I owe you one. Just remember, no one can hear about this outside the island."

"Discretion is my middle name. Eduardo Discretion Romero."

Bethany chuckled, and after one more thank you, returned to her own space. Was Eduardo right? Had Derek asked because he had some sort of interest in her, even subconsciously? No, impossible. Even if she hadn't been buried in her boxy uniform, her hair hidden, without any makeup, his taste clearly ran to more supermodel. Even so, she ran through her clothing options. Nothing revealing, nothing that made her look like she was trying to catch his eye. She couldn't imagine anything more humiliating than him thinking she was interested and having to let her down easy.

She would be as no-nonsense a tour guide as they came.

She raced to the kitchen to make breakfast, which was easy enough, considering Derek was the only one left on the island. She went off menu and whipped up a crab Benedict for him, sending it out with several types of toast and a selection of fresh tropical fruit. Then she cleaned up the kitchen in record time and hightailed it back to her bungalow where a handful of emails from Eduardo awaited her. He was a miracle worker to have pulled off all the changes to the itinerary in such a short period of time. Which, of course, was why he was the concierge on a private island.

Now she had just enough time to pull on the blandest thing in her wardrobe—khaki shorts, a black tank top, and hiking boots. She braided her hair severely away from her face, bypassed makeup in favor of the SPF 50 sunscreen she practically bathed in, and began to pack her backpack with the snacks she'd prepared last night. As soon as the clock read 8:57, she slung the pack over her shoulder and strode toward the boat dock where she'd instructed Derek to meet her.

He was already waiting when she arrived, dressed equally casually in a T-shirt, shorts, and a Dodgers baseball cap. His smile broke as soon as he glimpsed her, making her heart do a backflip into her stomach.

Easy girl. He's off limits.

"Hi." He looked her up and down for several seconds before he finally fixed his attention on her face. "Are we doing some tomb raiding today?"

Bethany flushed. She was no Angelina Jolie, though now that she thought about it, her outfit was a little Lara Croft-ish. "Nope. Sorry. I left my pistols at home."

His lips twisted in amusement. "Too bad. Are we waiting for a boat?"

"Oh no. We go first class on this island." She cupped a hand over her eyes and squinted into the morning sun. "As a matter of fact, here comes our ride now."

The speck in the sky grew bigger, the thwack of the helicopter's rotors audible before they could make out the details. And then it was hovering in front of them, the wash from the blades whipping the palm fronds and scattering sand as it landed in a grassy patch a few hundred feet away. Derek's eyebrows were nearly to his hairline.

"You're not afraid of flying, are you?" she shouted as they approached the helicopter.

"No. Are you?"

Bethany shook her head. "No. In fact, I want to learn how to fly one someday."

"I take it you won't need me to hold your hand then."

Bethany blinked at him, but he was plunging ahead, ducking unnecessarily beneath the rotors into the open cabin. Surely she had misunderstood him. It was only the effect of that smile on her poor addled brain that was making her imagine things. She climbed in behind Derek and pulled the door shut, then accepted the headsets the pilot handed back to her. She passed Derek one, and put hers on, motioning for Derek to turn the knob on the side.

"Welcome, Mr. Moretti, Ms. Hall," the pilot's oddly distant voice said through the headsets. "I'm Jason. It's about twenty-five minutes to Orange Walk Town, so just sit back and enjoy the ride."

Bethany leaned back against the seat, her stomach getting a little jolt when the skids left solid ground. She glanced at Derek, who was watching the island shrink below them, completely unperturbed. She hadn't lied about wanting to someday learn how to fly, but that was just because she felt better when she understood the mechanics of thrust and lift and all the other things that made an otherwise ungainly hunk of metal stay aloft. Right now, it felt too much like magic, and she didn't trust in anything that couldn't be explained by an equation.

"From this height," she said, trying for a knowledgeable tone, "you can see the natural lagoon on the west side of the island. That change in color shows the graduation in depth. It goes from a few feet to a few hundred in a matter of yards."

"The water is so clear," Derek said. "It makes me realize how sandy and murky the Pacific is, at least near the coast."

"It's a completely different animal, the Caribbean." Bethany leaned across him to get a better look at the turquoise expanse below. "See down there? That's a pod of dolphins."

She expected him to bend nearer the glass to see the dark, undulating shapes, barely more than a shadow, speeding away from them. But instead, he was looking right at her, a peculiar expression on his face.

Bethany jerked backward and cleared her throat. "I'll just be quiet now and let you enjoy the ride."

Derek nodded and finally looked away, giving her a moment to draw a deep breath. This might not be as easy as she'd thought.

Derek had always wondered how he was going to die, and now he had a fairly good idea. Bethany Hall was going to do him in.

He hadn't lied to her when he said he didn't want to spend his last days in Belize staring at the water and doing a post-mortem on his failed engagement. He'd really believed that he and his equally cynical chef could spend a few casual, friendly days together, seeing the sights.

But that was before she'd shown up in her Lara Croft getup, complete with dark red braid trailing down her back. That dumpy chef uniform hadn't prepared him for the long legs and slim waist displayed by her shorts and tank top. Nor had he been able to steel himself against the fact that every time she leaned across him, he got a tantalizing glimpse of—

No, he wasn't going to go there. He wouldn't be *that* guy, who leered at a woman he'd practically bullied into being his tour guide, even if every last molecule in his body seemed to have snapped to attention and begun screaming, "Beautiful woman nearby!" If only he'd figured that out twelve hours ago and not when she was six inches from him, wearing far too little clothing and smelling like an intoxicating mixture of vanilla and tropical flowers.

Bethany looked at him askance, and he forced a reassuring smile. Even if he couldn't immediately turn off the switch she'd somehow flicked, he owed it to her not to make her uncomfortable.

He managed to feign interest in the scenery as the coastline grew through the window and they left behind the bright, varied blue of the sea for the lush, overgrown mainland. He hadn't been paying attention when he landed in Belize City, but now he focused on the green jungle, interspersed with wide fields of green and brown bisected by the pale yellow ribbons of dirt roads. Beautiful as the island was, it could have been nearly anywhere in the Caribbean or Southeast Asia. For the first time, Derek got a sense of their location in Central America.

"It's impressive, isn't it?" Bethany's quiet voice through the headset startled him.

"It is. Reminds me a little of Panama." He laughed when Bethany frowned in puzzlement and explained, "I served there in the Peace Corps for two years after college."

"The Peace Corps? You?"

"Don't sound so surprised! I wasn't always a heartless corporate drone. Besides, I mostly did it to irritate my father."

"I never said heartless," Bethany shot back. "What did you do there?"

"Community economic development. Basically teaching business principles to farmers and beekeepers."

"I see." She nodded and sat back in her seat, but he could tell that revelation had thrown her. It gave him an unreasonable feeling of satisfaction. He might be a spoiled rich kid, but at least he had a few good qualities to offset that fact.

They didn't speak for the rest of the flight, until a small airstrip in the middle of a sugarcane field appeared in the window, completely deserted but for a tiny shack that served as a terminal. Jason set the helicopter down on a grassy pad not far from the airstrip.

"I'll be back for you at four o'clock," he said. "Enjoy your excursion."

Bethany said her thanks and hopped out of the sliding door, but no sooner did Derek's feet touch the ground than she was off, heading toward a waiting car a few dozen feet away. A young man wearing a logoed green polo shirt straightened from where he leaned on the hood and gave them a wave. Or rather gave Bethany a wave. From the way the guy's eyes were locked on her, Derek was pretty sure the guide hadn't even registered his presence.

Bethany was rattling off a rapid stream of Spanish, which she cut off as soon as he joined them. "Manuel says we're the only two on the tour today, so we can go into town first, or we can get a start now. Either way, it looks like rain this afternoon."

The mounding clouds from the north did threaten showers, but that was to be expected in Belize. "Let's just get on with the tour. We can explore the town when we get back if we have time."

They climbed into the back of the car, and then they were off down the bumpy dirt road which then turned to an equally bumpy paved highway. Jungle-like foliage crowded the shoulders, and every so often Manuel had to pause to go around an inexplicably stopped vehicle.

The silence began to feel awkward, as if Derek were purposely ignoring Bethany. Finally, he asked, "Where did you learn to speak Spanish?"

"Almost everyone in Miami is bilingual. Plus, it's practically a requirement for working in a commercial kitchen."

"I bet it would be."

"Where did you learn to speak Spanish, and why do you pretend not to?"

He snapped his eyes to Bethany's face, surprised. She just smiled.

"They wouldn't have sent you to Panama if you weren't already fluent. I know that much about the Peace Corps."

She was smart, he'd give her that. Not a single person had ever asked that question. "My parents were never around, so my brother and sister and I were raised by a Colombian nanny. As for why I don't speak it … sometimes it better serves me to listen when people don't think I can understand them." He caught their guide's smile in the rearview mirror. "Doesn't it, Manuel?"

Manuel chuckled. "*Sí*. Many visitors don't realize English is the official language of Belize."

"You keep surprising me," Bethany murmured.

"Is that a good thing?"

She studied him for a long moment before looking away. "I'll let you know."

six

BETHANY HAD PURPOSELY HELD BACK the details of the river tour, letting Derek think it was a lazy cruise down a winding waterway, but she still laughed at his shock when Manuel led them to the end of a dock on the wide Rio Nuevo where his speedboat was moored, its blue awning providing relief from the pounding sun, which at nine o'clock had already nudged the warm, humid air toward sweltering.

Derek clambered into the boat beside her, and despite the fact it was big enough for six or eight people, he seated himself directly beside her. If she'd thought she could move without seeming rude, she would have. It had been hard enough to keep her neutrality while wedged beside him in the helicopter and in Manuel's car, especially when she was continually teased by his cologne, turned downright sultry in Belize's heat.

Why, oh why, must she always be attracted to unattainable men?

Manuel guided the boat away from the dock onto the river, the breeze created by their forward motion bringing welcome relief to the sticky air. Once he got past the docks of the other tour operators, he opened the throttle and sped forward down the wide river.

"Keep your eyes on the banks!" Manuel called over the motor. "You may see crocodiles sunning themselves."

Bethany didn't spy any crocodiles, but she pointed out birds in the treetops and the dark faces of spider monkeys peering from the foliage. Gradually the river narrowed, no longer a broad glassy expanse but a winding Amazonian-type waterway, its banks choked with fallen trees and promising predatory creatures in the murky shallows.

"Look right there." Derek leaned forward to speak into her ear as he pointed at the opposite bank, where the top of a crocodile's head was just visible. Bethany shivered.

"Not fond of them, I take it?"

"Not so much." Let him think it was the crocodile that raised the goosebumps, not the dance of his breath on her skin.

Manuel guided the boat to a little inlet crowded with overhanging branches, then tossed Derek a banana.

"What's this for?"

Bethany twisted away from him and laughed, grateful for the distraction. "Look."

The curious face of a spider monkey appeared in the foliage of the low-hanging tree. When it spied the banana in his hand, the monkey swung down and gave an expectant chirp.

"Okay, fella. Hold on." Derek peeled the banana and broke it in half, then held one piece out. The monkey snatched it from his hand and began eating, its gold-ringed eyes never wavering from the other piece in Derek's hand.

"Here." He offered the second piece to Bethany, but she refused to take it.

"No way. Monkeys creep me out."

"Look, you hurt his feelings." Derek reached past her and held out the other half of the banana. The monkey took it and scrambled back into the tree.

"So," he murmured in her ear, ostensibly so Manuel wouldn't overhear, "You're afraid of crocodiles and monkeys. What else doesn't Bethany Hall like?"

Right now, she didn't care for the things the sexy timbre of his voice did to her will to stay detached. The fact he seemed to be treating this as a date rather than a business arrangement didn't help either.

Derek was looking at her with that half-amused expression, though, and she belatedly remembered his question. "Um … I hate cilantro. It tastes like soap to me."

Derek chuckled and leaned back in his seat as Manuel pulled back into the current. "That must be inconvenient for a chef."

"It is, actually, since some recipes require it. Did you know people are genetically predisposed toward a taste for cilantro, one way or another?

People like me have olfactory receptors that are oversensitive to the aldehydes that give cilantro its distinctive flavor …" She trailed off, flushing when she saw he was smiling at her. "What?"

"I think it's interesting that you can just toss off all these scientific details."

She felt the heat deepen, sure she was tomato red. Curse her Irish, cilantro-hating genes. "Culinary physics … science in general … has always fascinated me."

"Really? Why?"

"Are you pretending to be interested so I don't feel stupid?"

"No, I'm curious. Cooking seems like such a creative thing, the scientific slant surprises me."

"Oh, but cooking is very scientific. You see, when you understand the chemical and physical processes—for example, what searing does to different cuts of meat or what happens to the volatile oils in an onion when you caramelize it—you have a lot of freedom in creating new recipes. I know it's the citric acid in the lemons or limes that 'cooks' the fish in ceviche, so I can substitute orange or tangerine or grapefruit for different effects. For that matter, I could use straight citric acid crystals, though I've never seen a reason to try it."

Derek was still smiling, but he didn't seem to be laughing at her. "Can I tell you a secret? I hate cilantro too."

Bethany's mouth opened. "But I've been putting cilantro in half your food! Why didn't you say something?"

"I picked it out. I didn't want to be a jerk."

"It's my job as a personal chef to customize these things," she said reprovingly. "What else aren't you telling me?"

"Nothing, I promise. Just the cilantro thing. Well, that and my hatred of pickled herring, but I don't suppose you have any Scandinavian dishes planned, do you?"

"No, I think you're safe."

"For the record, I have enjoyed everything you've made, with or without cilantro."

"Thank you." *And thank you for reminding me this is not a date.* She could be friendly, but they weren't friends. She was doing a job, even if it was outside of her normal duties. Derek would leave the island on Friday, and she would be back home before he even boarded a plane. She should just be grateful that his continued presence meant she didn't have to scramble for another job to make up for the loss of income.

Manuel pointed out more animals, pulling her attention from the growing and thoroughly unwanted rapport she was feeling. Then the speedboat brought them into a wide lagoon surrounded by thick foliage. A long dock on the far side already held a couple of other similar speedboats. Manuel navigated to an open spot and hopped out to tie up the boat. Derek immediately followed suit and held out a hand to Bethany. No choice. She forced herself to ignore how nice her hand felt in his and let go as soon as she was on stable ground.

Thank God for Manuel at least. The guide kept up a steady stream of narration in English as he led them through the small visitor's center at the site and then back out onto the packed dirt path that wound beneath the jungle canopy. Bethany stayed up front near Manuel while Derek lagged behind. It was bad enough that she found him attractive. Even worse now that she'd discovered he was a genuinely nice guy. Why couldn't he be an arrogant jerk instead?

Bethany actually was beginning to sympathize with Anna. If Derek had looked at her with the focused attention he was using on Bethany and still maintained his "love is bunk" position, she couldn't blame the girl for being upset. Of course, that didn't excuse Anna's abysmal behavior, but if Bethany were in love with a man who didn't love her back, she'd probably be angry and hurt too.

Actually, there was no *probably* about it. She'd been both, so much so it required leaving the country. The problem was, Alejándro had believed in love. He'd just mistaken the feeling to originate somewhere other than his heart, and in a place that was disinclined to resist the temptation of every pretty girl who walked by.

No, she'd think Alejándro and Derek were complete opposites if getting involved with them wouldn't have the same demonstrated results.

After walking what felt like forever, winding between the crooked trunks of the impossibly tall trees, over roots and around jutting rocks, the path widened into a clearing. A breathtaking temple ruin spread before them.

"This is the Mask Temple," Manuel said, turning to address both of them. "Construction began around 200 B.C., and renovations continued through about 1300 A.D. The masks on either side of the stairs are unusual because they are carved from limestone rather than covered with plaster. The style is also distinctly Olmec. You'll note the crocodile headdress, which proves that the Spanish records are correct in calling this 'the place of the crocodile.'"

Bethany and Derek moved closer to the gargantuan structure, its flat-topped pyramidal shape still intact, even though the centuries had worn once-sharp edges soft. The closer she got, the more Bethany could get a sense of the carvings' massive scale. Her head didn't even reach the mouth of the mask. She brushed her fingers across the intricately detailed surface.

Derek looked at her. "What do you think? Are we going to climb the temple?"

"Of course we are. But first, pictures. You know, if you don't have evidence, it didn't happen." Bethany dug in her backpack and came up with her smartphone. "I'll get some shots of you."

"No, no," Manuel said, easing the phone from Bethany's hand. "Both of you."

Derek shrugged and he slid his arm around her waist and positioned them to the left of the mask carving. The fact that there were still several inches between them made no difference. The touch lit up her entire body, and she struggled to remain relaxed beneath his hand.

"Smile," Manuel said, then raised the phone to snap several shots.

As soon as he lowered it again, Bethany put some distance between them. "Okay, then. Race you to the top?"

Something mischievous glinted in Derek's eye. "Deal."

But *race* was a misnomer. They only got a dozen steps up the steep side of the pyramid before her legs began to warn her to pace herself. Derek slowed his climb beside her, looking decidedly unaffected by the exertion, even though his shirt was starting to stick to his back from the oppressive humidity. It was a mark that she had completely lost her mind that, even sweaty, he was almost unbearably sexy.

"So, how many times have you been here, really?" he asked.

"Once," Bethany said. "When I first moved to Belize."

"You seem so knowledgeable, I thought for sure you did this thing pretty often."

"Contrary to some people's beliefs, personal chefs generally spend their days cooking, not tour-guiding." She'd meant to be snarky, but the words still came off with a hint of flirtation. *Drat.*

"I'd say I'm sorry, but I'm really not. Isn't this more fun than being stuck at work?"

"You mean more fun than doing what I love on a private island? Yes, it's my own personal hell."

He chuckled. "I suppose it is a pretty good gig when you put it that way. How did you become a personal chef anyway?"

The subtext was clear, though he was too polite to ask his real question: *why aren't you working at a restaurant in America somewhere, rather than hiding out on a private island in Belize?* Only Mariska knew the real answer, so Bethany said, "I worked in restaurants for a while, but I needed a change. This pays much better, and I only work about fifteen days a month instead of seven days a week, sixteen hours a day. After a while that sort of thing starts to wear on you, no matter how much you love it." *Especially when you have to work alongside someone who ripped your heart out and ground it beneath his heel.*

"So what do you do on the other fifteen days a month?"

"Lie on the beach and work on my tan, of course." She held out one pale arm. "Can't you tell?"

"I recognize avoidance tactics when I see them."

Bethany arched an eyebrow. "Why all the questions?"

"What? I can't be curious about you? After all, we're going to be spending the next couple of days together. It seems silly not to get to know each other a bit."

She didn't answer, concentrating instead on keeping her breathing even as she climbed, even though she was beginning to get winded. She really did need to get more exercise. After a few minutes, she asked, "What about you? What do you do exactly? You said finance."

"I used to be a broker in New York."

"Used to be?"

"Yeah. My doctor advised me to downshift my career a little after I landed in the ER."

"Heart attack?"

He grimaced. "Ulcers. It's kind of embarrassing. But when the market collapsed a few years back, the pressure got immense. Expectations remained high, even though all the revenue sources had dried up. It's not really a healthy way to live long-term. So I moved back to LA."

"What do you do now?"

"Day trading." Her thoughts must have shown on her face because he laughed. "Hey, I already had the skills. This time I'm trading my own money."

"That sounds more stressful to me."

"I figure if I make bad trades, it's on me. I don't have to tell a client that their kid won't go to Yale because I misjudged a security. Money comes and goes. It's good not to be too attached to it."

"That's surprisingly sensible coming from a guy who rented out a private island for his wedding."

"Hey, it cost a lot less than the five-hundred-guest affair at the Ritz Carlton that Anna wanted. The alternative had to be pretty spectacular."

Bethany shook her head. These people were from an entirely different world. Yeah, her dad was a master jeweler, but that didn't mean they'd been filthy rich. They'd lived modestly in Coral Gables, a legendary traditional neighborhood in Miami that had been affordable when her parents had moved in. She'd gone to culinary school instead of college, then moved out as soon as she got her first job. She had been happy to make enough money to pay rent and afford the high end ingredients for which she'd developed a taste while working in top restaurants.

But Derek was shockingly down to earth despite his background, which made the fact he had planned to marry Anna all the more confusing.

"I really don't understand the two of you. It doesn't seem like a match."

"Apparently it wasn't," Derek said wryly. "But you have to understand, Anna wasn't always like this. She used to be sweet. Shy. Insecure. And I guess deep down, I kept looking for the little girl I'd grown up with. I saw glimpses of that girl every once in a while and overlooked the other things."

"Plus, she's gorgeous."

"Well, yeah. But I'm not sure that's enough over the long haul when you don't want the same things."

It sounded good. It was the kind of line a drool-worthy playboy type told the average girl to convince her that he was just a normal guy at heart. And it was convincing. She just couldn't figure out why he bothered. No matter what he claimed, a guy who could land a supermodel like Anna Elliston didn't bother with women like her.

Which meant either he was looking for a conquest to stroke his ego after being dumped or he was actually sincere. She couldn't decide which one unsettled her more.

It didn't matter, though, because they had finally reached the top. A breeze blew through the trees, ruffling stray pieces of hair that had escaped her braid. She filled her lungs and looked out over the green canopy. Then she made the mistake of looking down off the side.

"Whoa there." Derek steadied her with a hand on her elbow as she swayed, which didn't actually do much to steady her insides. "You're not afraid of heights too, are you?"

"Not pathologically so, no. Just a little vertigo."

He dropped his hand, but he didn't move away. "It's beautiful. You can see why the Mayans built these the way they did. It's like being in the clouds. It must have felt like they could reach out and touch their gods."

"Wait until you see the High Temple," Bethany said. "This is nothing in comparison."

"Wait, we have another one to climb? You might need to carry me back to the boat."

There he went again, being all cute and charming and acting like a normal guy, when just yesterday he had called his aborted marriage a joining of TV royalty. She knew better than to buy into that shtick a second time around. They could have fun, tease, be friendly, as long as she didn't read too much into it.

The climb down went slightly faster than the way up, though they were quiet on the descent. They met up with their guide where he sat on a bench waiting for them, then rejoined the path that would take them to the next ruin, the High Temple Bethany had mentioned to Derek earlier.

This time when they approached the ruin, Derek stopped short. "Wow."

"I know." They looked up at the structure, half again as tall as the Mask Temple. The last section was so steep that a rope hung from the top for support. Reaching the apex required ascending on hands and knees and practically rappelling backward to get down again. The very idea made her nauseous. But she wasn't going to let him know she wasn't that thrilled about the long climb.

"If you don't think you can make it …" she began.

"You know, you talk a lot of trash for someone who got winded climbing up the smaller one."

So much for charming. She placed her hands on her hips. "Really? Bring it, *gringo*."

"Gringo?" He burst out laughing. "This from possibly the whitest girl on the planet?"

"Hey, I may be Irish on the outside, but I'm Belizean on the inside where it counts." She grinned and took off for the temple ahead of him.

Before she could get more than a few steps up the ruins, he was by her side again, a look of challenge on his face. "Be careful, little girl. I wouldn't want you to slip and fall because you're too stubborn to admit you're out of shape."

"Out of shape? I'm not the desk jockey here. We'll see who's laughing when we get to the top."

As much as she was enjoying the trash talk, there wasn't much conversation once they made it past the lower section of the temple and approached the upper half. Bethany took the path to the left of the rope, while Derek took the right. Each of them threw glances at it, but they were both too stubborn to use it to pull themselves to the top. The stairs were so steep, it was one step short of rock climbing. She dared not look behind her as Derek did lest the sensation of falling overtake her again.

He made it to the very top of the platform several seconds before she did and squatted down to wait for her. When she got within reach, he extended a hand.

After a moment's consideration, she took it and let him haul her the rest of the way up to the top. She bent at the waist while she caught her breath. "I let you win."

"Sure you did. Now, look."

Bethany straightened, looked out around them, and inhaled in surprise. She hadn't climbed all the way to the top last time, and now she realized she had missed out. The jungle trees spread out around them, a vibrant, undulating green carpet. Beyond was the sparkling blue of the New River Lagoon, just visible past the farthest edge of the trees. She closed her eyes and lifted her damp face to the breeze. When she opened them again, Derek's gaze was fixed on her and not on the view.

"What?"

"Nothing, I just—" A throaty, otherworldly sound pierced the air, echoing through the trees. "What on earth is that?"

"Howler monkeys. They live here at Lamanai."

"That's creepy."

"You won't get any arguments from me."

Derek moved to a jutting lump of stone near the edge and patted the spot next to him. She lowered herself beside him, clasping her hands over her knees.

"This is fun," he said. "Thanks."

The sincerity in his expression melted her earlier suspicions about his motivations. "You're welcome. Are you thirsty?" She dug in her backpack and handed him a bottle of water before twisting the cap off of a second bottle and taking a long swig.

"What else do you have in there?"

"Trail mix." She pulled out a plastic baggie filled with nuts and dried fruit and passed it over to him. Just as she shook a handful into her palm, the first fat drops of rain struck the stone around them.

"Uh-oh," she said. "As nice as this break was, I think we need to get back down before it starts raining for real. I don't really want to be descending wet steps."

Derek stood and tucked his water bottle into his own backpack. He reached for her hand and pulled her to her feet, but this time he held it. "No racing down this time. It was funny on the way up, but I don't want you getting hurt."

She bit back her sarcastic remark when she saw the seriousness in his face. "Okay. Same here. Use the rope. That's what it's there for."

"Deal."

Derek went down first, but no sooner did Bethany begin to back her way off the edge of the ruin than the rain stepped up its pace from a sprinkle to a steady spatter. She gripped the rope, taut from Derek's hold on it below her, and gradually backed her way down each step, cringing every time her knee brushed the rough stone.

"You okay?" Derek called once they were halfway down.

"I'm okay," she called back. "Why wouldn't I be okay backing down what essentially amounts to a pyramidal-shaped cliff?"

"You know, I'm thinking you might have oversold your comfort with heights." Amusement tinged his voice.

"I'm fine with heights. It's falling to my death I'm not particularly fond of."

Derek let out a hearty laugh, and it brought a smile to her face. She was fine with heights, really, except for those few moments when she realized exactly *how* high she was off the ground and how much it would hurt should she do a header off the side. Right now, she was just grateful for the rope's support on the increasingly slippery surface as she made a slow and steady descent toward the central platform.

And then, just as she was congratulating herself for managing not to hurt herself, the toe of her hiking boot slipped on a slick patch, sending both feet out from beneath her. She clutched the rope, her heart leaping into her throat as her torso and arms slammed into the stone. The breath left her body with an *oof*.

"Bethany!" Derek's voice held a note of fear as he scrambled to where she was now sprawled full-length on the steps. "Are you all right?"

The only thing she could manage was a groan. She would recover, of course, but the damage to her pride was probably permanent.

Derek slid an arm around her waist, pressing her close to his body. "I've got you. Get your feet beneath you."

She let go of the rope and found a foothold on a lower step, then twisted herself into a seated position. Just looking at the distance they still had to descend made her head spin. Or maybe that was the fact that Derek was still holding her, a little too near for coherent thought.

"I'm okay. Just a little banged up." Their faces were so close that she had a hard time looking away, captured by the concern in his vibrant green eyes. Her breath hitched in her throat.

And then he looked down. "You're bleeding!"

Sure enough, scrapes marked her knees and shins and the backs of her forearms near the elbow. Not to mention the muddy streaks on her shorts and tank top from sliding against the wet stone. "I'll be okay. I've had worse."

"Make it a point to do regular rounds with a wood chipper, do you?"

His joking was making it easier to breathe, and she eased away from him a degree, making it seem like she was just testing the condition of her body. She held out her arms in front of her. "Occupational hazard."

He brushed his thumb over the silvery scars from numerous grease burns, barely visible on her pale skin. He turned her hand over to where a long oval scar still marked her palm. "What happened here?"

"Busy night in the kitchen, right after I started my first job. I grabbed a pan without a towel and burned myself. Probably second degree."

His eyes widened. "You went to the hospital, I hope."

"I wrapped it in gauze from the first aid kit and finished my shift. I wasn't going to leave the line shorthanded during dinner service."

Derek shook his head. "I'm getting the feeling you're a lot tougher than you look."

That brought a smile to her lips. "You have no idea."

"In that case, do you feel well enough to get the rest of the way down?"

Her embarrassment returned, though it was mitigated by the memory of how he'd caressed her skin. *Get it together, Bethany.* "Let's do this before Manuel feels the need to come up and rescue me."

Derek waved to the guide, who was standing at the bottom of the ruin, attention riveted on them. "I'll be right behind you."

"I'm fine," she said, even though his concern was oddly warming. They made it down to the platform, and then finally the ground, without further incident. Naturally, the minute they set foot on the dirt below, the rain tapered off.

"Are you okay, Ms. Hall?" Manuel asked, his eyes wide.

"I'm okay. Just a little shaken up."

"Maybe we should go back," Derek said. "I'm sure there's a first aid kit on the boat. You really should put some antiseptic on these scrapes."

"I'm fine. Really. Nothing to be concerned about."

Nothing except the fact that the longer she was in Derek's presence, the harder it was to remember why she'd instituted her No Men policy in the first place.

seven

"ARE YOU SURE YOU'RE OKAY?" Derek asked.

Bethany gave him a patient smile from her seat across the boat. "I'm fine. Like I was the last four times you asked."

He grinned sheepishly and turned back to his lunch of "stew chicken" and rice and beans, which Manuel had somehow managed to produce from an insulated container on the boat, still hot. Bethany had assured him this was the most Belizean of all food, even more so than the abundance of seafood she prepared on the island.

The girl was tough, he could give her that. Despite the fact that bruises were already blossoming over her body from her spill on the temple steps, Bethany hadn't done so much as flinch when he swabbed the scrapes with an antiseptic wipe and pressed on a Band-Aid. Then again, any woman who finished a kitchen shift with a second degree burn on her hand probably wasn't going to be fazed by a little scratch … even if she did almost fall halfway down a Mayan ruin.

Maybe she hadn't quite needed his help, but he'd acted out of instinct before he realized what a terrible idea it was to have her in his arms. It sent his mind down all sorts of paths he didn't have any business exploring, especially when he'd been set to marry another woman a mere two days earlier.

And yet he didn't regret it nearly as much as he should.

"What time should we get back to Orange Walk, Manuel?" Bethany asked in Spanish between bites.

The guide checked his watch. "Three o'clock? Enough time to explore the town before your pickup."

"Are you sure you feel up to it?" Derek asked Bethany.

Her eyebrows lifted. "Do you?"

"Sure thing, *gringa.*"

She rolled her eyes, but she was smiling as she forked another bite of chicken into her mouth. Oh yeah, he was growing on her.

The real question was, did he really want to?

It would be easier if the attraction just stopped at looks. He was a guy—he was going to notice a pretty face and an outstanding figure—but he knew firsthand that an attractive exterior didn't always indicate the person underneath. But the more he got to know Bethany, the more he liked her toughness, her humor, the way she challenged him on … pretty much everything. There was far more to her than he'd initially thought.

He looked away and sighed. It was all a purely academic question anyway. If they lived in the same city, maybe their connection would bear exploring. Assuming he were even looking for another relationship so soon after Anna. Bethany had the same cynical views on love as he did, but she was still fun to be around. Smart, humorous, beautiful. She seemed to prove what he'd been saying all along—desperate, all-consuming, can't-live-without-you love was the enemy of true compatibility, not an essential requirement. Then, when the attraction and the novelty wore off, you were left with someone you could actually stand to be around.

It was so close to what Bethany had said the night he'd been left at the altar, he wasn't sure whether the thought originated from him or from her.

"You're deep in thought."

When he turned, she was watching him with that guarded expression again. "Sorry. Just thinking that I really should fit some work in while I'm here."

"Not tomorrow, you won't. I've got one more day planned for you. You can work when you're on your own time. Right now, you're on mine."

"Yes, ma'am. I'm at your service. Or your mercy, if today was any indication."

Bethany bit back a smile. "You might come to regret that statement."

They made the return trip up the river, this time without the stops, and docked at Orange Walk Town just after three o'clock. Manuel helped them out of the boat and asked if they wanted him to give a tour of the small town before he took them back to the airstrip.

"There's something I want you to try," Bethany said to Derek. "The Orange Walk tacos are legendary. It's not far on foot to the best stand in town."

"We just ate! Besides, I'm not sure you want to be walking around right now. You're still limping."

"I'm fine." She waved a hand in dismissal, but her careful movements said she was probably in more pain than she let on.

Derek looked to Manuel. "Would you mind driving us? She's so stubborn she'd walk on a broken ankle."

Bethany stuck out her tongue at him.

He laughed. "Despite the bulletproof logic of that argument, I insist. I'll try your tacos as long as you sit back and relax."

"Fine." She heaved a sigh and gave Manuel the location of the taco stand, which the driver recognized immediately. Then they piled back into the guide's waiting car.

As soon as they were on their way, Derek reached out and ran a finger across her bruised arm, eliciting a flinch. "Sorry. Does that hurt?"

"No," she said, avoiding his eyes. "I just feel foolish."

She probably did, but he suspected that wasn't the real reason for her sudden distance.

Manuel drove them into town past the toll booth, the rutted road jolting them to their teeth. This part of Orange Walk looked like any other Latin American city, the old and traditional interspersed with pockets of modern stucco and wrought iron. When the guide turned onto the main street, the flavor changed again, the bright pastels of the old buildings suggesting Caribbean influence. At last Manuel pulled to the side of the road in front of a two-story building with arches on the upper story—a hotel if the blinking neon *Vacancy* sign was an indication.

"This is your taco stand?" Derek asked.

"Not here. There." Bethany pointed across the street to something that was not much more than a wooden lean-to on the side of the road, a picnic table providing limited seating. A line of waiting patrons wound around it.

Derek grinned. In his experience, the worse the appearance, the better the food. "Lead on, then."

Manuel stayed with the car, so they crossed the street together. Derek automatically rested a hand on the small of her back as they dodged the cross traffic. Okay, *automatically* implied something entirely different than the calculated need to touch her again.

Bethany moved away as if she'd been electrocuted. "Orange Walk tacos are a Belizean institution. You used to only be able to find them right here, but their popularity means there are taco stands all over the country now."

When it was their turn, Bethany placed a four-dollar order of tacos plus two *horchatas*—a cinnamon rice milk drink almost as ubiquitous as tacos in Belize—then requested a separate order to go for Manuel.

"Four bucks?" Derek asked. "I know I said we just had lunch, but I don't think you understand how much I can eat."

Bethany just gave him an amused smile. "You'll see. If we'd had time, I would have brought you here for breakfast."

"Tacos for breakfast?"

"Especially for breakfast. They're even more popular than Johnny cakes."

Derek didn't know what Johnny cakes were, but he assumed they were some sort of breakfast bread. When a woman passed a paper plate to Bethany through the window—the plate nearly buckling under the weight of its cargo—his eyes widened. There had to be a dozen tacos on there.

"Cheap and good," Bethany said. "Just a snack really."

"I'd hate to see how many you consider a meal. Where should we sit?"

"Oh, we don't sit. We stand." She chose a spot on the dirt and set her paper drink cup at her feet, then picked up one of the tacos. "Come on. Don't be shy. You snooze, you lose."

"You can't possibly eat more than three of those."

"Watch me." She took a big bite and let out a groan of pleasure. To distract himself, he reached for one of the tacos. It was simple, quite unlike the street tacos he habitually ordered from food trucks in LA: just a freshly made tortilla rolled around shredded chicken, onion, and cabbage, and then drizzled with picadillo sauce. One bite told him it was also some of the best street food he'd ever eaten.

Bethany was already on her second—or was it her third?—an expression he'd liken to ecstasy on her face. He bit his lip against a smile. When she opened her eyes, she frowned at him. "What?"

"I'm just enjoying watching you. You get into this, don't you?"

"I take food very seriously." She polished off the remainder of the taco in one bite and reached for another one. "Like I said, time's a-wastin' if you want any of these."

He grinned at her and applied himself to helping her finish off the rest of the tacos. Bethany tossed the plate in the trash can, retrieved her drink, and nodded toward the waiting car. "Let's get back so Manuel can eat before we go back to the airstrip."

And then she was off, striding across the street with her usual determination, looking even more like Lara Croft now that she was smudged in dirt and covered with scrapes and bruises. The fact it made her even more attractive surely meant he had some deep-seated issues. Or maybe it was just because had the same thing happened to Anna, she would be milking the incident for all it was worth.

Bethany seemed to be breaking all sorts of preconceptions today, whether he wanted her to or not.

eight

DESPITE WHAT BETHANY HAD TOLD DEREK, her body ached everywhere, from the scrapes on her arms and legs to the bruises that were already turning a brilliant shade of black and blue. Nothing she couldn't hide under her customary chef's whites, but ones she'd certainly have to answer to Mariska for.

The most pathetic thing was that every ache was worthwhile for the way Derek was now hovering in the periphery. Not to mention the experience of having his arms around her on the ruins. She might have lied to him about the severity of her injuries, but she'd be lying to herself if she said she wasn't daydreaming up ways to make that happen again.

They were at the airstrip for only a few minutes before the helicopter appeared in the distance and then landed on the grassy pad in front of them. Bethany thanked Manuel for his help and tipped him a little extra beyond what he'd been paid through the booking agency, then climbed out of the car. She was acutely aware of Derek's every move behind her.

"Welcome back," Jason said when they climbed into the cabin's seats. He did a double take when he saw Bethany's injuries. "What happened?"

She threw him a wry twist of a smile. "For future reference, rain and the High Temple do not mix."

The pilot winced. "We'll have you back to Halcyon Caye in no time."

The helicopter shifted as the skids left the ground, and Bethany caught her breath as she did every time. To cover, she looked at Derek. "So, what do you want for dinner?"

"You're still planning on cooking? You should go home and relax for a while. Soak in a bath maybe."

She gave him a reproving look. "This is my job, remember? It may be a vacation for you, but I'm still expected to cook."

"I couldn't possibly eat anything for hours after those tacos. So you're off the hook."

"Maybe just dessert then?"

"Only if you join me."

His tone was light and playful, but there was still something in his gaze that made the helicopter's air conditioned interior feel small and stuffy. She swallowed and looked away. "We'll see."

"Bethany …" Derek placed a hand over hers on the seat, and she jerked—so violently that she knocked her backpack onto the floor, spilling items from the open zippered compartment. She scrambled to pick them up before he could help. The only way this day could get more embarrassing would be to have Derek handling her feminine products.

Wrong. She looked up and saw him holding a paperback book, a peculiar expression on his face. Her cheeks burned, and she snatched the book out of his hand to shove it back in the depths of her backpack.

"Why, Bethany Hall," he drawled. "I never took you for a romance novel fan."

The heat intensified. "It's not what you think."

"It's not? You don't just read them for the sexy bits?"

"No!" If her cheeks got any hotter, they would spontaneously combust.

"Why else does a woman who claims not to believe in romance read about it in her spare time?"

She folded her hands in her lap and swiveled toward him on the seat. "Just because I don't believe in something doesn't mean I refuse to acknowledge it. I don't believe in Santa Claus, either, but that doesn't stop me from decorating for Christmas."

"That's a totally bogus comparison and you know it."

"Well, it's true." Bethany crossed her arms and made a show of staring out the window. In truth, she was too attuned to Derek's presence beside her and the searching way he studied her when she wasn't looking. What did he want from her exactly? This was supposed to be a casual, friendly outing, not something that had suddenly become more charged than an electric fence. The romance novel thing had just injected another horrible level of awkwardness.

When they finally touched down on the island what felt like hours later, she couldn't get away fast enough.

"I hope you had a good time," she said hurriedly. "I'll have Eduardo light the fire in the small palapa when it gets dark."

"I meant what I said. I don't like to eat alone. I don't want dessert unless you'll join me."

She lifted her chin. "Fine. Meet me by the bonfire at seven thirty then." She swiveled on her heel and marched toward her bungalow on the opposite end of the island.

Bethany gave up on her plan for rest after an hour of lying on her fluffy bed, staring at the ceiling. Instead she went to the tiny bathroom and filled the tub with hot water, throwing in some lavender-infused bath salts for good measure. It would sting, but it would help heal her scraped up skin.

As soon as the water level neared the top, she climbed into the tub, her paperback in hand. She squashed a vague sense of guilt. It wasn't as if reading this book—or any of the other two dozen stashed in a cardboard mailing box in the corner of her bungalow—meant she had changed her mind about men. She didn't need to agree with the worldview to enjoy it. It was pure amusement, just like those ridiculous TV shows that claimed the pyramids and Mayan temples had been built to commune with aliens.

That was the example she should have used with Derek. The Santa Claus comparison had just been lame.

Fortunately, she was getting to the part of the story where something completely predictable interfered with the main couple's relationship and the woman went off all weepy, sure that romance was nothing but a fantasy. If Bethany were smart, she would stop there to remind herself that in real life, the guy didn't come back. There were no dramatic proposals or frantic sprints to the airport gate or extravagant gestures. Just heartbreak and loneliness and …

Geez. Now she was even depressing herself.

She put aside the book and climbed out of the tub, wrapping one towel around her body as she dried her hair. When it was no longer dripping, she twisted it into her traditional knot, which she then topped with a clean black-and-white bandanna. Then she pulled on a lacy, form-fitting cami that disappeared immediately beneath her bulky white jacket and black pants. Some female chefs tailored their jackets to give them a little more shape, but Bethany didn't see the point. She was in the kitchen to cook, not to catch anyone's eye—one reason she always hired a female sous for these assignments. She might have been slow to catch on, but she did eventually learn her lesson.

Bethany hooked her clogs over two fingers and headed barefoot to the Grand Palapa's kitchen. When she arrived, she immediately began to pull ingredients from the walk-in refrigerator and the wire shelving. She plopped a bunch of plantains on the counter, along with wonton wrappers, several different kinds of sugar, and a plastic bin of cornflakes. Then she dropped two big scoops of virgin coconut oil into a saucepan to start heating while she got the caramel sauce going beside it on the range. Her favorite dessert was by no means Belizean or even traditional to any culture. She'd just been messing around with variations on the deep-fried banana that repeatedly turned up in Latin American and Asian cuisine, and she'd hit on a particularly successful rendition.

She first rolled the peeled fruit in layers of flour, crushed cornflakes, and cinnamon and sugar, then set them aside on the tray. When the oil was up to temperature, she dropped the pieces in for the first fry until they were golden and crispy, and set them aside to drain. Then she folded them into the wonton wrappers, which puffed up slightly during the second dip in the hot oil. A drizzle of hot caramel sauce went on the plate first, then several pieces of banana sliced diagonally, finished with a dusting of powdered sugar.

She cleaned smudges of caramel off the edges of the plates with a towel and reviewed them with satisfaction. The presentation only added to the enjoyment, even when it was simply dessert by the fire.

When she carried the plates out from the kitchen to the little palapa near the water's edge, she could just make out the outline of Derek on one of the sofas, intermittently illuminated by the flickering fire in front of him.

"Dessert is served, sir," she announced as she approached him from behind.

He twisted on the seat to face her. His hair was still wet from the shower, or maybe the ocean, dark splotches marking the collar of his tight blue t-shirt. She forced a smile and prayed she would be able to pull in a lungful of air before she suffocated.

Rein it in, girl. You'd think you've never seen a man before. Even if he is a particularly impressive specimen.

"Rest up?" His warm tone melted over her.

"Sure." She cleared her throat. "You like bananas, right? Plantains?"

"Of course. That looks amazing." He took the plate from her and patted the cushion next to him. She sat, making sure to leave plenty of space between them.

"I had a good time today." He dragged the banana piece through a pool of caramel. "Thank you."

"You're welcome." She hesitated for a minute before she bit into her own dessert. This felt weird. Sure, guests often wanted to offer their compliments in person. The foodies sometimes liked to watch her work in the kitchen. But the way he was looking at her now, like they were here together, was completely new and thoroughly unsettling.

He reached over and tugged her bandanna from her head. "Your hair is a pretty color. You shouldn't cover it up. I didn't even realize it was red until I saw you this morning."

"With these freckles? It was a sure bet."

"Then why hide it? It makes you unique, especially in Belize."

"I have to cover my hair in the kitchen, and I don't like wearing a toque in this humidity." It was also a convenient way to hide her femininity in a male-dominated industry, but she wasn't about to get into that with him now. Instead, she changed the subject. "So, we're set up for tomorrow. We'll be taking a boat to Ambergris Caye in the morning. You'll want to bring swim trunks, but dress for lots of walking. There aren't many cars on the island, so the choices are golf cart, bicycle, or foot. Since it's difficult to get back after dark, I had Eduardo make us room reservations for the night. We can return the next morning. If that's okay with you."

"It sounds perfect. Ambergris Caye is Belize's most touristy island, right?"

"Yes. Lots of expats too. But you'll enjoy it. Good food, live music at night."

"I trust you." He polished off the last of his bananas and set his plate on the side table. "That was really good, especially the caramel sauce."

"It's house-made," she said. "Though the wonton wrappers aren't. I just keep them in the freezer."

"I promise I won't tell." He smiled at her, and the way the firelight cast his face in alternating light and shadow somehow made his handsome face even more devastating to her determination to stay detached. He reached out and swiped his thumb against the corner of her mouth. "You have a little caramel right there."

She froze, her heart lurching to a full stop in her chest. Before she could formulate a coherent response, he gave her a mischievous grin and transferred the sauce to her nose. "There. That's better."

A laugh welled from her chest. "Oh, you shouldn't have done that."

"No?" Challenge glinted in his eyes.

Bethany dipped her finger into the caramel on her plate, intending to return the favor. Instead, his hand shot out and clamped around her wrist, holding it fast between them. She fought his grip, but he was too strong. And then he leaned forward and licked the caramel from her finger.

Bethany's mouth dropped open. "I can't believe you just did that."

"I told you," he said. "It's too good to waste."

Something in his tone loosened the gridlock in her brain. Before he could guess what she was doing, she dipped her other hand into the caramel on the plate and slapped it onto his cheek.

"You shouldn't have done that." He grabbed her plate and tossed it onto the table, then trapped her other wrist in his hand while she laughed and squealed and tried to break free. And then somehow, he had her on her back on the chaise, arms pinned beside her head, both of them out of breath and laughing.

"Stop!" she gasped, trying to catch her breath. "I give. You win."

She stopped wriggling, and only then did she comprehend her position beneath him. Apparently so did he. The mirth vanished from his face, replaced by an intense look that simultaneously terrified and thrilled her. He stared into her eyes for an instant that seemed to stretch to eternity. When his gaze dropped to her mouth, her insides gave a brutal twist.

He was going to kiss her. She wanted him to kiss her.

No. *No.* She dragged her mind back from that languid place that didn't give a rip about vows and past mistakes and focused instead on the fact that she was publicly pinned in a compromising position. With a guest. In full view of anyone who might walk by.

"What time is it?" Her voice came out breathless and wobbly. "I need to get the kitchen cleaned up before it gets too late."

The intense look disappeared from Derek's face, a tinge of embarrassment taking its place. He pushed himself to his feet and then held out a hand to pull her upright. "Are you okay? I forgot about all your bruises."

"I'm fine." She straightened her jacket and smoothed her hair, sure she was thoroughly disheveled. Of course, she wasn't the one wearing a streak of caramel down one cheek like war paint, something she wasn't about to point out while she was still within arm's reach. "Breakfast is at nine. We catch the water taxi at eleven."

"I'll be ready," Derek said simply. "And Bethany? Thanks again. Today was the most fun I've had in years."

She dipped her head in acknowledgment and gathered the plates, his words sending a wave of pleasure through her. "Just remember you said that when you look in the mirror later."

Before he could process the meaning of her words, she turned and hightailed it back to the kitchen, trying—and failing—to ignore his hot gaze on her back the entire way.

nine

DEREK'S FIRST THOUGHT upon landing on the dock at Ambergris Caye was that it was quite possibly heaven on earth.

The second thought was that coming to Ambergris Caye with Bethany was just short of hell.

He'd never met anyone who struck him as so effortlessly attractive, even when she was purposely downplaying her looks. Some women he knew spent hours in front of the mirror just to go to the supermarket. Bethany showed up in a simple white t-shirt and modestly-cut shorts, without a lick of makeup, and it was the single most alluring thing he'd ever seen in his life.

It was the very last thing he needed today.

He'd been close, so close to crossing their very precisely drawn line last night. Had he kissed her, she probably would have welcomed it, and who knows where the evening would have gone from there. The last thing either of them needed was an ill-considered night of stupidity, him just three days past a broken engagement. If ever there were a classic example of a rebound situation, it was this one.

And yet he could barely look at her without his attention wandering to her full, pink-tinged lips and imagining what they would feel like against his. Fantasizing about what they would taste like. Remembering how she'd felt pressed up against him on the temple steps, soft and warm and feminine.

Yep. Hell. Undoubtedly. Or if he wasn't there already, he'd be headed there soon.

"So, what do you want to do?" Bethany asked, hoisting her straw handbag over her shoulder. "Maybe check into the hotel so we can drop our bags, and then we'll do a little exploring?"

"I'll leave that to you," he said. "I assumed you made plans."

"Only loose ones. This is your vacation after all. I figured you probably didn't want to be scheduled on a precise timetable or anything on your last couple of days."

That's right. He was leaving on Friday. Another reason to get his unruly thoughts under control. Anything between them would be over before it even started.

True to Bethany's word, the island's golf cart taxis hovered at the end of the dock, waiting to pick up new arrivals. Bethany led him to the first one in the line and hopped into the back seat, leaving the space beside the driver for him.

"Where to?" the driver asked.

"Bay Breeze Hotel."

Derek stayed quiet, taking in their surroundings. In less than a day, he'd been transported from the Central American interior back to the quintessential Caribbean island town. Palm trees marked the street's margins, swaying gently in the tropical breeze. Golf carts rattled in both directions, passing pedestrians and cyclists, no one wearing clothing more formal than shorts and flip flops. The pastel-colored buildings that lined the cobblestone drive ranged from beach shack to Spanish style. Still, when the taxi stopped, his mouth dropped open.

Bethany grinned at him. "Didn't believe there was anything like this in Belize, did you?"

The hotel was a sprawling, U-shaped Spanish structure—all red clay roofs and stuccoed archways—that was completely at odds with the haphazard town they'd ridden through to get here. Bethany hopped out of the cart with her single small bag and waited for him to follow with his duffel, then led him into the lobby where a long expanse of Spanish tile led to the gleaming wood reception desk.

"Pretty impressive, huh?" she threw over her shoulder with a smile. "It was built by the same company who owns Halcyon. First class all the way."

"You know, I'm beginning to think that you think I'm a snob."

"Private island, remember?" But her tone was teasing, not reproachful.

They checked into their separate rooms—not adjoining, thankfully—and then climbed the single flight of stairs to the second floor. The covered walkway gave them a view of the courtyard below—which included a sparkling blue swimming pool, its edges as sinuous and curvy as the island itself, and a sandy expanse studded by palm trees from which rope hammocks hung.

"Even I love this place, and I'm used to the luxury on Halcyon. If you want to hang around the pool and the beach today, I'm perfectly fine with that."

"I could do that back on the island. I want to see the town."

She looked at him askance. "Really?"

"Yes. Let me drop my bag and I'll meet you below." He continued down the walkway and pushed through to his room, which was every bit as luxurious as his accommodations on the island: golden wood, crisp white linens, and a stunning water view from the French doors. He left his duffel bag on the bed, and when he emerged again, Bethany was waiting for him.

"Wearing your trunks?" she asked.

"I am. Lead the way."

He followed Bethany back down the stairs, through the lobby, and onto the street, where they were met immediately by the trade winds that cooled the island. They walked in companionable silence for several minutes while he took in the fenced-in homes and open storefronts along the side of the cobblestone road.

"You know, you're missing out on the snorkeling," she said. "The sea life is absolutely stunning. Are you sure you don't want to change your mind? I could still set something up."

"No, it's okay. I'm not overly fond of the ocean anyway."

She cocked her head. "This isn't just a lack of interest on your part, is it?"

She'd picked that up in his voice, had she? "I had a bad experience at the beach when I was a kid."

Her eyebrows flew up, and he was momentarily tempted to embellish the story for effect, to make his fear sound less irrational. But he didn't. "My whole family was on a trip to Hawaii. I must have been seven or eight. I was bodysurfing by myself while everyone else was up on the beach. There was a riptide that day, and I got pulled away from shore. By the time a lifeguard noticed, I was pretty far out, exhausted from treading water and trying to swim across the current. A little longer and I would have drowned. Ever since then, I don't like being in water over my head. Boats and kayaks are fine, but snorkeling and scuba diving are pretty much out."

"I can't believe your family didn't notice!" Bethany said, wide-eyed. "I mean, you were only seven. I wasn't allowed to walk to the mailbox by myself at that age."

"It was our first trip together after my mom died. I think we were all so focused on proving we could do it without her that no one was paying much attention." He shrugged and gave her a crooked grin. "If I want to see tropical fish, I'll go to an aquarium."

She didn't smile at the joke; she was still looking at him with sympathy. "I'm sorry. About your mom. That must have been difficult."

"It was." He nudged her shoulder with his. "How about you? Did you have a run-in with a monkey in your past or something?"

Bethany grimaced. "Nothing that rational, I'm afraid."

"Come on, tell me. I won't laugh."

She looked at him from the corner of her eye. "My dad made me watch *Planet of the Apes* with him when I was five."

He couldn't help it. He laughed.

"Hey! You said you wouldn't do that!"

"That's before I knew the reason. I figured a monkey had grabbed your hair at the zoo or something legitimately terrifying."

"Talking apes are terrifying!"

"Agreed, but last time I checked, primates in real life do not speak English." Another chuckle slipped from his lips before he caught her glare and smothered his mirth. "I'm sorry. I guess if you're five, that would be scary."

"Thank you. Even though you don't really mean it."

"I promise, I totally mean it." He held up two fingers. "Scout's honor."

"It's three fingers, and I bet you weren't even a Boy Scout."

"Nope. Not at all."

They continued down the street, Bethany pointing out her favorite shops and restaurants, occasionally greeting familiar street vendors in fluid Spanish.

She was different here, he thought. More relaxed, less guarded. The freckled redhead who should look like a tourist somehow blended seamlessly with the San Pedro natives. She hid when she was on Halcyon Caye: in the kitchen, beneath the voluminous uniform, behind her job. Watching her now, walking easily beside him with the trade winds blowing tendrils of copper hair against her pale cheek, he felt an unfamiliar tug in his chest that was completely unrelated to the wash of attraction he'd felt earlier.

Bethany looked up at him, her brows tugged together in a quizzical fashion.

He cleared his throat so he didn't have to explain his staring. "What now?"

"That depends. Are you hungry?"

"Always."

"And you're up for anything?" A twinkle of mischief lit her blue eyes.

"I don't know," Derek said slowly. "What did you have in mind?"

ten

BETHANY KEPT HER PLAN TO HERSELF, even though she'd begun questioning the wisdom of her idea from the moment it left her lips. Not only did this plan involve water, which Derek was a bit iffy about, but it also involved showing more skin than she was accustomed to in a professional setting. Had Derek not treated her with friendly detachment—a relief considering their charged moment the night before—she would have abandoned the idea altogether. But he would miss out on one of the unique experiences on Ambergris Caye.

"Here we are!" she said brightly as they stepped onto the pier. A long gangplank-style walkway led to a palapa, which stood on stilts over the turquoise waters. "Some of the best food in Belize, with perhaps the most unique bar."

Derek's handsome face broke into a smile. "Inner tubes?"

"Absolutely." The small palapa housed several tables around a central grill where seafood and barbecued meat was cooked, while a sea of black inner tubes bobbed on the water below. She watched the amusement on Derek's face as he watched a server lower drinks in an ice-filled bucket down to the floating patrons. "If you think it's too silly—"

"No, it's fun. Caribbean experience, right?"

"Right. But first, food." She took Derek's arm, trying to ignore the feel of solid muscle beneath her hand, and pulled him toward the round counter that circled the cooking area. "Hey, Michael."

"Beth!" The cook's face lit up when he saw her. "Long time no see!"

"I'm showing a friend around San Pedro today." She hoped by now she could at least call Derek a friend, even if it was only temporary. "What's on today?"

"Pulled pork and onions is always good, and I've got some cracked conch and snapper coming up."

"Conch po'boy for me then," she said immediately.

"For you?" Michael glanced at Derek, his smile slipping a little.

"Same as Bethany."

Michael nodded to them both. "Find a seat. Food will be out in a couple of minutes."

"Thanks, Michael." Bethany led the way to a table on the far end, which gave them an uninterrupted view of blue seas and white-clouded skies. She lifted her face briefly to the warm wind and sighed. If Derek didn't love it here, he was absolutely crazy.

Or maybe he traveled so much, he was no longer awed by turquoise waters and rosy sunsets. Curiosity got the best of her. "You said you've been to Hawaii and Panama. Now Belize. Anywhere else?"

He lifted a shoulder. "Mexico and Canada, of course. Europe a couple of times with my dad as a teenager. Nothing all that exciting. Belize is probably the most adventurous."

"And here I thought you were the globe-trotting type."

"Too busy working, I guess. I earned a lot of vacation time but never used it. Which is pretty pathetic, now that I think about it. How about you?"

"Believe it or not, the first time I ever left the country was to come here." She made a face. "I guess that's pathetic too."

"Seems pretty adventurous, actually. How'd you settle on Belize, out of every other place on earth you could have gone?"

"Mariska. She'd been here on vacation and fell in love with it. If you'd ever spent any time with her, you'd know she creates her own vortex. One minute you're agreeing to go on a little vacation with her and the next, you're packing up your life and moving out of country together."

"And your family didn't object?"

Her attention went to the scarred tabletop. They'd objected plenty, but it wasn't the move to Belize with which they'd taken exception. She'd just not had the heart to endure the I-told-you-so's when things with Alejándro fell apart.

"They were supportive," she said finally, not sure if that counted as an outright lie or not.

They fell quiet as Michael approached and slid their plates in front of them. "Here you go. Let me know if you need anything else."

"Thanks, Michael." Bethany loaded her sandwich with coleslaw, then took a huge bite. Conch could be a little tough at times, but when it was pounded thin and tender, then breaded and fried, it turned into flaky, buttery perfection. Add the tangy slaw and it was pure heaven. The po'boy might not be authentic Belizean, but that didn't make it any less delicious.

Derek wasn't eating, though, instead looking between her and Michael. "Let me guess. You two had a thing."

Bethany's eyes widened, and she nearly choked on her food. "Me and Michael? No! Why would you say that?"

"Because he's annoyed that you brought another guy here and he's trying not to show it."

Bethany glanced at Michael, who merely gave her a little nod and went back to the grill. "We're just friends. He helped me out when I first moved here."

"Yeah, well, he's thinking it's time to cash in the favor."

Derek's tone was so acerbic, she laughed. "If I didn't know better, I'd say you were jealous."

"Not jealous. Just insulted. For all he knows, you and I are together."

His words brought a flush to her cheeks, though she would be hard-pressed to say why. Michael was a flirt, sure. He was that way with every woman, whether local or tourist. But the protective edge to Derek's voice set a flutter in her middle that was wholly incompatible with the need to maintain her neutrality.

"He's probably insulted you haven't tasted your food." Bethany nudged his plate, desperate to change the subject. Thankfully, he took the hint and picked up his sandwich, pronouncing it amazing after his first bite.

After Bethany paid their tab—and she practically had to rip the check out of Derek's hands—he glanced over the side of the rail to the inner tubes. "So ... we going to do it?"

Her plan seemed even less appealing now. "We're going to sink like stones after all that food."

"This was your idea. And after all that walking, I think I should get to relax in the sun for a while."

It was his vacation. She sighed and nodded, then ordered a couple of Belikins to be sent down to them. She trailed Derek back to the stairs that disappeared into blue waters and hesitated.

Derek had no such reticence, pulling his shirt over his head immediately. And why would he be shy? Every inch of him was tanned and toned, and it was all she could do not to gawk as he plunged down the stairs into the water.

"You coming?" He flopped into an inner tube and patted the one beside him.

Now or never. She shimmied out of her shorts and t-shirt until she was standing in her favorite 1940's style bikini. She loved it, not in small part because it covered some of the pale skin that drew attention to her like a beacon. Today, though, it was the mottled spots of black and blue over her body that were on full display.

Derek kept the same indifferent look as he held the inner tube for her to sit, then pushed them both off the dock. Warm water lapped around Bethany's legs and midsection.

"See, you were right. This was a good idea." Derek winked at her and sent a splash of water her direction.

Sure. She was glad her sunglasses covered her eyes, because she was having a hard time keeping her attention off the well-defined muscles in his chest and shoulders. Why couldn't he actually be built like the desk jockey she had teased him about being? It would be so much easier to pretend she had zero interest in him if he didn't look like *that*.

Bethany grabbed the rope that tethered the inner tubes together and to the dock, intending to pull herself closer to where their drinks were being lowered in the bucket.

"Uh, Bethany? How deep is this water?"

Bethany looked back just in time to see him slip off the inner tube and disappear beneath the surface. She gasped. "Derek!"

He surfaced, spluttering, then slid under again. Just as she was beginning to panic, his hand appeared above the water … and pulled her in after him.

Bethany plunged straight to the bottom, warm water engulfing her. As soon as her feet hit the sand, she thrust upward toward the surface.

To the sound of Derek's laughter.

"You jerk!" she yelled, more shocked than angry. "I really thought you were in trouble!"

"Here? Look, I can touch the bottom." He grinned at her and slicked his wet hair back with one hand, looking all the more attractive when he was soaked and laughing.

"Well, I can't, thank you very much." She spluttered as her mouth dipped beneath the water's surface again.

"Sorry." He looked contrite, though his eyes still danced with mirth. He put an arm around her waist, the buoyancy of the water lifting her to his eye level. Automatically, she slid her arm around his shoulders. "Better?"

"Better." Her voice came out breathy, no surprise now that her heart was beating so hard she swore he could see it. They were barely touching, the water doing as much to keep them apart as push them together. Even so, his arm around her bare waist left a trail of fire in its wake. With her hand splayed across his upper back, it was all she could do not to give in to the urge to explore his water-slicked skin with her fingertips.

"Bethany?"

"Yes?"

He nodded toward the pier. "Do you want to get our drinks or should I?"

"Oh. Right." Her face flamed as she realized how quickly her imagination had run off with her. "You get them. Since you can actually touch the bottom."

Derek waited until she levered herself back into the inner tube, then half-walked, half-swam back to the waiting bucket. She used the time to do some deep breathing exercises and get her thoroughly inappropriate thoughts under control.

This was crazy. It needed to stop now. She was supposed to be thinking professionally and not aching for more than just an arm around her waist. Maybe it wasn't completely unexpected here—all sorts of "regular" people ended up in casual hook-ups they would never consider back home, influenced by the pulse of romance that seemed to beat just below the surface of warm trade winds and turquoise waters. But that didn't mean she'd ever been one of them.

Bethany had mostly talked herself out of her crazy thoughts by the time Derek waded back, a bottle of Belikin in each hand. He passed off her bottle and then struggled one-handed back into his inner tube.

"So, what do you want to do for the rest of the day?" Bethany asked, managing a casual tone.

"Is this an option?" He shot her another bone-melting smile, but this time she didn't return it. He aimed a splash of water in her direction. "What's wrong? Are you still mad at me for the trick I played on you? I swear, I didn't think you'd take me so seriously."

He wasn't acting like anything had happened between them. Maybe she was the only one who felt that magnetic charge. Or maybe Derek was so used to women becoming tongue-tied in his presence that he no longer noticed. That was probably why perfect guys dated models: they were immune to each other's gorgeousness.

Derek was still waiting for an answer, though, so she forced a smile. "No, not really. I'm not going to fall for it a second time, though, so try not to actually drown yourself. I won't save you."

"Noted." A rowdy group of college-aged kids splashed into the water, and Derek gave his and Bethany's tubes a push away from the dock. The cords that linked them together allowed them to drift far enough out to dampen the raucous laughter. "So tell me, Chef Hall, how did you choose this career? Being a chef, I mean, not in Belize specifically."

Derek looked legitimately curious, so Bethany took a drink and considered how to begin. She might as well lead with the truth. It was embarrassing, but maybe that wasn't a bad thing. "I was a fat kid."

Derek's eyebrows raised at her bluntness. She shook her head. "I realize now that I really wasn't, but I got teased a lot. You know, the chubby girl with red hair and freckles. I wasn't all that good at school or sports or art or anything else. I got kind of obsessed with food and dieting. My mom only knew how to cook one way—these hearty, greasy, fried sorts of things, and she was so rail-thin it never seemed to affect her."

"So you started cooking out of self-preservation?"

"Exactly. I combed cookbooks from the library for healthy meals that would pass muster with my parents, and somewhere along the way, I realized I was really good at it. It made me … special. It was a skill that people actually seemed to value. I guess when you're a fat girl who can cook, it makes all the difference."

Derek winced every time she used the word *fat*, which was a point in his favor. His eyes never left her face. "What then?"

"My grades weren't good enough for college—I barely pulled Cs because I spent my after school hours concocting new and better recipes instead of studying—so I went to culinary school. It was a whole new world. Finding something you're truly great at is a godsend for someone like me."

"Hey. Stop doing that." Derek gave a sharp shake of his head. "Stop minimizing yourself."

"I'm not," Bethany said lightly. "I'm just being realistic."

Derek grabbed the cord that connected their floats and drew her in until the black rubber sides bumped together. "Bethany. There is absolutely nothing wrong with you. Not then. Most certainly not now."

The way his gaze drifted down her body and back up to meet her eyes made her flush. Even though the attention didn't feel creepy, only appreciative, she had to avert her eyes so he wouldn't see the insecurity raised by his appraisal.

"Anyway. I graduated. Worked my way up from kitchen assistant to saucier to sous in some pretty well-known restaurants. And then I got offered the head chef position at a new restaurant in Coconut Grove. Not quite the same thing as my own restaurant, but it gave me the experience I needed to move forward. And then I came here."

She was leaving out a huge chunk of the story, and he had to know it. Before he could probe further, she asked, "What made you choose finance over the entertainment industry? TV royalty and all."

"I don't know. I grew up in Hollywood, so I was pretty unimpressed by it. Maybe it's like how children decline to carry on the family business. There's no challenge involved when you're following in someone else's footsteps."

"And numbers are challenging?"

"Wall Street is challenging. I imagine it's a very similar environment to a commercial kitchen. Only the knives are metaphorical." He laughed at her surprise. "Hey, I've watched *Hell's Kitchen*. And I've seen your scars. I bet you could give me a run for my money in the high-stress environment category."

"Except we both escaped before it killed us."

"I guess we did." Derek quirked a smile her direction and tipped his bottle to hers with a clink. "To our good sense."

"To our good sense," she echoed, though that felt like a lie too. When it came to Derek, all her better judgment seemed to be disintegrating by the minute.

eleven

THEY FLOATED IN THEIR INNER TUBES until the sun began to dip to the horizon behind them and the sweltering heat softened to something more endurable in the twilight. Derek was beginning to feel a little intoxicated. Too bad he hadn't drunk nearly enough to blame it on the alcohol.

Bethany Hall was unlike any woman he'd ever met. Funny, smart, beautiful, and so utterly without vanity that he let himself relax for the first time in ages. He'd always vaguely felt as if he was an accessory to Anna—someone to make her look good in photos, compliment her on her wardrobe, keep her company when she was lonely. Bethany actually seemed interested in what he had to say on all topics from serious to lighthearted. How she couldn't see how appealing she was remained a mystery, especially considering how he could barely keep his eyes off her.

All of the above made him wish he wasn't leaving in three days.

"So what now?" he asked as they stood on the dock, pulling their dry clothes on over wet swimsuits. The strings of twinkle lights beneath the palapa had just switched on, lending a festive atmosphere to the increasingly crowded bar.

"I made us dinner reservations at a friend's restaurant." She grimaced at the wet spots on her clothing. "I guess we need to go back and change first, though."

"We definitely need to change. In my family, you dress for dinner, even in the Caribbean."

"Good thing I brought something other than shorts with me," Bethany said with a resigned sigh.

"Come on. You can't tell me you don't like dressing up once in a while."

"I rarely have the need. I came to Belize to get away from all that. Miami has some serious night life."

"I bet." They started toward their hotel, walking slowly along the edge of the cobblestone streets. "So how do you know Ambergris Caye so well? You seem like you have a lot of friends here."

"I live here in San Pedro. You didn't know that?"

"No, you didn't tell me."

"Mariska and I share a condo on the north side of the city. We're only here part of the time, but it's nice to have someplace to come back to when I'm not on Halcyon. I pick up a few personal chef gigs when I'm here too."

"And the rest of the time you party like a freshman on Spring Break?"

She snorted, which made him laugh too. "Hardly. In fact, Mariska has to drag me away from my books."

"Oh? More romance novels?"

Even in the dimming sunset, he caught the color in her cheeks. "You aren't going to let me forget that, are you?"

He laughed again. "It's nothing to be ashamed of. It just makes me think you might not be as jaded as you like to pretend."

"Oh, trust me. I'm jaded. I've had firsthand experience with how those fairy-tale romances end. Doesn't make me hate the fairy tales, though."

"Fair enough."

"What about you? What made you so cynical? You said you were honest with Anna, so it had to happen before her."

Derek studied her as they walked. She'd been painfully transparent about why she started cooking. Maybe he owed her the same candor.

"My dad's been married five times," he said finally.

"After your mom died?"

He nodded. "The one right after Mom—Candace—I really liked. We all thought she was going to stick around. And then one day we came home from school and she was gone, like she'd never existed. No goodbyes. Just packed up her stuff and left.

"Turns out Dad was seeing his production assistant while he was married to Candace. She left him, and I can't really blame her. The production assistant, Fiona, became wife number three. And so on. As I got older, the wives and girlfriends kept getting younger."

"That's hard," Bethany said softly. "But just because that's the way it worked for him …"

"The thing is, I watched Dad chase that high of falling in love over and over. As soon as it wore off, he was on to the next woman, regardless of the wreck he left behind. I swore I would never be that guy."

"You could never be that guy, Derek. I've only known you a few days, and I know that. Even if you can't see it."

Derek shrugged. "Maybe not. But the best I could do with Anna is make sure she didn't have unrealistic expectations. That she wasn't looking for the fairy tale. We both know how that turned out."

Bethany sighed, but it sounded like resigned agreement and not judgment. "You're right. I just can't decide if we're lucky that we learned the truth early or if we should be pitied because we miss out on the parts that are actually pretty good."

"Maybe a little of both." He smiled at her as they slowed to a stop in front of their expansive hotel. "Meet you back in the lobby?"

"An hour?"

"Deal." They headed up the stairs and parted ways on the balcony, toward their separate rooms. Despite himself, he watched Bethany walk away, feeling unaccountably wistful again.

No use denying it. He liked her. He was attracted to her. And he absolutely could not have her. Because no matter what she said about love, no matter how badly she had been hurt, eventually her heart would heal and she would want the fairy tale.

Derek showered and changed into evening-appropriate tropical clothing, trying not to let regret chew on his insides. He turned on the television and watched the local news, which mostly involved things like a dispute between taxi drivers and the local government. When the clock finally ticked off a full hour, he shoved his wallet and room key into his pocket and headed down to the lobby.

And stopped in his tracks.

Bethany turned to him, an uncertain smile on her face. "Ready?"

"You look … wow."

No, *wow* didn't cover it, though his sudden lack of vocabulary reflected his tongue-tied feeling well. If he'd been shocked by her appearance yesterday, he felt knocked off his feet this evening. She wore a knee-length red sundress, its billowy long sleeves slit from elbow to shoulder, the waist cinched with a braided leather belt. Combined with her long hair spilling in loose waves over her shoulders, the effect was tropical and relaxed and so tempting he wasn't sure he'd be able to remember his own name if she asked.

"I meant, wow."

She fairly glowed with pleasure. "You said that already. The restaurant is on the north side of the city, so we're borrowing one of the resort's golf carts."

"Borrowing?"

"You're a VIP guest," she said with a smile, but he couldn't tell if she was teasing him or not.

She led him out to a dinky two-seater cart sporting the hotel logo and climbed into the driver's seat. He didn't object. He had no idea where they were going, and besides, the less attention he had to spend on the road, the more he could watch her.

Probably not a helpful thought right now.

Night had fallen, bringing with it slightly lower temperatures and an uptick in the winds that made the air feel downright cool compared to the sweltering heat of day. Bethany navigated the dimly lit streets with the sureness of a native, taking them to the other side of the island and then north toward the cluster of restaurants and nightclubs that hugged the shore. When she finally stopped the cart along the street in front of a wood-paneled, beach-front building, he jumped out first so he could help her down from the driver's seat.

Totally unnecessary, as was the length of time he held her hand. Even then, he only let go so he could place his hand on her back as they walked into the restaurant together. The interior straddled the line between elegant and Caribbean casual with lots of rattan and wood and dimly romantic lighting: candles and torches and hurricane lamps in every nook.

A young Belizean hostess smiled as they approached, but before she could ask their names, a dark-skinned man with close-cropped hair and a brilliant smile moved from the back of the small restaurant. Without a word, he put his arms around Bethany and squeezed.

"There you are!" he said finally in rapid, accented Spanish. "So nice to see you, Bethany!"

"Diego, this is one of my clients, Derek Moretti. We escaped Halcyon for the day so he could sample some of Belize's best cooking."

"Smart girl," he said to Bethany, then extended his hand to Derek. "Welcome. Come with me."

Diego led them to a table on the balcony, which was cantilevered over the beach and lit by flickering torches. Had Derek not known better, he'd say the restaurant had been chosen specifically for the ambiance.

Apparently, Bethany could read minds, because as soon as Diego left them with menus, she leaned forward and whispered, "It's a little over the top, I know. But hands down, this is the best food on Ambergris."

"Diego is the owner and not the chef?"

"Right. He's been on me to work here since I filled in a few nights when his chef's wife had a baby."

"Why don't you?"

"I like the quiet on Halcyon Caye," Bethany said. "I already escaped, remember?"

"True." It seemed funny that he'd once thought she needed to learn to relax. She seemed perfectly at home here in San Pedro. Maybe it was just around restaurant people that she opened up, despite being completely oblivious to the fact that most of her "friends" had more than simple friendship on their minds.

How could she not get that she was striking and interesting, and half the men who came in contact with her were wondering how they could capture her attention? And why did the idea of her taking a single one of them up on the offer send a spike of jealousy through him?

Derek was acting weird. Maybe she shouldn't have been so honest about her feelings today. Maybe she shouldn't have pressed him so hard about his reticence to believe in love. She definitely shouldn't have dressed up. She'd even put on makeup—full proof she'd baked her brain too long in the sun.

Now their earlier rapport was gone, replaced by this weird distance.

Derek had been so casual and fun with her and now he was staring at her like he expected her to …

Well, she had no idea what he expected, but the tension made her jittery.

"You can't go wrong with anything on the menu," she said. "But I particularly like the spiny lobster. It's got a Peruvian twist."

"Spiny lobster it is, then."

The food was as good as she remembered, but she hardly noticed as she struggled to make small talk and recapture some of the ease they'd enjoyed earlier that day. "Our boat picks us up to return to Halcyon at noon tomorrow. I thought that would give us enough time to eat breakfast and then hang out by the pool for a while."

"That sounds like a good plan," he said, but she had no idea whether he meant it or not.

Why must men be so difficult to read?

They finished their meal with a smattering of awkward small talk and declined dessert. Bethany's mood dipped lower as she paid the check—her insistence—and they walked back to the golf cart. Maybe she'd scared him off because she'd gotten dressed up, even though he was the one who insisted they be properly attired.

Or maybe he found her ill-advised attempt to be pretty for him pathetic. Because no matter what she told herself, that's what she was doing. She liked his attention, thought maybe that hint of attraction she'd sensed was real.

She steered the cart back through the streets of San Pedro to the resort, while Derek sat silently beside her, the nervous tap of his leg hinting he wanted to be anywhere but here. She bit back her humiliation and disappointment, shoved them down deep where they belonged with the rest of her ridiculous fantasies.

They returned the cart to the hotel's lot and left the keys with an attendant, then walked inside together. The lobby was nearly deserted, but whether it was too early or too late, she didn't know. Bethany fingered the strap of her purse uncertainly.

"I'm sorry if this trip wasn't exactly what you were expecting," she began. "I hope you at least—"

She didn't get any further in her apology because Derek pulled her behind a potted palm, took her face in his hands, and kissed her.

She was so stunned, she couldn't do anything but stand there, her heart pounding and her thoughts piling on top of each other, as gridlocked as Miami traffic. When he pulled away, she just stared at him, wide-eyed.

Derek looked equally stunned by his behavior. "I'm sorry. I thought—"

Bethany slid her hand behind his neck and guided his head down to hers again.

It took only a split second for him to react. One hand spread across her back so she was pressed up against him, his other hand supporting her head as he teased apart her lips with his own. Desire flowed through her, warm and slow as honey, his mouth more intoxicating than the wine she could still taste on his tongue, until she forgot about every worry, every warning, every reason why she'd sworn she wasn't going to get involved.

Then he pulled back, a fierceness in his eyes that simultaneously excited and frightened her. "Coffee," he rasped.

"Coffee?" Surely the kiss had dislodged the language-processing part of her brain, because she had no idea what he was talking about. Besides, she didn't want coffee, she wanted more of this—his lips on hers, his hands on her body …

"On the patio. In public. Because if we keep this up, I'm taking you straight back to my room. And I don't want to be the guy who sleeps with a virtual stranger on vacation any more than you want to be that girl."

Right. He was right. Even if the half-growled words and the naked desire on his face made her question whether she might want to be that girl after all.

"Coffee would be good," she said finally, proud that her voice only trembled a little.

He took her hand, lacing their fingers together, and led her through the lobby to the patio. Across the pool, another couple dined in candlelight, their heads tilted together in intimate conversation, taking every excuse to touch each other. She dragged her eyes away at the impossible longing the scene ignited in her.

"What do you want?" Derek asked. She just stared at him, unblinking, until he prompted, "For dessert."

"Oh." She picked up the menu and then immediately put it back down. "The chocolate mousse tart. I get it every time I'm here. It's excellent."

Derek caught a server's eye as he came onto the patio and ordered them each a coffee and a chocolate tart in rapid, unaccented Spanish. If anything, it only made him sexier.

Not that he needed help in that department. When he caught her hand on the table, his fingers warm and strong, that mere touch sent a shiver all the way up her arm and down her back.

"I think I was probably out of line," he said.

"Then so was I. You just shocked me. I was getting the impression you were having second thoughts about this whole trip."

"You short-circuited my brain with that dress and that hair and all … this." He gave a wave of his hand with a self-conscious chuckle. "You really should give a man some warning."

"It hadn't occurred to me. It's not like men pull me behind potted plants on a regular basis." Great. Now she sounded lame. And desperate.

He looked at her thoughtfully. "What happened in Miami, Bethany?"

"What do you mean?"

"You left because of a guy, didn't you?"

She pulled her hand away, a chill cutting through the leftover glow of their kiss. "I don't want to talk about it. Definitely not now. Certainly not with you."

He looked like he was about to argue, but the server returned with their coffees and tarts. She picked up her fork and focused on her food like it was the only thing that could save her from the uncomfortable conversation.

Come to think of it, that had always been her problem. She set down her utensil with a sigh. "I was engaged."

Derek looked startled, but he only gave her an encouraging nod.

"His name was Alejándro. He was the owner of the restaurant. A little older than me, gorgeous, experienced. I was so flattered by his interest, I never questioned the rumors I heard about his … extra-curricular activities. And when he asked me to marry him, I agreed. My family never trusted him, though. Tried to warn me that something didn't add up. But I was in love."

Derek listened quietly, but she toyed with her napkin, unable to look him in the eye. "One night I came in early to the restaurant and found him in a compromising position with our hostess. Our beautiful, sexy, Puerto Rican hostess. He admitted they had been seeing each other all along. He said he wanted to marry her, not me." Funny how saying the words could still bring a wash of humiliation, even three years later.

"So that's why you left Miami?"

She nodded, glad that her tears remained behind her eyelids. "I couldn't work with him anymore and I couldn't face my family. So I ran away. I just felt so foolish. I thought he loved me."

Derek opened and closed his mouth several more times before he seemed to decide on words. "Bethany, any man who would do that doesn't deserve you. To be stringing along two women ..." Then he paused, understanding dawning in his expression. "You weren't sleeping with him."

Bethany felt the heat rise to her face, but she shook her head. She was a good Irish-Catholic girl through and through: she'd done what was expected of her her entire life. Of course she would wait to have sex until her wedding night. But the whole time she'd thought Alejándro was respecting her decision, he simply hadn't been interested in her that way. And considering the nubile beauties that draped themselves over him at every opportunity, she could understand why. Almost.

"The guy was a creep, Bethany. If he wasn't willing to wait for you, he's not the type of guy you want to marry."

Her cheeks burned hotter than ever. Now he knew the truth. She was a twenty-seven-year-old virgin who had been jilted for a hotter, more exciting woman, and she still hadn't gotten over it. He probably thought her naive and pathetic, even though the only thing she saw in his face now was empathy.

Even so, she couldn't force down more than a couple of bites of the tart, her stomach twisted into knots. Instead, she sipped her coffee in silence and watched Derek consume his own dessert with enthusiasm. How could he switch gears so quickly? One minute, he was kissing her passionately in a corridor, and the next, he was sitting here as coolly as if it had never happened. Meanwhile, she felt like she had whiplash from the highs and lows she'd experienced in the last ten minutes.

When they were finished, he stood and held a hand out to her. "Come on. I'll walk you to your room."

She took his hand and let him lead her upstairs to her door, where he stopped and turned her to face him.

"Derek," she began.

"Shh." He gently pulled her closer, cradled her face in his hands, and kissed her with aching thoroughness that melted her bones and every last bit of resistance she had against him.

For the first time, her rules no longer seemed so important. Why had she bothered waiting for her wedding night when at the rate she was going, there never would be a wedding night? It wasn't like men were beating down her door to ask her out. What exactly did she think she was saving herself for?

And then Derek pulled back to look straight into her eyes, a mix of hunger and surprising tenderness in his gaze. "Bethany, I want to make one thing very clear. The reason I'm not trying to talk you into bed tonight isn't because I don't want you. It's because it would be completely wrong. In more ways than you probably realize." He leaned forward and kissed her one more time, then strode off down the balcony to his own room.

Bethany watched him go, bewildered and relieved and melancholy. If she wasn't mistaken, the words had been a farewell.

twelve

DEREK SHUT THE DOOR to his hotel room and scrubbed a hand through his hair. This evening had been … enlightening.

It had been other things, too, but best he didn't dwell on those if he wanted to avoid doing something incredibly stupid. Not only was Bethany still wounded by her creep of an ex, he was pretty sure she was a virgin … and embarrassed by that fact. He felt like he was walking a tightrope between doing the right thing and making her feel unwanted.

Maybe he wasn't the most intuitive guy out there, but he'd have to be blind not to pick up on how the combination of Bethany's childhood taunting and her playboy ex-fiancé had convinced her that she wasn't pretty enough or sexy enough or just plain *enough* for any guy. Completely untrue, of course, but he'd seen the same insecurities in Anna, who needed constant reassurance that she wasn't the gawky, bullied girl she'd been at age nine.

Crap. If Anna was even the slightest bit like Bethany, she'd probably taken Derek's willingness to marry her—but inability to love her—as proof she still wasn't good enough. He closed his eyes and dropped his forehead to the wall. Idiot. Before he started congratulating himself for figuring out Bethany, maybe he should have figured out his own fiancée first.

No. Ex-fiancée. Just because he realized how he'd inadvertently hurt Anna didn't change the fact he didn't love her enough to marry her.

It just meant he wouldn't be making the same mistake with Bethany. For a minute, he'd been about to ask her how she felt about a visit to Los

Angeles, or what she would think about him coming back to Belize. He'd been thinking only of how much he enjoyed her company, how he wanted to keep seeing her. He'd simply been operating under the wrong set of assumptions.

Bethany wasn't cynical. She was hurt. In time, she would decide she wanted the fairy tale, and she'd eventually find a guy who could give it to her.

No matter how much he wanted it to be otherwise, he wasn't that guy.

Bethany didn't sleep. She packed and unpacked and repacked her bag. She paced the spacious floor of her room. She ate a candy bar, American chocolate she'd been saving for an emergency. This definitely qualified as an emergency.

Despite all her protests to the contrary, her bulletproof security in her position that real relationships didn't exist, she'd fallen for Derek Moretti anyway. In a mere three days. When it came to abandoning personal convictions, that had to be a record.

Even worse, she'd been so sure he felt something in return that she'd considered sleeping with him, a total stranger.

She was such a fool. He'd made his position clear. He liked her. He wanted her. But that was as far as it went. It was a sign of how little she'd learned her lesson that once again she was projecting her own wishes on a man who couldn't possibly fulfill them. Yet she would be lying if she pretended the past two days didn't mean something to her. She just didn't know if she had the guts to tell the truth.

Bethany shimmied out of her clothes and slipped into her ratty pajamas. Then, despite her own internal warnings, she fished her paperback novel from the pocket of her bag. Time to see how this couple found their way back to each other.

When she finally closed the back cover with a sigh, she felt as conflicted as an addict who had fallen off the wagon. Feeding her delusions wasn't good for her, and yet it was still so satisfying. She put the book on the nightstand and clicked off the light, then fell immediately into restless dreams of romance and betrayal and repeated episodes of being late for work.

When she jerked upright hours later with a gasp, bright sunshine streamed through the crack in the curtains. She glanced at the clock. 9:05. She was already late.

She flung the covers back and grabbed yesterday's shorts, then pulled them on with a clean tank top. Thank goodness there was no need to dress for breakfast, not when people showed up on the patio in swimsuits. She brushed her teeth, splashed water on her face, and tied her hair back in record time, then practically sprinted down to the patio.

Derek was already waiting for her at a table for two, cool and collected, his eyes hidden behind the mirrored lenses of his aviator shades.

"Morning." He rose and greeted her with a kiss on the cheek, but she sensed the change between them immediately, a distance that had most definitely not been there last night. "I hope you don't mind. I ordered us coffee. I thought you might need it this morning."

"Thank you," she said, her voice cracking from disuse. "You're right."

A long silence stretched between them. Bethany cleared her throat, but it did nothing for the jitters in her stomach.

"Derek …" she began.

At the same time, he said, "I wanted to …"

She broke off into nervous laughter.

He cracked a smile and gestured to her. "You first."

She licked her lips, summoning the nerve to continue. Now or never. "I lied to you, Derek. Maybe I lied to myself. It's not that I don't believe in love. I convinced myself that what Alejándro did to me was somehow my fault, that had I been less naive or prettier or tried harder to keep his interest, it would have worked out. For three years I've been scared to trust my own judgment, to believe there might be some decent guys out there. But the past few days—"

"Stop." Derek's voice, gentle but firm, cut her off mid-sentence. He ran his hand through his hair in an agitated motion. "Bethany, what Alejándro did to you is unforgivable. You have every right to be furious with him and cautious about trusting another man. The truth is, there are guys out there who will treat you the way you deserve to be treated. They will worship the ground you walk on. They'll give up everything for you."

"But?" Her voice came out strangled.

"But I'm not that guy." He reached out and put his hand over hers. "Bethany, I'm the exception that proves your rule."

She clamped down on her lower lip with her teeth, willing the pain to intercept her tears before they could form. She pulled her hand from his. "I see. Thank you for your honesty."

"Bethany, I'm so sorry …"

"No." She shook her head. "I'm sorry. You've been very clear about things from the start, and I …" She swallowed until she could bring her voice under control again. "I just got caught up in … all of this. You have nothing to apologize for."

She rose as gracefully as she could manage. "I'm going to eat in my room so I can finish packing. Meet me on the hotel boat dock at noon."

She fled upstairs to her room, berating herself for letting herself buy into the fantasy that she'd been solely responsible for creating. He hadn't led her on. He'd kissed her, yes, but she was old enough to know that attraction didn't mean love, or even the possibility of love. Good thing Derek had principles, no matter how he might play them off. Had it not been for his restraint, she would have done something she'd be fiercely regretting this morning.

She quickly packed her nightclothes and did a once over of the room, where she came across the finished paperback novel. She looked over the cover, with its dreamy-looking couple, choked back a sob, and tossed it straight into the trash can. How could she have been so foolish? Real people didn't fall in love over the course of three days. That was purely the province of fiction. She'd always known it, and she'd chosen to ignore it.

By the time she met Derek on the dock, she had herself mostly together. He on the other hand, looked miserable. "Bethany, I—"

"Think nothing of it," she said brusquely. "Just a momentary lapse."

"Still, I—"

She sent him a look that made him clamp his mouth shut. Fortunately, a familiar shaded speedboat was cutting through the water toward them. Bethany moved to the end of the dock and raised a hand in greeting as Juan maneuvered the boat alongside the wooden platform.

"Bethany!" The captain favored her with a brilliant smile as he helped her onto the boat. "Enjoying playing tour guide?"

She summoned what she thought was a particularly convincing grin. "Better than kicking your sorry butt at canasta."

Derek climbed aboard and shook the captain's hand, then took a seat opposite her. For one brief moment, she allowed herself to imagine how the outcome could have been different, what it would be like to ride back with his arm around her shoulders, figuring out how they would continue what they'd just barely begun. Just as quickly, she shoved the image down where it belonged.

They passed the ride back in silence, and Bethany lifted her face to the sun and wind, stubbornly refusing to look at Derek even when she felt his attention on her. When they finally reached the island's dock, she had managed to shake off her feelings about the past few days and turn her mind to the meals she would cook for him before he went back to his life in Los Angeles.

She was so engrossed in her own thoughts that at first she didn't register the helicopter sitting on the pad just beyond the dock, nor the beautiful brunette waiting at the end. Bethany blinked, wondering if mirages came in supermodel form.

"Anna?" Derek murmured, his tone holding more confusion than pleasure.

"Derek, wait." Bethany grabbed his arm before he could climb out and she swore she could feel Anna's frown from there. "Don't forget she was the one who left you. If you want her back, make her work for it."

Derek's expression shifted, but without being able to see his eyes, she couldn't tell what he thought of her words. And then he was up on the dock, striding toward his ex-fiancée, leaving the captain to help Bethany out.

She shouldered her bag and rushed by them, determined not to intrude on their moment, but she still registered their embrace, Derek's arms encircling Anna's waist as they had done to her own not long ago.

She bit her lip until she tasted blood, but it did nothing to stem the tide of tears that streamed from her eyes. The little sprout of hope she hadn't realized she still harbored shriveled under reality, hotter and more devastating than the relentless Belizean sun. It left only the awful truth from which she could no longer hide.

Love existed. It simply wasn't meant for her.

thirteen

BETHANY HEARD THE HELICOPTER LIFT OFF the island, but she didn't know her suspicions had become reality until Mariska burst unannounced into her bungalow.

"He left! With her! Can you believe it? I guess when you're a literal supermodel, you can get away with dumping a guy at the altar and then waltzing right back in when you change your mind."

"Great job, Derek," Bethany muttered. "Way to make her work for it."

Mariska stared at Bethany, her expression changing. "No. You didn't."

"Sleep with him? No. I didn't."

"I didn't mean that. Worse. You went and fell for him."

Bethany shook her head and dumped the contents of her bag on the bed, sorting the dirty clothes into her hanging hamper and laying her few cosmetics aside. "Momentary lapse is all. I mean, I knew him for all of three days. It's not like you can make any sort of meaningful connection in three days, right?"

"Right," Mariska said, but her tone wasn't entirely convincing. "Did you have a good time at least?"

"I did." Bethany sank onto the edge of the bed. "I haven't had that much fun in years. The weird thing is, there was no pressure. I could do whatever I wanted. I could say whatever I wanted." She swallowed. "And he seemed to like that. We had a great time. Right up until I told him about Alejándro and he said there were good guys out there, but he was not one of them."

"He said that?" Mariska screeched. "Does he think the wounded and self-deprecating thing is actually sexy in this day and age? What a jerk!"

Bethany was all set to agree, but she couldn't. "That's the thing. He's not. He tries to pretend like he's this snobbish money-hungry type, but he's quite the opposite. He was in the Peace Corps, for goodness sake, even though he tried to play it off as rebellion. He was kind of perfect, actually."

Bethany tossed her chiffon dress at the hamper and missed. "Which is the whole problem, I guess. He's perfect. Anna's perfect. I most certainly am not. I guess I can't really blame him for going back to her. He was going to marry her three days ago after all."

Mariska grabbed her by the shoulders. "Listen to me, Bethany, because I'm only going to say this once. No one gets to tell you how to feel about yourself. Not me. Not Derek. Definitely not Alejándro. You are an amazing, beautiful, talented person, and everyone who comes in contact with you knows it. But until you can accept that for yourself, nothing anyone else says will ever make a difference."

"But Alejándro …"

"Alejándro's problem was Alejándro. And Derek's problem is Derek. You can either let them have power over you by thinking it's your fault, or you can chalk it up to a learning experience and live your life. You can be the person you were meant to be, and someday you might just find a man who appreciates how special that is."

Bethany stared at Mariska. Who would have thought that her flighty, man-eating sous chef could be so … deep?

"Then how do you explain the fact that I've been single for three years?"

Mariska just stared.

Right. She'd been so sure she had nothing to offer that she'd hidden in the kitchen and refused to take a chance. It was only with Derek when she felt she had nothing to lose that she'd actually let herself go. For the first time in three years, she had finally *lived*.

In that case, maybe she owed him a debt of gratitude. He'd cracked her heart open enough to accept the possibility that someone might be able to love her for who she was, bad metaphors and no makeup and romance novel obsession included, even if she'd shut that door almost immediately out of reflex.

It was just too bad he remained closed to the possibility. She hadn't imagined their connection, but they would never have a chance to see where it might have taken them.

"I guess we're done here if the guests are gone?" Bethany asked.

"Yep. I'm packed and ready to go. Juan is waiting to take us back to Ambergris."

"Fabulous," Bethany said, rolling her eyes to hide the sudden wash of tears.

"Trust me, Bethany. If Derek was dumb enough to walk away from you, especially for a woman who already left him once, he didn't deserve you. Better you know that now before you invest any more time and energy into him."

"That's what every friend is required to say. It's practically in the best friend handbook." But despite Bethany's immediate inclination to brush off Mariska's words, a tiny bit of that conviction burrowed in and refused to be shaken.

fourteen

A MONTH LATER, Bethany walked through the front door of her San Pedro apartment and nearly got bowled over by Mariska. "Thank goodness you're home! I need a favor."

"Of course you do," Bethany said with an amused smile. She set down the bag that contained her knife roll, aprons, and a case full of specialty seasonings she had ordered from the U.S. "What is it today?"

Mariska's hand stopped midway to her ear, a dangly earring swinging from her fingertips. "You're wearing makeup. For work."

Bethany shrugged, though her face heated with embarrassment. She'd also abandoned her bandanna, though her hair remained braided or knotted out of her face. Funny thing, when she stopped trying to be anonymous, people treated her like a person and not a faceless kitchen automaton.

"That's perfect," Mariska said brightly. "I really need you to take my private cooking lesson tonight. I have a date."

Bethany shook her head in disbelief, though her roommate rarely surprised her anymore. "Who is he?"

"He's a lawyer from Boston. I promised I'd show him the local sights before he left."

"I meant the student."

"Oh! It's an older lady. Retiree. An easy hundred bucks. US."

Bethany sighed. It had already been a long three days cooking for a particularly spoiled family in one of the huge new houses farther up the island. But a hundred bucks US was a hundred bucks, and it wasn't like she had anything else to do. Just because she'd started wearing makeup didn't mean she'd actually worked herself up to having a social life.

"Okay. I'll do it. Leave me the address while I shower and change."

"Already texted you."

Sure enough, when Bethany pulled out her cell phone, there was a message waiting. Mariska was nothing if not efficient in her quest to get out of work.

"I'm going to go now," Mariska said. "Don't wait up."

"Have fun and be careful." Bethany shook her head. For all Mariska's dating, she never seemed to get too attached to anyone, even though she had plenty of men declaring their undying love, some of whom even meant it.

Bethany didn't need dozens of men. She just wanted one.

One man in particular, if she were being honest.

Bethany went to the single shared bathroom, where the shower erased both the day's grease and its tension. It still amazed her that a man whom she'd known for only three days had taken up permanent residence in her mind, despite repeated daily attempts to evict him. Derek had been true to his word and had his father write a glowing letter to corporate on her behalf, but otherwise he'd had no contact with her. She had no reason, no right, to miss him like she did.

Twenty minutes later, she was walking out the door in fresh clothes, her hair twisted into a wet knot at the nape of her neck, the bare minimum makeup reapplied. It wasn't like a retired lady was going to care about her eye makeup, but to leave it off felt like a step backward into anonymity.

The address the golf cart taxi dropped her in front of was a beach house, significantly more modest than the one at which she'd spent the weekend, but with spectacular views of the sun setting over the water. Bethany walked to the blue painted door and knocked. No answer. From inside, she heard a faint clatter. Frowning, she tried the latch and the door swung open.

The smell of sautéing garlic and onion drifted to her, melding with the richer aromas of sausage and tomatoes. Italian, she thought, not Spanish or Central American. Had she somehow gotten the time wrong and her student decided to get started without her?

"Hello?" she called, creeping deeper into the house.

No answer. She followed the sounds to the kitchen in the back of the house, where a young man, not an older woman, stood at the counter, chopping something with a heavy knife. A frisson of fear skittered through her. And then he turned, and her bag fell from her suddenly lifeless fingers.

"Derek?"

"Bethany." He smiled warmly, and her stomach dropped straight to her toes. "You're just in time. Dinner is in ten."

"I don't understand." Surely she was imagining this. She cleared her throat. "What are you doing here? What happened to the cooking lesson?"

He grimaced. "I'm sorry for the lie. I was afraid you might not talk to me if I showed up unannounced. The lesson was Mariska's idea."

"Of course it was." Bethany crossed her arms over her chest as if the physical barrier could protect her heart, too. "You didn't answer my question, though."

Derek wiped his hand on a dish towel. Even—or maybe especially—wearing a green apron that said *Kiss the Cook*, he looked unbearably appealing. If he were here to ask her to cater his and Anna's second wedding, she would strangle him with the apron strings. In fact, he should be grateful her knives were still safely stashed in her bag.

"I needed to talk to you. In person."

She didn't even try to hide her skepticism. "You flew to Belize to talk to me? What does Anna think of that?"

"I wouldn't know. I haven't seen her in a month."

Bethany blinked at him, no more able to process those words than she could his presence in front of her. He sighed and took her hand, then led her to the small table where two places had been set. "Just hear me out, Bethany. Please?"

She lowered herself to the chair and folded her hands in her lap.

"I was wrong. About everything. The way I treated you ... the way I treated Anna. She came back to beg my forgiveness and ask for a second chance, but the truth is, she was right to call off the wedding. She said she was expecting too much from me, that I'd always been honest about what I could give her and that it was enough. But the time I spent with you made me realize she had been right. She needed a man who couldn't stop thinking about her, who would do anything for her. I'm not that man. I can't be that man."

Bethany stared at Derek, confused. He'd come all the way to Belize to tell her what she already knew? "I don't understand, Derek. What do you want from me?"

A smile rose to his lips. "I was getting to that. You promised to listen, remember?"

Bethany gave a bewildered sigh. "Sorry. Go on."

"So after Anna and I agreed to part ways permanently, I spent a few weeks feeling sorry for myself and buried myself in work. Made a few stupid trades that cost me a lot of money, too. I couldn't stop thinking about you, but I convinced myself it was better to move on and leave Belize behind. I could never be what you were looking for, so why put both us through unnecessary drama?

"And then my sister brought me this." He withdrew a faded snapshot from his pocket and passed it to her.

Bethany turned it over. The photo showed a beautiful blonde woman and a handsome dark-haired man who resembled Derek, both in 1970s formal wear. Their arms were wrapped around each other while they looked adoringly into each other's eyes. "Your parents?"

Derek nodded. "My mom used to be an actress. She was engaged to a big name director when she met my father. He wasn't in the industry; he was actually working with his family's import/export business in Italy. They fell for each other hard and fast, and they eloped. It caused a huge scandal that would have ended Mom's career had Dad not placated the director by helping finance his next film." Derek leveled a wry grin. "Had it not been for my mom's impulsive nature, Dad would never have gotten into the business in the first place."

Bethany smiled despite herself. It was a romantic story, the young American actress and the passionate Italian businessman. She opened her mouth to ask a question before she realized she'd agreed to let him finish his story.

"My dad was heartbroken after my mom died," Derek continued. "She had been his wife, his companion, and his business partner. I think he's just desperately searching for that again. I've been viewing Dad's marriages as proof that lasting love doesn't exist, when really it shows that my parents had something special. And by settling for a loveless marriage, I was *repeating* his mistakes, not preventing them."

Bethany realized she was holding her breath. She would never have thought Derek Moretti was capable of being this vulnerable. The kernel of hope blossomed in her heart, so fragile that a mere breath would crush it. "What are you saying, Derek?"

He took both her hands. "I would like nothing more than to sweep in and declare my undying love, but you and I both know it's too soon for that. We barely know each other. I guess I was just hoping …" He broke off. "I'm no good at this."

She squeezed his hands hard. "Just say it, Derek."

He swallowed and spilled the words out all at once. "Being jilted at the altar was the best thing that ever happened to me. Because meeting you made me believe in love again."

Bethany's breath left her in a rush. It wasn't a promise, exactly, merely a chance to pick up where they'd left off …

… when he'd kissed her and then walked away without a word. What was to say he wouldn't do the same thing again?

And yet he'd come back for her, enlisted her best friend to set up a meeting. Made her dinner. Those weren't the actions of a cynic who didn't believe in love. That was downright romantic, a page straight out of one of the novels he'd teased her about.

Bethany studied his face—so hopeful and anxious—and the tight grip she was holding on her emotions loosened. Maybe she and Derek weren't meant to be together. Maybe they'd learn that infatuation and attraction didn't automatically translate to love. But they would never find out if she didn't make the leap.

"Yes."

He blinked at her. "Yes, what?"

"Yes, I'll give you a chance. Yes, I would love to believe in love with you." She smiled at him and leaned forward to press a light kiss to his lips.

"Wow, that was easier than I expected. What happened to making me work for it?"

"What can I say? You're a really good kisser."

A laugh slipped from his lips, but it faded into a thoughtful expression as his eyes roamed her face. He pulled his chair close enough to reach her, took her face in his hands, and proceeded to prove her right.

epilogue

One year later

"Are you sure you want to do this?"

Bethany looked at the High Temple ruin that stretched upward to the tree line, then back at Derek, who wore a smug expression. "Why wouldn't I?"

"I don't know. Just the fact that you almost tumbled to your death last time we were here."

"I did not! I just … oh, never mind. We're going. Try to keep up." Bethany sent him a mock-stern look and started deliberately toward the steps.

"This all feels eerily familiar," Derek called after her. "Try not to slip this time. I'd hate for you to get all scraped up just because you want me to put my arms around you."

Bethany threw back her head and laughed, but she didn't pause in her climb. It had been exactly one year since she and Derek had come to Lamanai together. That part of her that had prompted her to take a chance on him, to take a chance on love, had been proven correct again and again. He was as funny and smart and sarcastic as she'd thought. He was also sweet and tender and caring … unless he was watching the World Cup, because he turned into an irrational maniac when the U.S. team was down, which seemed like always.

When she had expressed her desire to stay in Belize, he'd moved his life from Los Angeles to Ambergris Caye without question—after all, he could work anywhere with a laptop and an internet connection. When she'd made it clear she wanted to keep her condo with Mariska in San Pedro, he'd rented a house within walking distance.

Unlike what she'd once told her roommate, he wasn't perfect, but he was absolutely perfect for her.

"Lots of big talk, but it looks to me like you're already losing steam." Derek sent her a challenging look from a few steps above her. "Out of shape?"

Bethany winked. "Bring it, desk jockey."

That led to a race up the face of the temple, albeit one that grew slower as the steps grew steeper and they had to use their hands to scramble to the top. When they both made the final crawl up the last block at the same time, Bethany sent him a reproving glance.

"What? I'm just protecting your delicate feminine feelings."

"Right." Bethany snorted, about to retort, but he drew her away from the edge and wrapped his arms around her from behind.

She leaned back against his firm chest and let out a sigh. "It's beautiful up here. I didn't appreciate it like I should have the last time we were here."

"Too distracted by this view?" he asked, indicating himself with a downward sweep of his hand.

"That's what I love about you. Your modesty."

"If I were to list everything I love about you, we'd be up here all night and another day."

Bethany smiled to herself. There was a time when she wouldn't have believed those words, but the way he looked at her, like she was the only woman on earth, made it impossible to doubt his sincerity.

"Since you didn't fully enjoy the last trip, maybe I can make this one more memorable."

He let her go, and Bethany turned, puzzled. She didn't register the object in his hand until he lowered himself to one knee and flipped open the lid of the small box.

A diamond sparkled in a bed of gray velvet, drawing her eye and freezing the breath in her lungs until she realized Derek was talking to her.

"You know I'm not for doing things the traditional way," he said with a wry smile. "But you deserve every last romantic gesture from those romance novels of yours. Until I met you, I never thought love like this existed. But you showed me what I'd been missing, and now I never want to be without it.

"Bethany Hall, will you marry me?"

Her voice caught in her throat and all she could do was nod with tears in her eyes. He slid the ring onto her finger and then stood to pull her into his arms.

As he kissed her, two thoughts registered.

One, he really *was* that good a kisser.

And two, he was so much more than she could have concocted in her wildest dreams.

Starstruck

A Discovered by Love Novella

One

"Connor Bell is in the hospital."

Christine Lind stopped abruptly on the jetway at Los Angeles International Airport, causing the passengers behind her to veer past her like water around a rock in a stream. The crackle of static on the phone made her think she had somehow misheard her agent, Noah, even though his words were perfectly clear. "Connor Bell. As in the actor I'm supposed to be on a panel with in less than ninety-six hours. That Connor Bell?"

"Is there any other? Motorcycle accident in Manchester last night. Word is he broke his leg in three places."

A man behind her cursed sharply at her sudden stop, and she pushed herself up against the rickety jetway wall, wheeling her carry-on out of the way. "So what does this mean for filming?"

"Well, it means he won't be, naturally. Pretty physical part, and he can't be scaling Victorian brownstones if he's in a cast for months."

Christine pressed her fingertips to her eyes. This was not happening. In less than four days, they would be announcing the cast of a new cable series—a series based on her best-selling books—to a packed audience at London FanFest. As an executive consultant and co-creator of the show, she would be sitting up there alongside the cast and director, talking about why the English heartthrob was the perfect person to play her hero, Jackson Landry. She had spent days practicing her answers to the questions the moderator would be throwing her way. And now they didn't have a Jackson Landry at all?

"Why didn't anyone tell me?" she finally asked.

"I'm telling you now. And you're lucky you're perennially late to the airport. I called you as soon as I heard so you'd have time to prepare on the flight."

"So, they have someone new."

"They offered him the role tonight."

"Who is it?"

Noah hesitated. "You're not going to like it."

"Don't tell me they went with Rafael Montserrat. He's completely wrong, and he can't do an American accent to save his life."

"No, not Rafael." The silence stretched, and it brought with it a new beat of dread in her heart. "They gave it to Nick Cleary."

The blood rushed from Christine's face, leaving only the dull, watery thud of her pulse in her ears. The jetway seemed to waver around her for a moment. "Nick?"

"Listen, I know you weren't thrilled with the idea of him in the first place, but you have to admit he's perfect. And he lobbied hard for the part. He's exactly like you described Jackson."

There was a reason for that, one that Noah didn't need to know. "Forget it. I'm not coming."

"You have to come."

"No. No, I don't. They can do the panel without me." Christine was starting to hyperventilate, panic tracing an icy line down her back. Passengers began throwing her strange looks, so she turned away and lowered her voice. "I can't do this."

"I know you're not keen on public speaking, but you have to. That's why I gave you a few extra hours' notice. And what about your book signings? Are you going to disappoint all your fans?"

No, of course she wasn't. The fans were the only reason she ever left her beautiful little beach house in San Diego, the only reason she'd consider getting up in front of a packed theater. Noah certainly knew how to go for the throat. "How am I supposed to talk about how he's perfect for the part when I fought so hard against him?"

"You're a writer. Make it up. You should be comfortable with fiction. Just get on the plane."

"Fine. I'm going. I'll … I'll think of something." Christine clicked off the phone and stared at the screen as if somehow that was going to change the news. He was right. She didn't have a choice in the matter.

"Ma'am? We're finished boarding now."

Christine looked up and saw the flight attendant standing at the end of the jetway, staring at her with a mixture of concern and annoyance. Only then did she realize the line of passengers had vanished. She shoved her phone in her purse and strode toward the open hatch of the airliner.

She could do this. She could get on this plane and make up some line about why she was thrilled that Nick Cleary had gotten the role in her romantic steampunk adventure. She could feign a happy smile without letting on that she hated the man to the very depths of her soul, a conviction dating back to the days when she was a just a struggling, penniless author. The fact was, Nick was perfect to play Jackson Landry because the handsome actor had inspired the character, down to the rich brown eyes and the irresistible dimple in his left cheek.

Right before he had broken her heart.

By the time Christine landed in London ten-and-a-half hours later, she had managed to calm herself down. Well, to be fair, it was the sleeping pill her doctor had prescribed that had calmed her down, considering that she liked flying about as much as she liked speaking in front of a live audience. The benefit was that while she would have been chewing her nails to the quick over the prospect of having to face Nick again, she'd instead been blissfully unconscious for most of the flight. The wet spot on the shoulder of her sweatshirt indicated she'd been drooling as well, but as long as there wasn't any video evidence of the fact, she was comfortable ignoring it.

"I can do this," she whispered to herself, then gave a weak smile as the man next to her shot her a funny look. She retrieved her tote—a showy piece stamped with designer initials that she'd bought with her first advance check—and slung it over her shoulder, steeling herself for what awaited her.

She was over Nick. That wasn't a question. In fact, her longing had turned to anger when he got on network television and told the world that his first real love affair had ended in heartache because his fiancée just didn't have the same level of ambition that he did. Apparently, he couldn't be with someone who "wasn't constantly bettering herself."

Bettering herself. Somehow he thought sitting her butt in a chair for ten hours a day, writing novel after novel while she tried to find an agent or a publisher to take her on wasn't bettering herself. Back then, Nick had been struggling in his own career as much as she had, but his idea of bettering himself was getting his teeth whitened before yet another open call rejection.

At least she'd gotten her big break on the merits of her own work. Nick had finally given up and called in a favor from his childhood friend, Derek, whose father was a television producer. He'd been cast in a bit part as an angel or a demon or a vampire or whatever on one of those teen shows, and the female fans had demanded he be given a bigger role. So maybe the "self-improvements" had paid off after all.

Christine sighed and fell into line as the flight attendants opened the hatch to let them onto the jetway. No, she couldn't stoop to his level. Despite the fact he may have used his connections to get his break, he actually wasn't a bad actor. It was the only reason why a director of David Chan's stature would consider casting him in a series that was poised to be as big as *Outlander*.

Too bad the discussion wasn't over. She'd pulled up the contract for *Smoke and Glory* on her laptop at the beginning of the flight to double-check the language. Just as she'd thought, she didn't exactly have the final word on casting—the difference between the words *consultation* and *approval*—but there was a clause that required her to be formally notified of any changes before they were announced to the public. Noah's call was just a heads-up. Which meant that she still had time to make her case against him and urge David to choose someone else.

Vindictive? Maybe. But she knew one thing. Working with Nick on this project was likely to turn her dreams into a nightmare.

two

THIS HAD QUITE POSSIBLY BEEN the longest twenty-four hours of Nick Cleary's life.

When he'd gotten the call late last night from David Chan, he almost hadn't believed it. He'd been about to accuse one of his friends of doing an impersonation—albeit a very good one—of the director when Chan announced that their as-yet-unrevealed leading man had been injured and wasn't available to take the part of Jackson Landry. Was he still interested?

After Nick was done gaping like a fish out of water, he'd managed a calm, clear, "Yes, I'd be interested."

There was one catch, though, and it was the catch that now had Nick pacing the plush patterned carpeting of his hotel room like a restless animal. It wasn't a done deal until Christine Lind agreed to it.

And that was about as likely as him winning the lottery. Funny how he'd never thought that someone he'd hurt with his youthful stupidity would someday hold his career in her hands. He'd like to believe that Christine would be over it, that she'd forgiven him, but when you broke someone's heart and then stepped on it on network television, you had to be prepared for a little anger.

Nick pressed the heels of his hands to his eyes, and when he pulled them away, he saw stars. He'd never been so nervous in his life. As much as he hated to admit it, this was a dream role. Christine's book series had all the hallmarks of a hit: adventure, romance, steampunk flare set in an alternate history England. And Jackson Landry was a particularly juicy role. These days, the parts that came his way mostly involved looking smoldering with his shirt off—something that had him spending hours in the gym every day—but rarely any kind of character depth. By comparison, Landry was a quintessential antihero who found his redemption in the end. Nick knew this because he'd been reading the books as Christine published them. Not that he would ever admit that to her.

No, he would *have* to admit that. He had no pride to spare in this situation, not when Chan had made it clear that Christine had to sign off on him. Her executive consultant title probably didn't come with full cast approval, but everyone knew that all it would take was a casual remark on social media to her *millions* of fans and they'd never be able to get the series off the ground with him in the role. No, like it or not, Christine had the leverage to make or break this for him. Not only did he have to convince her he was right for Jackson, he had to convince her that he'd changed from the heartless jerk who'd left her for another woman shortly after he'd proposed.

Somehow, he didn't think she was going to take his word for it.

Chan promised that he would talk it over with her first so she wasn't blindsided by the idea, and then Nick could come up and make a case for himself. It shouldn't take long, he'd said. But as hours ticked by and Nick still hadn't gotten the call, the dread was starting to escape from him in a cold sweat. He was lucky he was already in London for the convention, where he could pitch himself—or beg, if it came to that—in person. If he were back home in Los Angeles, he'd have zero options.

He was checking his cell phone for the third time in case the call had gone straight to voice mail, when it sprang to life in his hands. He didn't even hesitate as he swiped to accept. "Nick Cleary."

"Nick, would you please join Christine and me in my suite? The Cromwell, top floor."

The director's calm request eased his nerves a bit. "Of course. I'll be right there."

Nick took a quick look in the room's mirror before pocketing his cell phone and his room key, then stepped into the dimly lit hall. He had to take a minute to orient himself. The St. Anselm Hotel was the closest accommodation to the convention center—and as a result, packed with the cast of at least four Hollywood productions—but it was a renovated school turned into a five-star hotel. To call the layout "labyrinthine" would be like calling Hogwarts "a little dangerous."

He finally remembered on which end of the hall lay the lift and strode toward it, wiping his damp palms on his pant legs. Chan hadn't sounded like it was going to be bad news. Maybe Nick was still in the game. He had to be. It wasn't that he wasn't grateful for the break he'd gotten on *Night Music*, but he was ready to prove he was more than a pretty face and a set of chiseled abs. Though if the other cable shows produced by this network were any indication, he probably wouldn't be changing his gym routine any time soon.

He emerged from the lift on the top floor and found the Cromwell suite, identified by a brass plaque on the extravagantly wallpapered wall. He rapped lightly on the door. It opened almost immediately, revealing a pretty middle-aged blonde who Nick remembered was the production publicist.

"Nick." She smiled warmly. "Please come in."

"Thank you … Remy," he said, digging her name out of his adrenaline-fogged brain. She offered him a bottle of cold water before leading him into the suite.

Sitting in a lushly appointed seating area that reflected the historic nature of the hotel was the director, instantly recognizable. Across from him was a beautiful brunette in leather leggings and a lace tunic. Had he misunderstood? Where was Christine?

David Chan smiled and rose to offer his hand. "Welcome, Nick. I understand that you and Christine already know each other. Which is, after all, the reason we're here."

Nick's mouth dropped open and he gaped at her, even more shocked than he had been when he'd gotten the phone call last night. "Christine?"

"I'd say it's nice to see you, Nick," she said in a low, almost sultry tone, lifting one shoulder in a shrug, "but I try never to lie."

"Shut your mouth, Nick, and have a seat," David said, not unkindly.

He did as he was told, still too stunned to form actual words. The Christine he'd dated five years ago had been a mousy brunette who would never have dreamed of wearing leggings, let alone ones made of leather. This woman had glossy chestnut hair that swooped over one shoulder of her lace tunic, drawing attention to the bright red streak that framed her face … which was fully made-up, he noticed, down to a fringe of false lashes. He trailed his gaze down shapely legs to strappy high-heeled booties, then back up to her face. At the moment, her look of amusement said she was enjoying his shock.

His stomach dropped to his feet.

He'd been thinking he could win her over with sincerity—and he truly was sorry for having been such a jerk—but somewhere along the line, his ex-fiancée had learned how to play the game. She was no longer the introvert who spent days and nights at her computer wearing a baggy sweatshirt dusted with Dorito crumbs. Now she was half-Hollywood-starlet and half-vixen … and completely in control.

"Christine has reservations about casting you as Jackson Landry," the director said by way of opening. Remy perched on the arm of the sofa beside Christine, clearly throwing her support behind her fellow female. Great. Were they back in elementary school? Girls against boys?

"I think reservations would be a nice way of saying it," Christine said, that sultry undercurrent still present in her voice. Or had it been there all along, and he'd merely taken it for granted during the three years they'd been together? "The fact is, while Nick is very good-looking, the role of Jackson is emotionally challenging, and Nick has made it clear that he is highly experiential in his approach to roles."

Nick stared. Had she just called him shallow? Had she implied that he wouldn't be able to connect with the role because he had no experience with actual feelings? He opened his mouth to protest, then realized that heated words would only prove her right. He swallowed down his pride once more and said levelly, "Based on your past experiences with me, I'd say I deserved that. But people change." He inclined his head toward her. "Clearly you have. Don't you think I deserve a chance to prove it?"

Pink colored her cheeks, and she seemed temporarily at a loss for words.

But David was not. "I think that's an excellent idea, actually. Christine, you know that I want this show to be as close to your vision as we can make it. But I've made it clear from the beginning that Nick is my top choice for this role. I'd consider it a personal favor if you'd at least hear him out."

Christine pulled her top lip between her teeth, a movement that brought up a flush of memory, a sign that the woman he'd known still existed inside this toned and polished and made-up version. Finally, she nodded. "Of course I will. But you promised me you wouldn't force this on me."

"I did." David favored her with what seemed to be a doting smile. He rose and they exchanged one of those ridiculous double air-kisses that everyone suddenly favored.

Christine's eyes brightened as she turned and crossed the room with a seductive sway that she'd evidently acquired since the last time he'd seen her. She paused and said in a low voice, "Don't get too comfortable here, Nick. You're not the only one with friends in this business."

He stared after her as she picked up her handbag from the entryway table and exited the suite. Chan looked amused at Nick's frozen, shocked state. "I'd go after her, if I were you. Do what you have to do to convince her. This is your big shot."

Nick gave him a nod, rose, and followed her. But for all the director's confidence in him, he was pretty certain Christine's mind was already made up.

three

CHRISTINE KNEW NICK WOULD COME AFTER HER, but she'd planned on being far enough ahead that he'd have to race to catch up with her. Unfortunately, the plush carpeting of the hotel's hallway conspired against her, the stiletto heels of her booties sinking into the pile and hampering her stride. Consequently, she was barely halfway to the lift before she heard his voice ring out behind her: "Chrissy!"

And despite herself, immediately came the little answering tug in her chest. Not good. Not good at all. It was even worse than her initial realization that he was still as good-looking as her memory and the television told her.

Still, she put on a supercilious expression, one eyebrow raised, and turned. "Yes?"

He seemed to be taken aback. Not that perceptive, was he? She'd figured even Nick would pick up that she had only been placating David.

"You said you'd give me a fair shot to change your mind. How can I do that when you run away from me?"

Christine crossed her arms, ignoring the way the dimple threatened at the edges of his wry half-smile. "Okay then. Convince me."

"In the hallway?"

"Why not?"

Now he crossed his arms, mirroring her stance. The fabric of his dress shirt strained at his biceps and shoulders. Reluctantly, she had to admit he had the build to play Jackson, and then even more reluctantly, admitted she'd lingered too long on the thought. "We have five years' worth of unfinished business to cover."

"No we don't. We have less than five minutes. The length of time it took for you to make me the object of pity and scorn on national TV."

"You're right. I should never have said that my last serious relationship ended because you weren't as ambitious or career-focused as I was. Not only was it unkind, it was untrue."

Christine blinked at him, taken aback. She had expected him to make an excuse, not own up to what he'd done.

"But can I at least explain a little?"

And there it was. The slight softening she had felt toward him disappeared. "Does it make up for the fact that I have to talk about 'the TV incident' every time I go home to see my parents?"

He grimaced. "Probably not. But it at least explains why I acted like an idiot."

She considered and then relented with a bare nod.

"They cut more than half of the interview. After she badgered me about rumors about my sexual orientation—there aren't any, by the way—she then detailed every woman I've ever dated, claiming that either I was compensating for being gay or I was more interested in running through the under-thirty Hollywood set than I was in my career. I was so angry and flustered by that point, I brought up our relationship. It was thoughtless, Chrissy, but it wasn't meant to be cruel."

Christine studied him, noted his body language. Unless he'd become a much better liar in the last five years, he was being sincere. "Okay. I accept your apology. I'm still irritated, but I believe you when you say you were just being a moron."

Something halfway between a grimace and a smile flickered across his lips, flashing the barest hint of that dimple and sending the most disconcerting twinge of … something … into her chest.

"So, does that mean you're okay with me in the role?"

"No. I meant what I told David. You might look like Jackson, but I'm not so sure you've got the ability to play the part."

He looked crushed. Was that another bit of acting? "What can I do to change your mind?"

"I don't know. And right now, I don't have time to think about it. I have a book signing at Waterstones in two hours and it's going to take me forever to get across the city."

"I'll come with you," he said. "I can help. I'll be your assistant."

"And you don't think your presence would be a distraction?" she asked wryly. "Sorry, Nick, but this time it isn't all about you."

She turned on her heel and walked away; this time he didn't follow her. Somehow the gesture wasn't nearly as satisfying as she'd envisioned it being.

The book signing went well. Better than well, actually. Waterstones Piccadilly was a London institution—the largest bookshop in Europe, in fact, to the tune of eight floors—and Christine had to pinch herself as she sat at a table behind fat stacks of books, signing for what seemed like a never-ending line of readers. Once she hadn't even dreamed of having this many fans, let alone ones who would show up for a signing in a single city. Still, looking at the almost entirely female demographic, she was glad she'd talked Nick out of his offer of help. Neither the shop nor the representative of her UK publisher hovering on the outskirts would have thanked her when the throng was more interested in getting selfies with the heartthrob-of-the-month than in buying her books.

That had always been the problem, she thought as she posed for her final picture and waved goodbye. Nick, especially as an aspiring actor, had been all about networking, being seen in the right places, meeting the right people. She could understand that, of course, but her brand of hustle on behalf of her career was quite the opposite—long hours in front of the computer screen. It was a bit like the fish/bird conundrum: they could fall in love, but one of them would always be out of their element.

Ironic, then, that Christine had crafted her public image to fit the daring, sexy feel of her books, complete with the sultry pen name, Cressida Lyons. Christine might be a bookish, nervous introvert, but Cressida basked in the adoration of her fans.

Now, though, she was at her limit of playacting. All she wanted to do was get out of this corset and the blasted leather pants, wrap herself in the fuzzy hotel robe, and watch Netflix on her laptop.

"Ms. Lyons?" One of the store managers, a middle-aged woman who had been assigned to her, approached hesitantly, a stack of paperbacks in her arms. Unlike the pristine hardcovers Christine had just signed, these were rumpled and dog-eared, the spines creased. "Do you think you might sign a few more? These are mine."

"Of course, Molly." Christine took the books and sat back down in her chair, pen in hand.

"I can't wait for the program," Molly said, her low-pitched British clip carrying a girlish hint of excitement. "I don't suppose you could … Do you know who's going to play Jackson Landry?"

Christine paused with her pen above the page. "That's such a huge secret, even I don't know."

"Right. Of course. It's just … I think he's my favorite hero. Ever."

"I can tell you one thing." Christine lowered her voice. "Jackson will be every bit as dreamy on the screen as he is on the page."

It might have been evasion, but Molly beamed as if she had been let in on a huge secret. Christine finished the inscriptions, making sure each was unique, then handed back the books, feeling oddly somber. The letdown from the day's excitement, she told herself.

Only when she was in the back of the cab, sliding through the dark London streets, did she manage to put a name to it. Guilt.

Maybe she wasn't being fair to Nick. She claimed her bias against him was based on his acting ability, but that wasn't true. Nick was an excellent actor. He always had been. It wasn't his fault that his roles so far required more looks than talent. Look at Brad Pitt. He'd gone from hunky eye-candy to Oscar winner in a handful of years.

The fact was, Nick was perfect for Jackson. She had written it with him in mind, first when she had been so in love with him that her enthusiasm spilled out onto the page, unbidden; later as she tried to redeem the character through hard lessons. She could admit that she had taken a twisted kind of delight in the torture she'd devised for Jackson in the later books.

So yeah, maybe she was letting her personal feelings interfere with her judgment.

And yet the idea of having to work with Nick, see him on a regular basis, made her feel a little ill. Or maybe that quiver in her stomach was an entirely different kind of sensation. She didn't want to examine that too closely.

But she didn't have to make the decision this second. David had given her another two days, and she suspected he had an alternate on speed dial, waiting in case she decided she just couldn't approve him for the role of Jackson. That, too, gave her a little twinge of guilt. She'd allowed Nick to believe her power came from the fact that her fans wouldn't support—and could in fact hurt—the series, when in reality it had a much more personal reason. When the first book in the *Smoke and Glory* series hadn't exactly flown off the shelves, she'd realized she needed a more consistent form of income and had taken a nanny job for a set of five-year-old twins. At the time, hired by the mother, Marilyn, she hadn't realized the twins' father was David Chan … nor had Marilyn realized that Christine was the author of the book she had just fallen in love with.

Fast forward three years and Christine was as much a part of the Chan family as if she were blood, even if the nanny position had been short-lived. She honestly didn't know if the books would have come to the attention of such a well-known director had there not been that personal connection.

But that's the way things are done in Hollywood, and in publishing for that matter. It's all about who you know. It's not any different than Nick using Derek to get a role on his father's show. Somehow that didn't comfort her. She'd always somehow thought she was above that.

Just like she'd never seen herself as the vindictive type.

When the cab let her off in front of the St. Anselm Hotel, she was thoroughly torn. She hoisted her tote bag onto her shoulder and made her way through the plush lobby to the lift. David had simply asked her to give Nick a chance to prove he deserved the role. So she'd give him a chance. And if she decided that he still had the emotional capacity of a four-year-old, rendering him incapable of playing the character, then she could tell David that with no ill will.

She rode up to her room, her heart lighter now that she'd managed to reconcile her feelings with her principles and let herself in with her key card. By now, the leather pants were making her feel like a sausage squeezed into a too-tight casing, and she was pretty sure that the spring steel boning in her corset was giving her a bruised rib. She threw the privacy latch across the door, pulled the pins out of her updo, and immediately began to work on the corset. Until it was gone, she wouldn't be able to bend over enough to peel herself out of the pants.

But when she put her fingers to the metal busk that closed the front of the garment, it didn't budge. She pushed both edges toward the middle, trying to free the posts from the hooks on the opposite side with no luck. Unfortunately, thanks to the corset, she couldn't see past her own chest to figure out what was hanging it up.

Groaning from the exertion and sweating like she was in a sauna, she moved to the full-length mirror on the back of the wardrobe. Dang it. The posts were bent, and there wasn't enough play in the stiffly structured garment to maneuver them free. She'd have to unlace herself from the back. She felt for the ties that crisscrossed the opening from the bottom up and the top down—she couldn't go with anything as non-traditional and déclassé as a zipper!—and tugged the knots free.

Nothing happened.

"No no no," she moaned, fumbling for the center of the thick laces. She twisted around, peering over her shoulder in the mirror. Even from here, she could tell that the knots she'd carefully tied were now tighter than a hipster's jeans. She slumped against the mirror, willing herself not to cry. What was she going to do now?

Remy. Maybe it was unorthodox to call a publicist to help her out of a corset, but the woman had become something of a friend while working on the preliminary publicity for the show. Plus, she was the only female Christine knew here in the hotel. She dug her cell phone from her discarded tote bag, found the number in the contacts list, and pressed *call*. It rang several times with the strange trill that indicated they were on an English network, before going to the woman's voice mail.

What now? She was tempted to cut the strings to get herself out, but her costume maker, Drew, would kill her if she somehow damaged the fabric in the process. Not to mention she needed this for a book signing in two days. What other choice did she have? If she had to, she would ask David to put her in touch with one of the costume designers he used here in London. No doubt they would be able to find a set of corset laces in the space of a day.

Just as she was about to call down to the front desk for a pair of scissors, a knock sounded at the door. With a sigh, she moved to the peephole and peered through, then jerked back.

Nick. What was he doing here?

Reluctantly, she opened the door just a crack. "Hi."

He hooked his thumbs in his pockets and sent her a charming smile, the one that had almost always gotten him out of trouble while they were together. "Hi yourself." Then he looked at her strangely, and she realized she was still breathing hard from her exertion with the corset. "Am I … interrupting something?"

Christine flushed when she finally followed his thinking and realized how it must look with her peeking her head out the crack of the door. She opened it wide to show she was indeed alone. "No, not really. I just got back from the book signing."

But he was now looking her up and down, his expression appreciative. "Wow. That is some getup, Chrissy."

Her spine stiffened, but his appraisal intensified the heat in her cheeks. "It's called cosplay. Haven't you ever heard of it?"

"Of course I've heard of it. But I never thought you were the type." The widening of his grin seemed to imply that he was very glad she was.

"My readers are the type, and that's what's important." She crossed her arms over her chest, which was probably a bad idea considering the way it emphasized the overspill from the corset. "Did you need something? And how did you find me anyway?"

"It wasn't hard. The hotel only has thirty-five rooms and you checked in under Chrissy Marie. You didn't think I'd forgotten, did you?"

And just when she thought she couldn't be embarrassed further, she felt the crimson spread over her chest and neck. "You promised you'd never tell anyone about that."

"Considering you're wearing leather pants and a corset, I didn't think you'd be ashamed of having written fan fiction." He held up his hands. "But no, I haven't told anyone about that. It just made you easy to track down in the hotel. I was actually coming to see if you'd eaten dinner."

In response, her stomach grumbled. Traitor.

"I'll take that as a no?"

She desperately fumbled for control of the situation, which had somehow slipped from her grasp. "I was just going to order up room service." Except she had been about to order up a pair of scissors in order to cut herself out of her corset.

She eyed him critically. No. That was probably a really bad idea. It would definitely send the wrong message.

The corset boning shifted as she moved and sent a twinge of pain through her ribs. "Okay. You really want to prove yourself?"

"You know I do."

"Then get me out of this corset and never speak of it again."

Mischief glinted in his dark eyes, and a wolfish smile spread across his face. She smacked him in the arm, hard. Unfortunately, it only served to hurt her hand. He really did spend all his time in the gym. "Stop that. I've been in this thing for six hours, the busk posts are bent, and the strings are knotted. I'm stuck."

He grinned at her and stepped inside, closing the door behind him. He leaned against the door, as if he were blocking her exit. "I have a condition."

"I don't think you're really in the position to have conditions."

He shrugged. "Fine. You're the one who's going to have to sleep in a corset." He pushed himself up and turned, his hand on the latch.

"Wait." She sighed. "What is it?"

"Nothing taxing. Let me buy you dinner downstairs at the restaurant."

She regarded him suspiciously. "Just dinner."

"Well, dinner and civil conversation. Like we don't hate each other. Because no matter what you might believe, Christine, I still like you. I always have. I admire what you've accomplished. Surely we can spend an hour or two together, getting to know each other again?"

She considered. His words and his tone seemed completely sincere, but then again, she had just finished convincing herself that he was a truly good actor. And she did have to eat … without the stupid corset compressing her organs into mush. She nodded.

"Okay, turn around. I'm assuming we're going through this because we can't just cut them?"

"Yes. The dress I'm wearing for the convention signing is fitted to this corset and I won't be able to get into it otherwise. I'm not sure I have time to track down more laces."

"All right, let me see what we're dealing with here." He gathered her hair with one hand and pushed it over her shoulder. It might have been intended as a businesslike motion, but the brush of his fingertips still raised goosebumps over her skin. That wasn't good.

"Mind if I sit?" He gestured to the chair in front of the nearby desk and then pulled it over behind her. As if that didn't make her feel more exposed. He was practically staring at her butt in leather pants. Then again, it was probably hard to bend himself close enough to see the knots. She kept her breathing as even as she could manage, though considering the situation—all elements of the situation—it was getting hard to manage.

"You know, this sort of thing usually comes *after* dinner," he murmured.

"Not funny," she said stiffly.

"Sorry. Just going for a little humor to lighten the mood." His tone didn't sound sorry at all, but she didn't dare turn to see what his expression looked like. His fingers tugged at the strings, and she struggled to stay still and upright as he worked at the knots that held her prisoner.

After what felt like an eternity, a triumphant "aha!" escaped his lips and she immediately felt the corset expand as the strings loosened in the eyelets. She let out a heavy sigh of relief. "Oh thank goodness. I thought I'd be stuck in this thing forever."

"I don't understand why you put yourself through it in the first place."

"It's part of the effect." Christine turned, her hands pressed to the front of the brocade material to keep it in place over her thin chiffon blouse. "The image."

"The image," he repeated quietly, his eyes meeting hers. "You never cared about that before."

She found she couldn't continue looking at him when he watched her with that soft, searching expression. Instead she turned and fled through the open bathroom door. "I'll meet you downstairs in twenty," she said, then shut the door in his face.

four

ONCE MORE, NICK FOUND HIMSELF WAITING on Christine and pacing the floor. Except now he was waiting to convince *himself* of something, not her.

He couldn't reconcile the woman upstairs with the one he had dated for three years. True, they had been in a different place than they were now, both struggling to start new lives, barely out of the undergraduate programs at the university where they'd met. He had still been scrambling to get an acting job—any job—and she had been enrolled in an MFA program while simultaneously trying to complete her first novel. They had been focused on completely different things.

Now it seemed like they were far more alike than they'd been when they split: both successful, both at the mercy of their fans and the images that came along with that success. Of course, she'd scoff at any suggestion that they had anything in common, just as she'd scoff at the thoughts that refused to leave his mind.

He should have found her someone else to help with the corset. He had only been thinking about how it was a way to leverage her gratitude into a chance to make a case for himself. He'd stupidly thought he would be unaffected by the soft skin of her shoulder as he brushed her hair away, that he could ignore the fact that he was essentially undressing a woman he'd once loved. A woman he was supposed to marry. It didn't matter how innocent the situation had been.

So he paced.

Finally, Christine appeared at the edge of the atrium, looking blessedly more relaxed and casual than she had in that eye-popping outfit twenty minutes earlier. Her long hair was twisted into a messy knot on top of her head, a loose silky blouse skimming her curves down to the tops of close-fitting trousers. A pair of leather ballet flats—he'd never admit he knew that's what they were called—peeped out beneath the hems.

"Better?" he asked, proud of how calm and casual his voice sounded.

"You have no idea. Be glad you're a man and you don't cram yourself into these ridiculous contraptions."

He gestured for her to walk with him across the lobby to the restaurant, an elegant white-tablecloth affair with silk draperies and crystal chandeliers. Even at this hour, the dining room was partially filled. "Why do you then?"

She didn't meet his eye, didn't respond. Had he said something wrong? The last thing he wanted to do was start the night off with her angry, not when this might be the only chance he had to convince her not to fire him from this part. He stayed quiet and led her inside to a free table near the corner where menus were already laid across the bread plates.

He held the chair for her while she sat, and she immediately picked up the menu. "Seriously?" she murmured. "*Foie gras* terrine and black truffle fondant?"

Nick chuckled. "What were you expecting exactly? Look at the place."

Christine sighed. "I knew it was too much to expect something like chicken nachos."

"I'm surprised you still eat them."

"Of course." She flashed him a tiny, knowing smile. "One does not just get over a chicken nacho obsession."

"We *were* pretty obsessed. You remember that little cafe we used to eat at in college? Sold half-price chicken nachos after ten?"

Christine grinned. "No wonder we all got a little soft around the middle that year. You can't eat like that after midnight every night and keep your girlish figure."

"It was fun, though, wasn't it? Our last hurrah before we were forced to act like grownups."

She smiled at him across the table, for once her expression free from suspicion. The fact she could reminisce fondly about their late-night snack spot gave him hope that not all her memories of him were bad. Maybe she would be able to see past how things had ended between them. Maybe she could forgive him for the mess he'd made of their relationship in public.

A woman arrived at their table, all English in a navy blue skirt, pressed white blouse, and bobbed haircut, and asked them for their drink orders. Nick immediately ordered a cocktail, but Christine opted for a sparkling water. His first misstep—he should have let her go first and followed her lead. As soon as the woman stepped away, Nick asked, "So how did this all come about? Seems you were three books in before I heard about the TV series."

Christine shifted in her chair, as if the question made her uncomfortable. "You remember that I'd gotten an agent for the first book when we … Well, that sold almost immediately, and I've been writing a book a year since. So number four just came out, which was what I was signing last night. David's wife is a fan, so that obviously helped along the option process. Once he was on board, things went rather more smoothly than most book-to-film deals go."

"They seem to be doing well." Nick thought they were at least. All four books were currently on the bestseller list, which he figured would indicate a pretty significant amount of sales, but he had no idea what that actually meant. Was it relative like movie openings, where rank depended on how bad the other options were?

"They are doing very well. I honestly thought I'd be looking at a flop, it started so slow, but then somehow they started gathering momentum. Once the first book hit the bestseller list, the others did too. And then the fourth opened near the top." She gave a little shrug, almost embarrassed. "It's inexplicable. It's a lot of luck, this business. But you know that."

"It helped that they're good books," Nick said.

She gaped at him. "You've read them?"

"Of course I've read them. Why do you think I wanted the role so badly? Jackson Landry is a perfect character, and *Smoke and Glory* is the perfect vehicle to prove what I can do. Steampunk, London, and a quirky, flawed, heroic male role. It's a great character in a great story, Christine."

A strange expression flickered over her face. Had she really thought he wouldn't do his homework? Any actor who really wanted a role would research the source material. Of course, he didn't tell her that he had read the books as they came out, one by one, eagerly awaiting the next volume. As skittish as she was around him, she would think he was stalking her, and then she'd never agree to work with him.

He thought she was going to comment, even thank him, but the return of their server with their drinks meant he'd never find out. Christine hurriedly scanned the menu, and Nick repressed a smile at the thought she was looking for a chicken nacho substitute. Of the two of them, Nick had always been the foodie. She'd never even had Chinese takeout before she'd met him.

A couple more seconds and she was beginning to look panicked, so he said smoothly, "We'll share the Chateaubriand for two with the truffle mashed potatoes."

The server smiled at him, her gaze lingering. "Green peppercorn sauce or garlic butter?"

"Garlic butter, thank you." He returned the menus to the woman and she hardly looked at Christine as she turned away. Maybe she hadn't noticed.

But Christine intoned in a sing-song voice, "Some things never change." She watched the server for a moment, then shifted her attention back to him. "You still like to order for me."

"Sorry, were you dying to try the squid ink spaghetti?"

"Funny. You know I wasn't. I'm sure what you picked will be good. It always is." She took a sip of her mineral water and then said, "Tell me how the role on *Night Music* came about. The real story, not the ones you always tell in interviews."

"Think I'm lying?"

"I think I've done enough interviews to know we all tell the truth, just little bits of it at different times as best suits the situation."

A little more cynical than he would have expected of the Christine he knew, but then again, he was beginning to think this wasn't the Christine he knew. "Essentially, I begged Derek to talk to his dad on my behalf. I'm not all that proud of it, but I'm not that ashamed either. He'd been offering for years, and I had this crazy idea that I would be able to land some big role on my own. And maybe I would have, had I kept at it long enough." He shrugged. "Sometimes I wonder if it was the best move, because now the only thing I get offered is supernatural, brooding, and shirtless."

"Yes, it must be rough to only be admired for your looks and your body," she said wryly, a hint of a smile playing around her lips.

"I don't know. How would you feel if people only came to see you in that impressive little corset and not because they loved your books?"

She pressed her lips together. "Point taken. But you enjoy the show, right? It can't be all bad."

"It's great. It really is. The cast is wonderful, with the exception of some diva behavior from certain actresses. Dante is brilliant when he's on set, and our showrunner is sharp. He knows what the audience wants and makes sure we stay on track each week. That's the only reason we're into our seventh season already." He folded his hands and leaned forward so he could pitch his voice low. "I wouldn't be up for this role if it hadn't been for *Night Music*, but I'm ready to show what I'm actually capable of."

He met her eyes, watched as they roamed over his face, presumably trying to ascertain his truthfulness. And then before she could say anything, the server came back with their arugula and goat cheese salads. As soon as they were alone again, Christine stabbed one of the leggy leaves with her fork and nibbled it experimentally.

Nick waited. "What do you think?"

"It tastes like weeds. Spicy weeds."

Nick chuckled and shook his head. "Somehow I expected your taste might grow up with you."

Instead of being offended, she merely smiled. "I made mushroom risotto last week."

"Oh yeah?" His eyes widened. "I'm impressed."

"Don't be too impressed. It came out gummy. But at least I tried."

"I'm impressed by the attempt then." He went back to the salad, noting that she was eating it despite her pronouncement. "What do you have planned this week leading up to the big reveal?"

A flicker of uncertainty passed over her face, like she was unsure if this was a way to pressure her into a decision. Finally she said, "The convention opens tomorrow, so I have a signing in the afternoon. Then very little beyond the announcement and the panel discussion afterward. Why?"

"I was wondering if maybe you wanted to do a little sightseeing with me."

She didn't say anything immediately and he realized he was holding his breath while he waited for the answer. Needy and pathetic. He exhaled slowly and took another bite of salad as if her response didn't matter to him.

Finally, she answered. "I'm not sure that's such a good idea."

"Afraid you might discover you actually still like me?"

"No, I'm afraid it would make it harder to kick you to the curb."

"That's kind of the idea. Come on, it will be fun. Casual. I promise I won't bring up the role unless you do."

After a long moment, she finally nodded. "I'm free after my two o'clock signing."

"Then I will be hanging around the hotel in case you need more corset assistance." He gave her a mischievous grin. He was saved from saying anything more by the return of the server, who set a platter of sliced medium-rare beef and crisped whole potatoes along with two dinner plates in front of them. A few minutes later, she brought him another cocktail and set it on a white napkin. He quickly moved the glass to cover the phone number scrawled in black ink on the corner.

But Christine was too quick. Her eyes followed the movement and a resigned smile crossed her face. "Like I said, some things never change."

"People do," he shot back, but it was too late. He could see that her mind was made up about him. And for the first time, he was absolutely sure her problem with him had nothing to do with his acting ability.

five

THEY FINISHED THEIR DINNER in the restaurant, keeping to neutral topics and pretending like they were merely old friends catching up on the past five years. When Nick asked her if she was seeing anyone, Christine made a non-committal answer about it being nothing serious. In truth, there was nothing to talk about, serious or not. She'd dated here and there, but somehow, despite the romance she wrote into her novels, a relationship wasn't at the top of her list.

Nick volunteered to walk her back to her room, and since she couldn't think of any polite way to say no, she nodded. He kept his distance in the lift and slipped his hands into his pockets as he trailed her down the hall.

"Thank you for joining me," he said, when they stopped outside her room.

"Thank you for … you know."

"No," he said, a twinkle in his eye. "I have absolutely no idea what you're talking about, just as instructed."

A tiny smile spread over her lips. "Thank you for that too."

"My pleasure." He looked down at her, his expression warm, and for a moment, she thought he was going to kiss her. But he only took her hand and lifted it to his lips, the kiss warm and gentle across her fingers. It was such a Jackson move that she knew it had to be calculated; the butterflies that erupted in her stomach didn't seem to care. "Good night. I'll see you tomorrow after the signing."

"Okay." She squashed the butterflies with the brutality of a neighborhood bully, but that didn't keep her from following his

133

departure. When he started to turn back, she panicked. He could not catch her watching him walk away. She waved her key card frantically in front of the door's reader. "Open open open," she hissed at the mechanism, refusing to look back even though she could feel Nick's eyes on her. When the light finally turned green, she shoved through the door and pushed it closed behind her.

"You're an idiot, Christine." She tossed her card on the desk, grabbed her pajamas from the dresser drawer, and strode into the impressive hotel bathroom. At least one thing was clear from that little show. He *was* an excellent actor. At least she hoped he was. Because the last thing she wanted to believe was that he was actually sincere.

She washed the last traces of makeup from her face, wound her hair into a bun on top of her head, which would help with the hairstyling in the morning, and then slipped on the oversized T-shirt and shorts that served as her nightwear. No doubt everyone imagined that the famous Cressida Lyons wore silky peignoirs around the house, lacy little nothings suited to a best-selling author with a sexy image. How disappointed everyone would be if they knew the truth.

When she finally made it back to the bed, the flashing light on her cell phone alerted her to a missed call. No message. She didn't even need to look at the number to know who had called. She hit *return*.

The phone on the other end rang twice and then an impatient voice came through the line: "Where have you been? I've been calling you!"

Christine laughed and pulled her legs up beneath her on the bed. Drew Price was one of her oldest and dearest friends, and even the fact she lived three hours north of San Diego in the San Fernando Valley hadn't dampened their friendship. "You called me once and texted me twice in the space of five minutes. A girl does have to use the restroom once in a while."

"Please, I know you take your phone in with you so you can check your Amazon rankings."

Christine laughed with a tinge of embarrassment, knowing how close to the truth that actually was. "What are you doing? It's after midnight here, so that makes it what … four p.m.? I didn't even know you Hollywood types got out of bed that early."

"Very funny. I'm looking at thirty yards of the ugliest green polyester I've ever seen. Remind me again why I'm doing this?"

"Because you are a good person and you want to give back to the community?" Christine ventured.

"Right. That must be why I'm spending the time I'd planned for my beach vacation sewing a billion tiny costumes. Because I'm telling you, I had no idea exactly how many Merry Men were in this production when I volunteered for it."

Christine smiled. Drew might be a tough-talking, in-demand Hollywood costume designer, but she was also a campfire-toasted marshmallow—a big softie wrapped in an intimidating all-black wardrobe. Which was the only way to explain how she was sewing costumes for a children's community theater on what would probably be her only two weeks off this year.

"Did you ever think we'd be here?" Christine asked. "Living the dream?"

"My dream did not involve draping Maid Marion in neon pink taffeta, but apparently we're working with donations from the community." Drew's tone was so flat it was all Christine could do not to laugh.

"Well, make sure you leave some time to fix my corset when I get back. My busk is bent and I almost got stuck in it today."

"Did you have to cut yourself out of it? I packed extra laces in that little pocket in the garment bag."

Christine's mouth dropped open. "You didn't think to mention that to me before I left?"

"What's the big deal? You're not still wearing it are you?" Drew gasped. "You did not cut the corset, did you? That took me two full weeks. I still have your pattern but—"

"Relax, I did not cut the corset. It's just that the only person around to help was—" she lowered her voice, not knowing why she was even doing so— "Nick Cleary."

"No!" Drew sounded scandalized. "I don't know what to ask first: how he had the guts to even get within ten feet of you or what he's doing in London in the first place?"

"Well, you know *Night Music* has a huge following. The whole cast is here at FanFest."

"No, there's more to this story. I know you. I can hear it in your voice."

Christine spilled the whole story, how Connor Bell was in the hospital with a broken leg, how David was pushing to have him replaced by Nick Cleary. How Nick was trying to play nice in order to get the role.

"You know, he'd actually be pretty good as Jackson."

Christine gasped. "Drew!"

"No, I know, we hates him, precious. But still … you did kind of write it for him …"

"Whose side are you on anyway?"

Drew's voice sobered. "Yours. Always yours, Christine. And I'm with you no matter what you decide. No one gets to dump you three weeks after your engagement, embarrass you on national TV, and still get everything he's ever dreamed of. At least not without a little payback."

There it was, the mischievous tone Christine knew so well. "What did you have in mind, exactly?"

"Oh, I have some ideas. It all depends on how much you want him to pay."

"Dearly. He needs to show me that he's truly sorry and he's willing to go to any length to get this."

Drew gave an evil giggle. "In that case, I have the best idea. Here's what you're going to do …"

Christine slept restlessly that night, partly from gleeful anticipation about the plan she and Drew had concocted, partly from nerves for today's book signing. It was one thing to put on a good show for Nick; it was another to keep it up all morning for the hordes of fans who came to cry, hug her, and take pictures while she signed books. She was immensely grateful for her fans—that was never in question—but for someone who was essentially an introvert and spent most of her time in her own quiet home office, FanFest felt a little like going into battle.

When she finally opened her bleary eyes after catching a short nap in the pre-dawn hours, it felt like she'd washed them out with sand. One look in the bathroom mirror told her she *looked* like she'd washed them with sand as well. Dark bags puffed out beneath her bloodshot eyes, her skin somehow managing to be simultaneously sallow and pale. Good thing she'd brought her train case, filled with more makeup than most professional artists carried with them. She had two hours to make herself back into Cressida Lyons, Bestselling Author, from little Chrissy, bag of nerves and self-consciousness. Which was exactly why she'd created this new image. She supposed she and Nick weren't all that much different in their ability to change themselves into different people; except she did it out of necessity.

Nick. As soon as she finished, she would put phase one of her plan into action. No doubt he thought he'd won her over last night, but she wasn't for a minute convinced that it hadn't all been for her benefit. They'd see how far he was willing to humble himself for something he really wanted. But not now. Now, she had more pressing concerns. As layer after layer of makeup went on, transforming her round moon face with blotchy cheeks and stubby eyebrows into the femme fatale in mink lashes, Christine began to disappear into Cressida. If today was a battle, this was her armor.

An hour later, she wasn't even the same person, her hair curled up into an elaborate updo, little stick pins with gears and charms dangling from the messy twists, her eyes now looking huge and seductive, pouty lips drawn on like a doll's. She slipped into the shift and crinoline that went beneath the striped Victorian style dress—historically accurate but for the front that cut up to the knee to reveal her stockings and lace up boots—then looked in consternation at the corset. Somehow, she'd forgotten about the bent busk pins, which meant the only way to get into the garment was to have someone else to lace her.

She certainly wasn't going to call Derek to do it. Instead she dialed Remy, who thankfully answered on the first ring. She led with, "I'm desperate. Can you help me?"

Five minutes later, Remy arrived at the door, already dressed for the day in a stylish black suit and towering nude heels. "Wardrobe," she trilled when Christine opened the door.

"Thank you. You have no idea how much you just saved me."

"Don't thank me yet," Remy said with a grin. "You look great, by the way. How did the signing go last night?"

"Wonderful. Sold out all the books they'd ordered. I'm hoping it's an indication of how today's going to go. There's nothing worse than sitting at a table all alone, trying not to look forlorn."

"And how was dinner?"

Christine looked at the publicist sharply. "Dinner?"

"I saw you and Nick at the restaurant downstairs, looking pretty cozy."

Fortunately, she got a hold on the blush before it could get started and gave a nonchalant shrug. "It was fine. He's trying to convince me that he can play the role. I'm trying not to be swayed too much."

"Why not? You know he'd be perfect."

"Yeah, but …" She found she didn't really have a response that didn't sound petulant or unnecessarily vengeful. Instead she nodded toward the heavily-boned brocade spread on the bed. "The instrument of torture is over there."

Remy picked up the corset unperturbed and handed it to Christine, who positioned it around herself and held the sides steady while the other woman threaded the laces through the eyelets and tugged. "You might want to hang on to something."

"I thought you've never done this before."

"I've watched *Gone with the Wind*." A glint of wickedness surfaced in Remy's smile. She should have figured the pretty, professional publicist had a sadistic streak. Christine clamped her hands on the bathroom doorframe and planted her feet as Remy pulled the laces tight up her back.

"Ow!" Christine exclaimed. "Did you just brace your knee against my butt?"

Remy laughed. "Stop whining. I'm trying to get the lacing even. The gap is supposed to be the same all the way down, isn't it?"

"Yeah, but it didn't take this much work to get into yesterday."

"You didn't eat dinner at ten p.m. the night before either."

"Yeah. Great. Thanks." When the laces were finally tightened and knotted in a way that Remy assured her would come loose without trouble, she turned. "I would say I really appreciate it, but I have a feeling you take a sick kind of pleasure from torturing me."

"What are friends for?" she said lightly. "Now get yourself ready. Your fans await."

"Don't remind me." Christine's stomach jumped with nervousness. She started to psych herself up for the signing, but Remy's hand was already on the door. "Don't take too long. I'll wait downstairs."

"You're coming?"

"Of course. Unless you'd like to field all the questions about the show yourself?"

Christine shuddered. "No, thank you. I'll see you downstairs then." She waited until the door clicked closed behind Remy and put on the striped dress, buttoning up the front and arranging the pleats of the skirt to show the right amount of leg and crinoline. When she was finally ready, she packed her touch-up makeup, a couple of extra copies of her recent release, her wallet, and her cell phone in a suitably in-character brocade carpetbag and made her way to the lift. A pair of businessmen waited in front of the doors, briefcases in hand; she struggled to keep a straight face as they stole looks at her, clearly taken aback by her outfit.

In the end, they merely gave her a polite nod and gestured for her to enter the lift first. She inclined her head like a proper Victorian lady, rather enjoying the experience. This was the reason for the Cressida persona. Christine would be humiliated, but Cressida was fearless. Cressida could handle anything, including a pushy actor who was sure that he could win her over. That was the mistake she had made last night. She'd attended dinner with him as Christine. Tonight, she would bring Cressida.

And yes, she was aware of how schizophrenic that sounded.

She joined Remy in the lobby, and they exited the stately brick hotel across the expanse of green lawn that separated it from busy Hammersmith Road. The July air condensed on their skin, warm and sticky thanks to the rare London heat wave. Thank goodness the convention center was only a couple of blocks away. Any farther and she was going to melt into a puddle on the sidewalk. Not for the first time, she felt sympathy for Victorian ladies with all their layers.

Half a block later, she was only feeling sympathy for herself. She dug in her satchel for a silk fan and ignored Remy's amused look when she fluttered it in front of her face. As they dodged backpack-wearing students and impatient office workers on their lunch breaks, Christine's thoughts turned inevitably back to Nick.

It was difficult to look at him and not remember the years they'd spent together, him as a struggling actor, her as a struggling writer. The date nights that consisted of cheap noodles at ethnic restaurants or staying out all night on the beach and then seeking out tacos for breakfast from one of the ubiquitous trucks that populated LA. The way he always brought her a single Gerbera daisy on Fridays to put on her desk while she worked, despite the fact that they were both barely making rent.

The way he dropped her for another woman with a helpless shrug and the explanation, "We just don't *match*. You see that, don't you, Chrissy?"

What she could see was that she hadn't been good enough for him until she became a bestselling author with a TV series and she once again had something he wanted. That thought brought up a wave of anger that carried her through the doors of the Olympia Exhibition Centre and into a wash of air-conditioned madness.

Long lines of people crowded around the doors, getting their badges scanned before they entered, dressed in all manner of cosplay. She lost track of the number of Marvel and DC characters she passed as she and Remy pushed their way through the throng to the exhibitor entrance where staff scanned their badges and waved them through into the main hall.

Voices melded into a dull rumble in the exhibit area, reverberating off the barrel-vaulted glass ceiling. Below stood booths crammed with memorabilia and costumes dedicated to various comic, TV, and film fandoms. Christine scanned the crowd and saw the steampunk contingent had made a good showing, no doubt helped by the cast announcement and panels for *Smoke and Glory*.

Too bad she still didn't know who would be sitting up there representing Jackson Landry.

"You okay?" Remy whispered in her ear.

"I'm great." Christine inclined her head just a tad, letting a half-smile come to her face. She was Cressida now, and these were her people.

"Cressida! Cressida!" She hadn't made it more than four booths before a teenage girl recognized her and came rushing toward her, a book clutched in her arms. "It really is you, I can't believe it! I tried to get tickets to your signing and the cast reveal but they were sold out and I …" She broke off, running out of breath before she could get the rest of the sentences out.

"What's your name?" Christine asked with a smile.

"Lindsey."

"Nice to meet you, Lindsey. Mind if I sign that for you?" Christine gently eased the book out of the girl's arms and flipped it open to the title page. Remy handed her a pen and she scrawled a quick message inside along with her signature. "Here you go."

"May I …" She held out her phone wordlessly, and Remy took the phone while Christine positioned herself alongside the beaming, gaping girl. The camera flashed and Remy handed it back.

"Thank you so much. You've no idea how much I wanted to meet you!"

"It's my pleasure, Lindsey. Enjoy the rest of your convention." Christine smiled warmly and let herself be pulled away by Remy.

"We're never going to make it to the signing if you stop for every single fan. There's a reason people pay for autographs here."

"Oh come on," Christine said. "She brought a first edition hardcover. And not even the UK version, the US version. You think I'm not going to sign it for her?"

Remy maneuvered her through the hall into the booth where she would be signing. It was simply a black-draped table in front of a standard convention logo backdrop with a single banner stand advertising Christine's books behind it. Ropes measured off the line for the signing, already packed with people. Her heart leaped and fell in relief as it always did. By now one would think she wouldn't worry, but a large part of her always was afraid that no one would show up. The bigger the deal they made out of her appearances, the bigger the risk if they didn't go well.

"Relax," Remy whispered as Christine enjoyed her last minute of anonymity. "They love you. They're all here for you."

And that was the other side of the fear. What to do with all the people who showed up.

But she put on a Cressida smile and walked confidently by the security guard who was manning the space between her booth and the neighboring one and gave a big wave. "Hello everyone!"

A cheer went up from the line along with an "I love you, Cressida!" She laughed and took her seat, where everything was already laid out for her as specified: a certain brand of pen, a stack of fresh yellow post-it notes. She settled herself behind the table and then the first person in line came.

As usual, it was mostly girls in their teens and twenties, but she was once again surprised at how many grown men were there at the signing with her books. They tended to gush over her even more than the girls, wanting a photo with her after she signed. Remy was there to move the line along, and security was there to hurry on anyone who got too handsy or clingy, yet it seemed like they weren't making any dent in the line. And then a tanned hand pushed a book across the table to her. "Would you mind signing my personal copy?"

Christine jerked her head up and found herself looking directly into the eyes of Nick Cleary. "What are you doing here?"

"I told you, I'm a fan. Would you sign it?"

Christine flipped the cover open—paperback, she noted, the cheapskate—and scrawled her name on the title page, then pushed it back. "There you go."

"A photo too, if you wouldn't mind?" He grinned, his eyes sparkling mischievously.

But Christine's narrowed in return. "I know what you're doing."

"Trying to show you that I really am a fan of your work?"

"Trying to get rumors started."

"What kind of rumors?" he asked innocently.

"Hey, are you going to take a picture or what?" A grumpy American voice from the line nudged them out of their personal squabble.

Christine sighed and stood. "Fine. You can have your photo."

But when Nick took his place with her and dug his phone out of his pocket, a whisper went through the readers in line. She distinctly heard the name *Nick Cleary* and more than once *Jackson Landry*.

"Smile," he said, passing the phone to Remy so she could take the photo.

Christine bypassed the smile and gave a pouty look that could be interpreted as sultry or angry, depending on how well the person in question knew her. But Nick just grinned as he swiped back to look at it. "That's great, Chrissy. Thanks for being a good sport."

"Oh you bet," she said, narrowing her eyes. "Now if you don't mind ..."

"Sure." He gave a wave toward the whispering fans that caused a titter to ripple through the line and then disappeared, leaving her shaking in frustration. Christine shot a worried glance at Remy and motioned her over.

"You know what that was about, right? He's stacking the deck in his favor. If he can get rumors flying about him being under consideration it makes it that much harder for me to turn him down."

"Do you blame him? He knows this role can make his career. And I hate to say it, but he could make the series too. Christine, look at him." Remy inclined her head toward where Nick stood taking selfies with a cluster of fans, beaming and schmoozing like a pro.

Christine didn't dignify that comment with an answer, even though she knew it was true. She settled back at the table, put on a bright smile, and took the next person's book for signing.

Inside, though, she was fuming. How dare he pretend to be all patient and reasonable with her last night and then try to force her hand today in front of the fans? It was a typical Nick Cleary move: play nice until you got what you wanted, then throw everyone else under the bus.

Fine. He might make this series successful. But that didn't mean she couldn't break him first.

six

Christine blinked at Remy as they walked out of the exhibition hall, the publicist's eyes—and thumbs—glued to her phone. "What kind of news?"

"Not sure yet. David wants to see us in his suite when we get back."

Christine took a deep breath and tried not to let the words send any more panic through her system than she was already feeling. Nick had thrown her off her game. There was no doubt about it. From the minute he'd shown up, she'd ceased to be the strong, successful woman she liked to think she was, pulled right back into the young girl who was still shattered by his betrayal. Betrayals. Because until he'd come back into her life, she'd been convinced she was completely over it.

But she wasn't going to show Remy that, because Remy didn't need to see the resurgence of those old insecurities. "That went well. At least I think that went well. What do you think?"

But Remy was staring at the phone, a funny expression on her face.

"Remy?"

"Have you seen Twitter?"

"Of course I haven't. Why? What is it?"

Remy handed over her phone and Christine's eyes widened. "Oh no."

"Oh yes." Remy took it back. "It's all over the Internet. Someone posted a photo of you and Nick together and now the speculation about the show is running wild."

"What does that mean?"

"I don't know."

But from the tone of voice, Remy did know, and Christine did too.

She managed not to ask—or show her growing panic—as they returned to the hotel and then rode the lift up to the third floor. She barely noticed the weird looks she got from another set of businessmen, though seriously … it was FanFest and they were at one of the closest hotels to the Olympia. Surely she was not the first cosplayer they'd seen?

"Breathe," Remy said. "You're not breathing."

"I'm wearing a corset," Christine bit out, but it didn't make any difference. She knew what was coming.

David was waiting for them when they entered the suite. "Christine, Remy, good. Come sit down. I have some news."

Christine lowered herself to the seat carefully, her spine held unnaturally straight by the corset's stays, and folded her hands in her lap.

"Connor Bell is out of surgery and it was not as bad as they thought."

Christine stared. "What? What does that mean?"

"It means that with proper rest and a careful exercise regimen, he could be on set in eight weeks."

She let out a long breath of relief. "That's great. It's great, right? Why are we even talking about this? We get Connor, I don't have to deal with Nick, everyone wins."

"Not so fast," David said carefully. "Even if he's ready to shoot, he won't be able to film the action sequences. Definitely not right away. Maybe not ever. So that means bringing in a stunt double."

"So? You already discussed having a double. Right?"

"Even so, we begin filming in five weeks. We'd have to rearrange the shooting schedule, which will cost us even more money. And I don't need to tell you that this is not exactly an inexpensive production, Christine."

She flopped back in defeat against the sofa, but the corset bit into her stomach and she popped straight up again like a jack-in-the-box. "So you're telling me I have no choice. You have to hire Nick."

"No." His expression shifted to something akin to sympathy. "Alastair MacCauley is still a viable option. But if the other producers are against sticking with Connor and we're passing on Nick, I need to be able to tell them more than 'Cressida hates her ex-fiancé.'"

"Right."

"And then there's the matter of this photo." David held up his phone and Christine groaned. "His fan base is going crazy, Christine. Do you have any idea how many viewers *Night Music* has?"

"Connor Bell won an Academy Award."

"And his last film was a box office flop. Nick is hot right now. He engages with his fans, he's got a reputation of being easy to work with—which, let's face it, Connor does not—and he wants this role. I would suggest you try to make peace with him, because from where I'm standing, none of us may have any real choice if you want this series made."

"And you better do it fast," Remy said, "because the cast announcement is in two days."

Christine searched for a response but there was nothing to say. Instead she levered herself to standing, picked up her carpetbag, and strode to the door.

David called after her. "Christine—"

"It's okay, really. I understand." She pulled the door open.

And found herself looking straight at Nick Cleary, his hand raised as if to knock. She shut the door behind her with an arch of her eyebrows and strode straight past him, her head held high.

"Chrissy, wait!"

She slowed and turned to fix him with an icy look. "What do you want, Nick? Haven't you done enough? Or are you just coming by to rub it in?"

He jogged toward her, apparently abandoning his errand. "What happened? You're ticked at me."

She stared at him. "You're unbelievable. What? I didn't give in to your 'reformed bad boy' routine fast enough so you decided to go behind my back to your fans?"

"What are you talking about?" Nick's brow furrowed. He looked completely baffled, and once again, she realized she'd underestimated his acting ability.

"I'm talking about this." She dug in her bag for her phone, then pulled up Twitter and searched for the hashtag #NickClearyIsJacksonLandry. Then held her phone two inches from his face.

Nick took a step back and held up his hands. "Whoa. I promise you, I had nothing to do with that. I didn't leak the photo. Someone else must have taken it."

"Which is exactly what you counted on when you showed up at my book signing and wanted to take a photo with me."

"No! Not at all. Chrissy, you have to believe me. I went there because I wanted to make a public statement that there are no hard feelings between us, at least on my side. But—"

"Why pass up a photo op if you can bend it to your advantage?" Christine shook her head, fuming. "I read you wrong, Nick. You really will do whatever it takes to get what you want." She hiked her bag onto her shoulder, turned on her high heel, and marched the last stretch of the hallway toward the lift. She punched the button, trying to get the car to arrive through sheer force of will. Of course the old-fashioned dial was fixed permanently in the middle, giving Nick plenty of time to catch up with her.

"Christine, I promise you, I was not behind this. I want this role, yes, but I know you well enough to know a stunt like this would only make you dig in your heels. Please, how can I make this up to you?"

"You can't. It's out there, and you can't take it back. And now I get to disappoint your fans, because it looks like Connor Bell is going to make a full recovery." The lift finally arrived and she darted inside, punching the *close* button.

He put his hand out to stop the doors and slipped onto the lift beside her. "I heard about Connor. And I also know there's no way he's going to be ready to shoot in five weeks. You'll have to delay production for him."

Christine shrugged. "He's worth the wait. He brings some needed gravity to the role."

"Come on. He's done nothing but snore-worthy costume dramas. He's probably the single actor I've ever met who is more interesting in real life than he is on screen. He's not right for Jackson Landry. Jackson has … life. Wit. A spark. Doesn't take himself too seriously."

"Oh, and you're perfect for the role? What prepared you for that, your impressive collection of Instagram workout selfies or four seasons of playing a brooding otherworldly incubus?"

"He's a shape-shifter, actually. But it's only a role."

"A role you play to perfection." She reached out and tweaked a piece of Nick's perfectly coiffed hair, then smirked as he reached up to smooth it back in place. "You're about the most image-conscious person I've ever met."

"You're wrong. Let me prove it to you."

She was about to shut him down and kick him out of the lift when she remembered Drew's plan. A slow smile crossed her face. "Okay, then. You want to prove it? Come with me."

"A bunny suit?"

"Shut up and put it on." Christine pushed the pink footy-pajamas thing into his arms and guided him back to the costume shop's dressing room, which was little more than a cubicle with a curtain. "I'll hold onto the head for you."

"I still don't understand what this is going to prove."

"It's going to prove that you're no longer the type of guy who puts himself and his career first in any situation."

"I didn't—"

Christine sent him a disbelieving look, and he snapped his mouth closed. She continued, "It's going to prove your willingness to do whatever is required to get this role. And what I require at this moment is a bunny suit."

Nick fixed her with a disbelieving stare and slid the curtain closed. She heard him mumbling the entire time he struggled into the costume, until the long hiss of a zipper indicated he was finally ensconced in the pink monstrosity. He pulled open the curtain. "Now what?"

Christine repressed a laugh. "Now, you put this on." She picked up the giant bunny head and plopped it onto his shoulders. "Perfect."

The shop girl approached, a forced smile on her face. Clearly she didn't know what to make of the giant pink bunny either. "So … how does it fit?"

"I think it's perfect," Christine answered. "We'll take it. Nick, give her your credit card."

"But—" his muffled protest came from the suit.

"Nick, credit card."

He sighed and fumbled for his back pocket, which really meant groping his own pink backside. "I can't get to it."

"You're going to have to get to it. This is your act of contrition. I'm not paying for it."

He sighed and dropped his head, but the bunny ears flopped onto his chest. He fumbled for the zipper and finally unzipped it all the way, then reached around inside the suit for his wallet. He handed it over to her wordlessly.

She flipped open the leather bifold and fished out an American Express card, then handed it to the girl. Nice, Platinum. Apparently he wasn't doing too badly for himself. Since he wasn't in a position to object, she flipped through the other items. An ATM card, a grocery store frequent shopper tag, his California driver's license. A handful of British banknotes. And then, tucked into the back, was one of those narrow picture strips from an old-fashioned photo booth. She tugged it out and sucked in a sharp breath.

The photos were of her and Nick, hamming it up for the camera with cheesy smiles, making bunny ears behind each other's heads, kissing. And in the last one, staring at each other, so wrapped up in their connection that it was almost painful to look at.

She remembered that night well. They'd walked around Santa Monica in the balmy summer air for hours, finally landing inside the arcade where they played Skee-Ball and air hockey for hours. It was the night that, sitting on a park bench, eating ice cream cones, Nick had asked her to marry him.

"Ma'am?" The girl was handing back the credit card. Hastily, Christine shoved the photos back into his wallet and replaced the credit card in its slot. She scrawled an unreadable signature at the bottom of the register receipt and grabbed Nick by the arm. "Come on, Harvey. This is only our first stop."

He followed along docilely—too docilely—making her want to check to be sure it was really him inside the suit. A silly thought, of course, because who else would it be? She ignored the looks they were getting on the street, a woman tricked out in steampunk garb leading a six-foot pink rabbit. Surely this wasn't the weirdest sight ever seen in Golden Lane Estate, considering this part of the city was devoted to 1950s council housing painted in garish primary colors.

Fortunately, it wasn't far to the Old Street tube station, though she had to keep a tight grip on his arm while they traversed the steps down to the platform. "You know," Nick said through the bunny head, "This would be a lot easier if I could take the top off."

"What would be the fun in that?" she asked. "Don't worry, I'm not going to let you fall down the steps. I only want to humiliate you, not kill you."

"At least you're open about your goals," he quipped, and she had to wrestle a smile off her face.

Londoners were truly reserved people, because despite the initial glances they garnered, no one commented or hooted or questioned what the mismatched pair was doing on the tube. This was *definitely* not the weirdest thing to happen on the London Underground. Fortunately, the train arrived immediately with a whoosh of warm air and the familiar warning to "mind the gap," which took on a new meaning as Nick shuffled into the carriage and just barely kept his ears from getting caught in the closing doors.

Unfortunately, Christine hadn't thought this out well, because it took two line changes and nine stops to get from Old Street to Marble Arch, where their final destination lay. The whole time, Nick stayed silent except to answer the questions Christine asked of him. She couldn't tell if he was merely showing his patience or if inwardly he was fuming. Probably the latter. Which was just fine. This wasn't supposed to be fun.

"Wait, I know this," Nick finally said when they breached the edge of Hyde Park. "We're going to Speaker's Corner!"

"We are. You do know London."

"I love this city. That's another reason why I want the role so much. To spend months in England filming, only a train ride away from London? I know you probably won't believe this, but LA gets on my nerves sometimes. When I was struggling along as an actor, I felt like the sunshine was mocking me."

At least that's what she thought he said, because the whole speech was muffled by the bunny head. She could have simply let it go, but instead she found herself responding, "I know. That's why I moved to San Diego. I mean, same amount of sunshine, just less …"

"Fakery?" he suggested.

"Yeah, I guess. My neighbors are old-time surfers, not celebrities, at least."

"You're a celebrity, you know."

Christine laughed. "Hardly. Unless I'm in a corset no one recognizes me."

"Is that why you do it? So no one will recognize you when they see you for real?"

"Look, here we are." Christine conveniently skipped over his question as they approached the famous Speaker's Corner, which was really just a section of Hyde Park with an iron railing and an ugly mushroom-shaped concession stand. She had to admit she'd been expecting something far grander given its storied history.

Currently, there was a man wearing a beanie, shouting something about the British government and Marxist economics, but she couldn't figure out whether he was criticizing or making suggestions and whether he was for or against. Eventually, as the watchers trickled away, he hopped down from his folding step stool, tucked it under his arm, and wandered off to buy a cappuccino. Christine and Nick looked at each other and started to laugh.

"Okay, your turn."

"What am I talking about?" he asked, seemingly unperturbed by the whole situation.

"You're reciting the Gettysburg Address, of course. Here, I've got a copy in my bag for you."

"Chrissy, how am I going to read anything through this thing? I can barely see an inch in front of me."

"Then you're just going to have to recite it from memory." She cocked her head. "Don't tell me you've forgotten it already. You were so proud that you could still remember your eighth-grade speech."

He made a sound that seemed like a sigh. "I remember. Okay, let's get this going." He marched over to the spot near the railing Beanie Guy had just vacated while Christine pulled out her cell phone and moved into position to video tape him. She snickered to herself as he adjusted the bunny head and tugged up the sagging pink legs.

"Four score and seven years ago our fathers brought forth on this continent, a new nation, conceived in Liberty, and dedicated to the proposition that all men are created equal ..." Nick's voice rang out, somehow clear despite the stupid suit. He projected like a Shakespearean actor. "Now we are engaged in a great civil war, testing whether that nation or any nation so conceived and also so dedicated can long endure."

Christine watched on, marveling that he was taking this seriously. And that somehow, despite the fact he was wearing a bunny suit, he was managing to give it the gravity it deserved.

"The world will little note, nor long remember what we say here, but it can never forget what they did here …"

All the amusement she'd felt in this whole endeavor drained away. It was childish and mean and probably more than a little disrespectful toward one of her country's pivotal moments. She was suddenly ashamed of having gone to so much trouble to set it up. When his final words faded away, he lifted the head off the bunny suit and grinned. "Did you get it?"

"Got it," she said, pressing *stop*. But as she attached it to the tweet from her anonymous account, she hesitated.

"What's wrong?" He marched over to her, his hair sticking out in all directions, a couple of locks clinging to his sweaty forehead.

"Why do you still have photos of us in your wallet?"

His eyes met hers, his face suddenly guarded as if he'd been caught at something. He took the phone from her hand. "Here, I'll make it easy on you. It's posted." He handed the phone back. "Now the whole world can see my epic oration and you don't have to feel guilty about it."

She didn't even look at the phone. "You didn't answer my question."

"And you don't want to hear the answer." He glanced down at himself. "If it's okay with you, I'm going to get out of this thing."

"Sure. Whatever. The deed is done."

He frowned. "I thought this is what you wanted. Or did you expect me to balk and prove that you're right about me?"

Her eyes leaped back to his face. "That's not what I was doing."

"Wasn't it?" He unzipped the costume and carefully stepped out, then draped it over his arm. "You wanted to prove that my ego was bigger than my desire for this role. That I was all talk. And you were wrong."

His eyes issued a challenge, and her first instinct was to argue. But she couldn't. "You're right. I *was* wrong."

Without another word, she walked straight to the street, flagged down a cab, and climbed inside.

Leaving him and his bunny suit behind.

seven

It would have been easy enough to grab a cab since he was no longer dressed like a big pink rabbit, but instead Nick took his time, walking what must have been miles around Hyde Park and finally ending up on the other side, looking out at the Serpentine. Christine confounded him. Christine of the leather pants and steampunk sass and quicksilver moods that could go from irritated to amused to sad in a mere moment. In the years he'd known her, she'd never been what he would have called passionate. Single-minded, yes. Determined, absolutely. But whatever passion she might have felt always seemed directed toward her characters, never outside herself. Never toward him. And that had been part of the problem, why it had been so easy to walk away.

But the fact she was still harboring this much anger toward him, this much *feeling*, made him think he'd woefully underestimated what was going on inside her.

He sighed and kicked a rock into the water, then turned around and began walking out of the park back to Kensington Road, where he'd be able to grab a cab to the hotel. This little outing of theirs had taken up a big chunk of the afternoon and he would have just enough time to shower and dress for dinner with his fellow *Night Music* cast members.

When Nick finally made it back to the hotel, he gave the bunny costume to the concierge with instructions to send it back to the costume shop, then rode the lift up to his floor. As the old-fashioned dial clicked upward, he changed his mind and pushed another button. Moments later, as he stood outside Christine's room, he wondered how it was that she'd attempted to humiliate him, and yet he was the one who ended up feeling bad about it.

Even so, he knocked sharply and listened for movement inside. Nothing. Either she wasn't back yet or she'd left for the night.

He shoved down the uncomfortable sensation of guilt while he showered, shaved, and changed, but it didn't make him feel any better. His assessment of guilt didn't matter—right now it was solely her opinion that counted.

He kept his eyes open for any sign of her when he returned to the lobby, but the only people waiting for him were his fellow cast members, looking like they were ready for a red carpet.

"Hey man." His co-star, Ethan Gray, greeted him with a handshake and a slap on the back. On the show, Ethan was the golden boy to Nick's brooding darkness, typecasting if ever there was an example. Ethan always reminded him of a retriever—overly-friendly and eager to please. Nick also thought at times he wasn't the sharpest crayon in the box, but he had an almost preternatural gift for remembering dialogue. What took Nick an hour to memorize, Ethan got from a single pass of the script. On set, it all evened out.

The other two were the actresses who played their love interests on screen, and *only* on screen, no matter what the tabloids said. Tatiana Smith, Ethan's character's girlfriend, was as dark as he was light, sinuous and sexy in a sparkly two-piece dress that showed a large swath of smooth, bare midsection. Nick greeted her with a kiss on the cheek before he turned to his own on-screen girlfriend, Megan Childs, red-headed, pale, and resplendent in a white halter pantsuit with a plunging neckline. She gave him a chilly smile and offered her cheek for a kiss as well, even though he could swear that she purposely shuddered when she drew away.

To say they didn't get along was an understatement. And made the words "long night" sound like a hopelessly trite cliché.

"Ready to go?" he said brightly. "Our reservations are at seven, and I'd venture to say the photographers will be upset if we're late."

Megan rolled her eyes and linked arms with Tatiana, dragging her ahead with an all-too-familiar swagger. Ethan stayed behind with Nick and gave a low whistle. "She's still mad at you, is she?"

"Still mad, mad again, hard to tell." Nick jerked his head in the girls' direction, indicating they should follow them. "I still haven't figured out what I did the first time."

"You exist," Ethan said with a grin.

Sadly, that was true. Nick had joined the cast late and quickly became a fan favorite. No one was thrilled by the way Megan's character, Alexandra, treated Nick's character, Victor—the writers' choice, not theirs—and so she had been quickly vilified by viewers. Not Alexandra, but Megan herself, the fandom obviously having difficulty separating the character from the actress. It had gotten so chilly between them that Nick had begged Dante to intervene and do something different with Alexandra, but he'd refused. The drama made good ratings; the social media frenzy only helped to draw attention to the show.

Were Nick to get this role, it would all be moot, because he would quit *Night Music* to star in *Smoke and Glory*.

Megan should be thanking him.

But she wouldn't, even if she knew the truth, and that made for a very long dinner in a very trendy London restaurant, Ethan and Nick chatting across the girls while they held their own conversation beneath them. And the whole time, he was thinking of Christine.

"What's up with you?" Ethan asked finally. "You've been distracted."

"Sorry. Just thinking."

"About *Smoke and Glory?*"

Nick blinked. "You know?"

"Everybody knows. Which is what you wanted, right? Why else would you have posted that photo of you and Cressida Lyons?"

"I didn't post it."

Ethan made a face. "Right."

"No, really, I didn't. Trust me, I know better than to tick off someone who has my role in her hands. And I know Chris—Cressida well enough to know that photo would infuriate her."

"So who did then?"

"Someone trying to make trouble for me? No idea."

"I'd say they did you a favor, man. Your hashtag is trending."

He took the phone that Ethan offered and scrolled through the long list of #NickClearyIsJacksonLandry tweets. He shrugged casually, even though his mind was spinning over the implications. When Christine showed him the hashtag earlier, he'd assumed it would fizzle out and die.

After all, it didn't exactly roll off the tongue. But he'd underestimated both of their fandoms. Of course news like this would blow up the Internet. Maybe it would grow big enough that she'd have no choice but to acquiesce to the casting. But he'd rather not have to go that route.

And that's when he realized that not only did he want the role, he wanted her approval. Her forgiveness.

"—isn't it, Nick?" Tatiana grinned at him, a mischievous sparkle in her eye.

"I'm sorry?"

"I said, I'll bet you twenty bucks that our audience tomorrow is seventy-five percent teenage girls cosplaying Alexandra in the hopes of getting a photo with the real live Victor."

Nick gave a half-hearted chuckle, knowing that the joke could very well turn out to be true. "I'm not willing to take that bet."

"On that note, I think we should get going." Ethan pulled out his wallet and shoved his credit card in the folder, then set it on its end on the table for their server. As soon as the waiter ran his card and handed it back, Nick collected Megan's coat check ticket and went to retrieve their jackets, then met her at the entrance to help her into it. Whatever the truth might be, most of their fans wanted to believe they were all just one big happy family off-screen.

"How do I look?" Megan murmured just before they broke free of the doors.

"Gorgeous as usual," Nick said and put on a bright smile before the flash of cameras followed them all the way to the taxi rank and into their hired cab.

"Well, that was fun," Tatiana said drolly, looking between the two of them. "Our panel is tomorrow. Think the two of you could look a little more friendly by then? You are supposed to be in love, don't forget."

"I think our love/hate dynamic is far more appropriate, considering Alexandra tried to kill Victor twice and he pulled her into the underworld last season." Nick flashed a smile. "Don't you think, darling?"

"I definitely understand my character's motivations," she shot back sweetly. "But I still think I was robbed. I deserved an Emmy for pretending to be in love with you."

Tatiana pursed her lips and sucked in a dramatic breath at the burn, but Ethan looked uncomfortable as he always did when their interactions turned too sharp. Nick felt a flash of guilt over his uncharitable thoughts toward his co-star; Ethan was a better, kinder person than all of them combined.

"You guys need to kiss and make up, because look what I got us." Tatiana pulled four tickets from her purse and looked disappointed when they stared at her blankly. "The Ministry of Sound? You know, the dance club? It's practically a London institution."

Ethan shrugged. "I'm game."

Megan looked pointedly at him, and Nick knew what she wanted. "I think I'm going to hit the sack early. I'm still jet-lagged."

Tatiana pouted for a second—nice to know someone cared—then looked at Megan.

"If he's not going, I'm in."

"Okay then." Tatiana clapped her hands. "We can meet in the lobby at eleven. If you change your mind, Nick—"

"He won't."

No, he wouldn't. In fact, he took his leave of them as soon as he hit the lobby, eager to get up to the safety of his room. But as he turned the corner and passed the hotel restaurant, his eyes were immediately drawn to a lone figure at a corner table, almost as if he'd been unconsciously seeking her out. Maybe he had been.

He should stick to his plan and go straight to his room, but instead he found himself winding his way through the tables and pulling up the chair across from her.

Christine glanced his direction briefly, but otherwise didn't move a muscle, her fingertips resting on the rim of her glass.

When the server came over to him—a different one tonight—Nick said, "I'll have whatever she's having."

"It's just sparkling water," Christine said. "You shouldn't drink when you're jet lagged. It messes with your melatonin production."

"I did not know that," he said.

"No reason you should. It's a completely random fact."

The server came back and placed the glass on a napkin in front of him. He took a sip. Its bitterness was welcome after the heavy meal he'd just eaten.

"So where did you go, all dressed up?"

"Dinner. I'd actually intended to see if you wanted to come. I stopped by your room before I left."

"Ah. Sorry."

"What did you do?"

She shook her head, obviously not inclined to reveal her evening plans to him. But she wasn't telling him to leave, so he sat there silently and sipped his water.

Finally, she spoke. "Earlier today, when I asked about the photos, why did you say I wouldn't want to know?"

Nick took a deep breath and let it out slowly, considering. "Because I know you, and you would feel guilty and then you'd be mad at me for making you feel guilty."

A faint smile crossed her lips. "Fair enough. But I still want to know."

"It's punishment."

Her head jerked up.

"Or maybe punishment is the wrong word. Penance might be better. I look at the photo, and remember how happy we were, and how I ruined it all. And then I think about the selfish jerk I was and how I don't want to be that person anymore."

"I don't believe you."

"Would you believe that I regret breaking up with you and I miss you?"

Now a harsh laugh slipped out. "No. I believe that even less."

"Okay, then. You pick which one you like better."

She toyed with her glass. "You read my books."

"Yes."

"You think you can play Jackson Landry."

"I know I can."

"Then tell me your favorite part of the series so far."

He fell silent, considering. There was the honest answer and the smart answer, the one that would swing her decision in his direction. Finally, he said, "I like the part where he gets taken away by Scotland Yard and Livia just watches him go."

She flicked a glance his way, her brow furrowed. "Why?"

"Because that's the moment he knows that he deserves what's coming to him. Not because he's guilty of the crime he's been accused of— because even without reading the next book, I know he isn't—but because of all the things he *is* guilty of." He met her gaze unwaveringly. "He looks at her and he finally understands what he's taken from her."

Christine swallowed. "What's that?"

"Her hope. Her belief in true love."

Christine remained stock-still, not even breathing, her lips parted in surprise. Nick broke the connection and leaned back in the seat. "Of course, then he gets taken to prison and tortured, which is always fun. I think that's an acting challenge I'd like to take on."

Christine laughed lightly, the spell—or whatever it had been—broken. She rose gracefully from her chair, then took a banknote from her purse and tossed it on the table. "Your drink's on me. I know you really didn't want sparkling water in the first place."

"Thanks." He waited until she was about to walk away before speaking. "Chrissy?"

She turned. "Yes?"

"Whatever you decide about the role, I'll accept it. If you're that dead set against me as Jackson Landry, then I'm not going to force it. But you should know … I did not leak that photo."

Christine licked her lips and nodded slowly, then walked away. Nick watched her. He'd done all he could do. Now he could only wait to see what she'd decide … about the role, and about him.

eight

CHRISTINE FLED THE RESTAURANT, feeling off balance and unsettled. She shouldn't have asked. She knew she shouldn't have asked, but curiosity had gotten the better of her, as Nick had to have known it would. All she'd been able to think about since Speaker's Corner that day was his cryptic statement that she wouldn't like the reasoning behind the fact he still carried old photos of them. It had dogged her through dinner with Remy and David and kept her out in the lobby hoping for a glimpse of him.

And now she knew.

She slumped against the lift's wall and watched the doors slide closed, praying no one got on with her. Cressida was done for the night, left up in her room with a mound of clothing; Christine was drained from the effort of being on all day. And by Nick's answer.

He couldn't have known it, but that scene was her favorite part too: she'd cried her way through the chapter as she wrote it, and again as she edited it before publication. The part where Jackson was taken away by the authorities while Livia stayed quiet with the information that could have saved him was the tipping point in the relationship. Unbeknownst to anyone but Christine, Livia had committed the crime for which Jackson was arrested and later tortured, but she couldn't bring herself to give herself up for him, not after all he'd done to her. Not after he'd repeatedly broken her heart.

And somehow, Nick understood the subtext, that Jackson's bad deeds had caught up to him and he was going to have to pay the price for them, even if it meant taking the blame for something he hadn't done. Christine still hadn't decided how she was going to get him out of the situation in the next book, taking a twisted pleasure in letting him rot in an alternate-history English prison while she formulated the next story. It was only fair, since Livia had reaped the consequences of Jackson's bad behavior. Since Christine had reaped the consequences for Nick's behavior.

Because it seemed silly to pretend that this wasn't their relationship played out on a fictional stage.

Christine heaved a sigh and pushed herself up from the wall when the lift dinged at her floor, then dragged herself down the hall to her room. She'd been trying to figure out how she would start the next book. Now was as good a time to decide as any.

She kicked off her shoes and climbed onto the bed with her laptop, opening a fresh file. She stared at the blinking cursor for a long moment and started typing.

> *The fine rain falling outside of Newgate Prison didn't seem to dampen the spirits of the spectators jostling to get a better view of the portable gallows set up outside Debtor's Door. There was a mean sort of reprieve from the misery of their own lives in watching the misfortune of others, a reminder that things could always be worse. No one questioned the slight figure who skirted the throng, the hood of her cloak pulled up to shield her face; she could be a flower-seller, peddling nosegays to take the edge from the stench that emanated from the prison, or a family member hoping to get one last look at a loved one before they passed into the Great Beyond. No one suspected that today, she was not a person, but Death. Death and Salvation in one.*

Christine paused. Okay, maybe it was a bit overwrought, but she did like to bring some drama in her openings. Livia, after all, was a dramatic character, a well-educated society lady who over the course of the series turned into an outlaw, so she had a tendency to think of herself in theatrical terms.

> *A buzz rippled through the crowd as the guards brought out the day's condemned, four men, all filthy and bloodied from their treatment in London's worst prison. Livia's stomach churned as she recognized Jackson. Not from his face, which was swollen and bruised beyond recognition, but from his walk, that cocky swagger that had so irritated her the first time they'd met. Even after*

his treatment at the hands of the guards, he was going to the gallows on his own terms.

The executioner was droning on about their crimes, but Livia blocked out the words as she moved into position. The executioner moved to the side of the gallows, his hand on the lever that would drop them to their deaths. She drew a breath, counting the moments as they passed in slow motion.

One: the trapdoor opened and the condemned men jolted downward to the end of their ropes. The drop was too short to break their necks—the condemned strangled to death at Newgate.

Two: an explosion somewhere behind them rocked the prison, covering the scene in black smoke.

Three: she whipped out her bow and nocked an arrow in one smooth movement, tracking Jackson's rope, which swayed to and fro as he struggled against the grip of the noose. She loosed, staying only long enough to see that her arrow had hit its target, then swirled away into the crowd before anyone could see what had happened. They were all too busy screaming in terror from the black powder bomb that her men had set off. A distraction.

It had worked.

Around the next corner, she tossed away her bow; farther down the street, she abandoned her cloak. By the time Livia met the nondescript black carriage at the end of the lane, she looked like nothing more than a wealthy woman in a violet day dress, out for a stroll.

"Good morning, Mrs. Barrett," her footman, Malcolm, greeted her. "I trust you found everything you were looking for? Your packages have already been delivered."

"Thank you, Malcolm," she replied, accepting his help into the carriage. "Let us away with all haste."

She gave him a vague smile and he closed the door behind her as she settled into her seat. Directly across from the bloodied, bruised, battered man she loved. The man she'd almost destroyed.

"You rescued me," Jackson rasped. He rubbed his throat as if surprised by the damage dangling from a rope could do to a man's voice.

"It was only fair," Livia said, "since I was the guilty one."

A faint smile stretched his cracked lips. "I know. I've always known."

Christine leaned back against the headboard of her bed, having surprised even herself. She'd planned on leaving Jackson to twist—both metaphorically and literally—for a bit longer before she rescued him, but it seemed that her subconscious had other ideas. After five books—five years' worth of rancor and power struggles and buried attraction—it was time to put them on the same side. It was time for Livia to let go of her anger against the man who had killed her husband.

She picked up her cell phone and dialed, not waiting for David to answer before she spoke. "Okay."

He didn't sound annoyed or asleep, which was a bit of a miracle considering the time, but he did sound confused. "Okay what?"

"Cast Nick Cleary."

A long pause. "Are you sure? You said—"

"I know what I said. And as much as I hate to admit it, he's better for the part than Connor Bell. He understands Jackson. And his fans will help make this a success, right?"

"Right." David heaved a sigh. "I'm so relieved that you came around, Christine. This is the right call."

"I know it is. And it was time for me to let go. Move on."

"Do you want to tell him or should I?"

"You can tell him. If I tell him, he's going to think he's being punked."

"This is great. I'll let him know right now."

"What about Connor Bell?"

"I was thinking he might be good for Captain Brown, actually. And he doesn't appear until the end of the season, so it gives him plenty of time to recover."

Christine nodded thoughtfully. Brown was an important, if supporting role, and a character utterly without a sense of humor. Connor would be great. "I'm good with that."

"This is going to be huge, Christine. So many of Nick's fans are at this con, it's going to make a massive impact."

"That's what I'm hoping." Christine forced a smile so it came through her voice and then clicked off the line. She'd meant what she said. Nick was the best person for the role, and deep down, she'd always known that. But just because she was willing to relent for the good of the show didn't mean she was actually prepared to have him back in her life, to work with him.

To be fair, she was only going to be on set on occasion; her life was back in California, and they would begin filming in Cambridge in a little more than a month. She basically had to make it through FanFest and they could go back to the arrangement that had worked so well for them for the past several years.

Once in love. Now strangers. As it should be.

Christine jerked her head up, her heart pounding. It took her several minutes to realize she'd fallen asleep against the headboard, her laptop on her knees. And then she realized the pounding wasn't just her heart, but the door.

She put her computer aside and stumbled to the door, too groggy to puzzle through who would be knocking after midnight. A quick glance through the peephole revealed it was Nick, still dressed in his clothes from earlier this evening. Somehow looking fresh and handsome despite the fact it was nearly one a.m.

She opened the door. "What are you doing here?"

He blew inside, picked her up, and spun her around. "Thank you, Chrissy."

His warm body pressed against hers, his arms around her waist, pushed away the last vestiges of sleep. "I take it you heard."

"I did. And you have no idea how grateful I am. I promise you, you won't be sorry."

Christine swallowed and extricated herself. "I know I won't. You're the right one for the role. You proved to me that you really know the character."

Nick beamed at her and shoved his hands in his pockets. He looked around, seeming to realize that he was interrupting something, that it wasn't normal to show up at her room this late. His eyes traveled over the rumpled but still-made bed, the laptop set on the side table. "Were you working?"

Christine rubbed her forehead. "Yeah. I was getting started on book six. I'm a lot behind, as you can probably guess."

Nick's eyes lit up. "Can I see?"

She laughed. "Of course you can't. That much hasn't changed."

"Then at least tell me ... do I survive Newgate?"

Christine hesitated and relented. "You spend all of book five in prison, untangling the mystery of your employer's identity, but you do eventually make it out."

Nick grinned. "Thanks for that then. I wasn't entirely sure what was going to happen to me. Would I be off the show in a couple of seasons?"

"Oh, it was close, trust me. Why do you think Jackson takes such a beating in the first four books? I was always debating whether to kill you off. I mean, kill him off."

He cocked his head. "So you really did write the character after me?"

She cocked her head the same way, mocking him. "You know I did. I started the series when we were still together. And when you left, it was very therapeutic to put you through the wringer."

"And now?"

"And now I realized I'm over you. Over it. So it doesn't matter." She smiled. "Don't get too cocky though. I still plan on making life difficult for him."

He held her gaze. "I really am sorry, Chrissy. It wasn't a ploy to get you to cast me. I've been trying to find a way to apologize to you for years."

"You should be sorry. You devastated me. Made me question everything about myself. But you know what? If it hadn't happened, this series wouldn't have happened. You gave me the motivation to prove myself. Your leaving made me realize what I'd been missing in myself. Some drive. Fire, maybe."

"Passion?" he suggested softly.

She licked her lips. "Sure. Passion. As mad as I was about what you did, I realized you had this … desire to succeed that I was lacking. You were willing to do anything to make it. And you have. That's why I was so mad about the TV interview. Not because you drew attention to me, but because you were right."

Nick stepped closer. "No. I wasn't."

"You were. I was always dedicated to my writing, but that's different from really putting myself out there and taking a risk."

He lifted a lock of hair that had fallen across the shoulder of her T-shirt and rubbed the strand between his fingers. "Is that why you came up with Cressida? To reinvent yourself?"

She caught her breath. As they'd been talking, he'd edged ever closer to her, and now he was mere inches away. Close enough that if he lowered his head a little and she turned her face up to him …

She stepped back and looked at the patterned carpet before she was tempted to act on the thoughts cascading through her head. "You've got a panel in the morning, and I've got to get back to work."

"Right." He cleared his throat. "Can we … would you be interested … There's something I'd like to show you. Maybe after I'm finished tomorrow?"

"Show me where?" She couldn't help the skepticism that came through in her voice.

"In the city." He nudged her arm. "What did you think I was talking about?"

"With you? I couldn't possibly guess." She moved to the door and opened it for him. "Maybe. Text me in the morning."

"I don't have your number."

"I have a feeling you can get it. Good night, Nick." She waited until he stepped outside the door and shut it firmly behind him.

And then exhaled.

She'd been right about one thing. She was done being mad at him.

But she wasn't even close to being over him.

nine

Nick wanted to take her somewhere.

It was the first thought that popped into Christine's head when she woke, before she remembered where she was or managed to look at the clock. Of course, the glowing red numbers quickly swept that thought away, because it was almost one o'clock. She never slept the day away. She did her best work in the morning, which meant she was always up by six and sitting at her desk by 6:45. But she wasn't in San Diego, she was in London. By California time, that meant she was up early. And she'd only slept in because she'd been up well past dawn, pounding out the first seven chapters of the next novel.

She threw aside the covers and swung her legs to the padded carpet, forcing herself to think past her jet-lagged grogginess. The blinking light of her cell phone pierced the fog. One missed text from Nick.

Panel discussion at 2pm, then photo call until 4. Meet me outside the convention center at 5:30?

Christine hesitated. He didn't even question the idea that she was going to join him; then again, she'd gone along with the idea when he proposed it last night. Finally, she typed in return: **Where are we going? What am I wearing?**

She dropped the phone on her nightstand and went to the bathroom to put on some makeup and brush her teeth. When she came back, there was already a reply.

Bring Christine, not Cressida. No photo ops today.

A faint smile came to her lips. Maybe she should be mad that he'd so easily figured out the truth about her split personality, but she shouldn't be surprised. Other than her parents and Drew, Nick was the person in the world who had known her best. Still knew her best.

Okay, she typed back, Meet you at 5:30.

She should take advantage of her one day off before the cast announcement tomorrow to make more headway on the book, but instead she found herself dressing for the convention floor. Not as Cressida, but in a way that would make her look like she belonged without drawing any attention to herself. Dark jeans, a gray T-shirt with bold white letters that said *You had me at the proper use of you're,* and a fitted black blazer. She cuffed the jeans and slid her feet into a comfortable pair of ankle boots, then grabbed her purse and convention badge.

"What are you doing, Christine?" she mumbled to herself on the way to the exhibit hall in a cab. She knew this was a bad idea but she couldn't help herself. Then again, he didn't need to know she was there. She could slip in and right back out without him ever suspecting a thing.

She put her badge on backward so the casual observer couldn't see her name until she flipped it around, as she had to do to gain entrance to the hall. Once inside, no one gave her a second look. She wasn't Cressida, decked out in steampunk splendor, larger than life. She was just some girl in jeans and a blazer, her hair in a braid and wearing next to no makeup, looking like someone's publicist, agent, or exhibit manager.

The place was huge, though, and she had to ask directions more than once to make her way to the exhibition center theater where they were holding the panel discussions. At the door, a long line of ticket holders stretched down the hallway behind a red rope, all waiting for their chance to file in and get their seats. Christine hovered in the periphery until the line started moving and there was nothing but a scattering of people left behind. Then she went to the man standing at the door and flipped over her badge.

She saw him read the name and start connecting the dots. Of course, an exhibitor badge could get you in pretty much anywhere; it didn't hurt to have the name of her show and the network beneath. He gave a little nod and gestured for her to go in.

The auditorium lights were low, the only illumination the spotlights on the stage, highlighting a long, draped table with a handful of chairs. Christine took advantage of the darkness to slip into a space along the back wall, amid a cluster of similarly-dressed people tapping away at their cell phones. The audience, on the other hand, was buzzing with excitement, more than half of them cosplaying characters from the show. She caught a glimpse of one guy in full Victor regalia, in shape-shifter form, of course, and wondered suddenly if she'd made the right call about Nick.

No, just because she secretly thought his show was silly didn't mean he wasn't the right actor for the job. And if the fans of the show showed half the devotion to *Smoke and Glory* as they did to *Night Music*, they would be in good shape for seasons to come.

The house lights went down completely and spots came up on the stage, bathing the whole auditorium in a silvery blue light. Then the theme song of the show came on and the audience went wild. Slowly, one by one, the cast members emerged from a side door and climbed onto the stage.

Christine had to admit it was a show filled with beautiful people, not the least being Ethan Gray who lit up the place like a beam of sunshine when he walked out. But the minute Nick made his appearance, she couldn't take her eyes off him. If she wasn't mistaken, the female screaming got a bit louder at the same time as well. She evidently wasn't the only one who felt a little breathless at fifty meters.

The executive producer, Dante Moretti, emerged last, taking a microphone from one of the con's staff, and beamed out onto the assembled crowd. Trim and handsome with only the gray hair giving a nod to his age, he had clearly been a heart-stopper in his younger days. When he held up his hand to quiet the room and then began to speak, traces of his Italian accent showed through.

"Thank you so much for joining us here at the Olympia!" He spread his hands wide. "Look at all you beautiful people!"

A cheer went up, and Christine smiled to herself. She'd done cons all over the world, but London tended to be far more reserved than San Diego, which had almost a festival atmosphere. He was warming them up, amping up the enthusiasm before he turned over the stage to his actors.

"Now, I know you're all anxious to hear from our stars—" some hoots and whistles— "but before we do that, I don't suppose anyone wants a sneak preview of the season seven trailer, would they?"

Now the response was deafening. Christine laughed out loud as the screen came down behind the tables and the lights lowered again. Images flickered onto the screen with ominous music, teasing the setting, then moved on to flashes of the Big Bad story arc that the characters would face in season seven. Some interpersonal drama, lots of hand-to-hand combat with mystical weapons, and then the money shot: Victor taking Alexandra by the shoulders and declaring, "I would give up eternity to spend one life here with you."

She was pretty sure the entire auditorium exhaled in one simultaneous sigh.

And then it was over and the lights came up to applause and more female screams. Yep. Nick was the fan favorite, and Ethan, sitting down the table from him, didn't seem to mind.

She wasn't all that interested in the panel discussion, which mostly involved a recap of season six and what the actors thought about their characters' arcs from the previous season. They were consummate professionals, friendly yet polished, accessible yet still somehow untouchable in their glamour. It was Nick who really shone when it was his turn at the mike, however: he was personable and funny and just flirtatious enough that every woman in the room wished they could be the object of that dark gaze for just a few seconds. He had that "it factor" that no one could define, but everyone recognized the moment they saw it.

He'd always had it, and she knew just how easy it was to become starstruck in his presence, because she'd experienced it firsthand.

She murmured her apologies and slipped out of the theater.

After Christine left the exhibition center, she found herself wandering West Kensington without any real destination in mind, ogling the Victorian and Edwardian buildings and trying not to inhale the pervasive diesel haze. Nick was right. It was silly that she'd set an entire series in England and yet never experienced it herself. If she were smart, she'd hop on the tube and use her free hours to wander the National Gallery or explore Piccadilly Circus. Instead, she walked residential streets and gazed up at the attached brick row homes, wondering about the lives the owners led. This wasn't the most upscale part of West London, but it was certainly beyond what any average citizen could dream of, just as it had been in Livia's day.

When she got tired of her meandering route, she ducked into a small cafe where she ate a panini by the plate glass window and scrawled notes for the next few chapters in her pocket notebook.

Waiting on Nick as you always did, huh?

She silenced the mocking voice in her head. That wasn't what she was doing. She could have done anything with her day, texted Nick to meet her somewhere else. But the heat wave had lifted, leaving them with pleasant, overcast warmth even in the unair-conditioned cafe, and she was getting some work done on the next book.

She didn't like to admit that until she'd finally agreed to let Nick go forward as Jackson Landry, she'd been hopelessly blocked.

Now the ideas were flowing, and she filled page after page with plot points. She only liked composing on her computer, but she had the feeling she was going to spend the entire eleven-hour flight home on her laptop now that she knew what was going to happen next.

Maybe it was finally the time for Livia and Jackson to succumb to their attraction.

The idea gave her a thrill that wasn't entirely esoteric; there was way too much of herself and Nick wrapped up in these characters. It was what had made them come alive, why the passion and the hatred and the angst seemed so real and palpable to readers. She'd meant what she said: she owed much of her success to what had happened in their relationship.

A few minutes after five, she paid her check, packed up her things, and made her way slowly back to the exhibition center. Her heart picked up a rapid beat when she saw that Nick was already waiting for her out front, a baseball cap pulled low over his eyes to disguise his face. Even from a distance, she saw his expression light up when she appeared.

"You came." The low timbre of his voice sent a little shiver down her spine. No, that couldn't be what had caused it. It must be the sudden coolness of the breeze as the sun began to dip.

"How was your panel?" she asked as they moved together down the street, she presumed toward the tube stop.

"You tell me."

Her cheeks heated. "You saw me?"

"You're hard to miss."

Christine laughed harshly. "I don't buy that for a second. Someone told you."

"Oh, no, I spotted you the moment you walked in. I was standing off stage watching the crowd. My question is, why did you leave so soon?"

She shrugged. "I'd seen enough."

"Convincing yourself you made the right decision?"

"Something like that. Even if I didn't think you'd make a good Jackson, the fans' response to you would have convinced me. You had them eating out of the palm of your hand."

"Part of the job," he said. "Fans are the difference between a good show that goes nowhere and a smash hit."

"I have a feeling Dante is going to be very unhappy to hear he's losing you."

Nick didn't say anything, and Christine threw him a curious look. "He already knows?"

"I owed him as much. Better he hear it from me than tomorrow at the panel. I suspect the writers are figuring out how to kill me off at this very moment."

"Are you sorry to be leaving?"

He shook his head. "No. I'm grateful for the show, but I'm ready to move on. And more importantly, Megan is ready for me to move on."

"Funny, you two always look so cozy."

"That only proves that we're good actors. Trust me, it's hard to act like you're in love with someone on screen when they hate your guts in real life. I imagine Megan will get a good, heart-wrenching scene over my death that will boost sympathy among the viewers … or maybe Victor will do something horrible and she'll kill me."

"Does that mean you'll go back to shoot some final episodes?"

"I imagine I will. We haven't really discussed it in any depth yet." They'd come to the Underground station and descended the cement stairs side by side.

"So, do you want to tell me where exactly we're going or am I supposed to guess?" Christine asked.

"And ruin the fun? Why would I do that?"

"So it's something fun?"

"I guess that would all depend on your definition of fun."

"So not the London Eye."

He cast her a wry look. "Even I know that isn't your definition of fun."

"Then you should know that surprises in general aren't my definition of fun. Are we going to dinner?"

"Maybe later if you play your cards right."

She squinted at him.

"Listen, if I told you, you would be completely unimpressed and think I've lost my mind. It's really something that's better as a surprise. I promise you, it doesn't involve bunny costumes or historical speeches."

Christine felt her cheeks heat again. "Yeah. I feel like maybe I owe you an apology for that."

He shrugged. "I walked into that one."

The train rumbled into the station, its doors sliding open to let off a trickle of passengers. They slid onto the train and nabbed two seats by the doors.

"Besides," Nick continued, as if their conversation hadn't been interrupted, "You obviously haven't seen Twitter."

She threw him a curious look and he pulled up his app, then handed his phone to her. She scrolled down through all the mentions and sighed. "Seriously? A bunch of teenage girls sighing over your humility and sense of humor?"

He took the phone back and pocketed it with a shrug, though a smile played on the corners of his lips. "What can I say? My fans love me."

"Unbelievable," she muttered. Of course, now that they'd really cast him, it was good that her little stunt hadn't caused him any problems; then it would be *their* problem and she'd have to answer for it.

He nudged her. "Come on. Admit it. I do a pretty good Rabbit Abraham Lincoln."

She made a face but she couldn't help but laugh. "I was actually impressed that you remembered the entire Gettysburg Address."

"Believe it or not, I know a good chunk of FDR's first inaugural address too. Not the whole thing, of course. That thing is like three and a half minutes long."

The train went around a curve, jostling her against him, and he steadied her automatically. She carefully separated from him before asking, "Do you make it a point to memorize famous presidential speeches?"

"I learned them for speech club in high school."

Christine stared at him. "I didn't know that."

"Oh yeah, I was a gigantic nerd. Figured any attention was better than not existing, so I did debate team, speech, and theater. Never helped me get any girls, though."

"A fact that they are all lamenting this very second, I'll bet."

His eyes twinkled. "If I'm not mistaken, that sounded like a compliment."

"No, not a compliment. Just an observation. You're kind of famous."

"So are you." He reached out and tugged the end of her braid. "So much so you have to go around in disguise."

When the train stopped at Earl's Court a few minutes later, Nick straightened. "We get off here and change to Piccadilly."

Christine followed him as the door slid open and they stepped off the train onto the ground floor, atrium-roofed platform. "So you really do know London?"

"A bit. I've been here half a dozen times, so at least I kind of get the Underground. You write books set in England but you've never actually come here?"

She shook her head. "I do all my research on the Internet. Between Google and YouTube, you don't really need to go anywhere."

"So you've never been to Piccadilly Circus or Trafalgar Square or the National Gallery—"

"—or the Tower of London or Buckingham Palace. No to all of them."

"Had I known that, I wouldn't have gone for something so obscure." He squinted at her. "You've been here for three days and you honestly haven't left the hotel?"

"I did see Hyde Park …"

"Yes, I suppose you did. You just acted like you knew where you were going, so I figured you'd at least gone exploring."

"Google." It had been Cressida in charge then, anyway, carrying out Drew's silly revenge fantasy.

They took a short flight of stairs down to the Piccadilly Line tunnels and arrived on the platform just as another train arrived. Several more stops and Nick was leading the way out and down the street among block after block of impressive London row houses. Nick pulled up at the end of a long line forming along the homes' fences, opposite a large park. "Here we are."

She peered around the line, trying to get a glimpse of where it began, at least fifty people deep. "I don't understand. Where are we?"

"It's Sir John Soane's house."

She continued to stare at him.

"He was an architect from the Napoleonic Era. He designed the Bank of England and the Dulwich Picture Gallery, among other things. He bought three houses here in Lincoln's Inn Fields and combined them to make a … I guess you could call it a home, but that doesn't quite describe it."

Christine went back to peering at what looked like a rather ordinary block of houses. It was a weird destination for Nick; he didn't strike her as the type to take an interest in historic architecture. "So we're spending the evening at a museum."

"Oh ye of little faith. Just wait. I promise it's going to be worth it."

And wait they did, which was a little awkward considering how little they had to discuss. They found themselves recapping bits and pieces of their lives that the other had missed in the past five years: how Nick had gone from a bit part to a starring role on *Night Music*; how Christine had settled on Cressida Lyons as a pen name. At last, the queue started to lurch forward in fits and starts, she assumed because they were only taking a handful of people in at a time. When they finally filed in through the wrought iron gate and up the steps, they were greeted by a cheery docent in a navy blue suit who introduced himself as Clive, his eyes sparkling with mischief. She flung a doubtful look at Nick as they began to move into a rather normal-looking nineteenth-century hallway. Did he think because she wrote alternate history that a tour of a period house would be inspiring?

It took only two rooms to realize that this was no normal house, once inhabited by a normal man. Rather, it was the dwelling of either a madman or a genius, the British Museum in miniature, all packed into high-ceilinged rooms and narrow hallways. There were spaces devoted to models of classical architecture. Rooms filled with ancient corbels and frescoes, busts and sculpture. One room, the portrait room, featured painting after painting mounted on movable walls that opened and closed, Transformer-like, to reveal layers of old masters. And in every room, candles and dim electric lights gave an eerie, moody atmosphere to the eccentric collection.

Christine hung back at the end of the group, examining the elaborately patterned wallpaper, and Nick hovered at her elbow. "I don't know what you intend for the character, but I've always kind of envisioned The Collector living someplace like this. It's like an episode of *Hoarders: Rich English Dudes*."

Christine laughed. She'd been thinking the same thing, and his read on the eccentric inventor and explorer in her series was spot-on. "I can absolutely see Lord Parrish living here. Though this is slightly less macabre than his house would be."

"Oh, never fear. There's a sarcophagus in the basement."

"Really?"

He grinned. "Really."

By the time they made it out of the house, Christine was brimming with inspiration. She'd planned on making Parrish a greater part of the next book, and this trip had spun out ideas so fast she could barely wait to jot them down in her notebook. The sun was all the way down when they set foot on the sidewalk again, the queue still spilling down the street.

"I'm told there's a historic pub within walking distance. Are you game?"

Christine hesitated for a long moment. A large part of her didn't want the night to end, and that was exactly why it had to. "Sorry. I have to get back to the hotel."

"To the tube then." They moved back toward the station, dodging the pedestrians moving the opposite direction on their way home. The glowing red and blue sign of the Underground station was in sight before Nick spoke again. "Are you glad you came, at least?"

"Absolutely! That place was amazing. Weird, but amazing."

"I know." He grinned as they came to the escalators that took them down to the intermediate concourse. "They didn't mention it on the tour, but Soane actually sealed his bathtub with instructions not to open it for fifty-some years after his death."

"What was in it?"

"Just a bunch of junk. Papers. The newspapers of the time thought it was his idea of a joke."

That, too, sparked an idea. "I can only imagine what Lord Parrish would seal up in his bathtub."

"The bones of his enemies?" Nick suggested.

"That and his failed experiments." She looked up at him, searching for the truth in his face. "You didn't lie. You actually are a fan."

"Guilty as charged. Any news on who's going to play Parrish? I know my opinion doesn't count for much, but I've always envisioned him as Jeremy Irons."

"Yeah, he'd be good," Christine said. "Do you think he'd do it if he was offered the role?"

"I hope so. I'd kind of like to say I was on a TV show with him." Nick grinned at her, and in that moment, she saw a glimpse of the young man he'd been years ago, dreaming of how he'd someday like to make a living as an actor. Boggling at the thought of being on set with someone famous and hoping he didn't make a fool of himself. And today he'd been the object of hundreds of screaming fans.

They finally arrived at the Piccadilly line platform and stood waiting, a little awkward in the sudden silence. Christine cleared her throat. "You ready for the announcement tomorrow?"

"Sure. The fan ones are fun. The press panel on the other hand ..."

"You're great with reporters," Christine said. "What are you worried about?"

"Leaving one successful show for an untried one? They'll be trying to dig up dirt on the situation on *Night Music*, and you know it's only a matter of time before they figure out you and I had a prior relationship and try to make that into something."

He was right. The legitimate industry reporters probably wouldn't latch onto it, but the sites who did their trade in celebrity gossip would have a field day. "So we make an end run around it. Turn it to our advantage."

"How do you propose we do that?"

"I'm working on that." She had some ideas, but she wasn't about to disclose them to him now. There was no way around the gossip mags' interest in any sordid details attached to a production this buzzy, but at least they could try to turn the interest to their advantage. Better that she keep it to herself in case Remy attempted to nix it.

The train's approach killed any further conversation, along those lines anyway. They were able to grab two seats together again, where the jostling of the train caused their knees and shoulders to rub with each sideways sway of the carriage. She stole a surreptitious glance at his profile. Once upon a time, this was all she would have wanted—a quiet life, happy with Nick, maybe some occasional travel to a city like London where they would see the sights and ride the tube back to their hotel, hands entwined. And now, years later, she could see that she hadn't dreamed big enough. He had been all about the big picture, and she'd been too content with her simple, tiny vision. Not that contentment was a bad thing, but when it held you back from pursuing your dreams …

"Do you have any idea how lucky we are?" she asked suddenly. "I mean really. When we used to talk about this stuff, it was only dreams. No substance. Did you really think we would be here?"

"Here in London together? No." He caught the face she made and grinned. "But I never had any doubt we would make it. Both of us."

"You had more confidence in me than I did, then." She cast him a sideways look. "If it wasn't for my lack of ambition, why did you leave me?"

Nick chewed his lip for a moment, like he was considering. Too late, she realized she might not really want to know. Finally he said, "Because I wasn't sure if I would ever be as important to you as the people in your head, and my ego couldn't handle the idea of finding out the truth someday."

Her mouth dropped open slightly. "Are you serious?"

"One hundred percent. You already had everything you needed. You were so happy, so self-contained, with your laptop and your novels. And I still felt this … emptiness. Or maybe emptiness is the wrong word. Restlessness, like there was something wrong with me because I hadn't found the thing that I was really meant to do. You were my bright spot. It made me feel like I needed you too much, and you didn't need me at all."

Her breath left her in a soft *whoosh*. "Wow." All this time she'd thought he'd vanished on her because she was lacking, and in truth, it was because he'd thought she didn't need him.

"So there's my big secret. All that confidence was just bravado." He looked her straight in the eye, bare to her gaze in what she realized might be the first time in their lives, and she had to look away.

"I was always jealous of your actor friends," she murmured. "They were beautiful and confident and flirtatious and I figured it was only a matter of time before you started to wonder what you were doing with me instead of one of them. So I hid inside my book. It was easier to write us into the story so I could control the outcome. Jackson would always be faithful to Livia because I could pull the strings."

"Chrissy, I'm sorry. I feel like that's my fault. If I ever made you feel—"

"You can't apologize for *my* insecurities, Nick."

He shot her a wry look. "Maybe communication wasn't our strong suit back then."

"I'd say definitely not."

The speaker overhead announced their station, and Christine used the pole to pull herself upright as the train ground to a stop. Nick followed her, holding onto the same pole, his other hand coming to rest on the small of her back as they waited for the doors to slide open. And then somehow, as they moved off onto the platform, dodging the boarding passengers, their hands brushed. And held, their fingers twining together.

It felt illicit. Forbidden. Stupid maybe. And the last thing she wanted to do was let go.

They walked hand in hand to the stairs, and disappointment flooded her when he released her so they could hold onto the railing as they ascended to street level. There in the throng that surrounded the Baron's Court station, he found her hand again and squeezed it hard, pulling her into his side.

"Sure I can't convince you to have dinner with me?" he said.

She wanted so badly to say yes, but her rapid heartbeat and breathless anticipation told her that was the absolutely wrong course of action. "Remy is going to be waiting for me. I need to get back."

Nick nodded and said nothing. As soon as they got within sight of their grand hotel, he let her go. They walked the rest of the way with a respectable amount of distance between them. He hung back as she entered the arched brick atrium so it wouldn't be apparent they'd arrived together, but he caught up to her at the lift. "Can I at least see you to your room?"

She still knew him too well. Knew what he was really asking. And she nodded anyway.

They rode the lift up a single floor and Nick followed her down the corridor to her room. She fumbled for her room key, then stopped and turned toward him without knowing what to say.

He beat her to it. "Thank you."

"For what?"

"For taking a chance on me. Honestly, I had pretty much given up on your approval for this role, and I've wanted it more than almost anything else in my life."

Christine studied his face, determining his sincerity. "*Almost* anything else?"

He lifted his hand and brushed the back of his fingertips against her cheek. She stood there, so still she was rocked by her own heartbeat, unable to move away. No, not unable. Unwilling. He lowered his head and brushed her lips gently with his own, then pulled back to look into her eyes, to gauge her reaction. To give her a chance to shut him down, to tell him this wasn't what she wanted.

Instead, she moved closer and laid a hand on his chest, the warmth of his body radiating into her palm, the hard beat of his heart telling her that his cool patience was merely a facade. There was really no point in pretending any longer that this wasn't what she wanted. When their lips met again, she twined her arms around his neck and gave herself to the moment, letting herself be swept away. She expected his kiss to be familiar, but it wasn't; she expected it to feel like old times, but it didn't. He slid his hands into her hair, taking control of the kiss in a way that made her head swim and her limbs loosen. She'd loved him before, but he'd never weakened her knees like this. He'd never made her feel this needy.

He wasn't the same and neither was she. Maybe in order to let the past go, she had to embrace who they were now.

"That's one way to seal the deal," came a wry, familiar voice behind them. Christine disentangled herself from Nick and looked over his shoulder to where Remy stood with raised eyebrows, watching them.

Christine pulled away, her face heating furiously. Nick on the other hand, simply shot the publicist a placid smile. "We're celebrating."

"I can see that." She looked at Christine. "I was just coming down to see if we were still on for dinner, but I can guess that answer for myself …"

"No, we're still on. I just need to …" She waved vaguely toward her hotel room door, still unopened.

Remy struggled against a smile. "Yeah, I guess so. Why don't you get ready for dinner? Nick and I have some things to discuss anyway. Meet you in the lobby?"

"Sure." She smiled at Remy in a way she hoped looked innocent, then softened as her gaze shifted to Nick. He kissed her cheek and whispered, "Good night. Have fun."

She tapped her card to the door lock and a green light flashed as it disengaged. She slipped into her room and shut the door behind her, then tossed her purse on the dresser.

She and Nick Cleary.

Three days ago she would have said that sounded like madness. And maybe it still was.

But the bubble of happiness inside her made it impossible to care.

ten

"ARE YOU READY?" David sidled up beside Christine backstage in the Olympia auditorium where they were only minutes away from the cast announcement.

"Yep, never been better." She shot him a bright smile and gave the end of her braid a flick. She'd bypassed on the cosplay today, given the event, but she still looked sufficiently on-brand in a pair of washed leather pants, knee-high boots, and a flowered Bohemian blouse. She had the full face of Cressida makeup though. Her disguise only worked when she wore it; appear on camera barefaced and natural and she'd never be able to walk a convention floor unnoticed again.

"Okay then. We're on."

Music came on then—not their theme, because they didn't have one yet—but one that sounded epic and sufficiently exciting. David climbed the stairs to the stage and thunderous applause vibrated through the high-ceilinged room. To have someone of his stature appearing on a FanFest stage was a big deal.

"You're really ready?" Nick's soft voice came in her ear, his breath tickling her neck and sending a shiver through her whole body, along with an inconvenient spike of longing.

She didn't turn toward him, pitching her voice low. "I could ask you the same thing."

"Oh, I've never been better." The glance he sent her was far too knowing to be innocent, but she had no time to explore it, because David was introducing her. She straightened her blouse, threw Nick a "here goes nothing" look and stepped out on stage to a very flattering round of applause. She waved, trying not to look as uncomfortable as she felt, and seated herself in the chair nearest David.

"And now, we are pleased to reveal the cast of *Smoke and Glory* for the very first time here. Ladies and gentlemen, I give you your Professor Mulroney!"

One by one, David announced the cast, working his way back from the smaller characters until there was only Jackson and Livia left.

"Your Livia Barrett, Rebecca Romano."

Rebecca stepped out onto the stage, beaming and waving and looking stunning in a black sheath dress that showed off her slender figure. Whispers rippled through the audience at the announcement of an unknown actress, then exploded into applause again. They were determined to embrace their Livia, even if they didn't have any frame of reference for her. Christine absolutely trusted the casting; not only did Rebecca look like the book character come to life, she had a strong stage background that would serve her well. Christine had seen a clip of her playing Portia in *The Merchant of Venice* and thought she had both the strength and vulnerability that the character needed.

"And now, the announcement you've all been waiting for… your Jackson Landry, Nick Cleary."

Nick walked out on stage, smiling and waving and looking utterly comfortable with the adoration that came his way. And adoration it was, because the response nearly brought the house down. Christine could swear a few teenage girls swooned in the audience. She couldn't blame them. Right about now, it was proving fairly difficult not to feel the same way, especially when she remembered the way he'd kissed her outside her door last night.

"Your cast of *Smoke and Glory*!"

It took a fair bit of time for the audience to settle down enough to call it silence. David threw her a smile. "We're going to start with the author of the book series that spawned the show, Cressida Lyons. Tell me, Cressida, what do you think about your cast?"

She leaned forward slightly toward the microphone set up on the table. "I think it's amazing, David. I couldn't ask for a better group of actors to bring this show to life. And that goes for every member of the production crew as well. It really is a dream come true."

"And I have to ask … what do you think about our heroic couple down there?"

Christine grinned and leaned forward to give Nick and Rebecca a little wave. "Hi guys." They laughed. They really did look good together. If they had half the chemistry she suspected, every viewer would be shipping the characters by the end of the first episode.

"Really, I'm thrilled. For those of you who don't know Rebecca, she has an amazing stage background, and I think she will bring the gravitas that Livia really needs. And of course, we all know Nick. He does brooding and sexy well, but he's also quite funny, which is an essential characteristic for Jackson."

David looked like he was going to move on, but Christine continued. "What you might not know is that Nick and I have some history together. We've known each other for years, and when I was looking for someone on whom to model Jackson Landry, Nick was the first one to come to mind. So when I say he's perfect for the role, it's because it was custom-written for him. I just never dreamed I'd actually see him play the character on screen."

"Are you together?" someone yelled from the audience.

Christine flicked a look at David who shrugged as if to say, "You opened the door to this one." She answered, "No, we're not. But we're good friends." If she were Pinocchio, her nose would be a mile long, but she knew full well what she needed to say. Besides, how was she going to answer that? *No, but he gave me the kiss of my lifetime last night and I can't stop thinking about him?* Honesty was not the best policy here, especially surrounded by swoony female fans.

"Good! He's available!" another girl called out, and laughter rumbled through the auditorium in response.

"Let's hear from your cast and then we'll open up to questions from the floor."

The cast members said the usual things, how they were fans of the books, how they were honored to be working with someone like David, how they knew this was going to be the opportunity of a lifetime and they were privileged to be part of it. They were all professionals, knew how this kind of thing worked. Then the convention staff activated the mike at the front and brought up members of the audience to ask their questions.

Most of them were directed to Christine, which she should have expected given the fact there was no show yet; she was still their main link to the stories. But mark her words, next year with a season's worth of episodes behind them, it would be the opposite. The TV show always eclipsed the books as the audience spread beyond the original readership. That was just fine with Christine. She'd rather be home writing than here anyway.

The panel finally wrapped up, and they all filed off stage. The press panel was going to begin in an hour, but Christine didn't need to attend that one. Most of the questions would be directed toward the cast and producers.

"You made the right decision," David said, clapping a hand on her shoulder. "It's going to be wonderful."

"I know it is." She automatically sought Nick in the small crowd where he was chatting animatedly with Rebecca, who looked more than a little smitten. Christine really couldn't blame her. When Nick turned on the charm, he was magnetic. "We're going to have to give Rebecca some time to get used to him. Livia can't be making eyes at Jackson when she's supposed to hate his guts."

"I think she'll be just fine," David said with a wink. "She's just giving her leading man an ego boost."

Christine chuckled and David moved on, leaving her by herself, a little island in the sea of activity. She didn't kid herself. She was here because David liked her and her contract required them to hire her as a consultant for the show. But she didn't really belong here. She was a writer. She performed her magic alone at her desk, in her own head. The actors tolerated her because she wrote the vehicle and signed off on their best chance to become rich and famous.

"What's that serious look all about?"

Christine lifted her head, pulled from her reverie by Nick's voice. "Oh, sorry. Lost in thought. I think it went well, don't you?"

Nick nodded. "I see what you had in mind now. Did an end run around our deep dark secret?"

"Oh, they're still going to dig and see what they can find out, but I doubt they'll be able to get much. We didn't live together, so it's not like there are rental agreements or utility bills in our name for them to parade across the web. The best they might do is find a picture of us together at that writer's conference you attended with me years ago."

"I forgot about that," he said with a smile. "You won an award. And you wore that short little red dress."

"And felt self-conscious the entire time."

"You were beautiful back then too," he said quietly. "It just took you a few years to realize it for yourself."

Christine's cheeks heated, and she forced down the embarrassment. "Cressida's the confident one."

"You realize how crazy that sounds, right?"

She shrugged. "No more so than admitting that I have the voices of imaginary people in my head. What's one more?"

Nick grinned and glanced around, realizing now that they were alone in the corridor off the stage. "So, I have this press thing right now. What do you think about dinner?"

"I generally like it," she said. "Did you have something more in mind?"

"Dinner with me? Tonight? I can meet you back at the hotel. No reason for you to stay around here if you don't want to."

She looked up through her false lashes at him. "Nick Cleary, are you asking me out on a date?"

A flicker of discomfort crossed his face. "Yeah, I guess I am."

"In that case, yes."

"Yes?"

"Against my better judgment, yes." She laughed, unable to keep the happiness in her chest from welling up into her voice. "Text me when you're back at the hotel and I'll meet you."

"Deal." He took a quick look around and then bent to quickly press a kiss to her lips. "If we weren't in danger of being outed right now, I could express myself a lot better than that."

"Hmm. I might hold you to that."

Surprise flickered over his face, and then he grinned. "See you tonight then."

"Good luck at the press panel."

He gave her a little salute and then disappeared down toward the exit to join his fellow cast in the conference rooms set up not far away. Christine stood there for a bit longer, letting her fingertips drift to her lips as if to remind herself that she had kissed Nick Cleary not once but twice. The guy who had broken her heart. The guy who had been on her mind every day, for better or worse, for the past five years. It felt both unbelievable and perfectly fitting. She would be publishing her last book in the series just as the first season aired. It seemed somehow appropriate that he bookend the era of her life that had been both the most exciting and the most painful.

She made a slow exit from the exhibition center, stopping every dozen feet to take pictures with fans who had been in the cast announcement session, then made a break for freedom when she glimpsed daylight through the building's glass doors. With any luck, she could get a bit more done on her first draft. It was as if making peace—okay, it was more than that—with Nick had opened the floodgates of her creativity, especially since this book would finally reconcile Jackson and Livia's relationship once and for all. Jackson had proved himself worthy of her time and attention by taking the fall for Livia's own crimes—which she'd repaid by rescuing him from execution at Newgate. The slate was wiped clean, their debts were paid, now they could move forward … and she hoped, find true love.

Hoped, because no matter how much she might think she was in control of her characters, they always seemed to seize the reins and surprise her.

And yes, that sounded *totally* schizophrenic.

It took a mere six minutes to reach the nearby hotel, where she went to her room and immediately kicked off the high heeled boots. She sighed in relief and dug her throbbing toes into the soft carpet. As soon as she was back in San Diego, she could retire Cressida's wardrobe until the next con and go back to her blessedly comfortable collection of cut-off shorts and flip flops. Her feet could only take so much abuse.

In the meantime, she would throw herself into the world of alternate-history Victorian London, where Jackson was currently being taken to Livia's Mayfair townhouse to be cleaned and bathed and deloused … Newgate Prison being what it was.

Things were just starting to heat up between the newly reunited enemies/lovers when a text message beeped on her cell. Just got back to the hotel. Need to change and then meet you in the lobby in 15?

Christine glanced at the clock and found it was already after six. She'd never managed a shower when she got back. Apparently, it would be

Cressida going out on the date with Nick, because there wasn't enough time to remove the makeup and false lashes and reapply something less stagey. Instead, she dug through the clothing on hangers in her closet and swapped out her frilly blouse for a vintage concert tee and the blazer she'd worn yesterday. Less dressy, more casual cool. Knowing Nick, she'd fit right in.

She quickly touched up her smeared eyeliner, swiped on some lip gloss, and then grabbed her handbag and keycard, her heart fluttering in anticipation. A date. With Nick Cleary. The man who had broken her heart.

She needed to stop thinking of him that way if there was to be any chance of … anything. The years seemed to have matured him, and after his revelation last night on the tube, she couldn't deny that maybe she'd played as much a role in their breakup as he had. They were no longer struggling young artists; they were successful professionals. Certainly they could put aside their differences and make a new start.

The lift took its time coming down from the upper floor, so she fussed with her hair, double-checking her reflection in the mirror on the wall. When it finally arrived with a ding, the doors slid open to reveal a man in a dark suit. She stepped inside, keeping her eyes fixed on the lift's patterned floor.

"Excuse me, but you're Cressida Lyons, aren't you?"

Christine lifted her gaze. He didn't look like a FanFest attendee, with his nicely tailored suit and European-accented English, but one never knew. She smiled. "I am."

"My daughter is a huge fan of your books. She's never going to believe we were staying at the same hotel. Would you mind …?" He pulled his cell phone from his pocket and held it up almost apologetically.

"Sure, it's no problem." She moved to his side while he extended his arm for the selfie and smiled at the camera. He took several, then replaced the phone in his breast pocket, looking embarrassed.

"Thanks. I've never done a single cool thing in my life according to her, but this might be the thing to turn it around."

"I'm happy to help." Christine smiled, but she didn't buy the story for a minute. She wasn't all that recognizable out of costume, even with the makeup. His daughter might be a fan, but she had no doubt he was a reader, too, maybe more. She had a fair number of men who were closet devotees, mostly the guys who were afraid that any hint of romance qualified a book as a chick read.

When the lift arrived at the ground floor, they exited and went their separate ways, and Christine started scanning the lobby for any sign of Nick. She finally found him speaking with Remy by one of the massive brick posts, partially hidden by potted foliage.

She made her way toward them, a bright smile forming on her face as she approached, but they were both too engrossed in their conversation to notice her arrival. And then she caught Remy's words.

"—have to hand it to you, Nick. You worked this thing hard. I had my doubts it could be done."

"Well, you almost blew it by posting the photo. But you *are* the one who told me to talk about the books. She just needed to be convinced that I was committed to the spirit of the role. She takes her characters pretty seriously."

Remy laughed, but it had a bit of a vicious undertone. "Writers, am I right?"

Nick cracked a vague smile, but Christine must have gasped or made some sound of outrage, because they both swiveled toward her. Remy recovered faster than Nick, smoothing over her surprise. Clearly she thought there was a chance that Christine hadn't heard anything.

"Hey, there you are." Remy smiled between Nick and Christine, but her eyes never landed on their faces. "I'll leave you two to your dinner plans. I'll catch you tomorrow." She gave a little wave and then click-clacked across the atrium in her heels.

Scratch that. She knew full well what had been overheard, but she was leaving Nick to deal with the fallout. Classy.

Nick's expression showed he knew exactly how bad things looked. "Christine, it's not what it sounded like—"

"Oh no? Because it sounded like you and Remy have been working together to make sure you get this role. Pretending to be my friend—*handling me*—since the beginning."

"It wasn't like that, Chrissy, I swear."

"Then what was it like?" She crossed her arms over her chest and waited while Nick's mouth opened and closed several times, but nothing resembling an explanation spilled out.

She shook her head in disgust. "I'll make it really easy for you. You did what you had to do to convince me that you were right for the role. And you know what? You're a brilliant actor, Nick. You actually made me believe that you still felt something for me. That deserves some sort of reward. So congratulations. You're every bit as much a con artist as Jackson Landry."

She turned on her heel and took a few steps away from him before she spun back. "But I wouldn't count on Jackson making it through book six if I were you."

The words seemed to unfreeze Nick. Typical. A threat to his career was always more effective than any appeal to his sense of personal integrity. He rushed toward her and scuttled next to her like the cockroach he was as she strode toward the lift. "Chrissy, I screwed up. Let me make it up to you."

"What could you possibly do that would make it up to me?"

Nick deflated. "Chrissy, I never meant to hurt you. Yes, Remy coached me on what to say to you. But the rest … the Soane House, the kiss … that was all sincere. I did that because I wanted to."

The lift doors slid open and Christine stepped on. "Remy was right. You were trying to seal the deal. Consider it done." She punched the *close* button and the doors slid together, shutting him out. For good this time.

eleven

NICK WATCHED as Christine disappeared behind the lift doors, his heart in his throat, dread sitting squarely where his stomach used to be. Had someone tried to script a heart-wrenching betrayal scene, they couldn't have done it any better than what Christine had just witnessed. From her perspective, it looked like he'd manipulated her from the start.

And she wasn't entirely wrong.

Nick punched the lift's *up* button and tapped his foot impatiently while the car delivered Christine and then returned to the lobby. He had to explain. He couldn't leave her thinking that he'd betrayed her again for the sake of his career. It would taint this whole production, something that was supposed to catapult both of them up the next rung of their careers.

Even worse, it would ensure that she'd never speak to him again.

The car finally arrived, and he stepped on and pushed the button for Christine's floor, his gut churning the whole way up. Funny how only a few days ago, it was the idea of losing the role that had him in knots and now it was the thought of losing her.

The idea stunned him before it was chased by a secondary thought: he'd never really had her in the first place. He'd given up any right to her affections five years ago due to his own selfish stupidity. He'd cast himself as the wronged party in that situation, but he'd been the one who'd gotten scared and fled the relationship only weeks after proposing. The fact she'd even consider forgiving him should have come as more of a surprise that the idea she might jump to the worst possible conclusion.

The lift dumped him off on her floor, and he slowly approached her door as if she might sense him coming and flee the scene. *Don't be stupid. Just knock.*

As soon as he did, he heard a rustle behind the door, followed by a muffled, "Go away."

"Christine." He leaned closer to the door. "I need to talk to you. I want to explain."

"We've got nothing to say to each other."

Nick sighed, then raised his hand and knocked harder. And kept knocking until his knuckles throbbed. Finally, the door jerked open and Christine stared at him.

Dry-eyed and furious.

Somehow he imagined her at least sniffling a little, but right now she looked to be contemplating how best to murder him and throw his body into the Thames.

But she'd opened the door, so he asked meekly, "Can I come in?"

She turned on her heel. "Fine. Whatever. But make it quick."

Nick caught the door before it slammed and followed her in. When he saw the suitcase lying open on the bed, he faltered. "You're leaving already? Fanfest isn't over yet."

"My part is." She went to the wardrobe and began extracting her steampunk wardrobe carefully from the hangers. Everything else looked to have been shoved haphazardly into her luggage, but now she took special care with the corsets and petticoats. "So? What is it you wanted to say?"

"I'm sorry."

"Good to know. There's the door." She didn't even look at him, just kept packing with those spare, precise motions.

"Remy did tell me that I needed to show you I had a personal connection to the character. She did tell me I needed to win you over. But I swear to you, Chrissy, everything I said to you was the truth. That's why I want the role. I do love the character. And the fact that I would recite the Gettysburg Address in a bunny suit should tell you that I would do anything to play it."

"Even get cozy with the author for a few days," she said flatly. "No one is questioning your commitment here, only your motives."

"Why would I need to manipulate you? I'd already been given the role."

"Because it hadn't been announced yet? And until I publicly endorsed your involvement, you couldn't be sure you really had it?" She fixed him with a pointed stare and a raised eyebrow.

"Wow. That's cynical, even for you."

"What can I say? I've learned from my past experiences." She straightened from the suitcase and tried to brush by him. "If that's all—"

He grabbed her arm. "Chrissy—"

She sighed. "Look. We both know you're only here to assuage your guilt and make sure things aren't awkward on the rare occasion we cross on set. So consider it mission accomplished. Yes, I'm furious. I think you're a jerk. But I'm more convinced than ever that you're perfect for the role." She threw him a smirk. "I know it's hard for you to wrap your ego around the idea that two kisses with you didn't ruin me for all other men, but I've made a pretty good life for myself. I'm not the same naive girl whose heart you once broke. So if you'll excuse me, I've got an early flight to catch."

A flicker of memory nagged at him as he peered into her eyes. Doubt surfaced in them before she steeled herself against his gaze. And then he realized why the words sounded so familiar. *I know it's hard for you to wrap your ego* ...

It was a line directly from book four, right before Jackson was taken off to prison, when Livia decides to punish him for his string of betrayals. Where Livia puts aside her conscience and her soft heart and reaches for vengeance instead, making herself into the person she'd been resisting all along. And at last he thought he understood.

"I'm sorry I hurt you, Chrissy. Then and now. But if you're dealing with things so well, maybe you need to ask yourself why you felt the need to create a whole new personality."

The doubt changed to fury in a flash. "Get out."

He nodded slowly. "For the record, I take full blame for what happened between us. I was an immature, cowardly jerk. But no matter how much you may try to make yourself into Cressida, there was never anything wrong with Chrissy."

He didn't look at her again, just slipped out of the room and stood for a long moment, stock still, in the hallway.

It was time to finally take responsibility, show her what she didn't seem to comprehend from his words. He knew what he had to do.

Christine stared at the door, trembling but unable to put her finger on what infuriated her more—the fact that Nick thought a simple apology could erase her anger or the implication that he knew her better than she knew herself.

She went back to the bed and laid out her long velvet overcoat. How dare he imply she was hiding behind Cressida because she was still broken-hearted over him? The pen name had been a strategic decision, nothing more. She'd known from the beginning that this series would someday generate its own fandom, one that would appreciate the tough, sexy Cressida Lyons. Her popularity at this con clearly proved she'd known what she was doing. European businessmen didn't stop Chrissy Lind for photos in a hotel lift.

Her hands stilled on the coat, rolled into a neat cylinder, when she realized what she'd just thought. It was one thing to cosplay for fun, even to keep her public and private lives separate, but she'd clearly taken it further than that. Didn't she mentally don Cressida when she couldn't deal with an uncomfortable situation? Hadn't she created the pen name because she knew that crushed, pathetic Chrissy who couldn't keep a man certainly wasn't capable of writing a bestseller?

Of course, the pen name had also been intended to shield her from the speculation of friends and family when she rewrote her Nick Cleary/Jackson Landry character with the sole intention of making him suffer.

Could Nick be right about her?

Christine sank down on the edge of her bed, confronted by a reality she'd always instinctively known but never wanted to address. Her being over Nick, her triumphant single life—all of it—had been the biggest fiction of all.

Tears welled on her lower lashes and she swiped them away before they could trickle down her face. If she could admit that, she could admit that she had been hoping for a different outcome with Nick, not because she wanted a relationship with him, but because she wanted to prove to him that he'd made a mistake leaving her all those years ago.

After all her successes, she still wanted his approval.

She sat there frozen, stunned by the realization. Stunned by her own weakness. Stunned that two days with Nick had revealed an entire facet of her life to be a huge lie. What was she supposed to do now?

The answer came to her instantly: nothing.

Or rather, she would do exactly what she had already planned. She still had a book to write. A TV series that would begin shooting in five weeks. And a few more cons this year, where Cressida Lyons would have to make an appearance in her full steampunk glory. There would be no grand, external transformation that would signal to her friends and family that she was Moving On, that she'd had a Revelation.

Just a quiet olive branch to the broken-hearted girl named Chrissy, what she should have told herself long ago: failing didn't make her a failure and grieving didn't make her weak. And just because the love of her life couldn't see what he'd had didn't mean she needed to be anyone other than who she was.

twelve

CHRISTINE HAD ASKED HER ASSISTANT to book her the first flight out of Heathrow, but she hadn't taken into account that she'd have to be at the airport by five a.m. She made it through security bleary-eyed and yawning and feeling like the messy bun on top of her head was only one sharp move from sliding to her ear. She liked to travel comfortable, but even for her, this was taking things too far.

She went off in search of coffee and then made her way to her gate with plenty of time to spare. She pulled out her laptop, set it up on her knees, and opened her file to the last page she'd written.

The kiss between Jackson and Livia.

Christine flushed as she read it, recognizing the similarities between the fictional interlude and the kiss outside her hotel room door. Remembering Nick's lips on hers, the feel of their bodies pressed together. Realizing that as amazing as it had been, it would remain merely a memory.

She might have once been tempted to break apart the heroic couple, but that wasn't the right thing for the story, no matter what she'd said to Nick in anger. This was their time to put aside past differences and work together for the greater good. She was so engrossed in the story that she didn't notice the man who sat down beside her until he peered over her shoulder to look at her screen.

"Well, that's a relief. I thought for sure Jackson was going straight back to Newgate."

Christine jerked her head up to look directly into a pair of familiar brown eyes. "What are you doing here?"

Nick settled back again the seat. "Going home, same as you."

She blinked. "Don't you have press panels and photo calls?"

"Nope."

Christine stared at him, uncomprehending.

"I take it you haven't checked your messages."

She glanced at her phone, which was still on silent, and saw she had several voice mails. Looking back at Nick, she punched *speaker*.

David's voice streamed out, tight and bewildered. "Christine, call me. Nick backed out. Do you know anything about this?" The next two messages were more of the same.

Christine lowered the phone, unable to process what she'd just heard. "You quit."

He nodded placidly. "I did."

"But … why?"

"Because this is your big break, what you've always dreamed of. You don't need me to spoil what should arguably be a highlight of your career."

"But we've announced. Your fans—"

"—will get over it." Nick folded his hands and looked into her eyes. "Do you really think I could enjoy the role knowing I'd hurt you to get it?"

"I'm thinking the huge salary would probably go a long way to dampen the guilt."

That got him. He shifted in his seat and rubbed the side of his nose. "That's true, it would. But I'm hoping now that I'm not attached to the project—thus proving I have no ulterior motives— you might be willing to have dinner with me."

Christine blinked. "Let me get this straight. You quit the role that could make your career in order to have dinner with me. Are you insane?"

"Beginning to think so, yeah."

"Why?"

He reached out and caressed her cheek like he'd done that night after their field trip, his expression softening. "Because I've always wondered what might have been, had I not been such a jerk. I knew I made a big mistake. And I was hoping maybe you would be willing to give me another chance to prove myself. To maybe go back to the way we were."

Christine took a deep breath and curled her fingers around his hand, then lowered it to the seat between them. "We can't go back to how we were."

His hopeful expression faded, and he turned an unnatural shade of pale. He pulled his hand away. "I see. Well, I always knew there was a chance I'd messed up too badly. I'm sorry, Chrissy, I really am."

"We can't go back to how we were, because we're not the same people we were. Would you really want to go back to a place where we both were so afraid to say what we were feeling that we let it drive us apart? Is that the kind of relationship you want?"

Hope rekindled on his face. "What are you saying?"

She licked her lips and took a deep breath, unable to believe what she was about to propose. "I'm saying that if we want to give this a shot, we need to start over. From the beginning. No assumptions. No shortcuts." She drilled him with a look. "I don't kiss until at least the third date."

"Can we count the one in London as our first, then?" At her stern look, he smiled. "Okay. Three dates. I can live with that."

"Also, you're going to have to pick up that phone and tell David that you made a terrible mistake and you do want the role. Blame it on a hangover or the fact that you're an idiot, but just get it back."

"Really?"

"Really. No matter how this, *us*, turns out, you were born to play that role. I'm not letting you give it up."

"Is that all?" Amusement sparkled in his eyes.

"One last thing." She held out her hand. "I'm Christine. Not Cressida, not Chrissy. Just Christine."

A slow smile spread over his face as his fingers closed around hers, warm and firm. "It's nice to meet you, Christine. I'm Nick. I'm looking forward to getting to know you."

epilogue

Eighteen months later

"CUT! I THINK WE'VE GOT IT NOW. Reset for number thirty-nine." The first assistant director, Levi, pulled off his headset and stepped away from the monitor. Under his direction, crew members began to rearrange furniture and props for the next interior of the Victorian drawing room.

They were on location today at a Mayfair row home, something Christine was thoroughly pleased about considering the fine snow that fell gently like sugar from a giant sifter. She removed her own earbuds and hopped out of her chair for a stretch. Had she been back home in San Diego, she'd be recovering from turkey overdose on this Friday after Thanksgiving. Instead, she was in London, witnessing what would be the last day of shooting before they wrapped season two of *Smoke and Glory*.

To say it was an unmitigated success would be an understatement. The show had lived up to its name by becoming the cable channel's number one scripted series of all time, and it had launched a fandom that surpassed anything Christine could have ever imagined. Much was due to the gorgeous English locations and fabulous acting, but she couldn't deny the larger part was owed to the charisma of its leading man. Who was flagging her down right now.

"Christine! Could you come here for a second? We have a question."

She hopped out of her seat and pulled together the lapels of her wool cardigan against the house's drafts as she cast around for David. Technically, she wasn't supposed to be giving direction to the actors, but now he gave her a little nod of assent. She maneuvered herself through cables and equipment to where Nick stood with Rebecca.

He smiled warmly when she approached, making her melt a little inside. Eighteen months together, and that look still affected her as strongly as ever. But they were on set, and while their relationship was no secret, they still had a duty to keep things professional.

It was Rebecca who spoke up when she stopped beside them. "So, Livia is telling Jackson about the theft. Is she still really in the dark? Or does she know and she's just playing dumb?"

"Livia knows. She's trying to catch him in a lie. So when he answers so sincerely that he had nothing to do with it, it casts everything else he's just told her into question too."

Rebecca nodded. "Okay. Perfect. Thanks."

Christine turned to go back to her chair. Only then did she realize that half the cast and crew were crowded around them, including the camera operator, who was practically holding the rig six inches from her face. "What's going on?" She searched for David again in the crowd. "Are you shooting footage for the behind-the-scenes promo again?"

"Not quite," Nick said behind her.

Christine turned slowly, and her hands flew to her mouth at the sight of him kneeling on the rug in front of the fireplace. He had a velvet box in his hands.

"Nick, what—"

He stretched to grasp her hand. "Christine, seven years ago, I made the biggest mistake of my life by letting you go. The past year and a half has been the happiest I can remember ever being, and I can't help thinking there's only one thing that could make me happier than being your boyfriend."

Christine looked around at all the expectant faces. "You all knew about this?"

Cast and crew alike put on innocent, wide-eyed looks. The squeeze of Nick's hand brought her gaze back to him.

"Christine, you are the most interesting and intelligent woman I've ever met—whether you call yourself Chrissy, Christine, or Cressida—and I love every minute I spend with you. Would you do me the honor of becoming my wife?"

Tears pricked her eyes, emotion swelling up inside her. She nodded wordlessly, and he slipped the ring onto her finger, a slender old-fashioned band of filigree and diamonds. And then she pulled him to his feet, threw her arms around his neck, and kissed him.

The crowd around them cheered, and he broke off the kiss to draw back and look into her eyes. "I take it that's a yes?"

She nodded wordlessly, happiness bubbling up inside her and spilling out in a smile that threatened to crack her face. "Yes. Yes. Yes." She laughed and planted a quick kiss on his lips before drawing back with a mischievous grin. "From all three of us."

Snowbound

A Discovered by Love Novella

One

THIS PLACE WAS A TEARDOWN.

That was Meg Anderson's first impression of the house when she pulled into the cracked asphalt driveway and stepped out of the car. It wasn't just the state of the house, a few square feet short of a mansion, because despite the peeling paint and piles of fallen leaves drifting into the corners, it wasn't in that bad of shape. It was the unholy mix of styles that could have only come from the mind of either an insane or drunk architect, a sort of faux-English country mixed with mountain rustic and seasoned with an ill-advised sprinkle of Austrian chalet.

Meg had never wanted a job so badly in her life.

She slammed the door of her Jeep and pulled the lapels of her down parka together against the sudden rush of frigid wind. Her deep determination to win this project for her architecture firm—and prove her worth once and for all—was the only thing that could have compelled her to drive into the Colorado mountains eight hours before what meteorologists were saying could be the storm of the decade. Vail was less than two hours from her home in Denver, but she wasn't stupid … she'd booked herself a room for the weekend in case the weather shifted and she couldn't make it home. She might be ambitious, but she wasn't about to die of hypothermia on the side of the road, waiting for a snowplow to dig her out.

With that cheery thought in mind, Meg marched to the front door and punched in the code she'd gotten from the client. The lockbox snapped open with a reassuring click, revealing a brass key. The fact she was even being given the chance to bid on this project was something of a miracle. Eleanor Gratz was an eccentric heiress who owned homes all over the United States and Europe just in case, on a whim, she decided to summer or winter outside her native Austria. Right now, Mrs. Gratz was living at her house in the Hamptons while she took bids for the full remodel of her Vail ski home; apparently, the first batch of bids had displeased her so much, she'd dumped them all and started searching for what she'd called in the brief "lesser known talent."

You couldn't get much lesser known than Meg.

That thought propelled the key into the lock, and she shoved her shoulder against the door to dislodge it from the frame. It creaked open on disused hinges, disgorging a plume of dust that floated around her head, dusted her shoulders, and made her sneeze. Clearly Mrs. Gratz didn't employ a caretaker for the home and hadn't for the past ten years.

Technically, Meg didn't even need to be here. If this really was a teardown, it meant abandoning the house's original footprint, scraping the lot, and pouring a new foundation. She could have drafted all that from her office or her own cozy home in Denver instead of walking through a house so cold she was surprised she couldn't see her own breath.

But despite her flippant attitude when she'd first seen the exterior, now she wasn't so sure. The soaring wood-paneled ceilings with their reclaimed wood were meant to be rustic, but they could go fully contemporary when paired with the massive panes of glass with which she intended to replace the far wall to frame views of the valley. And there was no real reason to close off the foyer with solid wood paneling when she could tell at first glance that the walls weren't structural.

The wheels started turning in her head, even though she'd just added to her own workload. A teardown was easy to sketch and lay out. Working with the existing structure was harder, especially considering her previous requests for a floor plan had gone unanswered. She wandered around the great room, wishing she'd brought her laser measure with her so she could take some actual dimensions.

She was so focused on the vision in her mind's eye that she didn't immediately notice the footsteps outside the great room. Hair lifted on her arms. Her first wild thought went to ghosts, but as quickly as it surfaced, she shook off the thought. "Hello? Who's there?"

No answer. For the first time, she realized how isolated she was out here, a full three miles outside of Vail city limits, on the edge of twenty acres with no neighbors nearby. Feeling foolish even as she did it, she reached for the fireplace poker and wrapped her fingers around its comforting heft. As quietly as she could, she moved through the room and back out into the shadows of the foyer … and let out a yelp when she came face to face with a stranger.

His hand came up automatically to grip the poker. "What are you trying to do? Take my head off?"

Meg froze before she could begin to put up a struggle. She knew that voice. And the stranger scenario was preferable to the presence of the man in front of her.

Declan McKenzie.

"You," she whispered. "What are you doing here?"

"Meg Anderson. I thought that was you." Amusement tinged his voice, deepening the Irish lilt that she had once—against her will, of course— found irresistible. He eased the poker out of her hand, retraced his steps, and then flicked a switch near the door. Instantly, warm light flooded the foyer.

Meg flushed in embarrassment. Of course Eleanor Gratz wouldn't do anything as plebeian as turn off the electricity in one of her homes. And of course Declan, with his prep school upbringing and his famous father, would know that.

The heat in her cheeks intensified as she looked him over properly. She'd seen him at parties and open houses over the last few years, infrequently and distantly enough to convince herself that he couldn't possibly be as good-looking as she remembered.

She was wrong.

Worse yet, he looked even better than she recalled. Last time she'd spent any length of time with him, they'd just completed an internship straight out of their graduate architecture program at the University of Colorado, Denver: she, twenty-five; he, almost twenty-seven. Now, six years later, the roundness of youth had sharpened into planes and angles, highlighting his high cheekbones, drawing attention to dark-lashed gray eyes that had never failed to enchant his multitude of female admirers. He did wear his hair shorter now, almost military-cropped, with none of those irresistibly youthful curls that just begged a woman to bury her fingers in them.

She shook her head angrily against the errant thought. Her youthful fantasies about him had no business remaining so close to the surface after all these years, especially considering how well-acquainted she was with ugly reality. She would have thought all that had happened between them would have destroyed any lingering attraction.

She cleared her throat and repeated, "What are you doing here?"

"Same as you, I'd imagine. Leave it to Eleanor Gratz to send out a design brief at two o'clock on a Friday before a snowstorm." He thrust his hands into his jeans pockets and rocked back on his heels. "The consequences of being second tier, I suppose."

"I never thought I'd hear you call yourself second tier."

He shrugged. "Even I have my moments of humility."

And only he could be so casual that even that statement seemed arrogant. She rolled her eyes. "Do you happen to know if we're expecting any other … competitors?"

"Are we competitors now?" His eyes danced in a way that made it clear he was laughing at her. Then he sobered under her pointed stare and cleared his throat. "No. I think we're the only two people mad enough to drive up here at the last minute. But since we're here …" He gestured ahead of him, as if he was gallantly allowing her to precede him. Unsurprisingly, it irritated her.

At this point, his very living, breathing presence was an affront.

It hadn't always been that way. Once upon a time, she'd thought they could be friends. They both had lived all over the world as children; they both had done degrees in architectural engineering, which set them apart from their B.S. and B. Arch classmates. And for about five seconds, she'd thought maybe they could be more than that.

No, that was a lie. *He* had acted as if they could be something more for all of five seconds. She, on the other hand, had spent an entire semester gazing longingly across a classroom at him, hopelessly infatuated. The situation was all the more embarrassing because she'd never been the type to … pine. She'd dated, she'd had relationships, but they'd all been easy, mutual, and they'd ended that way too. Until she'd laid eyes on Declan McKenzie the first day of her graduate design program, she'd thought the overwrought stories of instant, overwhelming chemical attraction were simply fiction.

But then he'd proved himself to be an arrogant tool. He'd rebuffed her every friendly overture. Argued with her in class. One-upped her in presentations. And most unforgivably, sabotaged her during their shared summer internship at Klein & Company, a top architectural firm in Denver, so that he got an offer of a permanent position and she got an unceremonious farewell. It had taken her eighteen months to land somewhere half-decent after that, at a boutique firm called NCO Architecture with a good reputation but few high-dollar contracts … where she was still languishing as a junior architect while he, if rumors could be believed, was up for managing partner.

She'd thought that, finally, all the anger she'd felt toward him had broken that inexplicable draw. Apparently, she'd been wrong.

Meg waited until they were both gazing at a stone fireplace that would have been more at home in a theme restaurant than a multi-million-dollar Vail retreat to say, "I'm surprised they called you in. Wasn't your firm the one who designed this monstrosity in the first place?"

The barb struck, but didn't seem to wound. "The old managing partner. As you might guess, they're ready for some fresh ideas."

And just like that, he deflected her jab and reminded her of the disparity in their positions. Declan had always been much better at this game than her. She might have a gift for snark, but she had neither the confidence nor the bearing to pull it off. Seemed to be one more advantage bestowed on him by his father.

Meg bit back her sharp response, raising her phone instead to take a photo of the fireplace. She was getting dangerously close to petulant and that was never a good look on anyone. For one thing, it made her a victim, and she was not a victim. She was a winner.

She was going to win this bid and end this competition once and for all.

She led the way through the rooms, Declan trailing behind her. She didn't know why he kept on her heels—making sure she didn't discover something super-secret and exciting?—but his very presence made her edgy. She kept expecting him to say something, but he seemed content to walk in her footsteps and take photos of the same things she did. The whole time, she resisted the impulse to break the silence, make small talk.

Ask him if he was married, for example, as if she wouldn't have heard about that through the grapevine. Ask if he already had an idea of how to handle the joist configuration. Comment on the weather.

Which, she suspected, was his whole plan. Make her break first. She wouldn't.

They toured the entire house that way, all eighteen rooms including a master suite the size of her entire first floor, an enormous kitchen, and a media and game room in the walk-out basement.

In the end, she was too eager to escape to wait for him to break the silence. "So I guess that's it." The fireplace poker was leaning by the front door where he'd left it, but she wasn't about to draw his attention to it by putting it back. "May the best architect win."

He smiled—smirked really—but she didn't wait to hear what he had to say. Instead, she fished the key from her pocket, yanked the front door open, and took a step outside.

Into a solid wall of white.

It would be funny if it weren't so inconvenient.

Declan McKenzie watched the shock on Meg's face turn to dismay as she realized that the whole time they'd been touring the massive home, they'd been quietly getting snowed in.

"So much for the storm arriving at midnight," he said blandly.

She fixed him with a glare, and he held up his hands in surrender. "I'm just saying. I checked the forecast before I ever got in the car. It wasn't supposed to start for another six hours, let alone accumulate—" he peered around her to check the depth of snow on the porch— "four inches."

Meg straightened her back and zipped up her jacket, pulling locks of her long brown hair free of the collar with an irritated flick. He recognized that stubborn look all too well—it meant she was preparing herself for a battle. "I only have to make it three miles. I got a room in Vail just in case."

"Smart," he observed. "But I don't think you're going to make it three feet, let alone three miles."

That determined glare again. "Watch me."

Declan sighed and zipped up his own jacket. "Okay then. If you're so determined, we might as well both give it a go." He was driving a sedan, but it had all-wheel drive and the snow wasn't yet deep enough to give him a problem. It was better than being stuck here with her. Not because he minded so much, but because he wasn't sure she wouldn't try to murder him in his sleep.

He'd had plenty of people dislike him in his thirty-two years, but he wasn't sure he'd ever been hated with such pure, unadulterated passion before Meg Anderson. In all fairness, he probably deserved it. But it would have been so much easier if the feeling was even remotely reciprocated.

Meg waited, shivering on the porch, until he turned out the lights and shut the door behind them. Then she locked up and replaced the key in the lockbox. He made a mental note to include smart house functions in his proposal, then followed Meg into the swirling maelstrom of white.

"Meg—" he began dubiously, but she was already marching to a Jeep SUV that looked only slightly more capable than his BMW. "I'm not sure it's—"

She climbed in and slammed the door.

"—safe." He stood there for a moment until she flicked on her headlights, illuminating him in a swirl of white, then realized just how cold it was. The temperature had dropped at least twenty degrees when the sun went down, and it hadn't been much above freezing in the first place. He trudged across the driveway, opening his car with the remote, and climbed into its usually cozy interior, which was now only one step above frigid. Slowly, he turned his car around and followed Meg away from the house.

The drive was a quarter mile of packed gravel, so neither vehicle had a problem gaining traction, though the ten-foot visibility was another story. The snow was coming down in clumps now, so thick that his headlights created a white glare that Meg's taillights could barely penetrate. He flicked off the low beams in favor of running lamps and side markers and said a prayer that their stupidity wouldn't get them stuck or killed.

At the stop, Meg turned left onto the county road with confidence. He prepared to hang a right to rejoin the highway. Meg's taillights were already fading into the blizzard, but still he sat, motionless, torn. Which was stupid. She only had three miles to go. She had a four-wheel-drive Jeep. Surely she'd be fine. He was the one who should be worried, especially if it had snowed heavily enough on his path to turn the front bumper of his low-slung car into a snowplow.

He turned left.

"Mental," he muttered to himself, but his conscience demanded that he follow her all the way to town and make sure she got to the hotel safely. Or if not conscience, then a sense of equity. He couldn't deny that he owed her. It was the least he could do.

He drove slowly along the paved road, feeling the instability beneath his tires that told him there was a layer of ice under the snow, and he reduced his speed even further. Judging how fast Meg had pulled out and how long he'd vacillated, he'd be lucky to catch up with her before they reached town.

But it was only a few minutes before a hazy red glow caught his attention. He headed straight for it, unable to see beyond the dim circle of his running lamps until he realized the lights weren't on the road. They were coming from a ditch.

Declan braked too hard and immediately the grinding sound of the ABS system kicked in as he skidded to a stop on the shoulder. He put on the parking brake and threw the car door open, then scrambled to the side of the road where the Jeep was tilted at an awkward angle. There didn't seem to be any major damage, but that didn't mean Meg wasn't hurt.

He slid down the slope, his heart hammering, and rapped sharply on the driver's window before brushing the accumulated snow from it. No airbags. A good sign. Slowly, the window slid down.

"Are you all right?"

Meg looked pale and shaken and her lack of a flippant answer proved it, as did the fact she actually seemed happy to see him. "I'm okay, I think. It was more of a slide than a crash."

"What happened?"

In the dome light's dim illumination, he saw her color flood back. "An owl swooped down in front of me. I braked automatically and ..." She waved a hand with a grimace.

"Okay, well, let's try and get you out. There's a tree stump right outside your door, so it's either going to be through the back or the window."

Meg cast a look over her shoulder, clearly weighing the contortion required to get over the seat versus the fact he would have to help her out the window. "I'll go through the back."

Declan held up his hands in acknowledgment and stood back as she rolled up the window, climbed into her backseat, then lowered one side to let herself into the cargo area. She popped out the back, surprisingly unperturbed, a backpack slung over one shoulder and a tote bag in the other hand. At his questioning look, she said, "My computer and some snacks. It was a long drive. I don't suppose you could grab my suitcase?"

"Suitcase?"

She shrugged. "I believe in being prepared. Looks like I was right."

Fortunately, the suitcase in question was a tiny roller bag that could fit beneath an airplane seat, not the behemoth he'd been envisioning. He took it without complaint, scrambling up the slippery hill to his car. At least half an inch of snow had already accumulated on his windows.

Meg followed him up less confidently, falling to her knees once or twice, but he didn't offer to help. She wouldn't like any reminder that he'd come to her rescue. Only when her things were safely stowed in his trunk and she was sitting in his front seat with the heater on high did he turn to her.

Even shivering, with clumps of snow melting in her hair, she was beautiful. Not for the first time, he felt a pang of regret that things had turned out so badly between them. For a brief period, during their internship, he thought they'd finally established a friendship. He thought she might be interested in becoming more, had been summoning up his courage to make a move. And then …

And then he'd been an idiot and had blown it all up, even if he hadn't intended to. The situation had quickly spiraled out of his control.

He cleared his throat and his regrets along with it. "So. Your call."

She looked at him questioningly.

"We can try the two-and-a-half miles to town. We'll probably make it, barring any more owls." He gave her a faint smile. "But if we don't, we're stuck in the car all night until a plow comes through, and considering we're supposed to get two feet by morning, it might be a while.

"Or we head back to the house and wait it out there. Even if we get stuck, we're close enough that we could walk back if we had to."

Meg glanced down the road. Clearly, she was inclined to take the first option, where they could be rid of each other and on with their lives—albeit stuck in Vail for the weekend. Then she sighed. "The smart move is the house, isn't it?"

"Probably."

Meg bowed her head. "House it is." She shot him a wry look. "Guess we're going to be doing our proposals hands-on this time, aren't we?"

He managed to make his expression neutral despite the images the phrase *hands-on* summoned. She didn't need to see how much he'd been hoping she'd make this decision. "Seems so." He turned the car around carefully and began the drive back to the house.

It was now snowing so hard that their tracks had already been covered by a fresh coat of white, and he had to rely exclusively on snow markers to find his way back to the drive. Meg said nothing, but gripped the door in silent anxiety. When they finally made the turn onto the Gratz property, Meg said quietly, "Thanks, by the way. I know you weren't going my direction. You must have followed me. In the chivalrous way. Not the creepy way."

He shot her a grin. "That might be the nicest thing you've ever said to me."

Meg flushed again, but she managed a weak smile in return.

And that was the last thing they said to each other until they reached the front of the house and let themselves in with the key, showering snowflakes and dropping bits of muddy ice on the hand-scraped hardwood and Oriental rug.

"I'll go find some towels," Meg said, setting her bags in the corner.

"And I'll get the heater turned on."

They went their separate ways, Meg to the mudroom around back, where they should have entered in the first place, and Declan to the thermostat in the hallway beneath the stairs. It was an old-fashioned unit with actual buttons, but he turned up the temperature from its forty-degree minimum setting, and somewhere deep in the house, a fan thrummed to life. It might smell like burning leaves for a while, but at least they'd get warm. Eventually. The amount of energy it took to heat a five thousand square foot house from near-freezing was staggering.

Meg was still rummaging, so Declan wandered back into the home's enormous, if outdated, kitchen. Hickory cabinets encircled the whole room, accented by a once-fashionable black and brown granite. A huge island big enough to seat six people dominated the center. Behind the island was a door he was pretty sure led to a pantry. Now to see if it had been cleaned out or if Eleanor still kept staples on hand.

Declan walked into a space the size of a small bedroom fitted with floor-to-ceiling shelves. Jackpot. There was a full section of canned goods left, most of them expensive and many of them foreign, acrylic containers full of rice and pasta, and an entire shelf full of imported mineral waters. He scanned the provisions and began pulling down ingredients: some bucatini, a couple of packets of tuna in olive oil, and an unopened bottle of capers. At the last minute, he chose a small, expensive bottle of extra-virgin olive oil from the shelf.

He was going to have to reimburse Eleanor a small fortune for this, or at least replace it all before anyone was the wiser.

"Declan? Where are you?"

"In the kitchen." He pulled down pots and pans and set them on the eight-burner Viking range. He sensed, rather than saw, Meg pull up short in the doorway.

"I cleaned up the— what are you doing?"

"Cooking dinner. If we're going to be stuck here a while, I'd like a real meal."

"You can cook?"

"I can cook. Just don't judge me entirely on this meal because there's no fresh garlic, onion, or lemon here and they're all fairly essential for Spaghettoni al Tonno." He twisted on the faucet behind the stove to fill the pot, relieved at the immediate flow of water. He'd been hoping that since the heater had been left on low, the house hadn't been fully winterized. "Why the tone of surprise?"

Meg came fully into the room and pushed herself up onto the counter, her legs dangling. "I don't know. You didn't strike me as the type."

"The type to eat food?"

"The type to … do things. Regular things, I mean."

"Ouch."

"Oh, come on, don't pretend your upbringing wasn't privileged."

Declan sighed. So they were on to this. Meg had always pretended she didn't care who his father was, but of course it was a lie. It was always a lie. No matter how far he got from Ireland, Colum McKenzie's reputation preceded him. "We had plenty of money, yes, if that's what you mean."

"What else could it mean?"

"Spoken like someone who's privileged without knowing it."

"I don't understand."

He swore he could hear Meg frown without looking at her, a side effect of spending so many hours studying her expressions when she wasn't looking, hoping for some clue as to what actually went on in that brilliant head of hers. He stole a look, and sure enough, it was just as he'd predicted.

"I'm sure you don't."

Meg paused for a long moment, then hopped off the counter. "I'm going to go look around a bit. Call me when dinner's ready."

A pang of regret struck Declan as Meg vanished. He hadn't meant to antagonize her. Or maybe he had. Everyone thought it was so easy, such a privilege to be the son of Colum McKenzie, famed architect, the man behind some of the best-known Brutalist public buildings in Europe. Sure, there had been money and expensive trips, but there had also been empty houses, holidays spent at boarding school, and an impossible-to-meet set of expectations.

No one, Meg included, could believe that they, with their normal houses, nuclear families, and middle-class worries, were the privileged ones.

He shook off his silent whingeing and turned his attention to the meal. The pasta water was now boiling, so he salted it and measured out two portions of bucatini. Then he stared at the hot pan and wondered what he could do to make up for the lack of fresh aromatics. He was searching for a bottle of Calabrian chilis in oil that he'd seen in the pantry earlier when the room went pitch black, all the appliances powering down with a deflated whine.

And somewhere in the house, he heard a shriek.

two

MEG WAS REACHING FOR THE SPACE HEATER on the top shelf of the master bedroom closet when the lights abruptly blinked out. She tilted precariously on her tiptoes, momentarily dizzied by the sudden darkness, her fingers grasping for the heater before she became completely disoriented. She just about had it—and then the entire contents of the closet shelf came tumbling down.

Meg screamed as the heater, half a dozen blankets, and what felt like a pile of books dropped onto her head and back.

From down below, Declan's voice drifted: "Meg? You all right up there?"

She rubbed her scalp gingerly before replying. "Yeah! I'm okay."

"Good! Dinner in five."

She pulled her cell phone from her back pocket and flicked on the flashlight to review the carnage. She'd gone in search of a space heater once she realized it was going to take all night to get the house to a comfortable temperature, but this power outage made the whole search moot. She knelt in front of the mess and attempted to fold all the blankets as they'd been before. Not only had she and Declan raided Eleanor Gratz's pantry, but now she was rooting around in her closet as well.

She gathered up the books on the floor before she realized that they were leather-bound photo albums. Some were filled with color photos of trips abroad—she recognized the Eiffel Tower and the Trevi Fountain— but the other was filled with creased black and white photos. She flicked through the pages, angling her phone's light for a better look. Gradually, she realized that the photos had been taken at this very house, though not in its current iteration. All the interiors had the look of an English country manor with dark paneling, staid antiques, and fusty draperies. She must have gotten distracted by trying to pick out details in the background, because Declan's voice carried to her again: "Meg? Dinner!"

She quickly shoved the other photo albums onto the shelf, then hurried downstairs with the house album under her arm. She charged into the kitchen, invigorated by her find, then stumbled to a halt. Two plates of delicious-smelling pasta sat on the island counter along with glasses and a bottle of mineral water, the whole thing illuminated by the flickering light of two tapers in stone candlesticks.

"This looks very …" *Romantic*, she wanted to say, but she was afraid he would take that as a positive thing.

But he seemed to read her mind, because he looked abashed. "I know. It was all I could find. I'm sure there are some lanterns somewhere around here." He gestured to the empty chair in front of her plate. "Sit. Eat while it's hot."

Reluctantly, Meg sidled over to the island. He'd left a chair between them, she saw. Apparently, he wasn't any more enthusiastic about this arrangement than she was. Declan poured her some water while she took her first bite.

"It's … it's really good!"

"Again with the surprise."

"Sorry, I just …" She took another bite. "If this is what you did with pantry items, I can't imagine what it tastes like with fresh."

"The Calabrian chili helps. I'm going to make a spicy sauce tomorrow with the rest of the jar. Assuming we're still here tomorrow," he amended.

"About that. How much snow so far?"

"Seven or eight inches last I checked."

"Whoa." That made something like four inches an hour. "I wonder what happened to the power. That's not enough snow to down a line."

"Hard to tell what it's like elsewhere." He took a bite of his own pasta, seeming to be evaluating it, before he gave a shrug that she took to mean *it's okay.*

"Doesn't this place have a backup generator?" Meg asked. "It's going to get cold fast if we can't rely on the furnace. I was looking for heaters upstairs, but the only one I found was electric."

"I think the fireplace in the den is gas. Which is better anyway because it's a smaller room to heat. If the power doesn't come on, we'll have to camp out there."

"Great." From the way Declan flinched, Meg realized she'd hurt his feelings. She cringed. She might still harbor plenty of bitterness toward him, but he had, after all, rescued her from the side of the road, where she'd still be if he hadn't decided to check up on her. "I just meant, I'm kind of a baby about my sleep. I'd really been hoping for a proper mattress."

He flicked a glance at her. "There's another fireplace up in the master bedroom, but it would mean sharing a bed."

"Uh, no. I draw the line there." Her response was so emphatic that she thought she might have offended him again, but he just laughed.

"I see. Afraid you can't control yourself, huh?"

"Please." Meg rolled her eyes, but found she had no comeback. Just because she'd spent the last six years cursing his existence and her own naivete didn't mean she didn't feel a quiver of anticipation in her middle at his very proximity. She'd learned a long time ago that her head and her hormones had very different tastes in men.

Declan grinned as though he knew exactly what she was thinking. If she was half as transparent as she'd once been with him, he probably did.

She grasped for another subject. "Seriously, though. Are we the only two architects bidding on this project?"

"Why do you think I would know?" Meg sent him a look and he caved. "Yeah, I think so."

"Why us?" Meg asked, then amended, "I can understand you. But why me?"

He raised a shoulder. "Would you rather have not been considered?"

"No! I just mean … NCO isn't a big firm like Klein. I'm not even a senior architect."

"Yeah, but you've done a couple of noteworthy structures. The Breakwater House, for example. It's a beautiful piece of architecture. Modern, elegant, maybe a little challenging, but in an interesting way, not an off-putting one."

Meg slid him a dubious look. "How do you know about that?"

"There was that little feature in *Altitude Magazine*. Mentioned your name. But I would have recognized your style anywhere. It's always been very … innovative."

"Now you're mocking me." There was no way anything she did would be considered innovative by the son of Colum McKenzie, standard bearer of the revived European Brutalist movement. She drained her glass, picked up her half-finished plate, and took them both to the sink.

"I'm not mocking you!" Declan insisted. "It takes guts to look at a pristine wilderness location and say 'I'm going to design in steel and glass.' And it takes talent to make it actually work. Intellectually, it's no more out of place than an icicle in winter. Just because something is hard and shiny doesn't mean it's not also organic."

It was, perhaps, the nicest thing anyone had said about her work and the closest anyone but she had come to articulating her style. She looked at nature and saw not only soft lines and warm materials, but the sharp edges—the strata of a rock cliff, the sharp bright cut of a stream through a valley.

What was surprising was that it was Declan saying it. He was the master of traditional: he made places the way builders and architects would have done centuries ago, if only they'd been able to plan ahead for electricity and running water and the desire for open living spaces. Walking into one of his homes was like walking back in time to any genteel European country house, just without the inconveniences of low doorframes and water closets that were down the hall from the bath. And though that style wasn't to her particular taste—it was, in fact, the polar opposite of her taste—she could admit that he was good at it.

In that way, the request to have them both bid on this project made perfect sense. Two opposing viewpoints, two radically different visions. No middle ground. If the design brief could be believed, the first batch of architects had failed because they tried too hard to be everything to everybody. And if there was one thing she knew about Eleanor Gratz, it was that the woman was her own person. No matter what anyone thought

Meg flipped on the faucet and began to wash the dishes, surprised when Declan appeared beside her and took over, handing her a dish towel instead. They worked silently in tandem for a minute until Declan said, "Can I ask you something?"

After his compliments, she was beginning to thaw toward him. "Okay."

"What's this perfume you always wear? You're the only person I've ever smelled it on, and I've always wondered what it was."

"Oh." She'd expected him to ask her how she fell in love with architecture, why she wanted this job; she'd never envisioned something so personal. "It's Chanel. Bois de Iles. It's a 1920s fragrance that they reissued in the noughties. My mom bought a bottle for me for my high school graduation and it just kind of became a thing." She threw him a sheepish smile. "I don't usually like perfume, but I like this one. It's not blended. It's … built."

When she glanced over at him, he was looking down at her with warmth in his eyes. That annoying quiver built to a full-blown vibration, making her breath catch.

"That is a very architect sort of response," he said with a smile. He finished washing the last pan and left the water on at a trickle, no doubt to prevent the pipes from freezing now that the heater didn't work. "I'm going to go see about that generator. Wish me luck."

"Good luck," she said absently as he left the room.

What on earth was happening to her? She'd only been in the house alone with him for four hours and already she had Stockholm Syndrome? Even more shocking, it seemed to go both ways. As if a shared meal and cleaning up together had made them forget they were rivals, forget all the cutthroat things he'd done to get where he was. Maybe he wanted to bury the hatchet out of guilt, but all things considered, the only place she should want to bury the hatchet was his head.

She wiped down the countertop, put away the dishes and glasses, and went to inspect the adjacent den, willing the lights to turn back on and the house to power up again. All she needed was enough electricity to retreat to separate rooms, forget the unexplainable moments of connection, and refocus on what was really important in this scenario—winning this bid for her firm and getting the promotion she absolutely deserved.

The den did indeed have a gas fireplace, this one trimmed out more formally in figured mahogany, along with two overstuffed sofas, a large wall-mounted TV, and layered Oriental and cowhide rugs. A weird combination, but at least if they had to sleep in here, they'd be comfortable.

Ten minutes later, Declan reappeared, just as Meg was trying and failing to manually light the fireplace. She glanced up hopefully. "What's the generator situation?"

"There is a generator. But it's out of diesel, and if there's a tank anywhere, I can't find it. I can barely see a foot in front of me."

Meg sat back on her heels. "That's disappointing." Only then did she notice he was shivering, his heavy wool coat soaked. "Come here and get warm."

"In front of the invisible fire?" he quipped.

"Very funny. You try lighting a fire through a space meant for a screwdriver."

He dug in his pocket and pulled out a Swiss Army knife. "Here, take off the glass before we asphyxiate from all that gas you're pumping in here."

"I turned off the valve when you walked in, thank you very much." She disassembled the front of the glass screen easily, twisted on the gas valve, and lit the flame on the first try. Quickly, she replaced the screen and handed him back the pocketknife.

Declan knelt on the floor next to her and held his hands out to the warmth now pouring out of the fireplace. "Bet you wish you'd risked the drive into town."

She shrugged so she didn't have to think her way through that statement. "Upside? We get to see how the house actually lives. I'll admit it, I'm not a fan of the architecture or the decor, but it is pretty cozy."

"Wait, what? Did Meg Anderson actually admire comfort over aesthetics?"

Meg leaned back on her hands and laughed. "I've never only been about aesthetics. I just think there should be a way to marry the two where neither plays a backseat role. Me saying 'At least it's comfortable' is like you saying 'At least she has a good personality.'"

"Ouch again. Who's accusing whom of only caring about aesthetics?"

She conceded that point. "You have to admit, though, your work relies heavily on memory and tradition." She held up a hand to stop his inevitable protest. "I'm not saying there's anything wrong with that. I just meant that when you rely on nostalgia, innovation—and by extension, aesthetics—are bound to suffer."

He shifted a little closer to the fire. "I'm going to disagree with you on that point."

"What a surprise."

Declan grinned. "You are laboring under the misapprehension that something nostalgic can't be beautiful, as if novelty is the only criteria for beauty. But science tells us the opposite. Our minds appreciate the familiar, which makes it beautiful but also opens up the possibility of moments of surprise. Whereas something too novel can be rejected because our minds can't adequately categorize what we're seeing."

"Small minds, perhaps."

Declan threw his head back and laughed. "Ah, I've missed sparring with you, Meg. We used to have some of the most fantastic arguments."

Meg stilled abruptly and stared at him. "I don't know what you mean."

"Surely you haven't forgotten how much fun we had in design studio. I argued that good architecture isn't necessarily good placemaking and used Frank Lloyd Wright as an example. You about took my head off."

Reluctantly, Meg smiled. "I don't remember what was surely a reasoned argument, but I do remember saying I was surprised that he wasn't your idol considering you shared the same level of arrogance."

"That's right! I'd forgotten about that." Declan grinned at her with something she could only call fondness. "In that whole class, you were the only worthy opponent. Everyone lacked the passion of their convictions."

She blinked at him, momentarily confounded. Was that really how he remembered it? All this time she thought he was attacking her personally when he thought it was good-natured sparring. How had he thought anything so heated could be a game? She'd literally thought he hated her for the entire semester.

Oblivious to her thoughts, he went on. "It's no wonder maybe five of them are working in the field now."

"You've kept up with everyone?"

"Some of them. Some fell off the face of the earth, at least in the architecture world. As far as I know, the only working architects are you, me, Joel Robison, Mina Law, and that guy … the one who always had coffee. What was his name?"

"Mark something."

"Yeah, him. We're it. Everyone else got downsized or never got a job in the first place. It's been a hard few years for construction."

That put her life into unwelcome perspective. She'd kept her head down except for the occasional jealous peek at Declan's career, so she hadn't fully grasped how bad it had been for everyone else. She'd been beating herself up for her failures when maybe she should have just been happy to have a job.

"Anyway," he said, pushing himself to his feet. "We should try and get a little work done. At least I need to."

"Yeah. Work. Right." Meg got up as well and went back to the foyer to retrieve her things, using her phone's flashlight to illuminate her steps. The difference in temperature between the den and the rest of the house was already noticeable. She settled on the sofa closest to the fire with her sketchbook, her first step in any project. She needed to download the ideas from her brain to the page, see them visually, before she could even start to think about drafting them in SketchUp and Revit.

But except for the initial impressions she'd had of the great room, nothing occurred to her. Instead, her mind kept drifting back to the conversation with Declan. Their impressions of grad school varied so much, it was like they'd gone through a completely different program. Had she really misread him that badly? Or was he just giving her the revisionist version because they were stranded here together?

When it became clear that no substantial work was going to get done, she pulled out the photo album she'd brought down from the bedroom and began flipping through it. She moved closer to the fire to see more clearly, fascinated. So the weird architectural mishmash had been the most recent update. If she wasn't mistaken, these photos were from the 1940s, not long after the original house had been built, with no sign of chalet or mountain rustic anywhere in sight. It could have been taken in England or Germany if not for the handwritten inscription identifying it as this structure.

"What have you got there?"

Meg looked up. "Photos of this house in its original form."

"Can I see?" In seconds, he was down on the floor with her. She passed the album over.

"This reminds me a little of my aunt's place in Killarney," he said slowly. "Same heavy furnishings, dark wood."

"Good memories?"

His gaze flicked to hers. "Not particularly. Those were the days after my mom left and my dad didn't know what to do with me. Didn't last long because I was soon old enough for boarding school."

Meg gaped. "Your mom left?"

He kept flipping. "When I was ten. Went back to America." He threw her a look. "Bet you didn't know I'm a dual citizen, did you?"

She shook her head.

"About the only useful thing she ever did for me. Made staying here after uni easy at least."

There were depths here at which she would never have guessed, but she wasn't sure now was the time to explore them. "Do you miss it? Ireland, I mean?" Maybe that was why he was so fixated on traditional forms.

"Ireland, sure. Sometimes. England, not so much. Denver feels much more like home to me than London or Somerset ever did." He handed the album back to her. "Thanks. Not so much help, though, is it? Not very much of that era left here. We're basically starting over."

Meg retreated to the sofa again, where she sat with her sketchbook open on her lap, staring into the fire. She should be taking advantage of this enforced work time, but instead of roof pitches and sight lines, all she could think about were those words: *starting over.*

Did she want to start over with Declan? It seemed like she'd gotten him wrong, at least in some aspects. Maybe it was simply that they'd both grown up, or maybe he was trying to make amends, but for the occasional flash of overconfidence, he was no longer the brash, arrogant guy she'd so hopelessly fallen for and then spent all her free time berating herself over. Now he seemed friendly, even considerate. And despite the fact she apparently had an enduring weakness for his bad boy swagger, she was finding the real him—if indeed that was real—even more attractive.

Heaven help her.

Meg drifted off to sleep in front of the fireplace, but Declan was wide awake and thought he'd remain so for the foreseeable future. He'd always wondered how things had gone so wrong between the two of them when by all accounts they should have been friends, and now he had an insight into why Meg hated him so much.

He'd never dreamed that she had taken their daily debates as a personal attack. He supposed he had focused on her to the exclusion of the other students, but that had only been because she was the sole member of their grad program who could put up a good fight. She was intelligent and passionate and she wouldn't back down when she thought she was right, which was pretty much always.

That would have been enough to draw his attention, but she was also stunning, with her dark hair worn loose around her shoulders, warm brown eyes flecked with gold that sparked with fire when he made her angry. Somehow, she was even prettier now, even when she was glaring at him. Maybe especially when she was glaring at him.

He put aside his laptop and rose, pausing beside her sleeping form for a moment. Her sketchpad was about to slip out of her hand, so he placed it on the table beside the sofa with her fallen pencil. Then he took a throw blanket from the arm of the sofa and draped it over her. She stirred, but didn't awaken.

He was about to walk away when he caught a glimpse of the half-finished sketch on the table. Even though he knew he shouldn't be snooping, he lifted the pad for a closer look. It was the home's rear elevation, the part that housed the great room and kitchen. It was just the kind of thing he'd expected of her. It had the pitched, asymmetrical roofline that characterized many of her homes, as well as the wall of windows she so liked to show off the vistas. To him, it looked like she intended them to slide and stack away to remove all boundaries between the home and the view. Surprisingly, she'd extended it along the entire back end of the house, even throughout the kitchen. He immediately grasped what she was thinking: cabinets against the whole back wall, with the cooking and prep area facing outside. Knowing her, she would use just enough wood to link the indoors with the outdoors, the house itself becoming a barely perceptible vessel for the people and things inside.

It would be stunning.

He put aside the sketchbook again and moved out into the hall, immediately hit with a heavy rush of cold air. It felt late, but it was actually only nine o'clock. He pulled his phone out of his pocket and dialed.

"Hey, Nina, it's me."

"Declan. Hi. What's wrong?" The sounds in the background suggested his boss, Nina Klein, was at a restaurant. He immediately felt stupid for assuming she would be home on a Friday night just because he would.

"Nothing's wrong exactly. I got stuck up at the Vail house for the night at least." He quickly filled her in on the situation, then added, "Meg Anderson is here too."

Nina paused, obviously surprised. Then she laughed. "I didn't think you still had it in you. Fraternizing with the competition?"

"It's not like that."

"Sure it's not. Enjoy your cozy weekend. Just don't let anything slip and make sure your butt is back in the office on Monday morning. I don't care if you have to snowshoe home. It looks bad if the future managing partner is taking long ski weekends while the rest of us toil away in the mines."

"I—"

"Have to run now. Try to get some work done up there, will you? You've got less than a week to get this bid in, and I don't have to remind you what's at stake here."

"No, you don't. Thanks, Nina." Declan clicked off the line, slightly troubled by Nina's assumptions. He wasn't sure if she thought his plan was to have a sexy weekend away with his rival or to do some subtle reconnaissance on Meg's design, but either way, he didn't care for the implications. He was surprised Nina would assume such things. But then, why wouldn't she? She'd already seen what he would do to get a job with her firm, and even if it had been somewhat accidental on his part, she'd approved. Said that if Meg would put her personal feelings ahead of achieving her dream, she didn't have the killer instinct she needed to succeed there. After seven years at the firm, Declan would have to agree.

The only thing was, he wondered if *he* had the killer instinct to succeed there.

He'd been wrong about Meg. He'd thought she was just like him. But she had something different and more powerful driving her: love for what she did, passion, vision. He … he had ambition and the need to prove himself as more than just the son of Colum McKenzie. There was no question which motivation made the better architect.

If he didn't step up his game, he was going to lose everything he'd worked for, and then it would have all been for nothing.

Declan crept back into the den, the warmth luring him for a bare minute, but he steeled himself and grabbed both his coat and laptop before returning to the cold kitchen. He found a kettle in the cabinet and put on some water to boil; though he'd found tea bags, he'd have to do without milk. No matter. It was the warmth and the subtle hit of caffeine he wanted right now. As soon as he had a steaming mug beside him, he settled at the island with his laptop and got to work.

He knew without a doubt what he needed to do. No matter how much he might be rooting for Meg to succeed, no matter how much he might want to assuage his guilt, he owed it to himself and Nina to make this his best work. Everything he'd ever wanted was riding on it.

three

MEG WOKE SOMETIME IN THE EARLY MORNING, disoriented but toasty warm thanks to the fire still blazing in the fireplace. Pale blue light filtered in through the window, making it impossible to tell the time—with the swirl of snow still falling outside, it could have been seven a.m. or noon. She reached for her phone and was relieved to find it was only a little past eight. With any luck, the plows had been out all night and she could get roadside assistance to winch her Jeep out of the ditch.

Only when she sat up and threw the blanket aside did she notice its presence. Had she pulled it over herself during the night or had Declan done it? She thrust her feet into her boots, which were even warmer from sitting next to the fire all night and pushed herself off the sofa with a groan. She'd meant what she said last night—she really was sensitive to her sleeping accommodations. As cushy as the sofa might have been, she'd be feeling it in her neck for a week.

Meg wandered out of the den into the hallway and convulsed in a full-body shiver as the cold air hit her skin. She dashed back for her coat and shrugged it on, then zipped it up to her chin. It had definitely been the right choice to sleep in the den. It was barely above freezing in the rest of the house. She moved into the kitchen, half-expecting to see Declan, but the room was quiet and still with only a used mug and a wet teabag to show that she hadn't stayed here alone.

"Declan?" she called cautiously, her voice ringing through the cavernous house. No answer. No sounds of movement anywhere either.

A sudden sick feeling cut through her middle, and she dashed to the window, expecting to find his BMW missing from the driveway. But no, it was still there—an indistinct lump, already covered with more than a foot of snow, as if saying that there was no way it was going to be moving anytime soon.

But if Declan hadn't left her, then where was he?

She pulled out her phone automatically, intending to call him, before she realized she didn't have his number. She hadn't thought she'd need it. They were snowed in together in a large, but not infinite, house; there were only so many places he could go.

Her stomach rumbled, reminding her that she'd been so taken aback by the unfamiliar side of Declan McKenzie that she hadn't finished her pasta last night. Leaving the door open for light, she rummaged in the pantry for a few minutes until she came up with a handful of ingredients that she knew would work together. An unconventional breakfast, for sure, but a hot and filling one, at least. For both of them. If he came back.

"Don't be silly," she said aloud, "Of course he'll come back." Up until then, she hadn't realized how much comfort she'd drawn from his presence. Well, not *his* presence exactly. Anyone's presence would have done. It was creepy being in a big house alone, without the hum of electric appliances, with only the snow steadily falling outside the window. It felt almost as if she'd been taken back in time—or out of time—as if she could be stuck here forever without anyone being the wiser. She had to check her phone to see if she had a cell signal. She did. Of course she did.

"Now you're really losing it," she told herself. She filled a pot with water from the faucet, then set it on the stove. It took her a second to rummage in a drawer for matches to light the burner, but in minutes, the water was simmering away happily on the stove.

And then, just as her mind was turning back to Declan and where he could possibly have gone, the front door opened and closed with a thud.

"Declan!" she exclaimed before she could stop herself. "Where have you been?"

She heard the rustle of fabric and the thud of boots dropping on the floor before he made his way back down the hall to the kitchen. He was wearing a cap pulled low over his ears, with a muffler around his neck and face, his wool jacket covered with wet spots from rapidly melting snow. "Ah, you're up. I thought I'd just take a look around."

She stared at him, uncomprehending. "A look around where?"

"A look around the house. You were asleep." He grinned at her, his lips, nose, and cheeks cherry red from the cold. "You snore, you know."

"I do not!" she said hotly, but she felt her cheeks flame in response. "At least I don't when I have a proper bed."

"You're welcome to the one upstairs tonight, then. Just make sure you wear your coat. It's barely even forty in here."

She started to retort, then processed what he said. "Tonight? You think we're going to be stuck here again?"

Declan shrugged. "I'm not sure, but I wouldn't count on your car getting pulled out before then. I found some snowshoes in the garage and went down to the road to see the situation. I think we're up to eighteen inches and the plows haven't even come this way yet."

"Great," she said, all her hopes of getting out of here today deflating. "Maybe we could call the county and get an update? Or roadside assistance?"

"I'm going to bet they're probably busy clearing the highways, but we can try." He unwound his muffler, but he left his hat and jacket on. He sniffed the air. "What is that? It smells delicious."

"Breakfast couscous," Meg said proudly. "We used to bring it with us camping when I was a kid. Couscous, brown sugar, cinnamon, and whatever dried fruit and nuts we had on hand. I used the cherries and pecans from the trail mix I brought with me."

Declan moved to the stove and was about to lift the lid on the pot, but she smacked his hand before he could touch it.

"Don't take the lid off. You'll let the steam escape and it won't cook."

He grinned and leaned back against the island. "Fine. What do you want to do today?"

She stared at him. "What do you mean, what do I want to do today?"

"After we call the county and they tell us they're not going to get to us until tomorrow. How do you want to spend the day?"

"Normally, I would say binge-watch Netflix, but that's not exactly an option."

Declan rolled his eyes. "It's beautiful outside. We've got all this fresh powder. And you want to stay indoors?"

Meg pulled out her phone and held it up so Declan could see the weather widget. "It's six degrees outside."

He waved a hand. "It's above zero. It's totally fine. You know, there are several sets of snowshoes in the garage. I was hoping to find cross country skis, but they must have taken them with them."

"Or you know, Eleanor Gratz isn't crazy enough to ski in sub-zero weather."

"*Do you want to build a snowman?*" He sing-songed the phrase so gleefully that she groaned.

"Please don't …"

"You know you want to go out and play," he paraphrased, staying in tune.

"You know you want to be murdered if you keep singing."

Declan laughed. "Seriously. We could stay inside all day and work, or we could act like children and play in the snow. I don't know about you, but I know which one sounds like more fun."

Easy for him to say. He didn't have the result of this bid hanging over his head every minute like a dark cloud. Meg lifted the lid off the pot. "Breakfast is ready. Grab some bowls." She rummaged in a drawer for a serving spoon and halved the contents of the pot between the two large bowls he brought to the counter.

He didn't even wait to sit down before he grabbed a fork and started shoving the couscous into his mouth. "This is amazing. Fortifying for a day in the snow."

Meg couldn't help but laugh. "You never give up, do you?"

"Nope. Not when it comes to snow. I spent more than half of my life thinking it was only something that happened in movies."

"Come on. It snows in England. Occasionally in Ireland, too, I'm told."

"Yeah, but not very often and not to this degree, at least not where I lived. And then I moved to Alabama, which is not exactly the snow capital of America."

She smiled despite herself. Even with the slight accent, he spoke so much like an American, it always surprised her when he said something that was typically British. No one living in America actually *called* it America.

"What?"

She turned her attention back to her couscous, embarrassed at being caught in her thoughts. She couldn't let herself like him. Couldn't feel fondness toward him. After all, he had been her nemesis, and now he was her competition. The last thing she needed was to mess around all day in the snow with him, instead of working on her design. In fact, that was probably his idea. Given that this house was originally his firm's project, he might have even known the design brief was coming on Friday. How did she know he didn't have a head start? Or was she just being paranoid?

"I'll make you a deal," he said finally, almost as if he'd read her thoughts. "We spend half the day playing and we spend the other half working. Compromise."

She could feel herself wavering. "Work first."

"Fair. Work first." He stuck out his hand to shake and reluctantly, she took it.

"Geez, your hands are freezing. I'm changing my mind."

"No take-backs. You're committed. We will be good little worker bees this morning and then this afternoon, we're free."

"Fine. I'll keep my end of the bargain if you keep yours."

He winked at her. "I'll make sure you do."

Meg finished her couscous, all the while stealing looks at him. Why was he in such a good mood this morning? Last night he'd been nice, but unexpectedly subdued. Today he was downright … jaunty.

When they'd finished the couscous and washed their dishes, they returned to the den, which felt almost oppressively warm after the frigid kitchen. Meg contemplated turning off the fireplace, but that meant she'd have to light it again in an hour or two, which sounded like too much work. Instead, she left the door cracked open and settled down on the sofa opposite where Declan was sitting with his laptop. "Where's my—"

"Table behind you," Declan said without looking up.

"Oh." She twisted around and saw that her sketchbook had been closed and set aside with her pencil, which she didn't remember doing either. Had Declan picked it up when he covered her? Had he looked at it?

For some reason the idea made her feel off-balance, at a disadvantage. It wasn't like he would steal her design … It wasn't at all his style and that much would be obvious to anyone who looked at it. But the idea that he might have been looking at her preliminary sketches—just the random ideas that came to mind, might not even be used in the final project—made her feel uncomfortably vulnerable.

She pushed away that thought and opened the sketchbook to a fresh page. She might have said she wasn't going to use the drawing, but her initial instincts on a project tended to be pretty good, and she liked the concept that she'd come up with. It was perhaps slightly more organic, a little warmer, than her recent structures, but she could tell from the decor—like the sofa she was sitting on right now—that she'd lose Mrs. Gratz if she went too modern or too sterile. But that didn't mean she was willing to backtrack all the way to traditional. She began sketching as an idea for the front elevation occurred to her, so engrossed in her work that she completely forgot about Declan until he stood abruptly and shut his laptop.

"I'm going to work in the kitchen. It's too warm in here."

"The kitchen's freezing, though!"

"It's good for me. It gets my synapses firing."

"So that explains it," Meg said. "You design cozy houses because you won't let yourself be comfortable while you're working. I mean, imagine what you would do if you stayed in this room. You might have a sudden yearning for metal and glass."

He studied her for a second, then cracked a smile when he figured out she was teasing him. "Perish the thought. I might even turn into Frank Lloyd Wright."

She grinned. "I told you he was your spirit animal."

He waved her off and left the room for cooler climates, and Meg went back to her sketching. But his joking words had triggered a thought. Just because a material was traditional didn't mean it had to be used in a traditional way. If she just …

She flipped another page and started on a second iteration of the concept sketch, incorporating her slowly developing ideas. By the time Declan came back into the room, she was surprised to find several hours had passed and she'd filled half the notebook with drawings.

"Good work? I poked my head in here an hour ago, but you were so absorbed in your sketching, I didn't want to disturb you."

She closed her notebook, stood up, and stretched, feeling not just the kink in her neck from the night on the sofa, but the results of sitting cross-legged for hours without moving. "I think I've got a good start, yes. You?"

"I roughed mine out last night while you were sleeping. I think I'm squared away." He rubbed his hands together. "You ready for some fun now?"

She tucked her sketchbook safely away in her backpack. "I'm all yours."

She didn't mean it the way it sounded. Declan knew that. And yet there was a part of him that perked up with reckless hope. She was thawing toward him—no pun intended—losing that suspicious, guarded expression he'd seen since they arrived. He didn't have any right to feel so stung by it, considering he deserved it, but when she looked at him with that half-smile, her eyes unguarded, it was like the sun coming out.

He shook off the embarrassingly poetic thoughts. "So. Let's get going then. You have some extra layers in that suitcase of yours? You're going to need them."

Meg looked less than thrilled about what she'd agreed to then, but he wasn't about to let her off the hook. He knew her. Or at least he knew how she used to be. She'd coped pretty well with the idea of being locked in the house with him overnight, but the longer the day wore on, the edgier she would get. And the more annoyed she would get with him, as if it were his fault that they'd misjudged the weather on the single snowiest day of the year.

Or maybe that was all just an excuse. For a few minutes last night, they'd actually had a pleasant conversation where she didn't look at him with suspicion or contempt, and he'd liked it. A lot. When she laughed, it did something to his insides, and he was willing to brave all sorts of frigid weather to hear her laugh again.

"I'll just wait in the hallway for you so you can change." He slipped outside and then went to the front porch where he'd left his snowshoes, wondering if she'd actually emerge. He couldn't rule out the idea that she might just settle back on the sofa with her sketchbook and completely disregard their agreement.

So he was somewhat relieved that when he went back inside, she was waiting for him, bundled up like that kid in the Christmas movie who couldn't put his arms down. By his estimation, she was probably wearing three sweaters beneath her coat, in addition to a scarf and hat. He couldn't help but laugh. "You really don't like the cold, do you?"

"I'm okay with the cold. I just don't like *being* cold," she said. "So let's do this. What did you have in mind?"

He led her through the house to the attached garage, which was one floor down, built into the walk-out basement. It was a configuration he actually appreciated, so that was definitely staying in his design. As much as he preferred separate carriage house-style garages in temperate climates, no one wanted to have to walk through two feet of snow to get to their vehicle or be forced to shovel before they could leave home. Since Eleanor Gratz would never do anything as undignified as *trudge*, it was an important consideration.

He hit the garage door button before he realized that without electricity, it wouldn't do anything. He went to the garage door opener instead and pulled the release cord, then slid up the metal door manually. Pale light illuminated the cavernous space, which was nicer than most people's kitchens, with an epoxy floor and yards of interior grade cabinetry.

"Snowshoes in here." He began rummaging through a cabinet to find a pair that would fit Meg.

"Those are snowshoes?" she asked dubiously. "They look like giant skateboard platforms with bindings. I thought they were like tennis rackets strapped to your feet."

He stopped and stared at her. "Do you get all your sports knowledge from Norman Rockwell paintings?"

Instantly, she turned defensive. "No. I've just never had occasion to snowshoe. For that matter, I've never known anyone who had occasion to snowshoe. Why do you even know about this stuff?"

"I like the outdoors." He found a pair that looked right, the bindings adjustable enough to fit her smaller feet, but the platform large enough to help her stay on top of the powder. "Here, try these."

He helped her fit them then encouraged her to take an experimental step. She immediately tripped and he reached out to steady her. "It takes a bit of practice. You need to keep your feet farther apart, like so." He strapped on his own pair and demonstrated. "See? You just have to adjust your gait a little. Walk like a Neanderthal."

"So that's why you're so good at it," she said grumpily, but there was a glimmer in her eye. "Okay, if we're going to do this, let's get it over with."

Declan crossed his arms. "Listen, no one is forcing you. If you don't want to go out in the cold, don't. I just thought it might be nice to get out of the house for a bit. We can even go up the road and check on your car if you want."

She sighed. "It's not that. It's just … I keep thinking that I should be inside, focusing on this bid. It's the perfect opportunity to work with no distractions."

"I wouldn't say *no* distractions."

She made a face. "You *are* a very big distraction, especially with your love of Disney tunes." But she moved toward the garage exit, not the house, so he took that as a sign she was going along with him, at least for now. He hurried after her before she could realize how cold it was and change her mind, pulling the garage door down behind them.

It took a few minutes, but Meg finally settled into a somewhat comfortable stride, though she still grimaced when she banged the edges of the snowshoes together. He moved next to her and gently nudged her to turn down the driveway toward the road.

"So, why is this project so important to you anyway?" he asked.

She glanced at him. "Every project is important to me."

"I know that. But you wouldn't drive hours in the middle of a snowstorm for just any job. Why this one?"

For a second, Declan thought she wouldn't answer. "Eleanor Gratz is high profile. And I need to prove to my firm that I'm capable of dealing with high-profile clients."

"Your other projects have been high profile," he began, but she shook her head.

"After the fact. The one I did in Boulder only got attention because two years later, the owner sold his tech start-up for a kajillion dollars and everyone wondered where he'd come from. But the media was about him, not about his house and his architect. And I designed a multi-family in Idaho Springs that got a huge amount of attention, but the buzz went to the managing partners, because I was only one part of the team and they were never going to give credit to a junior member. So yeah, this one is important. If I win the bid, *I* win the bid. *I* bring that client to the table, not anyone else."

"It sounds to me like your firm really doesn't appreciate your talent."

"Yeah, well, beggars can't be choosers. After I lost the job at Klein, I was lucky to get anything at all." Bitterness hung heavy in her words.

"Meg, I—"

"I know, you're sorry. You never meant to sell me out, blah blah blah."

"I did, though."

She stopped short. "What?"

"I knew exactly what I was doing." Declan's face heated at the admission. "I mean, I didn't go into it planning to hang the whole project management disaster around your neck, but when you took responsibility for it, I knew what it meant if I didn't step up. I knew it wouldn't reflect well on you."

Meg was shocked into silence. "I can't believe you just admitted that."

"Why should I lie about it? You already know it's the truth. You already hate me for it."

"I don't hate you."

"But you resent me."

She bowed her head a little. "Yes."

Declan started walking again, but slowly, waiting to see if she would catch up. She did. "Here's the thing you don't know. You were never getting that job."

She blinked. "Of all the arrogant—"

"No," he interrupted gently. "Because of my father. I was all set to step up the next day with you and take responsibility for our screw-up. But then my father called and told me it was all arranged. He and Nina Klein go way back."

She gaped at him, mouth opening and closing like a fish out of water. "So I never had a chance?"

He shook his head. "No. So you're right that I hung you out to dry, because there was no point in starting off a job having them think I was incompetent. But it didn't cost you the job. You could have done absolutely everything right and they still would have picked me. Because that's how my dad works. I told him over and over that I didn't want him to interfere, that I wanted to do this on my own, and he went behind my back and did it anyway."

"You could have turned it down," Meg said, but her tone said she knew how unlikely that was.

"I could have. But I didn't. And I have to live with never knowing if I could have made it on my own." And that was the crux of it. Meg thought that the situation had only messed up her career, but it lingered over his as well. He would never know if they would have chosen him or Meg for the position; he would never know if he would have been promoted to Senior Architect if he didn't have a famous surname. And he certainly would never know if he had true talent or if people just expected him to because of his father.

That was the funny thing about architecture. Just like art, it was so subjective that the line between brilliance and trash was razor-thin and entirely in the eye of the beholder. It was just that people tended to look at him through Colum McKenzie-colored glasses.

Meg kept walking, the snow crunching beneath her snowshoes, while she digested this information. "You know I'm not going to feel sorry for you."

"I wouldn't expect you to."

"But I kind of understand." She glanced up at him, and surprisingly, he didn't see suspicion in her face. "You're here for the same reason I am."

"What's that?"

"To prove ourselves. Me, I have to prove myself to my firm. You have the harder job. You have to prove it to yourself."

Declan smiled. It was a far more gracious take on the situation than he deserved. He might not have meant to hurt her, he might not have actually taken her job since it was always meant to be his, but she was right. He could have turned it down. He could have made his own way, without his father's help. He could have changed his name and cut off contact with his dad, had he really been so concerned. But it had been convenient. All their classmates had gone on to find jobs, but few of them were working in the field they'd originally intended. And when it came down to it, if Klein & Company had judged exclusively on merit, he'd be hard pressed to guess whether he or Meg would have come out on top. He was good, he had no doubt about that ... but he had a suspicion that someday Meg would be great.

"You know, I give you a hard time, but you're really good, Declan."

Wait. Was she actually trying to make *him* feel better?

"I've been mad because you sold me out, but I really think it could have gone either way had your dad not intervened. I was hoping I'd get it, because of course I was. But it's not like you're dead weight. That house you did up in Bennett … what was it called?"

"Little Creek?"

"Yeah, Little Creek. It was …"

"Don't say innovative. It was *not* innovative."

"But it was exactly what the owners wanted. It was cozy and warm and fit with the landscape and …" She shrugged. "I'd totally Airbnb it."

He threw back his head and laughed. "That's a high compliment, coming from you. How do you even know about it?"

Her cheeks were pink, but it was hard to tell whether it was because of the cold or the question. "I might sometimes follow your work on Klein's website."

"Really?"

Now her expression turned wry. "Don't give me too much credit. I think I've always been hoping to see something really horrible so I can say you only got ahead because of your family connections. Alas, no such luck."

He couldn't help but grin. "Now that really *is* that's the nicest thing you've ever said to me."

"What can I say? The bar was set low."

They exchanged a grin and then settled into companionable silence, the crunch of snow underfoot melding with the sound of their breathing. Puffs of frozen air clouded around their heads as they approached the markers that indicated the end of the estate's driveway and the start of the county road. And then Meg pulled up short. "Look."

Declan followed her gaze, and though he knew it shouldn't, his heart sank.

The road. It was plowed.

four

OF ALL THE THINGS MEG EXPECTED TO FEEL, disappointment was last on her list.

But there it was. She'd convinced herself that she had no choice but to stay another night at the house with Declan, something that she was going to endure rather than enjoy, but the sinking in her heart seemed to indicate something completely different. Something complicated that she wasn't quite ready to confront.

"Do you want to keep going and see if they've already tagged your car?" Declan asked.

She glanced at him questioningly.

"You know, they put a little streamer on to indicate they've already checked for stranded people."

"Oh. Yeah. Sure. Why not?"

"Unless you're already tired ..."

"No, I'm fine." She seemed incapable of speaking in anything more than two-word phrases, but Declan apparently attributed that to her being out of breath rather than completely taken aback by her realization.

She actually enjoyed Declan McKenzie's company.

That really shouldn't be a surprise. She'd always enjoyed Declan's company, when he wasn't being a jerk. And why shouldn't she have? He was smart and funny and handsome. It wasn't exactly a chore to be in his presence. And for a while there, while they were both interns at Klein & Company, they were starting to become something she would have considered friends. Which was why his actions had hit her doubly hard.

To be betrayed by a rival was one thing; it was cutthroat but not particularly surprising. But by a friend?

She had already bought him a birthday present by then, a sleek fountain pen that she'd had to sell on eBay just so she didn't have to stare at the reminder of him.

"I guess this is good timing," she said finally. "I still need to digitize my sketches for my proposal and finalize a floor plan. Which would be a lot easier if I'd ever gotten the drawings I asked for."

He frowned at her. "No one ever sent you the architectural drawings from the current house?"

Meg shook her head. "No. I asked about them but no one replied."

"Well, I just got them last night. Maybe your signal isn't good up here or something." He pulled his phone out of his pocket and tapped the screen a few times before she heard the whoosh of an email being sent. "There. I just forwarded it."

"Thank you." Meg frowned and studied his profile. He could have just held onto them, made her job harder, forced her to turn in an incomplete proposal. But that idea hadn't even occurred to him, it seemed. Maybe he really was sorry about his previous actions.

She was still mulling this thought when she caught a glimpse of the bend where she'd slid off the road. Sure enough, there was her car, cocked at a strange angle in the ditch. Except, instead of having the two feet of snow that had fallen on it, it was buried in a snow drift, courtesy of the plow that had come through and shoved the entire contents of the road up against her driver's side door.

Meg blinked and stared. "What am I supposed to do with this?"

Declan started to laugh. "Wait for the spring thaw?"

"Not funny."

"It's a little funny."

"It's annoying is what it is." She clomped closer. "Were there any snow shovels in the garage?"

"Given what I've found so far? I'm sure there are. But maybe you should call roadside assistance and see when they can come out to help. No use doing it now and then having to do a second round before they can winch it out of the ditch."

Now Meg pulled out her own phone and saw that the email Declan forwarded had arrived, but she ignored it in favor of her phone book, where she'd stored the number of roadside assistance. She'd never actually had to use it—had been thinking of canceling her membership, actually—but now she was glad she'd kept it around. Not that it would help her much if they found damage and her Jeep wasn't drivable. She shuddered to think how much it would cost to have it towed to her mechanic in Denver.

With some help from Declan to brush the snow off the mile-marker sign just ahead, Meg managed to tell the dispatcher where her car was and what kind of assistance she would need. She was beginning to think she would be on her way back home within the hour when the dispatcher said, "Great, we've got you in the system. We should be able to get to you by tomorrow morning, but we'll call you before we come out."

"Wait. *Tomorrow morning?*"

"There are cars stranded all up and down I-70, and unfortunately, that's the priority. But don't worry, we'll get to you. You can call and check with us later tonight if you want a more accurate estimate."

"Thanks," Meg said, not a little sourly. She clicked off the line.

Declan raised an eyebrow. "Not rushing over here, I take it?"

"Apparently, there are cars stranded all along I-70 so all the tow trucks are busy."

"That seems unreasonable to me. Why should anyone need to drive on the interstate?"

Meg shot him a look and then rolled her eyes. "I understand it, but that doesn't mean I have to like it."

"Well, look at the upside. You've got a chance to sample another one of my delicious pantry meals."

Meg turned herself around on the snowshoes and started off the way they'd come. "Just because I'm stuck here doesn't mean you have to be. Now that the roads are plowed, you can go anytime you want. Don't let me keep you here."

Declan stared at her as if she'd grown another head. "There's no way I'm leaving you here by yourself."

"Why? I'll be fine. I would have been fine if you hadn't been here. I did figure out how to light the fireplace, remember?"

He held up his hands. "I never said you wouldn't be fine. I'd be happy to drive you back to Denver, but you probably want your vehicle."

"I do. But still. Really. Don't stay on my account."

"What if I want to?"

She glanced at him, expecting him to look teasing or even mocking. But his face was serious, intense. A chill rippled over her skin, one that even she couldn't convince herself was due to the frigid temperatures. "Why would you want to?"

He didn't answer immediately, and the silence stretched, filled with the crunch and squeak of their snowshoes on the hard packed road. "I really have always regretted what happened between us. How the whole internship thing went down. I'd thought that if things were different … well, I thought we might have been friends." He looked a little abashed. "I thought we *were* friends."

"Yeah," Meg said slowly. "I thought we were too."

Declan just nodded, a melancholy mood falling between them as they reached the turnoff to the house's drive. As Meg stepped onto the deeper, unplowed snow just past the gate, she lost her balance for a second, and Declan grabbed one of her flailing arms to steady her. But when she righted herself, he didn't let go, his gloved hand sliding down to wrap around her cold, bare one. Her heart gave a frantic little flutter, her cheeks burning suddenly hot in the cold air, but she made no move to pull away.

Having her hand in his felt more right than she could have possibly imagined.

When they reached the house, they circled around back to the garage again, where they divested themselves of their snowshoes, stamping off the snow from their boots and leaving them by the back door as they entered the house in their stocking feet. After the frigid air outside, even the cold house felt warm, and slowly, the feeling started to come back to Meg's fingers. For a second, she allowed herself to feel disappointed that her hand wasn't still wrapped in Declan's, but there was no way she was actually going to touch him. Maybe what she'd interpreted as a subtle overture was simply him not wanting to watch her struggle through her first experience in snowshoes all the way back up to the house.

"I'd normally suggest hot chocolate, but that is the one thing Mrs. Gratz doesn't actually have in her pantry. We do have tea, however."

Meg threw him a teasing look. "You Irishmen and your tea."

He laughed. "I do not apologize for it. Though, technically speaking, I'm just as American as I am Irish, and I've lived here for longer."

"Then what's with the accent?"

"Oh, that? That's put on to pick up women."

A smile threatened at the corner of Meg's lips. "Does it work?"

"Not as well as you'd imagine."

"Now I know you're a liar."

"Why? Because it works on you?"

"*Worked* on me. Past tense." Meg brushed by him and started up the stairs to the main level of the house. Declan hung back and then rushed to catch up with her.

"Wait, what? What are you talking about?"

She paused on the step and threw a chiding look over her shoulder. "Come on. You knew I had a—" she waved her hand—"thing for you in grad school."

His eyes grew wide. "I certainly did not know about any *thing* in grad school. I thought you despised me."

That was later, when he didn't respond to any of her friendly overtures, she wanted to say. When she thought he was purposely picking on her in class, which she now knew not to be true. She was embarrassed to let on how much she'd built up a history and an animosity that might not have actually existed. "No. I may have felt many things, but I did not despise you." She turned and kept on climbing, then headed for the kitchen.

"Wait a second. I want to talk about this."

Meg took the teapot from where he'd left it on the range and filled it with water, just for something to do. "There's nothing to talk about. It was ages ago. We're ..."

"We're what?"

"Rivals." She didn't know what she'd been about to say, but this word explained the situation as well as anything. They were rivals, and there was too much water under the bridge and too many years to roll back time to where they might have been friends.

"We don't have to be rivals, you know."

She lit the burner under the teapot with a match and then turned to face him, an eyebrow raised. "Is this where you suggest that we join forces and design this house together?"

He laughed and it turned into a snort. "Hardly. Not even if we were at the same firm. I still want this job and so do you. But just because we're in competition for the same job doesn't mean there have to be bad feelings between us."

"There are no bad feelings between us. At least not on my side." Maybe earlier, but now Meg realized that it was true. Her fury and bitterness had begun to evaporate the moment he revealed the truth about the internship. After he apologized. She still thought it had been a crummy thing to do, letting her potential boss blame her for something for which they'd both been responsible, but it hadn't really affected her. She'd still gotten a decent recommendation from Klein, she'd added some work to her portfolio, and if she really hadn't had a chance at the job, it made no difference. She just wished he had communicated that a lot earlier. It would have saved her from wasting all the energy disliking him.

Which, now that she thought about it, was really more of her problem than his. She'd conflated his unfriendliness in school into a concerted campaign to make her life miserable. It seemed that she was as much a conspirator in her own unhappiness as he was. "I do have a question for you, though."

"Anything."

"Why were you so dismissive of me the first semester during our design seminar?"

Declan settled onto a chair at the island. "I didn't know I was, to be honest."

"How is that possible?"

"I was preoccupied. There was something messed up with my financial aid, and I didn't know if I was going to be able to stay in school. My dad certainly wasn't going to pay for it—he's all about using his name to get me ahead, as long as it doesn't involve his money—and I was already working part-time to pay for my housing."

"I had no idea."

"How would you? I didn't tell anyone. In the end, I managed to find a grant to make up the shortfall and all was well. But by that time, apparently I had pissed you off." He threw her a rueful smile. "I missed my window."

Meg just gaped at him. She was forming some sort of meaningful response to that statement when the teapot's quiet purr escalated into a full-fledged whistle. She whipped around and turned off the burner before looking for cups. Declan beat her to it and pulled out two mugs and a selection of teas.

"Maybe we should go into town and replenish all the things that we've swiped from Mrs. Gratz's cupboards," Meg said wryly.

He looked at her. "You know, that's actually not a bad idea. The road is plowed, we have my car …" He raised his eyebrows. "How do you feel about a field trip?"

It was a Hail Mary, that was for sure. But something had shifted between them in the last few hours, and Declan wasn't about to lose his chance.

The fact was, he'd been interested in Meg for much longer than she knew, but the ever-present contempt she'd radiated had always stayed his hand. He was confident, but even his ego was not that suicidal. He'd never in a million years make a move when he thought she would reject him faster than a knife fight in a phone booth.

He grinned at the metaphor. Seemed his four years in Alabama really had left their mark.

But Meg still seemed doubtful about his suggestion. "I don't know. I really think I should stay here in case roadside assistance calls."

"It sounds like you'll be lucky to get a call from them by the time it's dark." Declan pulled up a listing on the map on his cell phone and showed it to her. "Look. There's a market about twenty minutes from here, thirty at the most considering road conditions. Even if we mess around in the store, we'll be back in an hour and a half." He fixed her with a significant look. "And I can do much better than dried pasta and jarred chilis for dinner if we go."

Apparently, a man's heart wasn't the only kind unlocked by food, because she looked sorely tempted by the offer. "I don't know …"

"I bet they have ice cream …"

She narrowed her eyes. "Who told you?"

"Lucky guess," Declan said with a grin. "You in?"

After a moment's hesitation, she nodded. "You have to let me pay my fair share though."

"Wait, you're not paying? This whole thing is off then."

Meg gave him a playful shove, and he scooted away, laughing. The fact that she would even voluntarily make contact with him was a good sign.

They exited through the garage again so they could grab their boots and trudged uphill through the deep snow to the main level where he was parked. He made a mental note to look at the current configuration of the driveway on this side of the house—he couldn't completely ignore the reason for this trip—as he followed Meg up the hill, ready to catch her if she slipped. It was much safer to think of architecture than the fantastic view he had of her jeans-clad bum.

It took him a minute to shove enough snow off the car to get into the trunk and grab his snow brush, and another five minutes to completely clear the hood, roof, and windows. By the time they settled into the car, Meg was shivering. The car started with a shudder, the engine protesting against the cold oil creeping through its cylinders, and he reached over to flick on the seat heaters.

"You know I really thought the whole cold weather package thing was a gimmick until I moved to Colorado," Declan said wryly. "Makes me laugh to think that when I lived in Alabama, we used to pull out our sweaters as soon as it hit sixty-five degrees."

"To be fair, Auburn is in Alabama, not Colorado. It always feels colder in the humidity."

He cocked his head at her, studying her for a second before he put his car into gear and slowly backed down the drive. "I don't remember telling you I went to Auburn."

She threw him an apologetic smile. "I web-stalked you, remember?"

"Right. Hoping to catch me up in a compromising design position."

"Exactly. Out of curiosity, how *did* you end up in Alabama?"

"Tennis scholarship."

Her jaw dropped. "Tennis scholarship?"

"Yep. My boarding school was known for its sports programs, particularly tennis. Which was, of course, why my father sent me there in the first place. Wanted me to 'make my own way' and all that. Auburn came scouting—along with some other schools—and offered me a scholarship. The rest is history."

"Wow. I always wondered why you didn't go to Oxford or Cambridge or the London School of Economics."

He laughed. "I didn't have the A-levels for Oxbridge, and LSE doesn't have an undergraduate architecture program." He shrugged. "Besides, it was a way to get out from under my father's thumb. And I really did love tennis. America is the best place to play."

"So you must have been good."

"Division 1 champs two years running."

Meg seemed impressed, which hadn't been his intention, but he didn't feel sorry about it. "Do you still play?" she asked.

"Not really. No time." In that way, Klein & Company hadn't been his dream job after all. He'd never imagined that he'd have to give up everything else he enjoyed for work.

Meg fell silent for a few minutes, and he didn't race to fill the space. This time it was a comfortable silence, one he was content to enjoy. But then she threw him a curious look. "I know we aren't supposed to be talking about it, but what *do* you have in mind for this renovation?"

"Looking for ideas, are you?" He waggled his eyebrows so she knew he was kidding.

"Even if I was, I don't think I'd find them here. No offense."

"None taken. I actually caught a glimpse of your sketches when I picked up your notebook. You don't need my help."

"You looked?"

"Not intentionally. It was kind of hard to not see it."

"Let me guess. It's about the exact opposite of your approach."

Declan chuckled. "Pretty much. It's good, though. It's just going to come down to what she's looking for. And to be honest, she's given very little guidance in the design brief other than to make it 'significant' in the area, whatever that means. I think we're just going to have to bring our A-games and hope."

He could feel her eyes on him as he drove, thought she might be smiling. "Our own little battle of the styles."

"Something like that. But in answer to your question, I'm not really sure what I have in mind. I just know that the biggest problem right now is that the house lacks a cohesive identity. And before you say it, it's not because of the bad remodel in the '80s."

"So you agree it was a bad remodel! I thought you were going for solidarity with your firm or something."

"Seems to me the house is like a kid who wants to fit into the cool crowd and cuts his hair and chooses his clothes to make other people like him without any regard to who he actually is." He glanced at Meg and found she was grinning at him. "What?"

"Really? Anthropomorphizing houses? A house is a vessel for living. It becomes what you put into it. Nothing more, nothing less."

He looked at her curiously. "You seriously don't think houses have a personality? What about your childhood home?"

"I don't have a childhood home."

Now this was interesting. "Really? Why not?"

They were at the turnoff onto the county road, so he took the opportunity to pause and look at her. She was staring out the window as if she didn't want to meet his eyes. "We moved around a lot. I never lived anywhere more than two years until I was fourteen. I got to finish high school in the same place, but that was it."

"Wow. No kidding. Military?"

Meg shook her head. "No. My dad worked for a network security firm that set up computer systems for big companies. So he would get transferred to a regional office, say in Japan, and then he would work all over Asia for two years. And then we'd move again."

"That must have been hard." He thought he'd had it rough, but all told, he'd only lived in four places from birth to college. "Where all did you live?"

Meg ticked off the places on her fingers. "Osaka, Sydney, Prague, Berlin, and London. Oh, and of course, Colorado Springs. That's where I went to high school."

"Wow. When were you in London?"

"Moved there when I was ten. Left just before I turned twelve."

Declan did the quick calculations. "So for two years, we were only a hundred forty miles away from each other and we never knew."

She threw him another little smile. "A hundred forty miles is not exactly next door."

"When you consider that you're from America and I'm from Ireland, and we ended up within driving distance at the same time, that's pretty close. Besides, I spent summers in London. Where did you live?"

"Kensington."

Declan grinned. "Mayfair. We were literally three miles from each other. Can you imagine? We might have even passed on the street and never known it."

He finally accelerated onto the country road, his wheels slipping a little on the ice before he got the car back under control. When he looked back at her, she was studying him.

"You're a romantic," she said.

"You say that like it's a bad thing."

"It's not. It's just … not what I expected."

"Because you are distinctly not a romantic, and since we had similar childhoods, you think we should be completely alike?"

"No, because I always thought you were a cold-hearted, ambitious jerk, and come to find out that's just me."

Declan choked on a laugh. "I'll give you ambitious, but you are not cold-hearted."

"How do you know?"

How did he know? Because when she talked about her upbringing, there was a hint of sadness in it, despite how hard she tried to hide it. He was getting the feeling that a lot of what he saw on the surface of Meg Anderson was a mask meant to protect her. The fact that he'd never even known she fancied him showed how well she hid her feelings. "Tell me one thing you collect."

"What makes you think I collect anything?"

"Everyone collects something, even if they're not conscious of it. Ticket stubs, photos, cooking equipment."

She said nothing, which is how he knew he had her.

"Come on, tell me."

She sighed. "I collect coffee table books."

"Coffee table books?" Snow was beginning to fall again, melting on the warming window, so he flipped on the windshield wipers. "Like, architecture books?"

"Not quite."

"Come on, tell me. Is it something embarrassing? Do you collect every pictorial on china dolls or something?"

"No." She laughed. "Okay, you know all those really nice, hardbound books you see in museum gift shops? The ones that show the exhibits and some information on the building and all that?"

"Sure."

"I collect those."

"That isn't embarrassing at all. How many do you have?"

"Like … four hundred?"

"*Four hundred?*" His jaw dropped. "How many museums did you go to?"

"Four hundred," she said matter of factly. "Give or take. I think it's actually like four hundred eight at last count."

"Wait, you still collect them?"

"Oh yes. The first three hundred or so were from my childhood. My mom and I used to spend our weekends going through all the museums in a city … and then in the surrounding cities … And really, once you've collected three hundred books, it seems silly to stop just because you don't like them."

He blinked. "Wait. You collect coffee table books and you don't even like them?"

"Affirmative. My mom started buying them for me."

"And you've kept on, simply because you already had three hundred … which you didn't like."

"Yes."

He took his eyes off the road long enough to look at her. "That's pathological. Why not just stop?"

She shrugged. "Dunno. I've never cracked any of them open, but when I look at them all lined up on the shelf, it's like a chronology of my childhood. I think, 'Reina Sophia, that was the time I lost a molar and almost swallowed it. Osaka Science Museum, that was the weekend that my dad told us he was being relocated from Japan to Australia.'"

"So they're big expensive postcards."

"Pretty much." Meg sighed. "I guess it is kind of pathological."

"No," he said slowly. "It's *sentimental*." He took another moment to stare hard at her. "It's—dare I say it—romantic."

Now she was grinning. "You're projecting."

"I'm completely open about my sentimentality, but then again, I'm not the one with four hundred exhibit books on her shelves at home. Please tell me they're displayed in your living room or something."

"In my library actually."

"In your … You have a library?"

"Yeah, my house was built at the turn of the last century. Everyone had a library."

Up until this point, he'd just been teasing, trying to get her to open up a little. And despite the fact she still managed to hide behind that no-nonsense exterior, she'd told him something he'd bet she didn't volunteer to anyone. "You have a historic home in Denver?"

"I bought it as an investment. It's a 1908 Victorian in Capitol Hill. I intended to renovate it, but I haven't had the time to get to it. The kitchen and bathrooms are truly awful, but the rest of it is pretty close to the original, just needs to be stripped back and polished up."

He shook his head in amazement. "You realize that we live right next to each other, right? I live in Cheesman Park."

"Let me guess, historic home as well?"

He grinned at the reversal. "High-rise condo conversion. Penthouse, of course."

She laughed. "Of course."

"But it's a rental. Ultra modern. My neighbor owns half of the top floor, rents out the other units."

"It surprises me that you haven't bought anything here yet. I mean, the time to buy was five years ago or longer, but still …"

"I don't know. I keep thinking if I bought something now, I'd be basing it on my current lifestyle and then I would be stuck with it." The words spilled out before he considered them, and he felt the sudden sickening sensation of having revealed too much to the wrong person. Given that he had the job—the life—that Meg wanted, to even give a hint of dissatisfaction would be a slap in the face. But now that he'd said it, the truth of the matter hit him square in the chest.

He didn't particularly like his life.

He liked parts of it, of course. His job, in the broadest sense of the word—he liked designing buildings and working with contractors to see them come to life. He liked the intellectual challenge of jobs like the Gratz project—acting as an archaeologist, sifting through previous design choices, finding a way forward that stayed true to the original while giving it a cohesive identity. But he didn't like the quiet echo of his empty condo when he came home at night, which was part of the reason he spent so much time in the office. He didn't like taking out random women that he met through friends or at parties or bars just because it passed the time. He didn't like the feeling that somehow, some way, he had stepped into someone else's life and he didn't know how to get out of it.

"Declan?" Meg reached over and put her hand on his arm.

Her touch snapped him out of it, and he felt suddenly exposed. "You know, I always think that maybe one day I'm going to wake up and decide that I've had enough of Denver and move back to Dublin. Or London. Or, I don't know, you mentioned Prague, I've always wanted to go there."

"It's a nice city," she said mildly, but she was just mollifying him, he thought, playing along with his sudden change in mood.

It was kinder than he'd expected of her, but now that he'd spent a little time with her, now that he could picture her standing in a Victorian library with four hundred souvenir coffee table books she'd never opened, he realized he'd had her all wrong all this time.

And as much as he thought he'd liked the old Meg, he liked the new one even better.

five

SHE'D ACTUALLY TOLD HIM ABOUT HER BOOKS.

It wasn't like it was a secret, exactly, it was just … private. Her books were her way of giving her transient childhood some substance, when so much of it had felt ephemeral, unstable.

And in return, he'd given her a glimpse inside his current reality, the suggestion that even though he'd gotten everything he'd worked for, things weren't quite as perfect as they seemed.

Before she could find her footing again with this new transparency between them, he put on his turn signal and made a left turn off the county road into a parking lot that sported two gas pumps at an island and a small timber building proclaiming the name in a font more suited to a backwoods summer camp: *Mountain Market.* Huge mounds of snow bordered each edge of the parking lot, the rest of the asphalt scraped clean except for the bare dusting of snow that had just begun falling again.

"How did you even know this was here?"

"I worked up here a while back. House in Beaver Creek." He glanced at her with a mischievous smile. "But you wouldn't know that, because I wasn't the primary, so it wasn't in my portfolio."

"Ha, very funny," she said, but she felt her cheeks burn all the same. Maybe she shouldn't have confessed that she'd been keeping tabs on his work; he was never going to let her live it down now. "Are you sure this place is going to have what we need? It looks more like a convenience store."

"Just wait. You're going to be surprised."

She was indeed surprised. While the outside looked like a typical mini-mart, the inside looked like a shrunken Whole Foods Market, with a small section of fresh produce and meat on the right side, and several aisles of high-end groceries on the left. She followed Declan as he grabbed a black plastic wheelie cart from by the door and trailed it behind them as they perused the store's offerings.

"Most expensive real estate per square foot in the Rockies up here. They're going to have a decent high-end market without having to drive to Vail or Beaver Creek." He looked over the meat in the case. "What do you feel like having for dinner?"

Meg shrugged. "Chef's choice."

"Really? I thought you were going to think up a *Chopped* challenge for me. Incorporate Skittles into a steak dish or something."

"I can if you want to. But I really want a good meal if we're going to be stuck here again."

Declan grinned at her. "Oh ye of little faith. I thought about becoming a chef, did you know that?"

"No. Really?"

He nodded. "I cooked at a local chain restaurant in college." He saw the question in her eyes and shrugged. "Influence, not money, remember? Anyway, I liked it, thought I might stick with it. But it turns out that the son of Colum McKenzie was not going to be a line cook."

"So you went into architecture to make your dad happy?"

He shrugged. "Not really. It was more that I was going to go into cooking to make him mad. He won, and in the end, it wasn't the worst thing."

"High praise for the discipline to which you've dedicated your life."

He drilled her with a look. "You can't tell me you go into work every single day, thrilled to be there."

Meg thought. There were days when she was irritated at her coworkers or frustrated by her lack of upward momentum, but when it came to the actual work … "If it weren't for office politics, it would be like Disneyland. I truly love what I do."

He nodded thoughtfully. "If you take out the politics, most people would love what they did. Except maybe garbage collectors, and I imagine there are probably politics in the sanitation department too."

"Probably." Meg leaned over the case. "Do I have a price limit on my dinner selection?"

"You're buying, remember?"

Meg grinned. "Then I want lobster."

"No. We're landlocked. You don't buy lobster in a mountain store in a landlocked state. Especially not during a snowstorm."

Okay, he had a point there. "Those porterhouse steaks look good."

"You're an expensive date, do you know that?"

"I thought I was buying." She crossed her arms. "I was just trying to go easy on you. It's not hard to impress with expensive meat. But if you really want a challenge, here's one. Twenty-dollar limit, not counting the stuff we have to replace in the pantry."

His eyes glinted. "Fine. You'll be sorry you doubted me." He looked around for some help and caught the eye of someone working in the deli toward the back. "Excuse me, can you help me with the meat?"

Twenty minutes later, he had a handful of ingredients in his basket, that, to Meg's eye, didn't have anything in common with each other. Other than the farfalle, which indicated it was going to be a pasta dish, she really didn't know what he was going to come up with. She tracked down the things that they'd used from the pantry, surprised they actually had Calabrian chilis in a jar, then added two pints of ice cream, some coffee, and a carton of half-and-half.

"You know we don't have a freezer, right?" Declan said.

Meg grinned and waved a hand toward the outside. "The world is our freezer."

"Good point." He moved toward the checkout counter, which did look suspiciously like a convenience store with a scale, and began piling his things up on the counter. "Can you ring these up first?"

When the man behind the counter had finished, the total was $19.72. Declan whistled. "Just under the wire. What do I win?"

"Bragging rights?"

"Not what I was thinking," he murmured, and for reasons she could only guess at, she blushed yet again.

"You get dinner, I get the rest," she said, deflecting, and he didn't argue.

Three minutes later, they were each carrying a plastic bag out of the store, back to Declan's BMW, which sported a fluffy layer of snow on its windshield again. She paused and stared at the misty sky, snowflakes dotting her face. "Think we're going to get more?"

"Not according to the news, but you saw how accurate they were last time."

They climbed back into the car, and Meg settled into the seat, feeling suddenly drowsy. Between the awkward sleeping arrangements, the snowshoeing, and the constant tug at her emotions, she was feeling worn out, like a rubber band stretched too far and too often. She leaned back against the leather headrest and her eyelids sank downwards.

When she opened her eyes again, she was alone in the car, the windshield completely covered with snow. She jerked straight up and checked her phone. By her estimation, they should have gotten home forty minutes ago. Had he just left her here? She flicked on the wipers to clear the windshield and realized the car was parked in the driveway of the Gratz home.

And then she noticed the car was still running with the heater and seat warmer on, and the blanket from the den had been draped over her. Clearly it had been Declan. But why?

She leaned over to push the ignition button and found Declan's keys sitting in the console. She gathered her things and the blanket and climbed out, then feeling foolish, locked the doors behind her. After all, who was going to come and break in?

When she opened the front door, a delicious smell was already drifting from the kitchen. She followed her nose to where Declan was cooking by the light of a camping lantern. She must have made a sound, because he turned in surprise, which then melted into pleasure. "Evening, Sleeping Beauty. Have a good nap?"

"Why didn't you wake me?"

"You looked so peaceful, I didn't have the heart. You tossed and turned so much last night, I figured you needed the sleep."

"How do you know I tossed and turned?"

He looked slightly abashed. "I didn't sleep. I was up working."

So that explained why he was so cavalier about work time today. He'd already gotten a head start on the project. For a second, she thought that had been his plan all along, then had to abandon that idea. Just because her knee-jerk reaction was to distrust him didn't mean it was right. It seemed like she owned her own fair share of the blame for their enmity.

Instead, she sidled up beside him and peered into the pan. "What are we having?"

He shook his head. "No questions. Just remember that you were the one who set a twenty-dollar limit on this dinner. You could have had steak, but no, we're having pasta again."

"But I like pasta."

"Good, because it's too late now." He waved a spatula at the pot of boiling water. "Now shoo. You can light the fire in the den before it gets dark again if you like."

She'd been banished, but the sparkle in his eye softened his dismissal enough that she didn't feel bad about it. She instead returned to the den, which had equalized its temperature with the rest of the frigid house, and started a fire in the hearth. Maybe she could get a little work done before dinner.

But instead, her eyes were drawn to his computer, open with a screensaver set to a retro string-tangle animation. She knew she shouldn't, but after his admission that he'd peeked at her own drawings, surely it was only fair that she get a look?

Glancing back at the closed door, she walked over to the computer and tapped the track pad, almost like it was an accident. The screen lit up right away, didn't even ask for a password. It was open to the CAD program pretty much everyone except she used for concept sketches, a half-finished drawing on the screen.

It was … not what she expected from him. She'd thought he'd go with English hunting lodge or something equally heavy and storied, but the drawing instead was for a straight-up mountain rustic retreat, a mix of stacked stone and wood. Plenty of large windows opened up the house to the view. For a split second, she was tempted to say he'd incorporated some of her ideas, but no … this was more a matter of them having similar solutions to the design brief's directives, filtered through their own personal style. Of course you were going to do a lot of windows with a view like that. Any architect who didn't frame the sights would be out of a job before they could blink.

She'd been hoping for something old-fashioned, something that would reassure her she was going to win this bid, but she had to reluctantly admit that his concept was as good as hers. Different, of course, but good.

Like she'd said in the car, this really was going to be a battle of styles and of whose vision was the clearest.

A sharp sound from the kitchen made her start, and she quickly walked away from the computer, hoping it would switch back to screen saver before Declan came in. He probably wouldn't be mad at her for looking, but the last thing she wanted was for him to think she was so competitive she would steal his work.

Work, no. But ideas? His drawing had reminded her of something she'd overlooked, a small change she wanted to make to her facade … She grabbed her sketchbook, a pencil, and an eraser and started to modify her original vision.

She was so engrossed in her sketch that she didn't notice the door open or Declan move through it until he knelt down before her with a plate of pasta. "Dinner is served. I thought we might have a floor picnic." He handed her silverware wrapped in a paper napkin. "I think the storm is clearing out, but it's getting colder. The kitchen is freezing."

She accepted the flatware and the plate and settled cross-legged on the rug beside the fire. "So, twenty-dollar pasta. What's in this?"

Declan mirrored her position, facing her, and took a bite. "Farfalle with chicken, bacon, and sun-dried tomatoes in a Parmesan cream sauce."

Meg took a bite, the flavors of salty and tart and creamy melding on her tongue. "This is delicious." She took another bite. "But I feel like I've had it before. It's not pasta primavera because there are no vegetables. What am I thinking of?"

Declan grinned. "I ripped it off from a certain restaurant known for their desserts."

Meg's eyes widened and she covered her mouth as she laughed. "I knew it! I love that dish. I order it almost every time I go."

"Yeah, me too." Their eyes met and the warmth in the space was not entirely due to the flickering fire a foot to their left. "It's nice to cook for someone. You know?"

"Yeah, I do know." Then she smiled. "Actually, I don't know because I can't cook. But I like being cooked *for*." Her eyes never left his, communicating something that did not yet have words.

But whatever he might be seeing there, she was not letting a delicious plate of pasta go to waste, so she turned back to her food and savored every last bite of it. Declan ate more slowly, watching her with a small smile on his face, but she didn't feel self-conscious. The pleasure practically poured off him over her enjoyment, and who was she to try to ruin his triumph? She'd bet him he couldn't pull off a twenty-dollar meal, and he'd proven her wrong.

He'd proven her wrong about a lot of things in the past twenty-four hours. For once, she was happy to concede the point.

"Declan, I'm sorry." She reached out and touched his knee, suddenly seized by the need to make things right. Yes, he'd made a mistake with how he'd handled their internship, but she hadn't made it easy on him. She'd thought he'd rebuffed her overtures of friendship and she'd been cold, competitive, and occasionally hostile toward him. Why wouldn't he have worked things to his own advantage? If she were being honest with herself, given the state of their acquaintance, she probably would have done the same thing.

"No, I'm sorry. Whatever happened between us, I take full responsibility." Declan placed his hand over hers, still on his knee, and gripped it firmly. "The fact is, given the option between making my father mad and upsetting you … you were the easier choice. But that doesn't make it right, and it certainly doesn't make me proud." He sent her a crooked smile. "At very least, I should have talked to you about it afterward. I should have … done a lot of things."

Her gaze drifted down to their linked fingers. The fact she was holding hands with her sworn enemy should seem strange, but she could only focus on the warmth of his skin and the way his touch sent a delicious tingle through her entire body. She'd always been acutely attuned to his presence, whether it was the way he brushed his arm against hers while they sat side by side at a drafting table or the faint drift of familiar cologne that said he'd been in a room just moments before her. She'd had more than one fantasy about what might happen if they got locked in a darkened classroom together.

It seemed that now she'd gotten her wish.

It felt inevitable then, when he leaned forward to brush the backs of his fingers against her cheek, tentatively, as if asking a question. Her eyes drifted closed, warmth flooding her body as his fingertips grazed her lips, making her draw in a breath. When he finally pulled back and dropped his hand to his lap, she was achingly aware of his warm presence just inches away, even though he wasn't touching her.

Slowly, she opened her eyes and found herself looking into his clear gray ones. "I don't know if this is a good idea." The protest sounded weak, even to her ears.

His gaze flickered to her mouth and then back to her eyes. "You're probably right. We're bitter rivals, after all."

"I think it's safe to say we've called a truce," she whispered. "Maybe … maybe it's time to begin again?"

He smiled slightly. "In that case, I can do what I've thought about since the day we met." His eyes never left her face as he slid one hand behind her neck, tangling through her hair, and tugged her just a fraction of an inch closer. Giving her one last chance to pull away.

She moved to meet him, her heart beating so hard in her chest she thought it might burst. And when his lips finally met hers, not tentative and gentle as she'd expected, but firm and assured, a shudder rippled through her entire body, an acknowledgment that this was exactly what she wanted. *He* was exactly what she wanted. And for the first time, there was no good reason to deny it.

She met the hot demands of his mouth with equal fervor, her fingertips digging in his hair, feeling his sharp intake of breath when she caught his lower lip between her teeth. For a bare second, he pulled back, a flash of amusement in his eyes at her boldness, and then they were kissing again. But the way his mouth devoured hers, the skim of his hands over her body, just reinforced that there was still too much space between them. She rose on her knees to straddle him, his hands gripping her hips, their bodies now pressed so close that she could feel the heat coming off his skin, the frantic thump of his heart.

She'd somehow known this was what it would be like to kiss him. Knew that the moment his lips were on hers, she would lose all rational thought. Maybe that was why she'd resisted so much. Maybe that's why she'd been determined to cast them as rivals, because then at least, she had some control.

Right now, her control was slipping away as quickly and surely as her anger had.

She didn't protest, wouldn't have been able to find the words anyway, when he shifted her gently back onto the floor, his mouth leaving hers to trail down her neck, follow the line of her collarbone, drift ever downward to the neckline of her sweater. Just when she thought her heart might burst from the anticipation, the wanting, his lips were on hers again, teasing, tempting.

From somewhere beyond them, a buzz blending with the faint tinkling of wind chimes penetrated her desire-fogged brain, but she couldn't resolve them into logical thought. Wind chimes? Inside?

Declan lifted his head, his breath coming just as heavily as hers, but he wore a regretful smile. "Saved by the bell … or the wind chimes as it were?"

"What?"

He jerked his head toward the sofa. "Your phone."

"Shoot, that's the tow truck." She scrambled out from under him and dove for the phone before it stopped ringing. "Hello?" Her voice was raspy, sounding like she'd been … well, doing exactly what she had been doing. She winced and cleared her throat before trying again.

"Ms. Anderson?"

"Yes?"

"This is Clint from Aventura Towing. A driver is going to be coming your way in about forty-five minutes. Can I just verify your make, model, and license plate?"

She fumbled through the conversation, giving him the information he needed, though she had to repeat the license plate number three times before she got it right. The whole time, she pointedly ignored Declan's satisfied grin. He knew he was the reason she'd temporarily lost her grasp on the English language, and he'd done it without a single item of clothing coming off.

Finally, she hung up with the towing company and looked back to Declan, who was still wearing that grin. "I don't suppose you want to pick up where we left off?" She shot him a reproving look and he laughed. "You're right. I seem to lose all my good sense when it comes to you."

Ditto, she thought, but she was still feeling shaky enough to doubt her judgment, so she took a moment to straighten her sweater and smooth back her hair. "The tow truck is going to be here in forty-five minutes. I suppose that means we should start cleaning up?" She pushed herself to her feet and started to collect her personal items from where they littered the sofa and side table.

"Hey, wait." Declan caught her around the waist and turned her to face him, then dropped a slow, lingering kiss on her lips. "Just because you make me lose my good sense doesn't mean I regret kissing you." He pressed his lips to hers again, and she felt herself melting as surely as a candle in a flame. "You can't deny there's something between us."

"There's chemistry, yes …"

"More than that." Now he held her gaze, serious, intense. "I don't want to walk out of here and go straight back to how things were before."

"I'm not sure we could if we wanted to," she said ruefully.

"How about we clean this place up, I follow you back to Denver, and—"

Her eyebrows lifted.

"—you let me take you out on a proper date tomorrow night."

She didn't know why this surprised her, but it did. For what might have been the thousandth time, she'd underestimated him. "You want to date me?"

"Yes, Meg Anderson, I want to date you. I mean, if I'm being honest, I want to do a lot more than that, but let's start with the date, shall we?"

His tone and his expression were completely sincere, composed. How he'd managed to get a hold of himself so quickly when her hands were still trembling, she didn't know. But he was waiting for her response, so she gave a single nod. "Yes. Dinner would be nice."

"Good. I'll pick you up at seven." He bent to brush her lips one more time and it was all she could do not to sigh. Seven years of pent-up anger, resentment, and frustration turned out to be merely the tinder to his match; it had only taken the lightest touch to go up in flames.

And despite the fact that he had burned down every last resistance she had against him, she couldn't find it in herself to object.

One part of Declan was sorry they'd been interrupted by the phone call from the tow truck driver, but the rest of him had to admit it had been a timely intervention. Neither of them had been thinking straight, acting instead on instinct and long-repressed attraction. But a mere day ago, Meg had pretty much hated his guts. Moving too quickly was undoubtedly the easiest way to ruin the new rapport they'd established. Especially since they had no idea what the future might bring.

Declan still wanted this job, for example. Just because now that he'd kissed Meg, he wanted to do nothing more than to pull her into his arms at every turn didn't mean that they weren't still competing for the same contract, one that would have serious repercussions for the career of the winning architect. And while he was pretty sure he'd be able to move on and date Meg even if she was the one who had won the contract, he wasn't sure he could say the same for her.

They managed to get the house straightened up in record time—dishes and pots washed and returned to their cupboards, bathrooms wiped down, blankets, tools and snowshoes put back where they belonged. When they exited the front door and Meg replaced the key in the lock box, he felt suddenly disappointed that they were leaving. The past day and a half had been a respite from real life, a cocoon in which the normal pressures of their world didn't intrude, regardless of their original reason for being there.

He wondered if this ... *thing* ... between him and Meg would survive the transition.

But he didn't have much time to dwell on it, because the tow truck was already waiting on the road when he and Meg arrived there in Declan's car. She jumped out to talk to the driver, who looked dubious about the snowdrift until Declan volunteered to help dig it out. Between the two men, they managed to clear a path to the back of the Jeep. Then he and Meg moved back to watch the tow truck driver attach a hook and winch Meg's vehicle back out onto the road in a shower of snow. Declan winced at the creak of metal when it finally came to rest on flat ground and circled around the front to see the damage.

"It's ... not bad," he said finally.

Meg stared at the Jeep with a helpless look on her face. "I mean, it's only a bumper. Is it drivable?"

Declan knelt in the snow to peer underneath the car. "I think so. It's crushed, but nothing is going to hit the wheel at least. We're going to have to take it slow on the way home anyway, so I think it will be okay."

He only allowed himself a second of disappointment that the car wouldn't be traveling home by tow truck, leaving Meg to ride with him, but that was probably a good thing. She was carefully not looking at him, at least not *looking* looking, a sure sign she was already regretting their interlude at the house. He'd give anything to be back there now, kissing on the rug by the fire, instead of out in the cold, separated, with far too much time to think about practicalities.

Though why there should be anything to think about, he didn't know. The spark between them had practically burned the house down around them. They were no longer enemies, now that they'd sorted out their miscommunications and Declan had apologized for the way she'd left Klein & Company. They didn't work for the same company, so there were no interoffice conflicts to worry about, and there were lots of architects who were married to others from different firms. Though to be fair, most of them had started out in the same firm and left because they were rising through the ranks at unequal rates.

There was no good reason for them not to explore whether or not they had a future together.

Unless, of course, he'd misread her completely. Just because she was attracted to him didn't mean she actually liked him. How many dates had he been on that proved that very point?

And now he was really glad they hadn't gotten any further before the phone rang, because he was suddenly reminded that *he* was the sentimental one between the two of them.

Once Meg had confirmed that the car would start and drive without grinding any essential components together, she signed off on the towing company paperwork and then stopped between her Jeep and his BMW, illuminated by her vehicle's headlights. "So, this is it."

"You sound like we're on the surface of the moon," Declan said wryly. "I'll follow you home to make sure you don't break down. And then I'll see you tomorrow."

She smiled, but she didn't make any move toward him. "Deal."

Fortunately, Declan didn't have much time to dwell on how they'd left things, because despite Vail Pass being open and the roads recently plowed, the drive was still treacherous all the way down I-70 into Denver. He followed the white Jeep at a safe distance, watching for any sign that her steering or drivetrain components had been damaged, but the SUV pushed on, throwing up chunks of snow and ice at regular intervals, the brake lights flashing in the dark whenever she started going too fast.

Apparently, she drove the way she entered relationships … too hard on the gas, then backing off sharply. The thought made him huff out a laugh. But then it made him consider how she'd responded to his kiss with a passion he hadn't known she possessed, matching him for intensity and upping the ante. He shouldn't be surprised. Anyone who could hold a fierce grudge like she had felt things far more deeply than she let on to the outside world.

When they finally pulled up in front of her house three hours later, nearly double the time it would ordinarily take them, his eyes felt gritty from the glare of oncoming headlights, and his shoulders ached from keeping constant alertness to road conditions. He parked at the curb behind Meg's Jeep and then looked up at the house. Sure enough, it was a traditional Victorian, and in just as rough condition as she'd implied. The porch was sagging, the gate was rusted, and from what he could tell beyond the coating of snow, the brickwork could use repointing. It was, in short, a mess. And it made him instantly want to draft up drawings for how it could look with a little effort and TLC.

Meg exited her car and walked around to the cargo area, so he stepped out of his car and took her roller case before she could lift it. "Thanks," she said with a touch of surprise.

"My pleasure. Drive okay? Nothing feels strange? No weird noises?"

Meg shook her head. "Besides the bumper, you mean? I think it just needs an alignment. I'll take it in to my mechanic in the morning to be sure." She moved ahead of him to open the hip-height wrought iron gate, and he lifted the suitcase free of the snow piled on her sidewalk. The front porch light clicked on automatically.

After he deposited her suitcase on the front porch, he stepped back and studied her face, trying to read some hint of what she was thinking or feeling.

She cocked her head. "What?"

Oh, forget it. He was going to press his chance before she had time to overthink it. He closed the two feet between them, took her face in his hands, and kissed her again.

It took only moments for her to respond, wrapping her arms around him and returning the kiss with the same enthusiasm she'd shown back in the Gratz house. One taste of her, and he was forgetting every reason he was glad they'd been interrupted. Only when her back hit the front door with a thud and a rattle of glass did he come to his senses. He lifted his head and dropped his hands. "Sorry. I can't seem to help myself."

Meg licked her lips, looking mussed and appealing and a little dazed. "That makes two of us. See you tomorrow, Declan." She fished a key from her pocket, fitted it into the lock, and went into her house without a backward look at him. The door shut with a soft scrape, the message unmistakable.

"Good," he told himself as he moved down the stairs onto the snow-covered walkway. "Didn't need the temptation."

But that was as big a lie as any he'd told. Regardless of which side of the door Meg was on, she was nothing but a temptation.

six

DESPITE THE FACT THAT MEG WAS EXHAUSTED from the drive and from her restless night on the sofa, even a bath and her warmest pajamas couldn't settle her nerves enough to sleep. It wasn't just the lingering adrenaline from their interrupted encounter or the tension from the slippery drive home. It was the way Declan had looked at her when he left her on the porch. Like he couldn't believe his good fortune that they'd put their past behind them and embarked on a new ...

What? What was it exactly they'd done? They'd definitely made inroads to being friends. If friends made out on an antique Persian rug like the world was going to end, that was. The recollection put a smile on her face and a flush on her cheeks.

The man could kiss, she'd give him that much. That didn't surprise her at all. What surprised her was how much of a gentleman he turned out to be, acting as if he regretted pushing things too far more than he regretted getting interrupted in the first place.

Meg rolled over and pulled her down comforter more securely around her, forcing Declan out of her mind. He was the last thing that would lead to drifting off to sleep, when now the very thought of him had her pulse racing in anticipation for tomorrow night.

In the end, exhaustion won out, and Meg woke late the next morning to a clear blue sky, another inch of snow on the ground, and a text message from Declan.

Can't wait to see you tonight.

She smiled. Her face was liable to get stuck that way, as giddy as she felt at the prospect of a real date with him. But if she were going to take the evening off, that meant she had little time to waste on her design. Fortunately, she wasn't required to do more than exterior elevations and a floor plan for her proposal, but now that she'd glimpsed what Declan had in mind, she knew she was going to have to bring her very best work. If she lost this bid, it was going to be because Eleanor Gratz preferred his style of architecture, not because she'd been too preoccupied by the stirrings of new love to properly concentrate.

The word stopped her in her track: *love*. Was that what this was? Not in the real sense, of course. But in the potential sense. There was a difference between going into a date just hoping to have some fun versus thinking about the long term. Which did Declan think this was? For that matter, what did *she* think this was? She'd gone out with a few guys in the last several years, but it had all been very casual, and none of them had stuck around for more than a few months. That had been fine with her. Women were already underrepresented in her field, and she wasn't going to reinforce the stereotype of female architects being more devoted to family than they were to work. That made men a distraction she was all too willing to bypass.

But now, she thought, maybe she just hadn't met a man who was worth being distracted over.

"Not today, Meg," she told herself sternly. She pulled on a fuzzy cardigan over her pajamas, slipped her feet into wool socks, and padded across the cold hardwood floors, down the stairs to her kitchen. She puttered around making coffee, but as she braced herself against the counter to pick up a dropped coffee filter, one of the 1980s ceramic tiles broke off in her hand. She stared at the tile in bewilderment. She'd managed to ignore the state of the kitchen for the last two years, but if she were honest, she felt a little embarrassed by her neglect. She'd been paralyzed by the question of whether to restore or modernize, take down walls for the current ideal of open living spaces or retain the integrity of the original floor plan. And while she'd been waffling, it had begun to disintegrate around her.

Declan would have an idea of the best way to treat it. Maybe she'd ask him in and get his opinion on the right way to handle the remodel. After all, traditional styles were his forte, and while she was familiar with them, she didn't love them the same way he seemed to.

Then again, if she invited him in, they might never make it to the kitchen.

Meg pressed her hands to her quickly-warming cheeks. He was turning her into a lovestruck teenager with a perpetual flush and she wasn't even sorry. The last time she'd felt so buzzed on just the prospect of someone's nearness was …

… in grad school when she'd first met Declan, still thought there was the chance for them to be more than just classmates. Had she really spent a chunk of her adult life waiting on a guy she hated, whether she realized it or not?

But she didn't have time to dwell on what she might or might not have done subconsciously. She had exactly six hours to get some work done on this proposal before she had to start getting ready for her date with Declan. Which meant wrangling some focus out of her scattered thoughts, doing her best work, and proving once and for all that not only did she deserve the senior architect position, she deserved to be a woman in architecture, period.

It turned out she didn't need the pep talk. As she began transferring the details of her sketches to her software program, the ideas started flowing. The house itself wasn't bad; it had decent bones, and it had been sited properly to take advantage of the views as well as the heat from the sun during the winter. It was just like the heroine of one of those teen Pygmalion comedies, where the girl was already pretty, she was just hiding it behind terrible hair and wardrobe and big ugly glasses. Which was proof that Declan was already rubbing off on her. Now she was the one anthropomorphizing inanimate structures.

By the time she paused at one thirty to eat leftover Chinese food from the fridge, she'd put together renderings of all four elevations of the house and just had to fill in a little landscaping to make it feel finished. That little landscaping, of course, put her down a rabbit hole of small changes, and before she knew it, she was edging toward six o'clock without having made any move to change out of her thick socks and plaid pajama bottoms. She glanced at the clock, trying to judge realistically how long it would take her to get ready. She was looking forward to the date no less than she had earlier, but now that she'd hit her stride, she was loathe to walk away. She could at least get to work on the small changes she intended to make to the floor plan.

She opened her email inbox and sorted through the cascade of junk mail that had piled in since Declan had forwarded the email. She found it a couple of dozen lines down and double clicked on the attached file to download it. While she was waiting for it to save, she skimmed the message. It looked as if it had been forwarded to Declan from someone in the company. Her eyes widened when she saw the name on the top: Nina Klein. What was the owner doing getting involved in the details of a bid? Of course, Eleanor Gratz was a long time client of the firm. It made sense that she would have gone to the top first, even if she intended on having one of the junior architects work on the project.

And then she saw the words that were written below: *Here you go. Don't get too distracted by your little game in Vail. Get the information you need and then get back to work! I'm expecting your best on this one. I don't want any accusations of favoritism.*

Meg read and re-read the words, trying to understand what they meant. As much as she was tempted to read ill intent just because of her past experience with Nina and Declan, when she really parsed the message, it sounded like Nina was impatient with the fact that Declan had gone up to Vail when he already had the information he needed. She wasn't sure what the favoritism thing was about, but surely it had something to do with the fact that Declan's father had gotten him the job at the firm. Was it possible that someone other than Meg had taken exception to how he'd gotten it?

But that wasn't the end of the email. There were several back-and-forth conversations below. She scrolled all the way down to the end and started reading from the bottom up. The first one was just the original message from Mrs. Gratz, who seemed to be on a casual first name basis with Klein: *Nina, let's give your wonder boy a try on this one. So far my other bids have been sore disappointments. See what he can do with this.*

Then one from Nina to Declan: *Thoughts?*

Declan: *I'd love to take this on, but Craig is complaining that you show too much preference for me already. Better suggest she open it up to other architects so it's a fair bid.*

Nina: *Suggestions?*

Declan: *How about Meg Anderson? She's at NCO now and she'd jump on this, but Eleanor doesn't particularly like her work. She says she's always designing museums.*

Meg stared at the words, uncomprehending. Surely she was misunderstanding this. It couldn't mean what she thought it did. But she was feeling so many levels of betrayal and hurt that she couldn't even begin to unravel them. Forget the fact that Eleanor Gratz thought she was designing museums. That was fine. She'd heard it before from architects of Declan's ilk, who believed that post-modernism should only apply to public spaces. But if she was reading this right, Declan was the only reason she'd gotten invited to bid on this project in the first place.

Even worse, she'd been invited because she posed no threat to him.

The betrayal sliced deep, like a blade so sharp that it could kill you before the wound started to bleed. Everything Declan had said to her was a lie.

No, but that wasn't true either. He'd been completely honest, even as he didn't let on that she didn't have a chance in hell of winning this bid. He'd talked about what *he* liked about her work. He'd talked about how this would be a battle of styles. He just hadn't said that he already knew which way Eleanor would fall. He'd been one hundred percent honest while being one hundred percent devious.

It took a special kind of person to balance on that kind of razor's edge. It just wasn't special in a good way.

The biggest question was why he'd forwarded the email to her. She glanced at the time stamp, the one on Nina's email. Friday night. After ten. That meant at some point after she'd fallen asleep, he'd asked Nina to forward him the files. And then he'd immediately sent them to Meg when they were out for a walk. He probably hadn't scrolled all the way down on his phone to see the original email thread. There was no way he would have outed himself like this otherwise.

Meg sat back in her chair while her heart vacillated between anger and hurt. For a brief second, outrage flared, along with wild thoughts of retribution—stealing his ideas, doing a Declan McKenzie design better than Declan McKenzie, proving herself a contender for this job. But just as quickly as they came, they dissipated. She didn't want the job if it meant copying someone else's style, didn't even know if she could do it. It would be selling out in the highest order, a betrayal of all her professional ethics.

The thought of professional ethics made her laugh bitterly. Apparently, she was the only one that cared about the ethics of the situation. Even if Declan had been truthful, he hadn't exactly been ethical. One could even say he'd practically lured her to Vail under false pretenses and then taken advantage of her.

But even in her hurt, she couldn't go that far. Whatever had happened between her and Declan had everything to do with pent-up attraction and bad choices, not premeditation.

She sat there so long, turning the issue over in her mind, front and back and inside out, that she was caught off guard when the doorbell rang. She jerked straight up in her chair, her heart thrumming in her chest when she glimpsed the clock. Seven on the dot. Declan was here for their date. For a brief moment, she considered ignoring the doorbell and the knocks that would likely follow. Let him stand out in the cold, as bewildered as she felt now, wondering how she could have ditched him after that goodnight kiss on the porch.

But that would rob her of the pleasure of seeing his face when he found out she knew about his betrayal. She sprang out of her chair, marched across the room, and yanked the door open.

He was standing there in an actual suit, holding flowers, like an old-fashioned beau come to take his sweetheart for ice cream. He flashed her a wide smile and leaned in like he was going to kiss her hello. Then he took in her stony face and her pajamas and his expression shifted to one of concern.

"Are you sick? Do we need to reschedule?"

She crossed her arms and leaned against the door frame, saying nothing. His brow furrowed in confusion. "Did I … did I say something? Or do something?"

"Declan, how exactly did I get included on this bid?"

He froze, his eyes flicking around the porch for help before they landed on her face again. "Eleanor Gratz is a fan of your work, I image."

"Now I know that's a bold-faced lie. Do you know how I know it's a lie?"

If she hadn't been so angry, the shifts of expression on his face while he sorted through the possibilities might have amused her. At last it settled into understanding and he deflated. "The old email was attached to the file I forwarded, wasn't it?"

She gave a single, sharp nod.

"Then you know that I recommended you. No one else."

"I know that you picked the single person you could think of who wouldn't be a threat to you, who couldn't possibly beat you in this bid."

"That's not true. I had to say something to Nina. She would never agree to expand the bid if she thought I could lose it."

"Oh come off it, Declan," Meg snapped, losing her temper at last. "We both know you want this job, and once more, you're confident that your connections and your insider status will carry it off for you. But just like before, you can't stand for anyone to know the truth. So you make things up. Just like you made me take the heat for our mistake all those years ago, now you're using me as a decoy so no one in your office complains about how often you get the plum projects."

She studied him for a long moment. "You know, you're something else. It's one thing to be ambitious. Even cutthroat. I can respect that because it's honest. But you slink around, acting like you're the nice guy who's just misunderstood, who's afraid of disappointing everyone. If you had one honest bone in your body, you would own up to who you really are. But you won't do that, because it would take an iota of self-awareness, which you clearly don't have. But at least now *I* can own up to who you really are."

The whole time Meg was speaking, Declan seemed to sink a little bit more inside himself. Now he looked at her with resignation. "And what exactly is that?"

She looked him up and down, then straight in the eye. "My biggest mistake."

And she shut the door in his face.

Declan stared at the door for a long moment, hardly able to comprehend what had happened. He'd shown up, practically giddy over the change in their status, ready to show Meg a wonderful night out, and walked in to this.

The worst thing was, he knew he deserved it.

He should probably knock again, pound on the door until she had no choice but to open it, and explain in minute detail exactly what had happened. Once she heard there was a reasonable explanation for all of it, she'd still be mad, but at least she wouldn't think that he'd purposely betrayed her. Lied to her. Discounted her. But even as he lifted his hand to knock, he knew it was no good. There were too many of these incidents in their past. Any credibility he might have once had was now gone. He would just look like, once more, the guy who couldn't take responsibility for his own actions, the guy who would say anything not to have people mad at him.

The embarrassing thing was, it was all true.

Slowly, he set the flowers against the threshold of the door, though he knew that the cold would kill them almost immediately, and made his way back down the walkway. As he climbed into his car, he sorted through his options.

In a movie, this was where he'd plan a grand gesture. He'd do something stupid like steal her plans, submit them as his, and then when he got the job, make a big reveal about how it was really her work and she was being overlooked because of her gender and her less-recognizable name. But not only was that sort of thing trickier to pull off than the movies led you to believe, it was also quite possibly illegal. Not to mention stupid. They were both adults here, not teenagers in the midst of a high school tiff. The only thing that would give him another chance with her was if she won the bid fair and square.

Which meant throwing the job was out of the question, because if she found out, she would be so insulted she'd never speak to him again anyway. Besides, he could never do that. He still had a responsibility to Nina Klein and her company. He still had a responsibility—as much as he hated it—to his father who had set up the opportunity. And he had a responsibility to himself, because however he had screwed up his personal life, he believed in his own work. He wanted this job. He thought he could do exactly what Eleanor Gratz's house needed.

And right there was the answer. He couldn't control what Meg thought of him. She was determined to believe the worst, and he'd given her no reason to think otherwise. So the only thing he could do was put his head down, finish his proposal, and let the chips fall where they may.

Declan returned home, parking on the street in front of his building, and rode the elevator to the fifteenth floor. Laughter filtering from the unit next to him told him that the landlord and his chef wife were having one of their fabulous dinner parties that frequently spilled over to the shared roof deck above. The sounds of merriment only made him feel more alone. He pulled his keys from his pocket, fitted one into the lock, and let himself into the expansive, modern space.

It was ironic that he and Meg had each chosen homes that were the complete opposite of the kind of spaces they liked to design. Meg might say that she had purchased the house purely for investment reasons, but she looked at home there, crumbling wreck though it may be. The Meg who would stay in her pajamas while she worked on a snowy day fit with the historic Victorian.

His reasoning for his choice of accommodations was far less romantic than she might think: he didn't like it. And he'd found that longing and discomfort were the key driving forces in designing good, livable traditional spaces. All he had to do was look around the concrete floors and vaulted ceilings and spiral staircase to the roof and think about what he really wanted in the moment. While the snow was falling on the city fifteen stories below him, while he was as removed from life on the street as if he were in an airplane, he dreamed up spectacular double-sided fireplaces and insulated sunrooms that would bring his clients into the middle of the wonder. When the lights glinting off stainless steel and concrete and glass were cold and sterile, he called out wood timbers and organic materials and made spaces that begged for warm textiles and finishes. After all, it had been his stints living in his father's coldly constructed London flat that inspired him to become an architect in the first place. He'd never lost that need for the contrast between what he had and what he wanted.

It was just too bad that what he wanted now was so far out of reach.

Declan went to his bedroom toward the back of the unit, changed out of his suit and dress shoes, and pulled on a pair of sweat pants and a soft, threadbare Auburn t-shirt. Then he settled at his kitchen island with his laptop and a notepad and got to work.

seven

MEG WENT THROUGH THE MOTIONS for the next five days. She went to work. She dropped off her car at the mechanic to have a once over before the bumper was fixed. And she spent every minute of each evening at her dining room table, working on the bid for Eleanor Gratz.

All the while the ache in her chest grew steadily stronger.

It wasn't so much heartbreak. Heartbreak implied that there had been something more between them than attraction and the new, fragile hope of something more. It was deeper than that. It was knowing that someone she wanted for a friend, someone she respected as a colleague, whose approval—she might as well admit it—she desperately wanted, hadn't given her the courtesy of treating her as a person. Instead, he'd treated her like a pawn, a means to an end, all without looking like the bad guy. Relationships fell apart every day, flings fizzled, attraction died. There was no shame in romantic expectations that suddenly fell flat. But to be treated with so little care that she might as well be disposable? That was the thing that hurt.

Or so she told herself. But when she was lying in bed at night, her mind no longer occupied by the demands of work or everyday life, she remembered the feel of his lips on hers, the press of his hand on her back, the feeling of rightness when she was with him. In a mere day and a half, he had given her a glimpse of the Declan she had always wanted to believe existed and then he'd turned around and proved it was all an illusion.

She was a fool to have thought otherwise.

She supposed it was either a mark of her professionalism or the fact she'd never really made personal connections at work that no one picked up on the turmoil behind her eyes. Or maybe it was that they were all working more than fifty hours a week and no one had time to blink, let alone connect. She was in the middle of a tear-down in Boulder, which was taking up all her time, between communicating with the project manager and making the client's almost daily changes. She had no time to think about Declan or what might have been. She was just trying to keep her head above water.

On Friday morning, as she was putting the finishing touches on her renderings in preparation for sending her bid to Eleanor Gratz, the firm's managing partner, Edward Nelson, poked his head into her cubicle. "May I have a word with you in my office?"

Meg's eyebrows lifted. "Of course. Do I need to bring anything with me?"

"Just yourself. I'll see you in five."

Meg leaned back in her chair, her stomach fluttering with nervousness. What did Nelson want to talk to her about? Had Eleanor Gratz caught wind of the fact she and Declan had stayed overnight in her house and been offended by it? It wasn't as if they'd had any choice, but then, not having choices wasn't something that a rich eccentric would necessarily understand.

Stop obsessing and go find out. She grabbed her notebook and a pen just in case she needed to write anything down, smoothed her silk blouse, and strode into Nelson's glassed-in corner office.

He didn't look up when she entered. "Have a seat."

Dread built in her middle. She sat.

"I've been hearing a lot of things about you lately."

The butterflies took a nosedive. Maybe her unhappiness hadn't been as undercover as she thought it had been.

"As you know, the Ballasteros family are personal friends of mine."

Wait, what? This was about the Boulder job? She shifted in her seat, her dread shifting to confusion.

"And they are absolutely thrilled with the work that you've done on their project. I will admit, I dropped by the site this weekend just to see how things were coming along, and I'm impressed. I was a little worried that you and John wouldn't get along on the job site, but you've made it work."

John was the project manager. No, they didn't get along. But yes, she'd made sure things were still getting done.

"And then this …" He held up a sheaf of paper, evidently the designs for the Gratz house that he'd printed from the file she sent him. "I think this is your best work yet."

Meg swallowed, barely able to keep from stammering. "Thank you. That means a lot to me. I put a lot of concentrated effort into it."

Maybe she wasn't in here to be reprimanded. Maybe he was finally recognizing her contribution to the firm, he was finally going to give her the promotion that she'd been working towards for six years. Her heart lifted for the first time in a week. Her personal life might be a shambles, but at least her professional one was going in the right direction.

"That's why I wanted to talk to you before the decision was made public. I've decided to promote Chris to the open senior architect position."

Meg had been poised to gush about how excited she was, how she wouldn't let him down, but now those thoughts came to a screeching halt. "Excuse me?"

"You are more than qualified. But Chris has been here for three years longer, and his work is more consistent. Clients ask for him. He has a more recognizable name in the industry." Nelson folded his hands on the desk and looked at her sympathetically. "I just didn't want you to be discouraged and think that your work was not being recognized. You're a valued member of this team, and we're happy to have you here."

Meg swallowed. "Thank you, sir. I appreciate you taking the time. I take it that my design for the Gratz project has your approval? I can submit it?"

"Yes. And good luck to you. I think you've got a good shot at this one."

That's what you think, Meg thought. For a moment, she was tempted to confide in him. Maybe it was better for him to know that she never had a shot rather than have him think she'd lost because her work wasn't good enough. But that would just be playing into his reasoning for promoting Chris over her—more name recognition, more experience, more seniority.

In the end, she settled on a vague *thank you* and then returned to her desk, even though there was a boulder sitting in her stomach.

So this had all been for nothing. Nelson hadn't even waited for the outcome of this bid before making his decision to promote Chris. She wanted to tell herself that it was favoritism, sexism, whatever kind of *-ism* might make her feel better. But it wouldn't change the fact that Chris was an excellent architect with more experience and a proven track record.

She just wasn't good enough.

The reality hung heavy on her. Had this promotion gone differently, she might have been able to dismiss Declan's most recent betrayal as a product of his own insecurity. But now it seemed that he'd been right. She was destined to be the second-tier player, there to support the shining stars, make them look even better by comparison.

"Well," she murmured with a bitter laugh. "You just got your wish." She took one last quick look at her file, attached it to an email, and sent it to Eleanor Gratz. Now it was all over.

She dashed away tears before they could form and opened another rendering, forcing her mind back to the project at hand.

Her hopes might be gone, but always the work remained.

The month between submitting his proposal and Eleanor Gratz's decision was the longest month of Declan's life. The whole situation had been irregular from start to finish, from the hurried bid period to the abbreviated design documents to the surprisingly quick decision. That didn't even account for the thirty hours he had been snowbound with his biggest rival. But Mrs. Gratz was rich enough and well connected enough to demand whatever she wanted, and people would do her bidding. People would kill for a chance to compete to do her bidding.

And Declan wished he had been left out of it altogether.

Sure, that meant he would never have reconnected with Meg, but that would have been preferable to the constant feeling of loss that dogged his days. It wasn't just that for a split second, he'd thought he'd found something special. That maybe, he'd finally connected with someone he understood and who understood him in return. Someone he might have a future with. It was that his own stupid actions were responsible for shattering all those possibilities.

It was hard enough to accept when things didn't go your way because of the random actions of the universe, but it was downright devastating when it was your own fault.

Which was why he wasn't paying enough attention when his office phone rang, and he picked it up without checking the caller ID. "Hello?"

"Declan, I'm so glad I've caught you."

The familiar Irish-accented voice made him sit straight up in his chair. "Dad. What a surprise." He knew he should make an effort to force some enthusiasm into his voice, but he didn't have it in him. It didn't matter. His father rarely listened to what he had to say; while Declan was talking, his dad was already planning his next speech.

Sure enough, Colum McKenzie plowed on. "I've got good news for you, son. Eleanor Gratz wants to go forward with the project."

Declan blinked. He looked around to see if anyone else in his open floor plan office was near enough to overhear, but his colleagues were too engrossed in their own work to pay him any mind. He lowered his voice anyway. "She called you first?"

"Of course she called me first. I was the one who recommended you. She just had a few conditions."

This was the cherry on top of an already bizarre sundae. "What kind of conditions?"

"She has confidence that you have the skills to pull off the project, and Nina has thrown her full support behind you. It's just that she's looking for something a little less traditional."

"Less traditional how?"

"Check your email."

Declan balanced the phone on his shoulder while he moused over to his inbox and clicked the email from his father. Attached was an anonymous numbered file, but as soon as he opened it, it was obvious what he was looking at.

Meg Anderson's design.

He clicked through the pages slowly, taking in the work that she'd somehow managed to create in a mere week. It was … stunning.

He'd always admired Meg's sensibilities, but this went beyond that. She'd somehow melded her usual modern design aesthetic with the warmth demanded of a mountain home, taking her cues from the views outside: organic materials and earth tones, the home's straight sharp lines softened with curving interior walls and surprising angles. It was both a departure from her earlier work and the culmination of it. Maybe masterpiece was overstating things—it was a private home in the mountains of Colorado after all—but he had a sneaking suspicion that this house would be the one that catapulted her into public attention. Once this hit *Architectural Digest*—and it would—she would have more work than she could possibly manage.

"She wants me to revise my proposal to be something more like this," Declan said slowly, not sure that he'd understood.

"Yes."

"Forgive me saying this, but if this is what she wants, why doesn't she just hire Meg?"

Colum chuckled. "That's not how this works, son."

"That is exactly how it works for ninety-nine percent of the world. The person with the best design and the capability of accomplishing it gets the job."

"Don't be so naive. You think you got where you are on talent alone? This Meg was all set to get *your* job at Klein & Company until I talked to Nina. You'd be languishing in some unknown firm like her if I hadn't stepped in."

The words nearly knocked the breath out of him. He'd known his father had pulled strings, of course he had. It was the reason Declan had decided to let Meg take the fall for their joint mistake, knowing it would make no difference to her but all the difference to him. But all this time he'd been thinking it was a contest between evenly matched equals. That it could have gone either way and he'd just slightly tipped the odds in his favor.

But now? His father was telling him he didn't deserve his spot, that he'd stolen a job from a more talented colleague. That everything he'd accomplished, he hadn't actually earned. That he was only here because of his famous name.

"That makes my decision somewhat easier then."

"I thought it might."

"You can tell Eleanor Gratz to hire Meg Anderson. I'm officially withdrawing my bid."

There was a pregnant pause on the other end of the line. "Declan, don't be stupid."

"I'm not being stupid. For the first time in my life, I'm having some integrity. I know you think you're just doing what a good father does, but I need to know that I'm here on my own accomplishments. Frankly, Dad, I need you to butt out of my life and my career."

"You don't know what you're asking." Colum's voice was tight with repressed anger. "If it weren't for me, you'd be nowhere. You'd be building tiny little vacation cottages in the backwoods of Idaho if you didn't have my help."

Declan didn't give himself time to think over his response. "If anyone deserves your help, it's Meg Anderson. You know that as well as I do. Just look at her proposal. That's what Eleanor wants, so that's who Eleanor needs to hire."

"Declan—"

"Dad, I've got to go." And before his father could say anything else, he hung up the phone. He was surprised to find that his hands were shaking.

He'd finally stood up to him. He felt stunned, but somehow not surprised. Deep down, he'd always known his father didn't believe in him and his abilities. Looked down on the fact that he favored local vernacular and historical styles. To Colum, architecture was all about innovation, pushing boundaries, conquering materials and the natural world equally. But that was only because he'd had the childhood that Declan had wanted, growing up on a croft in Ireland, surrounded by warmth and laughter and happiness. What had happened to make him this humorless, ambitious, hard-hearted person, Declan didn't know …

But no, he did know. Before his mom, Fiona, left, there had been rides on his dad's shoulders and summer trips in a caravan and bedtime stories. But after Fiona extricated herself from their lives, Colum had cut himself off from the rest of human emotion. It had been good for his career— that had been the period when he'd switched to the appropriately named Brutalist style, when he'd decided that he would take out his emptiness on society by designing public spaces that looked like prisons. He'd let his career become his whole world, forgetting that he left behind a boy who needed a father far more than he needed an expensive boarding school or the advantage of professional connections.

In some ways, in Declan's attempt to prove he wasn't anything like his father, he'd become exactly like him, letting the ends justify the means, no matter who it hurt, no matter who he stepped on.

He had no idea how long it would take for word to make it back to Meg, but he figured it wouldn't be long. Colum McKenzie knew his son well enough to know that he wasn't going to change his mind, and if he wasn't going to take the job, Eleanor would have no choice but to hire the architect she really wanted.

Declan searched for a minute on his computer, then picked up the phone and called the first florist he could find. He ordered the biggest bouquet of flowers she had and dictated a note.

It looks like the best woman finally won. Sincerest congratulations.

And because he couldn't help himself, he had her sign it, *Love, Declan*

She was fine. Really and truly fine.

It had been a month since Meg had submitted her proposal to Eleanor Gratz and she hadn't heard anything, which had to mean bad news. As hard as the client had been pushing for the designs, Meg would have expected a decision by now. Given everything she knew about the circumstances surrounding the bid, it wasn't too hard to guess which way it had gone.

Meg nabbed one of the rare street parking spaces outside NCO and climbed out of her Jeep, feeling as if she'd been permanently pressed into a sitting position. Traffic out of Boulder was heinous at the best of times, but add in a Friday night drive and a multi-car accident—a deer dashing into traffic could leave a lot of destruction in its wake, even when it escaped unscathed—and it had turned into a marathon commute. That was okay, though. It meant the office would be mostly empty. Even with their insane hours, most of the architects bailed the minute the clock flipped to five o'clock on Friday night.

Then again, they all had families or significant others or at least evening plans that involved more than Netflix and takeout Chinese food.

She pushed away her self-pitying thoughts and swiped her keycard at the front door, then climbed the stairs to the second floor. The expanse of low-walled cubicles was dark with only the occasional spot of brightness coming from task lighting someone had left on.

"Meg! Come back for your flowers?"

Meg jumped back reflexively as an older woman appeared from the shadows, her oversized handbag slung over her shoulder—Rita, the office manager. Meg pressed a hand to her galloping heart and tried to process the woman's words. "I've been on a jobsite all day. What flowers?"

Rita's eyes went wide. "I thought someone called you! Now I've gone and spoiled the surprise!"

Meg stared, still not sure what they were talking about. All at once, the exhaustion from her long week and horrendous commute tumbled down over her like an avalanche, and she decided it was too much trouble to unravel that statement. "Have a good weekend, Rita. I'll see you on Monday."

"Don't work too late!" Rita chirped before heading for the door.

Meg wandered over to her cubicle, slinging her purse off her shoulder, then stopped as if she'd suddenly been poured in concrete. In the center of her desk was an enormous bouquet of sunflowers, roses, and sea lavender in a sculptural glass vase. What in the world?

She managed to unstick her feet and plucked the card from the plastic pick nestled in the middle of the bouquet.

It looks like the best woman finally won. Sincerest congratulations. Love, Declan

Her eyes stuck on the last two words, scrawled in a feminine hand: *Love, Declan*. Her heart rose into her throat. Declan had sent her flowers.

Then the rest of the message sank in. She dove for her computer, flicking it on and drumming her fingers impatiently while it booted up. After what felt like an eternity, her desktop flashed onto the screen and she clicked the email icon a dozen times in a vain attempt to get it to open faster. And there it was, among a bunch of junk and spam and interoffice messages—an email from Eleanor Gratz, subject line: *Vail Remodel*. She held her breath and clicked it …

… and let out a scream that, had anyone actually still been in the office, would have had them speed-dialing emergency services.

She'd done it. Finally. She'd won. She'd beat Declan at his own game, not through connections or underhanded plotting, but through sheer talent and skill.

But as her gaze drifted to the flowers, she realized that the idea no longer held the savor it once had. The project, of course, excited her as much as ever. But the thought of besting Declan had lost its appeal.

He wasn't her enemy, even if she'd once thought of him that way. He was just another professional trying to make his mark on the world, however much he might have stumbled over his own ambition. Now, the anger she'd been holding melted away in the face of her victory.

That, of course, brought up another big question: what exactly *had* happened? The messages between Declan and Nina had made it clear Mrs. Gratz had already made her decision and Meg was just a decoy to make the whole procedure feel fairer. So how had they gotten from Declan being a shoo-in to Meg winning the bid? She couldn't very well ask the client and she didn't want to probe for information from Nelson. He'd be angry that she hadn't been straight with him about the situation from the start, when he might have been able to do something. (He wouldn't have been able to, but that was beside the point. Nelson liked to think he had a lot more influence than he actually did.) So she picked up her phone, found Declan's text message, and pressed the *call* icon.

And then hung up before the call could connect. To phone him now would just make it seem like she was gloating. Besides, even if she could forgive him his final betrayal, it was just a symptom of a larger issue. He might like her, he might be attracted to her, but it was clear that he didn't respect her.

And despite the fact that she'd never felt that raw, uncontrollable attraction for anyone else, she could never be with someone who thought it was okay to use her as he had.

Someday, she would look back on that weekend as a brief interlude in her real life, a funny story she'd tell when friends were sitting around talking about their biggest mistakes. At least, she would say, it hadn't turned into one of her biggest regrets. It was a story that belonged to the old Meg, the one who had been so insecure that she'd held onto a hopeless infatuation for six long years; the Meg who had almost let herself be taken in by an Irish lilt and practiced charm and beautiful gray eyes. But that Meg was gone now, and it was time to build a new life for herself.

It was time to prove just how strong and capable she could really be.

eight

Six months later

MEG STOOD ON THE GRATZ JOB SITE, wearing a hard hat and bent over a sheaf of drawings. Like all projects of this scope, it had taken twice as long as they'd expected to secure the initial permits and they'd been plagued by all manner of difficulties as they got started. What should have begun in May with the demolition had stretched through the summer, putting them into October for framing. An unseasonably warm October, to be certain, but October all the same. They were going to be racing the weather to get the structure dried in before the first snow so the crews could work inside through the winter.

It had been months of long days and sleepless nights, and Meg had loved every minute of it.

In the days after she'd learned she won the bid, she'd walked around in a combination of shock and glee. Despite the fact she still had projects to finish, the Ballasteros job chief among them, she dove straight into the construction drawings so they could begin pulling permits. It ate at her, then, that a tiny part of her still felt restless, dissatisfied. She'd finally gotten everything she wanted in life. Why should she be anything but over-the-moon thrilled?

But if she were completely honest, she missed Declan. It didn't make any sense. She hadn't had him in the first place, at least for any significant length of time. But those two days with him had shifted something in her. It had caused a crack in her hard shell, her firm conviction that her work was all she needed in her life, and no matter how she tried to patch and cover up that crack, it widened with each passing day. She'd tried going on a few dates, but none of those men had appealed to her enough to see them again. She wanted someone in her life with whom she could talk about her work. Who would understand why she whipped out her phone to randomly photograph buildings that triggered some creative impulse in her. Someone who would kiss her like Declan had, sweep her away and drive every thought but him from her mind.

Meg thought the last item on her list might be the toughest to fulfill.

She'd like to pretend she'd moved on without another thought, but in truth, it had taken less than twenty-four hours to start stalking him on social media, searching for some barometer of how he felt about losing the bid, how he felt about losing her. But ever since the decision had been made, it was as if he'd dropped off the face of the earth. No new projects on his Instagram, nothing on his company's online portfolio. Had losing this bid been the thing he needed to send him back to Ireland?

She realized now that she was daydreaming when she was supposed to be looking at the plans to answer a question for the contractor. What had first seemed like a straightforward renovation had turned out to be an engineering feat, and one for which she was both well trained and well prepared. Because she'd opted to remove many of the interior walls and the ones that hadn't been removed were curved and often partial height, it had brought a special challenge to normally simple things like electrical, HVAC, and plumbing. Far from being frustrating, she'd found it invigorating. Finally, this was a project that utilized her full breadth of skills and education.

Connor Williams, the contractor, ambled over to her, zipping up his jacket against the sudden blast of chill wind.

She didn't wait for him to speak. "Here's the problem." She tapped the drawing. "The framing crew transposed the measurements on this interior wall so it's cutting into the hallway."

"That's easy enough to fix."

Meg arched an eyebrow.

He gave a wry smile. "Relatively speaking."

"Glad to hear it. I don't think you need me on site for this. Everything else looks good. I'll be back in two weeks when it's completely framed."

She was rolling up the drawings when the sound of wheels on the gravel driveway caught her attention. She didn't look up. There were cars and trucks coming in and out of the job site all the time, especially as the general contractor rotated the trades through. So she was completely unprepared when a familiar voice called her name, laced with a hint of uncertainty.

Meg froze, her muscles going stiff with shock. Then she forced herself back into deliberate movement and rubber banded the plans together before she turned. "Declan."

Her first sight of him in six months almost made her heart stop. Just like the last time she'd seen him, her brain had to recalibrate to the idea that yes, he really was that attractive, it hadn't just been her imagination. He was wearing jeans and boots and a wool coat, a knit scarf wrapped around his neck, looking far more European than she'd ever seen him. But it was the hopeful, uncertain look on his face that really captured her attention.

And she realized on that first glimpse what she should have realized long ago: that she'd forgiven him for whatever he did or did not do, and the pain when she thought of him was from missing what they might have been together.

"Hi." It was a thoroughly inadequate greeting for the feelings that were flooding her body at the moment.

"It's looking good." He nodded toward the house. "You're further along than I thought you'd be."

"Come back in two weeks and you'll get a better idea of what it will look like." That wasn't at all what she wanted to be saying to him, but despite having thought about this moment for half a year, she found herself completely at a loss for words.

He seemed to be having the same problem, because he thrust his hands into his pockets and scanned the job site. After an awkward pause he said, "Meg—" at the same time she began, "Declan—"

They both laughed. "You first," she said with a smile.

"This feels about six months too late," Declan said, "but I just wanted to say I'm sorry. I know it's completely inadequate considering everything that's happened between us over the years but I still need to say it, because it's true."

"It's okay, Declan," she said. "I forgive you. I was angry, yes, but when it came down to it, it was because of you that I got this job in the first place. No matter what the intention might have been. And at this point, I think you might have been misguided, but I don't think you were malicious."

He dipped his head. "That's very gracious of you."

"What I don't understand is how it all came about. She was dead set on giving you this job. Why did she change her mind?"

"She wanted your design. I think she was never really interested in my work, just in my name. And what you submitted was better." He gestured toward the skeleton of the house behind them. "I knew it from the first time I saw your sketches. I'm not surprised. This is going to make your career."

Meg nodded slowly. She couldn't deny that those were the words she'd longed to hear, but she could also sense that he was holding something back. "Why are you really here? I appreciate the apology, but you could have called me at any point in the last six months."

Unexpectedly, his smile flashed. "I figured talk was cheap. I insulted your work and your reputation with what I did. It's one thing to say you're sorry and another to show you're sorry."

Meg blinked at him. "I don't understand."

He cleared his throat. "After losing the bid, I realized that I was tired of working so hard to please everyone around me. I wasn't doing my best work—no, don't protest, we both know it's true—and that was partly because I was designing for my anti-father. He wasn't pleased with me for not fighting for this job, and he let slip that you were actually going to get the position at Klein. He literally changed their minds for them. It wasn't because I deserved it at all."

Meg could only stare in shock. Sure, she'd thought that more than once, but it was one thing to throw bitter imprecations at a rival and another to hear it come out of his own mouth.

"So I quit."

Her eyes went wide. "You what?"

"I quit. I finished up my projects at Klein. And I went out on my own. That's why I'm here." He cleared his throat. "I'm here to offer you a job. No, not a job, a partnership. I'm hoping you'll become one half of the newly formed Arete Architecture. Arete means—"

"Excellence, I know," she said, staring at him. She couldn't quite believe what she was hearing. "I would have thought you'd go with McKenzie."

He threw her a wry grin. "This name has given me nothing but trouble. I think it's time to do something different."

"But … why? Why are you coming to me now?"

"Because you are literally the best architect I know. NCO has been underutilizing you for years, and you still haven't gotten that promotion you deserve. And I know that once this house is finished, you'll have made a name for yourself and you can pick your projects. I'm just hoping that you'll bring that name over to my company. *Our* company. You'll be a partner. You'll make your own rules, control your own destiny … but with half of the risk of doing it by yourself."

Meg had no idea what to say. This was the last thing she'd expected out of his mouth, but she couldn't deny the satisfaction it gave her to hear him finally acknowledge what she'd accomplished. "Can I think about it?"

"Of course. Take as long as you need. The door is always open." He cleared his throat. "I also wanted to ask you another question, and I'm hoping you don't have to think about this one for as long."

"Oh?"

He took another step toward her, held his hand out like he wanted to take hers, and then dropped it just as abruptly. "Will you go out to dinner with me this weekend? I feel like we're far overdue for celebrating your success."

"And your new company." Now a teasing note crept into Meg's voice. "Is that that only reason you want to take me out?"

"There are a lot of reasons, but let's start with that, shall we?"

She heard the echo in his words of what he'd said to her last time, flushed a little at the recollection of what had preceded it. She might not be able to give him an answer to his first question right now, but the second took no thought whatsoever. "I'd love to."

"Good." Now he did reach for her hand and lift it to his lips, the brush against her fingers making her body thrill to his touch as avidly as it ever had. As he held her eyes, the first fat snowflakes began to fall from the sky, dusting their hair and shoulders and melting on their clasped hands. "We probably should be going. We know how fickle the weather is, and we don't want to get stuck here."

A smile tugged up the corners of her lips. "I could think of worse things."

epilogue

Two years later

"I TOLD YOU IT WOULD BE BETTER THIS WAY. Didn't I tell you it would be better this way?" Declan grinned at Meg, and she wrinkled her nose in response.

"Yes, yes, you're brilliant. What would I do without you?"

He moved to her side where she sat at her desk and dropped a light kiss on her lips. "I somehow feel like you're less than sincere with that praise, but I'll take it anyway."

Meg smiled at him and grabbed hold of the front of his sweater to pull him down for another kiss, which he willingly obliged. When they'd decided to renovate her house shortly after their wedding, both to complete the restoration she'd intended when she purchased it and to make it the headquarters for Arete Architecture, she'd agreed to let him take point on the project. He had the most experience in traditional vernaculars, and he was the one who was most excited about the original details they unearthed when they began their careful demolition. But she had held onto her initial insistence that the attic space was far too cramped and dark to make a decent office for the two of them.

Now, looking at the results—the airy gabled roof with a new set of historically accurate windows on both the front and back to let in light and air—she couldn't deny that he'd been absolutely right. It was the cozy artist's garret she'd never known her heart secretly wanted, layered with a warm mishmash of antique furnishings that made her feel like she was working in an old library and not her own home. Since they'd moved into the renovated space two weeks earlier, she'd barely left this room except to sleep.

Okay, that wasn't entirely true. They'd spent a fair amount of time christening their new master bedroom too, but it was reasonable to say the design she fought tooth and nail the entire way was her favorite spot in the house. And not the least because it was the space she shared with her new husband and business partner.

It was hard to believe how completely her life had changed in less than three years from a snowbound weekend with a man she thought she despised. It hadn't taken long for them to work through their past misunderstandings and move forward with a relationship, but it had taken considerably longer for her to move on from her job.

Declan had been right—after the photos of her redesign of the Gratz house hit all the right periodicals, she was suddenly deluged with new clients and NCO Architecture, once an unknown "boutique" firm, was suddenly a major player. It was still hard to believe that she had anything to do with that. Nelson had immediately promoted her, as well he should have, but he balked when she talked about a future as a managing partner of the firm. It was a fairly easy decision from there to join forces with her soon-to-be husband.

"I got the specs for the Rizowski project today," she said, spinning in her chair to pull up the email she'd just received. "We're going to have our work cut out with them. They want a full-depth basement and won't take no for an answer, but the soils report suggests it's a bad idea. They keep insisting that we need to find a way."

Declan bent down and placed a kiss on the side of her neck exposed by her upswept hairstyle. "So we find a way. Or talk them into an attic."

She shivered, a smile coming to her face, but she refused to let him off this easy. "They saw one of those TV shows where they excavated an old Roman bath in the basement and thought that was exactly what their own place needed."

"Mmm." Declan took a finger and slid aside the neck of her sweater to press a kiss to the top of her shoulder. "Yes, clearly everyone needs a Roman bath in their home."

"You're trying to distract me."

"Is it working?"

She cocked her head as if she was thinking, but really it was to give his lips better access. "I'm considering it."

"Would it help if I told you something?"

"Told me what?"

He gestured toward the wide window, where the threatening gray sky had finally begun to loose its moisture in a steady stream of fat, fluffy snowflakes. "The forecast is for a blizzard. We might not be able to leave the house for the entire weekend."

Her smile widened to a grin. "That sounds terrible. I can't imagine how we'll pass the time, can you?" She let him pull her to her feet and kissed him full on the mouth. Then she whispered in his ear, "Do you want to light the fire or should I?"

He grinned back in equal anticipation, but then his expression sobered. He reached up to brush a stray lock of hair away from her face, his touch at once comfortingly familiar and wondrously new. "You know, I almost didn't drive up to Vail that day we got snowed in. I knew it was probably going to be bad and I could get stuck up there. I had just about talked myself out of it."

In almost three years, Declan had never spoken of this. She pulled away a little to look into his face, surprised. "Then what changed your mind?"

He smiled slightly and pressed a kiss to her lips. "I thought 'what would Meg do in this situation?' And then I figured that whatever happened, even if I was snowbound, at least I would be with you."

Sunswept

A Discovered by Love Novella

One

Bailey Jensen always allowed for some discrepancies when booking a vacation rental, but she didn't remember reading anything in the listing about a man in her bathroom.

She stood stunned in the bedroom for a long moment, then quickly backed out of the room before he could see her, her heart pounding. For a second, she was tempted to go back outside and check the house number, as if Upper Matecumbe Key, one of the four islands that made up Islamorada, Florida, might have two bright yellow houses with turquoise shutters with similar addresses … that shared the same electronic keypad code.

Clearly there had been some sort of mix-up. The last guest had overstayed his reservation and the host either didn't know or had forgotten to contact her. She was no stranger to these sorts of situations. She was a real estate agent, after all, and she'd walked in on things in supposedly empty houses that would make the bravest agents' hair curl. There was nothing to do but walk straight back in there and find out exactly what was going on.

Bailey steeled herself and marched back to the bathroom, where the man was standing at the sink, wearing board shorts even if he wasn't wearing a shirt. She cleared her throat once and waited.

Not a movement, not a flicker of awareness of her presence. Was this guy clueless or just completely transfixed by his own reflection? She tried again, putting on her most professional voice.

"Excuse me. I think you're in my bathroom."

That did the trick. The muscles in his back—rather nicely developed ones, some inane part of her brain noted—went rigid. Slowly, the man turned to face her.

She froze. The bushy beard didn't surprise her, not considering the sandy brown hair that brushed his shoulders from behind. But the eyes—long-lashed and almost gold like a cat's, widened in mild surprise at her presence—stopped her in her tracks. No man who looked like a beach bum should have eyes that beautiful.

While she was frozen in—what? Shock? Appreciation?— he looked her over from the top of her messy blonde bun to the tips of her pink pedicure. His eyebrows lifted, his expression remaining mild. "From where I'm standing, it looks like you're the one who's in my bedroom."

"Cute," she said. She kept her eyes fixed firmly on his face, slightly disturbed by all the tanned skin at the edge of her vision but not enough to drive out the faint impression of abs. "I see why you'd think that, but you're the one overstaying your reservation. I'm supposed to be coming in today." She glanced at her watch. "Two hours ago, actually, thanks to traffic in Miami."

Now he grinned, showing even white teeth. "Well, in that case, I should get out of your way."

Bailey blinked. "Really?"

"No, not really. I just got here an hour ago myself. I booked the cottage until Monday through Better Rentals. See?" He turned back to retrieve his phone from the vanity, scrolled for a few seconds, then held out what appeared to be an email confirmation for the cottage.

"But I booked it through Sunday on VacayAway." Bailey fumbled for her own phone, but he barely looked at the screen.

He crossed his arms and regarded her impassively. "Then it seems we have a problem."

She narrowed her eyes. Why did this guy look familiar to her? She searched her memory, sorting through filed images until something clicked. "*Point Break!*" she blurted with a rush of relief.

"Excuse me?"

Heat rushed to Bailey's face. It was a fault of hers, or a superpower depending on who you asked, this heightened sense of patterns. When some little similarity caught her attention, she couldn't rest until she sorted it out. And her vacation rental interloper bore a strong resemblance to a young, cat-eyed Patrick Swayze from the original *Point Break* movie.

"Never mind." Normally, she managed to keep her epiphanies to herself, but there was nothing normal about this situation. She shook her head, pulling herself back to the present. "What are we going to do about this?"

"One of us has to find a new place to stay."

"I don't have time to find a new place to stay," Bailey said, but she already had the VacayAway app open, her thumbs tapping and scrolling as if of their own volition. "My conference starts tomorrow, and I can't miss any sessions."

"Problem solved. Stay at the conference hotel." He brushed past her to the open suitcase on the bed, pulled out a faded T-shirt, and slipped it on over his head.

"I can't. It filled up months ago. And besides, I'm not spending any more time there than I have to."

Her tone must have given away more than she intended, because he cocked his head curiously. "Why not?"

"Because I … It doesn't matter. It's not something I'm explaining to a stranger."

"I can fix that." He held out his hand. "I'm Zane."

She hesitated for a moment and then took it. "Bailey. Bailey Jensen."

His hand was warm and strong, but he didn't linger on the handshake. "Well, Bailey Bailey Jensen, I'd love to be chivalrous and give up the place, but I'm here for a wedding, and I don't think the groom would appreciate his attendant showing up wrinkled and sand-covered from sleeping on the beach."

"You could find—"

"As I think you're discovering from your compulsive scrolling, there's nothing left. It's high season in the Keys."

He was right: all her half-hearted searching had shown were rooms in people's houses that were little more than a twin mattress on the floor and a bare bulb, compared to this beautiful jewel box of a cottage, with a massive iron king-sized bed and hardwood floors and an ocean view …

Bailey sucked in a breath. She'd been so distracted by the strange man in her bathroom that she'd completely missed the panoramic view of the ocean from the wall of sliding doors. She practically ran to the nearest one, threw the door back, and stepped onto the deck.

Blue stretched out 180 degrees before her, water lapping on the sandy ribbon of private beach that separated the house from the water. The soft murmur and break of waves immediately drained the tension from her body, even as it steeled her resolve. This was why she'd booked the cottage in the first place, for a respite from this long, frustrating, disappointing year. The conference was already going to be a test of patience and self-control, and she wouldn't even be here if it weren't her first step in extricating herself from her current predicament.

She turned and faced Zane. "I'm not leaving."

He crossed his arms. "Then we have a real problem. Because neither am I."

Zane Whitney stared at the woman, unblinking, and watched the emotions play over her face. He was being a little cruel, he knew, but he was enjoying the way he could predict her next sentence a split second before it left her mouth. She was like one of those machines that was encased in clear plastic, where you could see the turning of gears and blinking of lights as it worked.

It wouldn't have made a difference, anyway. He wasn't giving up his rental, despite the chivalrous impulses that kept delivering words he couldn't actually say. He already didn't want to be here in Islamorada, didn't want to be in this wedding, certainly didn't want to give a toast to the happy couple. This little beach cottage, so close to the ocean he could practically roll out of bed and dive in for a morning swim, was his one compensation for the whole debacle.

Though this southern pixie in front of him was a close second. In fact, he wished he knew what he'd done to deserve this kind of luck. She wasn't beautiful, exactly. It was more that she was unbearably cute. Petite. Dressed in a tank top and denim shorts that showed a fit but curvy figure, she could pass easily for a college student on break. She just needed a paper cup in one hand to hold her pumpkin spice latte. Until she opened her mouth and out came a smoky alto that made him think that latte would have to be spiked with bourbon.

Either way, he wasn't quite ready for this introduction to be over.

"I suppose we could flip for it," he said, feigning indifference.

She blinked. "Flip for it?"

Zane reached for the pile of change he'd left on the nightstand and held up a quarter. "Yeah. You call it. Heads or tails."

She didn't look convinced of this solution, but she answered anyway. "Heads."

"Okay then." He flipped the coin up in the air and caught it, then slapped his right hand over the back of his left. But when he lifted his right hand again, there was nothing there.

Her eyes flew to his.

He shrugged again and leaned forward to retrieve the quarter from the front pocket of her shorts. He held it up, frowning. "I don't know what we're calling this? Heads or tails?"

She stared at him in consternation for a moment, then broke into a smile. "How did you do that?"

He leaned forward to whisper. "Magic."

Bailey chuckled. "Fair enough. But it doesn't solve our problem."

It kind of did, because now she was calling the situation *their* problem rather than thinking *he* was the problem. Magic had a way of disarming even the most suspicious person.

"How did you do that, by the way? No, wait, a magician never tells his secrets, right?"

"An *illusionist*, but no, I'll show you. Come here." He plopped down on the edge of the bed and gestured for her to sit beside him, where he showed her how to palm the quarter, pretend to pass it to her other hand, and then push it to her fingers to produce it again. She was doing a decent French drop after a couple of minutes. More importantly, she was no longer looking at him like an enemy.

Then he sighed. "Listen. I really do need to do this wedding on Saturday. After that, I can just go home. You can have my other two days. Best I can do."

She bit her lip. "That's a really nice offer, but my conference ends Saturday. I have to drive back to West Palm Beach on Sunday."

"Well, it's either that or share the place."

Instantly, she stiffened, all the good will evaporating. "I really don't—"

"Relax. There's a sofa bed in the living room. I'd offer to flip you for it, but …" He produced the quarter with a flourish and made it disappear again. "I don't mind. You can take the bedroom, and I'll take the sofa. There's a powder room off the kitchen too, so you can lock your door." He held up his hands. "I'll be a gentleman. Scout's honor."

"That would be a lot more convincing if you hadn't just proven you're a con artist."

He pretended to be hurt. "Illusionist. Not a con artist. And I showed you how I did it!"

"Right, all part of your evil plan," she said, but she was smiling again.

"How about this? It's getting late. Let's grab a bite to eat. You can ask me questions and decide if I'm legit and then make up your mind."

"You know, Ted Bundy didn't seem like a serial killer."

He snorted. "First a con artist, now a serial killer? Tough room."

She bit her lip.

"Seriously. I have no options. It's a small wedding and all the other attendants brought their significant others, so I can't even bunk with someone. I just need to get through this godforsaken wedding and then get back to my real life." He broke off. It was far more than he'd intended to say to a stranger, but now it seemed like it might work in his favor.

She was looking at him thoughtfully. "I think I'm going to let you buy me dinner now."

two

She must be insane.

Bailey drove down US 1, windows down and music up, the wind and sound preventing conversation while she tried not to steal glances at the man sitting in the front passenger seat beside her. He was a stranger she'd met twenty minutes ago and quite possibly a beach bum, based on his attire and the fact he didn't even have a car. Who didn't have a car? When she'd voiced the question, he'd given that eloquent shrug of his and referenced the beach cruisers chained in the storage area beneath the elevated house.

Except she'd snooped around the bedroom while he'd been changing in the bathroom. Next to his wallet—no, she hadn't looked inside; she did have *some* scruples—was his watch, a nice-looking Rado chronograph she'd had to look up because she'd never heard of it. And in his closet beside a handful of dress shirts was what she assumed was his wedding suit, a lightweight summer wool. She didn't recognize that label either, but the tailoring suggested it was custom. Not to mention she knew how much she'd paid for the cottage, and it wasn't cheap. All pointed to a man who made a good living, despite his odd transportation choices.

Not that money ensured someone wasn't a serial killer, but it did mean he probably wasn't a freeloader trying to con a stay in a luxury beach house. She'd called the host to confirm that impression and to tell her of the mix-up, but she'd only gotten voicemail.

Zane seemed to know the island, though, because he already had a reservation at a casual seafood restaurant near the end of Islamorada on

Lower Matecumbe. She parked in the sand-strewn lot and waited for him outside the car so they could walk to the hostess stand together. Now Bailey did sneak a couple of discreet looks in his direction. He was attractive, for sure, given the resemblance to a young Patrick Swayze, but more than that, he was calm, self-assured, unruffled. Whereas she had been in a tailspin, even before arriving in Islamorada and finding her place double-booked.

Though considering the circumstances, she figured she was justified a little freak-out.

The hostess was wearing an impossibly short skirt and a polo shirt. She gave Bailey a once-over and settled on her companion. "Reservation?"

"Zane. It was for one, but my friend got here early."

The hostess shot Bailey another surreptitious look, decided she was no competition, and flashed a brilliant smile at him. "Not a problem. Beach, patio, or balcony?"

Zane looked at Bailey, who hesitated. Her inclination was to say beach, but she had the feeling they were probably romantic candlelit two-tops and he might get the wrong idea.

"Go on, you know you want to sit on the beach."

How did he do that? She nodded anyway. "Beach."

"Right this way," the hostess chirped and led them through the warmly-lit dining room to a strip of beach set with bistro tables and tiny hurricane lamps.

Bailey paused to kick off her flip-flops and dangle them from her fingertips, then continued down the rough sand in her bare feet. Once they were seated uncomfortably close at the table, she opened and closed her menu. "You obviously know this place. What's good?"

"The Florida lobster, hands down. With or without the filet."

"Big spender," she commented mildly.

"I'm hoping I might talk my way back into the bedroom."

Bailey's eyes jerked to his face in alarm.

"Oh, no … I didn't mean … I meant to switch. Not to … share." For the first time, he actually looked flustered. Maybe he was just a good actor, but she could swear above his beard his cheekbones were turning pink. Her stomach unknotted a tiny bit.

They both ordered—Bailey the lobster, Zane the surf and turf and Bahamian conch fritters to share—and then she turned her full attention on him. "So, what do you do?"

"I'm in IT," he said easily. Then a shadow passed over his face. "I *was* in IT. Right now, I'm in between projects."

"Aha! So you *are* a beach bum!"

He grinned. "Is that what you were worried about? I've been gainfully employed since I was nineteen. I got the opportunity to cash out of my last company due to a change in ownership and now I'm deciding my next move. Actually, I was thinking about looking at some real estate while I'm here. For my own personal use, of course, but mostly as an investment."

"It's a very convenient time to be in Islamorada, then." She smiled. "I'm here for a real estate conference."

"That *is* rather convenient. Tell me, are you a good agent?"

"I'm here to accept an award for highest performing agent in Florida." At the quick lift of his eyebrows, she added hastily, "At my firm, that is. But it's a big company."

Zane raised his water glass in a toast. "Congratulations. I happen to know it's an extremely difficult career. That's an accomplishment."

"Thank you." She smoothed her napkin in her lap and leaned forward. "Actually, that's partly why I can't miss anything. I have to complete my continuing education to renew my license and then I'll be able to start my broker's program. Go out on my own."

"I see." He looked closely at her. "You must really want to get out of your firm."

"I didn't say that!"

"But you thought it. If you're the top agent in your firm, you're probably doing well. Either you want the challenge or you don't like your boss." He narrowed his eyes. "It's the last one."

"Seriously, how do you do that?"

Zane dismissed the question with a wave of his hand. "What's wrong with the boss?"

"Nothing's wrong with the boss. He's a decent guy. Good-looking. Successful. That's why I dated him."

"Oh." For all his perceptiveness, she could tell he hadn't expected that. "In that case, I don't blame you."

"I can mostly avoid him on a day-to-day basis, but of course, I have to sit at his table for the awards dinner with—"

"His new girlfriend?" Zane guessed.

She pointed at him and tapped her nose. "I can't even prepare myself, because I don't know who he's bringing. There were a couple of them. Which explains why we're no longer together."

"Ouch." He crossed his arms on the table and leaned forward to speak, but just then the server brought their conch fritters. Zane waited until they'd both sampled the appetizer, murmured approvingly, then started again. "I can beat the boss-and-the-new-girlfriend scenario."

"Oh yeah?"

"Yeah. The wedding I'm in? I used to be with the bride."

Bailey's mouth opened.

"And she's marrying my college roommate."

"No," she whispered. "And they still asked you to be in the wedding?"

"They asked me to give the toast. The best man has stage fright."

"Tacky." She thought for a second. "You don't … still have feelings for her, do you?"

"No! Not at all. It's just a slap in the face. We broke up because after four years of dating, she didn't want to get married." He pulled a face. "They've known each other for eight months, and they're tying the knot."

"Ouch," she echoed. "That's …" She reached across the table and put her hand over his. "I'm sorry."

His gaze traveled down to their hands, and she jerked hers away abruptly.

"It's okay. I'm okay. There's just nothing worse than seeing your ex at an event when you're single."

"You're not kidding. Andrew had the gall to ask who I was bringing for my plus-one."

Zane refilled her water glass from the carafe on the table. "When's your awards dinner?"

"Friday night. Why?"

"The wedding is Saturday."

Bailey stared at him. "You don't mean …"

"Why not? We're already staying in the same house. We both need dates so we don't lose face with our exes. And if I may say, you're prettier than she is, so she'll be furious." He grinned at her. "This is where you say I'm prettier than your ex-slash-boss."

"Well, you have more hair, that's for sure." Inside, Bailey's thoughts were spinning. Now she knew she was insane. Not only was she seriously considering sharing a house with a total stranger, she was actually considering being Zane's date to the wedding and bringing him to a work function.

"Just think about it," he said, but there was a tension in his voice that said her answer actually mattered to him. That, more than anything, made her want to trust him.

That, and her instincts. Real estate was much more than properties and contracts; it was about people. The reason she was so successful wasn't because she found clients what they wanted. It was because she read between the lines and found them what they didn't know they needed. And that had given her a pretty good sense of when people were being honest with her. She had a feeling that Zane was being honest now.

Then again, that sixth sense had been nowhere to be found when she started dating Andrew.

"I'll think about it," she said finally. She didn't need to say anything else, because their entrees arrived, and her food was just as good as he had promised.

They were halfway through their meals when Zane looked up at her, cocking his head. "Tell me one unusual thing about yourself."

"Only one?"

"As tempted as I am to pursue that, yes."

She thought about giving him a fluff answer. But what the heck? She was probably never going to see this guy again, and in the meantime, they'd be sleeping twenty feet from each other in the same house. What was the harm in being honest?

"So, I have this weird thing …"

"Weird thing, how? Like an alien appendage? Or you keep a llama in your basement?"

"I wasn't going to tell you because I thought you'd think I was strange, but now it's obvious you're the one who's the weirdo."

He threw his head back and laughed, full-throated. "Sorry. I promise I won't interrupt anymore."

"Thank you. Anyway, I have this thing about … patterns, I guess. Like, I'll hear a couple of notes from a song that's similar to another song, and I can't relax until I figure out what it is. Or I'll see a feature in someone's face, and I have to think of who they resemble."

He grinned. "You think I look like Patrick Swayze in *Point Break*?" He ran his fingers through his hair. "It's this luscious mane, isn't it?"

She should have felt embarrassed that he'd seen through her so quickly, but he was so good-natured about it, she just laughed. "Pretty sure that's it."

"I don't think that's particularly strange though. It just makes you smart and curious."

"You don't talk like an IT guy. You talk like … an English major."

That signature shrug. "It's all just language. Learn the words and syntax to communicate appropriately. People, computers, makes little difference."

"What's your weird thing then?"

"I'm about twenty-five percent fluent in six languages."

Bailey laughed again. She seemed to be doing a lot of that with this guy. "Twenty-five percent fluent? How do you figure that?"

"I like to travel, so I learn enough of the local language to get around the city, read street signs and menus. Right now, I'm 'quarter-fluent' in Spanish, French, Thai, Vietnamese, Indonesian, and Afrikaans."

Bailey thought for a moment. "Would those be the languages spoken in the world's best surf spots, by any chance?"

Now he mimicked her finger-on-the-nose gesture. "That pattern recognition at work."

"So you're an IT guy on sabbatical who travels the world surfing and almost-speaks six languages. What else do you do?"

He regarded her, golden eyes sparkling. "I also like romantic movies and long walks on the beach, if that's what you mean."

"I'm serious. You surf—and I imagine probably scuba dive and snorkel—but do you really just drift around the world looking for the next wave?"

"Now I know you're obsessed with *Point Break*. I don't rob banks in a president mask, if that's what you're asking. To be honest, I've worked nonstop since high school. I didn't have much of a life—which was part of my ex's objection to marrying me, I suspect. So why shouldn't I travel while I have both the money and the time? Wouldn't you?"

"I don't know." Bailey thought, propping her chin in her hands. "I've worked hard to get where I am. I'm not sure I could leave it behind for any amount of time. I'd be afraid it wouldn't be waiting for me when I got back."

"A bird in the hand?"

"Something like that."

"Then if you're all about taking opportunities as they present themselves, you should take my offer. Come to the wedding with me and I'll be your date for the awards dinner. I have a suit and everything."

He'd made a compelling argument, and in the last hour, she'd decided that he was not a serial killer. Though she would take advantage of the bedroom door's lock. "I don't know. It feels a lot like lying, and I have a thing about honesty."

"Then say I'm a potential client. And it won't even be lying because there's a house I want to look at tomorrow. Think you could get away long enough to show it to me?"

She felt herself caving, and he knew it. He had probably orchestrated this appeal to her professional side because he'd guessed she was constitutionally unable to turn down a client. "I can do it after the conference tomorrow. Get me the address and I'll call the listing agent."

"So that means you're in? For all of it? Sharing the cottage? Being each other's plus-ones?"

Her stomach fluttered with an inexplicable emotion. Nervousness? Anticipation? She caught his expression—open, expectant, begging her to take a leap.

She couldn't do it though. "We'll share the place tonight. As for the rest? We'll see how things go."

"I can live with that," he said with a slight smile. "I'm going to be the best temporary roommate you ever had."

She couldn't help but chuckle. "I guess we'll see."

Zane could hardly believe Bailey had agreed to any of it, and he spent the entire way back to the cottage expecting her to think better of it and change her mind. Part of him—the part that had been raised with four sisters—wanted to chide her for being so trusting of a stranger. She hadn't asked his last name or even to see his booking confirmation or his driver's license, which actually worked in his favor, considering he didn't want her to put things together yet. At least *he* knew he wasn't a serial killer or a creep who wanted to worm his way into her bed by the end of the weekend.

That wasn't to say he had lied when he told her she was prettier than Meredith—that was true. She was the first person he'd ever met who actually had gray eyes, and they were the luminous color of a winter sky.

She was right on one account, though: he did talk like an English major. But unlike the typical English major, he had no romantic notions about how this weekend would go. After Sunday, they would never see each other again—sooner if she decided she was uncomfortable with the arrangement. There was no point in starting anything more personal than a surface level acquaintance. They were solutions to each other's problems, nothing more.

It had long since gotten dark when they arrived back at the house, and the crash of the tide on the shore greeted them as they stepped out of Bailey's car. He gestured for her to precede him up the stairs to the second floor where the living spaces were located, where she immediately opened the door and hovered awkwardly near the exit.

"Listen, if you're not comfortable with this …" he began, hoping she wouldn't back out. Despite all his protests, if she was really freaked, he'd have to do the chivalrous thing and let her have it. Never mind that it was high season in Islamorada and he'd be lucky to score a sofa in someone's living room … though, in fact, that's what he was doing anyway. But at least this was a comfortable sofa with a stunning view. The peek at the ocean he'd get from the kitchen windows wasn't bad either.

But she was already shaking her head. "No, it's okay. I was just thinking about the … logistics."

"How about I take a shower now so I can move my stuff out of the bedroom and get out of your way?"

"Leave it. The stuff in the closet, I mean. No use letting it all get wrinkled."

"Listen, I know this all seems crazy …"

"Not any crazier than getting involved with a guy I knew ahead of time wasn't right for me." She looked momentarily horrified at her openness, then took a page from his book and shrugged. "You're better looking than he is, too."

He wasn't going to lie—he liked that she'd come right out and said it. One step closer to avoiding making a fool out of himself at the wedding. He gestured to the bedroom. "May I?"

"Yes, of course. Please. Take your time."

He didn't, mostly because it didn't take much time to soap up, shampoo his hair, and brush his teeth. He pulled a T-shirt on with his shorts and collected his personal items from the bedroom. When he came out, she'd unfolded the sofa bed and made it up like something out of a catalog, complete with sheets turned down and a blanket accordion-folded neatly at the end of the mattress. She, on the other hand, was nowhere to be found.

He was momentarily puzzled until he thought of where he would be at this moment if it weren't for Bailey. He went out the kitchen door onto the wraparound porch, and sure enough, she was curled up on the outdoor sofa, her feet tucked beneath her. It was only when he got closer that he saw her eyes were closed and her breathing was deep and even. Sound asleep.

She looked too peaceful to wake, but it would get chilly in the morning, so he leaned over and touched her shoulder lightly. "Bailey?"

She stirred but didn't wake.

He tried again, softly rubbing her arm. "Bailey. Wake up. Time to go in."

This time, her eyes opened slowly. A split second before she was fully awake, she favored him with a smile. Then she realized where she was and jerked bolt upright. "Wow. I must have been tired. You done in there?"

He nodded. "All yours."

"Thanks. Good night then."

"Same." He moved toward the door from which he'd come, forcing himself not to turn back. Because while that split-second smile had meant nothing to her, it had hit suspiciously close to his heart.

three

WHEN BAILEY AWOKE THE NEXT MORNING, refreshed from a full night's sleep in an obscenely comfortable bed, she could almost believe she had dreamed the entire previous day. Sharing a place with a stranger? Having dinner with someone she'd met twenty minutes earlier? These were things someone else did. Not Bailey Jensen … methodical, focused, ambitious Bailey.

But the dark suit in the closet said otherwise, as did the smell of frying bacon from the other room.

She threw on a T-shirt and shorts, then padded out into the cottage's combined living-kitchen-dining area. Zane stood at the stove amid the crackling of breakfast meat, his hair wet and dripping down the back of a vintage Ron Jon T-shirt. He was barefoot, and even from here, she could see sand clinging to the lower half of his tanned legs.

The picture was so far from anything she'd ever found attractive that she was downright startled by the kick of her own heart. She shook it off and managed a question. "When did you go shopping?"

He threw her a smile over his shoulder but swiftly turned his attention back to the bacon. "I see you didn't snoop enough. I stopped at the market on the way in yesterday."

Curious, she moved to the refrigerator and pulled the door open, expecting to find beer and burgers, but the shelves held what she herself considered necessities—milk, orange juice, eggs, uncured bacon, plus a shocking compliment of fruits and vegetables. So her temporary roommate was a health nut?

"Not what you were expecting?"

"From a bachelor? No."

Zane grinned and nudged open one of the top cabinets. "This will make you feel better then."

Bailey laughed. The small space held two types of potato chips, cheese curls, a small bottle of bourbon, and a bag of Hershey's miniatures. "Whew. I was getting worried."

"All things in moderation," he said easily. "How do you take your eggs?"

"Sunny side up."

"Coming your way. There's fresh coffee in the pot."

Bailey took a mug from a rack on the countertop and poured herself a cup, black. Then she settled at the table. This was weird. Not because it felt weird, but because it didn't. It was comfortable. Nice even. Zane had been nothing but open, casual, and friendly since they'd met, and now he was acting like they were long-term roommates. If roommates made each other breakfast. Bailey didn't know. She'd always lived alone.

"So what's the plan for today?" he asked a couple of minutes later, setting a plate before her with two fried eggs, a couple of strips of crispy bacon, and a piece of toast.

"This looks good, thanks." She took a bite of the bacon and considered. "I need to be at the hotel to register at nine, and my last session ends at five. I should be back no later than five-thirty. Did you get the address of that house?"

"Yeah. It's right here." He rummaged around the countertop and then handed her a receipt with an address scribbled on the back. "It's only a few minutes from here."

"Great. I'll look up the listing agent and set up a showing."

"Shouldn't be hard. It's vacant."

"Did you peek through the windows?"

He gave her an indulgent smile. "Trust me on this one."

She wasn't going to argue with a man who could fry an egg this perfectly. "What about you? What are your plans?"

"Little of this, little of that." He took his plate to the small table and sat down across from her.

"Does that mean surfing?"

"Nah. Not much surfing in the Keys. You might get lucky on Key West on occasion."

"Snorkeling then."

"Maybe." He smiled at her. "Jealous?"

"Let's see. My first class is Ethics in Real Estate, so you tell me."

He smiled. "I couldn't begin to guess what you might find fun."

"Sitting inside on a beautiful island all day isn't among them. But I don't have much of a choice. It's the last thing standing between me and the next step."

"Then we'll just have to fit in some fun after hours."

"We?"

"Of course." He winked. "My goal is to show you what an amazing fake boyfriend I can be."

"Wait a second. I thought we were just talking a date. Now it's a full fake relationship?"

"Maybe it's a date on your end. But who takes a virtual stranger to a wedding?"

She arched an eyebrow. "Apparently, you do."

"Good point. And I'm not asking you to lie outright. But we don't need to volunteer how we met, do we?"

The sparkle in his eye was conspiratorial, and it almost made her forget that she hadn't actually agreed to this mad scheme. She hadn't agreed to anything beyond sharing the place last night. But he did cook a good breakfast. She couldn't remember the last time she'd had time for more than a cup of coffee and an apple in the morning. She always seemed to be running late. Including today. She glanced at her watch. "I need to get ready. I'm going to be late if I don't hurry." Her eyes flicked toward the sink and once more, he did all but read her mind.

"Go. Leave the dishes to me."

"Now I know you are too good to be true."

"Wait a second."

She paused, already halfway to the bedroom door. "Yes?"

"Your phone number? In case I need to reach you?"

"Oh. Good idea." She recited the number while he punched it into his phone. A moment later, her cell beeped from the bedroom.

He smiled. "Call me if you need me."

"If I have any fake boyfriend emergencies, you'll be the first one I'll dial."

Bailey hadn't been lying—she really did need to hustle. As much as she'd enjoyed an unaccustomed morning sleeping in as well as a hot breakfast, it had put her off schedule. She took the world's fastest shower, blew dry her hair as quickly as possible before twisting it up into an elegant knot, and slipped into a lightweight linen blouse and a pencil skirt. Some attendees took advantage of the balmy weather to show up in resort wear, but Bailey had long since learned that she could never show a break in her professional persona if she wanted to be taken seriously. She was petite, she was blonde, and she was southern. It was like the trifecta for condescension. It was, in truth, how she'd fallen into her relationship with Andrew in the first place. Once she'd had a drink with him after work then let him kiss her in the parking lot, she'd felt she had no choice but to see it through. Genuine office romances were acceptable; after-hours flirtations with the boss were not.

And yet, if she could go back and turn down that offer of a real date, she wouldn't be in the position she was now. Sure, there would have been some whispers among her colleagues who had witnessed the parking lot incident, but she wouldn't have become the butt of every office joke. Not that anyone dared say anything to her face—even without dating the boss, her place as highest-grossing agent won her the favorite status easily—but there were whispers aimed her direction before they were quickly covered by false smiles.

When she walked out the door, Zane was already gone, off to pursue his "this or that" for the day. It was a good reminder not to get distracted, to remember why she was here. Only eight hours stood between her and the broker program, her freedom. And no matter how much Zane might joke about his fake boyfriend status with those twinkling golden eyes and magnificent beach hair, he was a distraction, one she could ill afford.

The conference was being held at a resort on Plantation Key, the northernmost island that made up Islamorada, a short skip from Key Largo. It was the consolation, she thought, for being stuck inside on a beautiful sunny day while the trade winds sent fluffy white clouds scudding across the sky. Instead of the usual Vegas-patterned carpet and pseudo-classical acanthus sconces, the resort had driftwood-colored hardwoods and bright white stucco. A reminder that they were in paradise, even as they discussed contracts and appraisals and fiduciary responsibility.

A valet took her car—a nice touch—and then she made her way into the marble-floored lobby, which had been fashioned into a makeshift registration area. Sure enough, most of the agents and brokers and appraisers milling around the lobby were in some version of resort wear, badges on bright blue lanyards around their necks. As Bailey click-clacked her way across the lobby in her heels and heads swiveled in her direction, she wondered if she should have relaxed her rules for just one day.

"Jensen, Bailey," she told the woman at the desk, who was sorting through packets in a big plastic bin in front of her.

"Jacey, Jackson, Jensen. Here you are, hon."

Bailey clutched her hands in front of her while the woman collected all the items that came with her registration, trying not to show the spinning thoughts on her face. The woman's voice … She could swear she knew it from somewhere. Of course, she didn't, but it was close enough to something filed in her memory that it was going to nag at her. A comedy for sure …

"Hon? Are you okay?"

Bailey jerked her attention back to the woman and forced a smile. Apparently, she wasn't doing a good enough job of hiding her thoughts. "I'm fine, thanks.

The registration volunteer handed her a white envelope, a badge lanyard, and an ugly blue canvas tote bag. "Your schedule, your notebook, and your dinner tickets are all inside. The keynote will start in the ballroom in just a few minutes."

The answer came to Bailey in a flash: the red-headed, squeaky-voiced accounts payable lady in *Office Space*. The vocal resemblance—and physical resemblance, to be honest—was so uncanny she could barely keep a straight face. "Thank you so much," she said seriously, then spun before she could let out the giggle that was bubbling up inside.

The smile quickly slid from her face as she found herself looking straight into a familiar, gray-suited chest. Even before she lifted her eyes, she knew it was him. Her good humor evaporated as quickly as it had come.

But she had been playing this game for six months now, so by the time her eyes traveled up his red power tie to his face, she was already wearing a bright smile.

"All squared away, Bailey?" he inquired, giving her a once-over. At one time, she'd thought that sly up-down gaze was sexy, but then she'd also thought she looked good in high-waisted trousers, so her judgment on certain things was clearly suspect.

"Just checked in. And with—" She checked her watch—"fifteen minutes to spare until the keynote." She made to move around him, hoping he'd get the hint. Instead, he swiveled and fell into step beside her. She just barely managed not to show her full-body cringe.

It wasn't that he wasn't a handsome man, because he was—tall, fit, good-looking, with perfect teeth, a full head of dark hair, and pale blue eyes. He dressed well, held himself confidently, and had a way of making a woman feel like she was the only one in the world. And for at least those moments, he seemed to believe it too. It was the only way she could think to explain how her judgment had gone so far awry with him. It was hard to spot a liar when he truly believed his own lies.

At least she wasn't the only one who had been fooled—she knew of at least two other women who thought they were his one and only. It was just too bad she hadn't discovered them before he dropped her and she spent a full month wondering what she'd done wrong. It was only because his secretary had taken pity on her and whispered about his two "side pieces" in the ladies' room that she'd found out at all. He still didn't know she knew, because that would have meant outing Maureen, who needed her job even more than Bailey did.

"What's up, Andrew?" she asked briskly, trying to hasten this encounter along.

"I was just wondering if I could borrow your second dinner ticket. Kelly came and it would be nice if she could sit at our table. You're not using it, are you?"

Kelly. So that was the new girlfriend's name. The fact that he just assumed she'd come alone when they hadn't had a personal conversation in months had words tumbling out of her mouth before she had time to consider them. "Actually, I'm bringing a date."

Andrew stopped walking. "A date? I didn't realize you were seeing anyone."

"It's new. And it just so happened that he had to be here for a wedding this weekend. What are the chances?"

"Indeed, what are the chances?" Andrew repeated weakly. "It's fine. I think Carlos's wife stayed home with the kids. I'll ask him." And before she had a chance to process what had just happened, he was gone.

What *had* just happened? She was still supposed to be mulling whether Zane's proposition was a good idea, and instead she'd committed herself. And not to bringing him as a client, but as her date. Someone with whom she was in a new relationship. Never mind that she hadn't actually lied … her meaning had been clear enough for even Andrew to understand.

There was only one thing left to do. She pulled out her cell phone, found the unopened text from Zane, and prepared to send a message.

Then she read his earlier words.

Love, your fake boyfriend, Zane.

She smiled and shook her head then tapped out her reply.

Brush up on those boyfriend skills. You're on.

four

Zane had expected Bailey to cave. She had been halfway there last night, but he knew her better judgment and aversion to lying was holding her back. He didn't blame her. Heck, even he knew how crazy this idea was, but he also didn't believe in ignoring gifts when they were dropped directly into his lap. Bailey, on the other hand, struck him as the type to plan every move in advance, which was why it had been so amusing to see the dismay flick across her face when she'd inadvertently blurted something that slipped by her filter.

So he was not at all surprised to get her text message. He was just surprised to get it so soon.

It was perfect timing, though, because he was on his way to meet Tony and Meredith at the resort where the wedding would be held, and they would no doubt ask about the mystery woman for whom he'd RSVPed, but who hadn't actually existed until yesterday. If Meredith knew, she'd probably sprain her eyeballs rolling them. She'd never understood Zane or his blind faith that things would work out the way he wanted them to. And until the day she left him, his optimism had always been borne out.

He did take slight pleasure in imagining her annoyance when he arrived in jeans and flip-flops, having just biked five miles along the path that lined US1 rather than taking the expected route and coming by car. His beach bum tendencies—as Bailey had quickly identified—had always made Meredith a little crazy. It wasn't "appropriate for his status" she'd always said, which struck him as ridiculous. What was the point in being successful if you couldn't do what you wanted? Otherwise, it was just another form of the lifestyle tyranny he'd been trying to escape when he went into business for himself.

Phrases like *lifestyle tyranny* had also annoyed her.

Come to think of it, a lot annoyed Meredith. Never, even at the beginning of their relationship, had she regarded him with the bemused fascination that Bailey displayed. Put in those terms, it seemed like he'd dodged a bullet, even if it had taken a few years and a complete stranger to make him realize it.

Even with the stiff wind blowing off the water, the day was warm and slightly humid, and he arrived at Plantation Key Resort sweaty enough to make Meredith scowl, but not enough to draw attention to himself, which was just about the right level of disheveledness. He left the bicycle with the amused valet and chuckled to himself as he wandered into the resort's expansive lobby. It took him a moment to orient himself, and then a bellhop directed him toward the Bay Club Restaurant just off the back of the reception area. He strolled across the foyer, his flip-flops smacking the tiled floor as he walked.

He spotted them immediately in the partially-filled restaurant, Meredith's shining dark hair instantly recognizable, Tony's nondescript brown head no more distinct than any other white guy in chinos and a button-down.

The host—probably maître d' in this place—approached him, but Zane pantomimed his intentions and crossed the restaurant to his friend and the soon-to-be bride.

Tony rose immediately and pounded him into a hug. "Zane! You came! Part of me wondered if you were going to bail and cruise to Bimini instead."

"It crossed my mind," Zane drawled, then bent to kiss Meredith's cheek. "Mer, looking beautiful as always."

"Zane. Looking … like always." The twist of her mouth suggested a smile without her having to make the effort. Had she always looked this pinched or was it displeasure that Tony had insisted on this lunch? Zane suspected she was the reason he wasn't best man, so for that he really ought to thank her. His insanity extended only so far.

Zane took his seat across from them and accepted the menu a discreet server handed him, but he didn't open it. "So? How goes the last-minute wedding tasks? Everything in order?"

"A few hiccups, but Meredith has them under control. Right, Mer?"

Meredith flinched, probably because that was the nickname that Zane always had used for her. She did look tired, though. Weren't brides supposed to be glowing and excited? She looked like she wanted to be anywhere but here right now.

He didn't blame her one bit.

But Tony stuck to light topics until they placed their orders, including cocktails. Zane asked for an unsweet tea. The more they sat there, the more he sensed an ambush and figured he'd need his wits about him. He certainly wasn't going to make it easy for them. He prattled on about his beach house rental, his last dive trip to the Maldives, how he was going to be looking at a piece of property tonight on Islamorada. And as minutes passed, Meredith looked more and more uncomfortable.

Finally, halfway through their meal—a delicious seafood pasta in Zane's case—Tony put down his fork. "We're all friends here, right?"

Zane paused. "Until you opened with that, I assumed so."

Tony cleared his throat. "Mer—I mean, we—just wanted to make sure you aren't feeling pushed into this. We know it's a bit awkward. And it's really important to her—I mean us—that everything goes off without a hitch."

Meredith had shrunk as far into her chair as possible without actually disappearing while her fiancé bumbled what was no doubt supposed to be a casual chat between old friends. Instead, Tony seemed to be mentally regurgitating talking points from a previous conversation. Zane felt a little sorry for her in that moment but not too sorry considering she'd had plenty of time to discover that Tony was a lovable chowderhead, even if he was a successful one.

Finally, he decided to let them off the hook. "Do you mean, 'Am I going to object to the wedding and declare my undying love for Meredith in front of two hundred people?' No, I figured it was better to do that now, in person."

Meredith paled, and Tony looked alarmed.

Zane rolled his eyes. "Guys. How long have you known me? Really."

"I knew he wasn't going to take things seriously," Meredith muttered, pushing her chair away from the table.

"No, Mer, sit. Really. You can't expect me not to yank your chain. I've jumped through all the wedding hoops, written a toast, and come all the way to Islamorada for the event, and now you decide to question my sincerity? If you were worried about it, I'd say you should have voiced that six months ago when Tony asked me."

The glare Meredith sent Tony made him think that was indeed when she'd brought up her concerns.

"With all due respect, Mer, you are a beautiful woman with an impressive career, but I haven't exactly been sitting around and pining for you this past year. And I can honestly say, Tony, I haven't been pining over you either."

Tony grinned, his concerns—if he'd ever had them—fully assuaged. Even Meredith looked mollified. "I won't even mention our previous relationship in the toast, Meredith, if it makes you uncomfortable. I will make no such promises to you, Tony, because I have been saving up embarrassing stories for a decade for expressly this purpose." Zane tossed his napkin on the table and made to stand. "So thank you for lunch. I will see you tomorrow, but I will need to pass on the rehearsal dinner because I have other plans."

"Plans?" Meredith blurted. "What other plans?"

"Bailey has an awards dinner. But don't worry, I'll be there for the rehearsal itself."

He was already walking away when he heard Meredith's voice echo after him. "Bailey? Who's Bailey?"

He chuckled to himself as he walked out of the restaurant. He'd had a feeling something like this would happen, so he'd been prepared for it. However, he hadn't been prepared for the fact that he'd meant every single word. When he looked at Meredith, he felt nothing except regret that they'd wasted so much time with each other when they could have been happy with someone else. Whether or not this marriage was going to last, he didn't know: Meredith suffered no fools, and Tony was known to have his moments. But he was stable, dependable, and slightly predictable. And if today's luncheon had reminded him of anything, it was that Meredith didn't like surprises.

Put in those terms, it was hard to understand what she'd ever seen in Zane in the first place.

He collected his bicycle from the valet and headed back to the house. He had several hours until Bailey got back, which meant he had time to take out one of the kayaks beneath the deck. But by the time he reached the house, his inclination for outdoor entertainment had waned.

Something in Meredith and Tony's attitude was needling him. At first, he'd assumed they were concerned he'd make a scene because of his previous relationship with her. But there had been something else in their manner—like they were talking to a dissolute nephew who couldn't be trusted not to show up sloppy and wasted. Maybe it wasn't a perfect analogy, because he didn't really drink—the emergency bourbon in the cabinet notwithstanding—and he'd never been accused of showing up at an event less than appropriately turned out. But it was the first time anyone had looked at him with that mixture of concern and pity.

He, who had made his first million at nineteen, who had most recently built a second company from the ground up, employed more than a hundred people, and cashed out for an absurd amount of money. He who had routinely worked eighty hours a week for a decade, rarely taking a vacation or seeing anything but the inside of his office. It had, in fact, been one of the deciding factors in his break-up with Meredith.

Everyone had been supportive of his decision to take some time off and enjoy life, but then one year had turned into two, and it seemed that it wasn't respectable to retire at thirty, despite the fact people would work another three decades for that sole purpose, complaining about it the whole time.

Maybe the problem was that he actually seemed content to do nothing. Though if he were truly honest, it was getting a little … boring.

Zane left the bike below the house then climbed the staircase to the main level and let himself in the front door. He went straight to the shower, where he rinsed off this morning's saltwater and this afternoon's sweat, then slipped on his only informal, nonbeachwear—a pair of jeans and a lightweight, short-sleeved button-down. Then he settled on the sofa with his laptop and started researching.

He was still in that position when Bailey walked through the door, looking tired and rumpled. She stopped when she saw him on the sofa in the deepening shadows, face illuminated by the screen. "What are you doing?"

"Rethinking my life choices," he said with a smile, but he put aside his laptop. "How was your day?"

"Long. But okay. How was 'this and that?'"

It took him a moment to recall his earlier words. "It was …" Uncomfortable? Awkward? Enlightening? "Fine."

"Okay then. Well, are you ready to go look at the house? We should go before it gets too dark."

"Don't you want to change first?"

She looked down at her skirt. "What's wrong with what I'm wearing?"

"You didn't look up the listing, did you?"

"No, I asked someone in my office to set it up. Why?"

"I recommend closed-toed shoes."

Bailey looked mildly alarmed, but to her credit, she didn't question it. She just disappeared into the bedroom and came out a minute later wearing a pair of stylishly distressed jeans, a floaty sort of top, and ballet flats. Still about three notches dressier than the house demanded, but it would do.

"Okay, let's go see this dream house of yours."

His smile only widened when, fifteen minutes later, she pulled up in front of the address he'd given her. She looked at him in dismay. "This is it?"

"Yep."

"Well, it's waterfront."

That was about all it had going for it. The house had originally been two stories, not counting the ground floor garage, but now it was little more than studs and a partial roof. Debris cluttered not just the interior of the house, mostly open to the elements, but also the entire lot, which was contained somewhat depressingly by a chain link fence.

They climbed out of the car and approached the fence. "That explains the price."

"It does. But it has a hundred feet of canal frontage. Do you have any idea what this would cost if there was a livable house on it?"

She shot him a look that said she thought he'd lost his mind. "I do, in fact. I also know that this house will take at least $300,000 to rebuild to a minimum standard … which in this neighborhood, might not be sufficient."

He just stuck his hands into his pockets and smiled at her.

"You have several hundred thousand dollars lying around to fix a house?"

"I don't intend to fix it. I would knock it down and start over. But yes. I have the money."

"But why? If you've got that kind of cash, why buy this? You could get a pretty amazing beach house for the same price."

He shrugged. "Maybe I need the challenge. Maybe I've spent long enough coasting and it's time to find something else to do."

She was still looking at him like he was crazy, but he was beginning to get used to that. He unlatched the gate and stepped inside. Bailey followed somewhat reluctantly.

It looked as if someone had at least started to clean up the lot, because there was a clear path on the left side of the structure. It was there that he headed, gesturing for Bailey to follow him as he navigated around the occasional debris. "From what I understand, this was hurricane-damaged. A flipper came in intending to renovate it, but they didn't get much further than demo before they figured out it was almost a total loss. Then another tropical storm hit and pretty much did the rest in. I would just be buying this for the lot." He stopped and gestured to the real reason he was interested in the house.

"It's on a deepwater canal," Bailey said. Indeed, a dark swath of blue cut between two rows of houses, facing spectacular mansions with their own docks. Large fishing boats and small yachts floated peacefully in the still water.

"Which leads to Florida Bay, with some pretty spectacular sunsets." He nodded toward where the canal joined with open water and was gratified by her intake of breath at the watercolor sky.

"I take it back," she said finally. "This would take you $600,000— maybe seven—to build here." She looked at him curiously. "You have more than a million dollars for this project?"

He just crossed his arms over his chest and looked at her.

"What don't I know about you?"

Now he laughed. "Just about everything, I'd venture to say. So what do you think?"

"I think if you have the money to put into it and a smart contractor, you could make half a million dollars on the deal. Or would you live here?"

"Live here for two years to avoid the capital gains, then move on, I'd think," he said. "Anyway, I've got a lot of research to do before I make a decision, but if I decide to go forward, do you want to be my agent?"

Bailey blinked, but he could tell she was tempted. "You barely know me."

"I know enough."

"I barely know you."

He smiled. "You know enough."

Reluctantly, she smiled too, and it turned to a laugh. "Let's talk about it over dinner."

Zane suggested another of his favorite restaurants, which Bailey looked up in her GPS, and then they were heading down the island again in the swiftly darkening evening. The whole time, he could tell she was holding herself back from appraising glances—she kept turning her head to look at him, then jerking her eyes back to the road. He wondered if he shouldn't have just left things the way they were. This was the reason he never told anyone who he was or what he had done before. True, there was only a small subset of the tech industry who would know the details, but anyone who read *Forbes* or *Fast Company* or any of those entrepreneurial publications would know at least the broad strokes of his story. And in his experience, once people knew that, they started treating him differently. Less like a beach bum, more like a unicorn. Or worse, like a potential investor.

If he were honest, though, maybe he'd wanted Bailey to look at him a little differently, especially after seeing the fleeting pity in Meredith's eyes.

The place he'd picked for dinner was a dive bar, somewhat rowdy even on a Thursday night, filled with vacationers and boaters that had made the run from Biscayne Bay to Islamorada for drinks and fish tacos, their impressive array of watercraft docked at the marina next door. Bailey didn't even blink as he ushered her through the entrance and selected a vacant two-top by the window.

"So, I know you've got a reason for bringing me here," Bailey said.

"I do. Conch tacos."

Bailey's mouth made an *ooh* of approval.

"We place our order at the bar though. You want something? A cocktail? A beer?"

"Tacos and a virgin margarita?"

"Not much of a drinker?"

She shrugged, and he suspected it meant, "Not with someone I don't know." He smiled and nodded as he walked away, but he couldn't help but feel slightly stung by the insinuation. He'd been nothing but a gentleman toward her so far, careful not to show an inkling of the attraction he felt in her presence. He glanced over his shoulder when he got to the bar and found her eyes fixed on him, though, like in the car, she quickly looked away.

Oh. Maybe it wasn't *him* she didn't trust.

He placed their orders, retrieved her margarita sans alcohol and a beer for himself, and ambled back to the table. He expected more small talk, admiration of the view, a comment about the rowdy group of middle-aged men at the table behind them.

He did not expect her to fold her arms atop the table, drill him with her sharp gaze, and say, "Are you going to tell me who you really are?"

five

BAILEY AIMED THE DART and watched it strike, hoping to see something flicker in Zane's face that might give away what he'd been hiding from her.

He only set the drinks down in front of them, completely unperturbed. "I'll tell you any time. My name is Zane Whitney. I'm a tech guy, like I told you. I made a lot of money at my last company, and now I'm enjoying early retirement while I decide what to do next."

Bailey stared at him, feeling a little deflated. Here she thought he was going to hedge and conceal, but he flat out told her what she wanted to know. And the name did not ring any bells at all. Maybe he was exactly who he'd said he was. It was just that she didn't often run into someone who rented other people's houses, rode a borrowed bike, and dressed like an islander when he had a million dollars sitting in his bank account.

But now that he was answering questions, she'd be stupid not to take advantage of it. "Where do you live?"

"Miami."

"Where exactly?"

"Coconut Grove."

So, yeah, he had money. Though the bohemian neighborhood fit him; it was expensive but not flashy by Miami standards, and it was right on the water.

"What was your company's name?"

"I'm not going to tell you that."

"Why not?"

"Because you're going to recognize it and look at me differently, and I think we're having a pretty good time the way things are."

"You know I could just Google it. You told me your last name."

"You could. But I'm hoping you won't."

"Tell me why."

He sat back in his chair. "I'm just a guy who knows how to do some things. People liked the things I did, and it was lucrative. But it drives me crazy when people look at me like I have some big secret to success. And let me tell you, it's usually people who already have a high degree of success. It's not enough for them. If they've made a million, they want ten. If they've made ten, they want a hundred. Do you know what I consider success?"

Bailey smiled slightly. "No, but I know you're going to tell me."

"Sitting in a dive bar at sunset in the Florida Keys with a beautiful woman who has no idea who I am but seems to like me anyway."

Her heart gave a little hiccup, because his words were true. She had no idea who he really was, but he was funny and kind and intriguing. "Is that right?"

"That is absolutely right." He sobered. "Everyone looked at me like I was crazy to walk away from my business. I could have had more, you know, had I made different decisions. But I wasn't happy. I worked all the time. Striving is exhausting to the soul."

It was really the last thing she'd expected him to say, though everything about him was beginning to make sense. All the standards by which she would have judged him or had judged him already—his car, his watch, his reputation—were about recognition. They had nothing to do with who he was. And the idea made her inexplicably uncomfortable.

"Do you think it's wrong to be ambitious?" She hadn't expected the words to come, but when they did, she was shocked to hear how insecure her voice sounded.

"Of course not. If it's because you like what you do and you want to push yourself." He met her eyes. "Is that why you want to be a broker?"

She'd never been asked that. For that matter, she'd never articulated it to herself. "I think I don't want to be reliant on someone else for my success. I want to ... control my own destiny."

He smiled. "Now who sounds like an English major?"

Bailey laughed. "Seriously, though. I love what I do. I can make a lot more money as a broker, once I open my own firm and hire some good agents, though I'll take a lot more risk. It's fun. I'm good at the business side."

"Sounds like you know exactly what you're supposed to be doing. Why the hesitation then?"

Bailey dropped her eyes and traced the water ring her glass had left on the table. "Andrew always told me I was overreaching. Made it all sound so difficult."

"Maybe Andrew didn't want to lose his best agent and probably some other ones, too. My guess is that Andrew's a tool."

Bailey's eyes widened, and she laughed. "Maybe."

"He probably also didn't want his girlfriend—or ex-girlfriend—as a competitor."

"Now *that* is definitely true. He's been resting on his laurels and his brokerage fees. I don't think he's done any actual work in the last two years. Too busy with his girlfriends, I'd guess."

"You really don't like this guy."

"Would you like someone who cheated on you repeatedly and you only found out from his secretary?"

"Ouch. No. Definitely a tool. That's why you broke up with him?"

"No, that's why he broke up with me. Actually, I don't know why he broke up with me. I'm assuming he had limited time and too many women to juggle. I only found out after the fact because I befriended his secretary."

"She isn't one of the women, is she? Because then you can add predictable to sleazy."

Bailey grinned. "No. She's sixty years old and not a young sixty either. I suspect she's extremely judgmental about his personal decisions."

"As well she should be." Zane leaned back in his chair and took a swig from the bottle. The noise behind him ramped up a few decibels.

"So what's your story? What's with the ex marrying your college roommate?"

"Well, I met Meredith when I moved back to Miami after college. We dated for about four years. When I started talking about marriage, she bolted."

"That's a reversal."

"Yeah, well, she's this big-time lawyer. So when someone like that tells you that *you're* too obsessed with your work, it might be a wake-up call."

"Is that why you left your company?" Things snapped into place and Bailey amended, "Why you *sold* your company, I mean?"

"Not the only reason, but yeah. I'd actually introduced Meredith to Tony at a party a while back, and when they ran into each other again, I guess they just clicked. He's a financial analyst, so their interests were … a little more compatible, I suppose."

"You mean they're both boring?" Bailey laughed. "Stable?"

He grinned. "Something like that. Though I wouldn't expect you to think of it that way."

"Because I have a boring job? I'm an entrepreneur, too. All it takes is a big recession and I have no income. Only a certain kind of person is willing to accept that risk. And it will be even more of a risk when I leave my job for my own brokerage, because I'll be responsible for everything: all the overhead, all the money collection, all the HR. No one to blame but myself if I fail."

Something like understanding—maybe even appreciation—lit his face, but before he could say anything, their tacos arrived. Bailey wasted no time digging into her food. He was right: they were fantastic. She'd never been a fan of conch before this trip, but so far, he was two for two with his recommendations.

They ate silently, but it was a comfortable silence, a companionable one. Despite the flirtation, which she suspected he could turn on and off like a light switch, she didn't get the sense that he had any agenda for her. Which was good. Because as she sat there, stealing occasional glances at him as she chewed, she realized she liked him.

Not in a "this guy would make decent husband material someday" way, because she wasn't sure he actually would. And not in a "sexy weekend fling" sort of way, because that wasn't her style. But in a genuine, "enjoy him as an actual person" sort of way. And she realized with a start how long it had been since she could say that about any of the men in the periphery of her life.

Certainly, she wouldn't have said that about Andrew. She had admired him to a degree, and she had been attracted to him, at least at first. But she wasn't sure that she ever could have said she liked him as a person. Nor could she have said that about any of her previous boyfriends.

Had her standards for men really been so low?

Zane caught her staring and lifted his eyebrows. "What are you thinking?"

"I was just thinking that you are unlike any of the men in my life."

"Is that a good thing?"

"Yeah. I like you." She felt the heat rise to her cheeks. "You know, as a person. You're nice to be around."

He threw her a wry grin. "Don't worry. I won't read too much into that. I can already see the wheels turning while you decide whether you regret having said that."

And there he went, reading her mind again. "I'm not sure I like how perceptive you are."

"I'm not that perceptive. You're pretty transparent to anyone who pays attention." When she opened her mouth to protest, he held up a hand. "I didn't say it was a bad thing."

"It sounds like a bad thing."

"Trust me, it's not. It's honest."

He smiled at her, his eyes locked on hers, and somehow the words and the look warmed her to her core. And beyond. She shifted and cleared her throat. "We should probably get going. I have an early day tomorrow and there's the dinner."

"Right." He picked up the check, cut off her protest with a look, and ambled back over to the bar, where he paid the bartender. When he came back, he waited patiently for her to gather her things then allowed her to precede him out the door.

When she stepped outside into the parking lot, they were immediately enveloped in blackness. Even the lights from the highway didn't seem to penetrate the dark. When she commented on it, Zane threw a glance at the sky. "It's a new moon." He shifted his gaze to her. "I know you said you wanted to turn in early, but there's something I want to show you. Are you game?"

She narrowed her eyes at him. "As long as this something you want to show me isn't a part of your body."

He raised an eyebrow.

"I had to ask. I've heard that line too many times not to be suspicious."

"Apparently, *all* your exes are tools, not just the most recent one." He held out his hand. "Here, give me your phone. It will be easier than giving directions."

She handed over her cell and watched as he tapped in a location and pressed *start*. She glanced at the route when he returned it to her. "We're going to Plantation Key?"

He put a finger to his lips. "Don't ask. You'll ruin the surprise."

She climbed into the driver's side and started the car, her curiosity piqued. He was probably taking her by another house he'd found for sale or a place for dessert. But she did not expect, when they arrived on Plantation Key, for the map to take them down to the bay side of a marina.

Zane directed her down a paved road, the water side lined with boats, then pointed to a spot on the grassy shoulder that doubled as a parking lot. When she turned off the car, he was watching her with anticipation on his face. "How do you feel about a little boat ride?"

Bailey couldn't hold back her surprise. "You have a boat here?"

He nodded once.

"Is it safe?"

"Winds are calm for once and the water's still. It's safe."

She licked her lips. She'd spent plenty of time on the water over the years, but only during the day. Somehow, the inky blackness beyond was far more intimidating. Yet Zane seemed supremely confident that it was safe. She finally nodded. "Okay. Let's go."

He smiled and led her across the road and another grassy shoulder to a wooden boardwalk behind the berths. Bailey's eyes widened as they passed. These weren't boats. These were *yachts*. Surely he didn't own one of these million-dollar behemoths. "Please don't tell me we're here to admire your yacht."

Zane laughed and stopped behind a modest-sized vessel, at least compared to the ones surrounding it, marked in dark blue script with the name *Celestine*. "Not a yacht. A fishing boat. And technically, since I've outfitted it as such, it's a dive boat."

"A large, expensive dive boat," she said, her eyebrows arched.

Zane shrugged. "Depends on who you ask. Ready to come aboard?"

"Aye aye, captain."

He grinned and held out a hand to steady her as she stepped onto the stern. It was low enough that she just had to step down to the deck. She watched as he loosened the dock lines and threw them onto the deck, then hopped aboard and made his way to the covered half-cabin in the center of the boat.

"You can sit there," he said, gesturing toward a comfortably upholstered bench seat behind the console. Then he turned a key and started flipping switches. The motors and electronics sprang to life.

"Tell me the truth," she said as he idled out of the berth. "Do you really use all this stuff?" She waved a hand at the console.

"Absolutely. There's some tricky navigation to get down here and the waterways aren't always well marked, hence the GPS. Having the radar is helpful in bad weather or narrow channels. There's nothing more terrifying than coming up behind a stopped boat in one of the smaller cuts."

"Do we need that now?"

He smiled at her. "Nah. We're not going that far anyway. Just out into the bay."

She wanted to ask him why but suspected that was part of the surprise, so she kept the question to herself. Once he cleared the marina's breakwater, he throttled up and the boat surged forward, cutting through the water smoothly with the hum of the outboard motors. The night was warm, but the air off the water was cooler, and she rubbed her arms against a sudden chill.

"There's a windbreaker beneath the seat if you're cold." He hadn't even turned his head, but somehow he'd caught the gesture.

"I'm okay," she said, but after another minute, she stood and dug into the storage space until she came up with a lightweight red windbreaker. As she thrust her arms into the sleeves and pulled the lapels shut against the wind, she was enveloped by a scent that she'd already unconsciously come to associate with Zane: salt, sunblock, a faintly masculine soap or aftershave. She inhaled surreptitiously then cursed herself for the answering shiver across her skin.

Suddenly, he throttled back. After a moment, he cut the motor completely until the only sound was water lapping at the hull. "Stay here," he said and disappeared out onto the bow, doing something she couldn't see. A second later, she heard the whir of a smaller motor and the clink of chains—he must be putting down the anchor.

When he came back, he was smiling. "We're here. Come look." He held out a hand. She took it reluctantly, letting him lead her back onto the deck. And then she gasped.

six

Her reaction was everything he'd hoped it would be. She tipped her head back to the sky, the light so dim around them that he felt rather than saw the smile that blossomed across her face. "I've never seen anything like this."

Zane tilted his head back as well. They were only about a mile offshore, but that mile was enough to eliminate all the ambient light from the relatively dimly lit key, plunging them into total darkness. Above them stretched the expanse of the heavens, so littered with stars that it was hard to believe so many could exist in the universe, the Milky Way a spill of diamond dust in the dark. He knew how she felt without her saying it—the first time he had escaped the lights of the city and realized how much those lights concealed, it was like finding out he'd been partially blind his whole life.

"Here." Zane pulled some of the cushions off the bench seat and spread them out on the deck so they could lay on their backs, side by side, staring upward. He pointed to the south of them. "Do you see those four stars there? The three blue ones and the warmer one up top? That's the Southern Cross. It points directly to the South Pole. This is the only place in the Northern Hemisphere that you can see it."

She turned her head quickly in surprise, though he imagined it was too dark to read anything in his expression. Then she looked up again. "It's beautiful. Not just that. All of it. I knew there were a lot of stars, but this … Why in the world are you staying in a beach house when you could be out here?"

He chuckled. "Because this doesn't have a cabin below, and it does get a little wet on deck."

"Ah." She stared up at the sky for a long moment. "Do you know a lot about stars?"

"A little. I mostly just like looking at them. It's peaceful."

"Do you see that one right there?" She pointed directly overhead. "Do you know what that is?"

Zane followed her gaze, then answered honestly. "I have no idea."

"It's Saturn," she said, a smile evident in her voice. It had been some sort of honesty test, he thought, and one he'd apparently passed. "You can also see Mars there, and Venus. Neptune also should be up, but we'd need a telescope or at least binoculars to see it."

"And here I thought I was going to be the one impressing you."

Her voice was soft. "Oh, you are impressing me. This was a good idea. I'm glad you turned out not to be a serial killer."

"As far as you know," he said teasingly, and she elbowed him hard in the ribs. After a moment, he asked, "So what else is up there that I should know about?"

"Hmm. Well, do you see that bright one? That's Vega."

"Okay …"

She chuckled. "This means nothing to you, does it?"

"No, not really."

"That's okay. I'm not really an astronomy expert either. Mostly I just like looking."

They lay there for several long minutes, just staring up at the universe above them. Then Zane rolled on his side to face her. "How do you feel about a swim?"

She turned onto her elbow and looked at him. "Right now?"

"Sure. It's still pretty warm out."

"Yeah, but I don't have a bathing suit."

He grinned. "Neither do I." He levered himself up to his feet and then made his way to the console where he flipped on the underwater lights. The sea around them lit up like semi-transparent blue-green glass. He pulled off his shirt and tossed it onto the bench, then kicked off his shoes. After a moment's consideration, the shorts went as well, leaving him in a pair of boxers. He grinned at Bailey in the dark, slid back the dive door, and took a step straight out into the water.

When he surfaced a couple of feet away within the glow of the lights, she was leaning over the gunwales, looking at him. He treaded water and slicked his hair back from his face. "Are you coming in or what?"

"You're crazy!"

"That wasn't an answer."

Bailey hesitated, but by now, he had learned to read her. That was the look she got when she was mentally trying to talk herself out of something she wanted to do.

"Come on. When is the next time you're going to find yourself in the middle of Florida Bay on a new moon night? You'll kick yourself if you don't come in."

That did it. She shook her head, as if not believing what she was about to do and then shimmied out of her top and jeans. Zane tried not to look too closely; merely knowing she was sliding out of her clothes was enough to make his heart just about stop beating. He caught the vague impression of a bikini-type bra and shorts-style panties before she plunged into the water.

And then she surfaced, spluttering a little.

"You okay?"

"Yeah, I'm fine. I just …" She wiped water off her face. "I can't believe it's so warm!"

"Water temperature is higher than the air right now," he said with a grin. "Told you you'd be sorry to miss it."

She treaded water, her arms outspread, her pale hair fanning out around her shoulders and bobbing in the current. "Do you do this a lot?"

"What? Swim at night?"

"No, I mean, yes … but take your boat out at night."

"Occasionally, if I'm without a place to stay. But mostly just day trips. Diving. Fishing. It's not the most comfortable set up for overnights."

"Why'd you buy it then? Seems to me you're happiest when you're out here."

"I am. But if I had a cabin, then I'd have no reason to ever go ashore, or at least farther than the marina. I spent too much of my life so far locked in an office alone. Part of the fun of boating is meeting strangers."

"Female strangers?" she asked casually, but there was the slightest hitch in her voice. Was she actually jealous? And why should that idea please him quite so much?

He answered levelly. "Sometimes. I've taken a couple of women diving. But I've never brought anyone out to look at the stars."

He caught a hint of her smile in the reflected glow off the water. "Good answer. Whether it's true or not."

That was enough to make him close the distance in a slow breaststroke, until he was close enough to see her eyes clearly. "I have not once lied to you, Bailey."

Her throat worked, her breath coming faster. "No," she said softly. "I believe that."

For the briefest moment, he was tempted to reach for her, but he clamped down on that impulse and instead stretched out an arm to grasp the deck of the boat through the open dive door. He held out a hand to her. "Ready to get back in?"

"Probably should." She took his hand and let him tow her back to the side of the boat, where she grabbed the deck as well. They stayed there, bobbing side by side for a second.

Then Bailey turned to push herself out of the water, but just as she managed to build up the momentum to get in, her hand slipped from the wet decking. Instinctively, Zane threw his arm out and caught her around the waist before she went under, hauling her to his side. One of her arms wrapped around his shoulders, bringing them face-to-face, her body near enough that he could feel the rise and fall of her chest. Instead of moving away, she stilled. Her eyes flicked to his mouth and lingered there, stoking the fire he'd been trying so hard to keep suppressed.

She kissed him first. Later, he would be sure of it. But in that moment, he only knew the softness of her lips, the taste of salt on her skin, the way her legs twined with his beneath the surface of the water. And then she pulled away, her eyes wide. "I'm sorry. I think that was a bad idea. I didn't mean to—"

"It's okay. You're right. It probably is a bad idea." But neither of them moved, and before he could think, he was kissing her again with an urgency that obliterated every warning sounding in the back of his mind.

It was probably good that his hands were occupied with keeping them both afloat or he would have been tempted to have them all over her, to feel her slick skin with his fingertips, to mold her curves with his palms. As it was, his breath was becoming ragged, his brain muzzy with desire.

And then the boat rocked. His grip on the deck faltered and they plunged downward into the saltwater.

It was as much of a shock as a cold shower. He surfaced instantly, bringing her with him, and her stunned expression told him she had been just as carried away by the moment as he had. He saw the instant her regret flooded in: she retreated behind her eyes, her expression guarded in a way it hadn't been since their first meeting. He wanted to curse himself for his stupidity.

He cleared his throat, but his voice still came out huskier than he'd intended. "Grab onto the boat. I'll get in first and help you up."

He levered himself out of the water and onto the deck. He reached for one of her hands then grabbed the other and hauled her easily up next to him. He didn't look at her, instead rummaging for two towels beneath the seat compartment. "Here," he said inanely. "Dry off."

He toweled himself dry then turned his back to her to pull on his shorts and T-shirt. She was patently not looking at him when he turned around.

"Is there someplace I can change?" she asked.

He was pleased to find that she seemed no steadier than he felt.

"The head, right next to the console." He waved vaguely, and she slipped by him, still not meeting his eye.

He was an idiot. He'd meant to be a gentleman. He really had. He'd managed admirably up until the point he had his arm around her and ...

She *had* started it, his inner voice reminded him.

True, but he'd most definitely taken it a step further. He toweled his hair until it was only damp then made his way back onto the bow to haul up and secure the anchor. When he returned to the cockpit, she was just stepping out of the head compartment, fully dressed.

"Ready to go?" he asked, forcing cheerfulness, and she nodded.

It was the last thing they said to each other. They made the trip back to the marina in silence, the drive back to their shared house in equal quiet. It wasn't until Bailey was standing in the doorway of her bedroom that she found her voice. "Good night, Zane."

"Good night, Bailey."

The door shut firmly in his face, telling him everything he needed to know about her feelings.

And in the morning, when he awoke, she was already gone.

seven

To say Bailey was off her game would be an understatement.

Before she'd even left the beach house—at an ungodly hour meant to preclude any conversation with her housemate—she'd burned herself with her curling iron, poked herself in the eye with a mascara wand, and chipped a nail while trying to zip her peep-toe booties. With that kind of evidence, she couldn't even pretend that the previous evening hadn't left her shaken and jittery.

She and Zane had crossed a line.

Not a physical line—though had circumstances been slightly different they might have blown past that one too—but a practical one. Before, they had been strangers, housemates, on their way to becoming platonic friends. But now? After that kiss that had burned down just about every barrier she had left against him? They were two people in close proximity, powerfully attracted to each other, just begging for trouble.

The only solution was to spend as little time with him as possible until they parted ways on Sunday. Easier said than done, considering they were supposed to be each other's dates for the next two nights.

But those were formal events. Staid. Posed. Not wildly romantic like stargazing on a boat in the bay, swimming in warm waters, seduced by the conceit that they were the only two people in the world.

If she stayed away from the wildly romantic, she'd be okay.

She even believed that. She stopped at a coffee shop near the resort for an Americano and bolstered her resolve with its double shot of espresso. She managed to make it through the keynote address in the morning and her first two classes without even thinking of Zane. Or at least not in more than the vaguest of terms. But midway through a seminar dealing with appraisals, she found herself focusing not on the speaker, but on the memory of Zane's lips on hers, the imaginary impressions his fingertips had burned into her skin. There had been something unbelievably erotic about that kiss, cradled by the ocean, nothing but a few layers of wet cotton between them, that had made it feel somehow illicit.

That's what it was, she decided. It was this idea of a vacation fling. She'd never in a million years have one. But she *could* if she wanted to. No one would know. There would be no whispers in the office, no professional fallout. No one to judge her but her own conscience, which she had found was unfortunately easy to silence when she really wanted to. It was dancing on the knife's edge of her own morality, the devil on her shoulder, that made Zane and his kisses so stupidly appealing.

It had nothing to do with him as a man.

Bailey was feeling much better about everything by the time she left the conference at four that day, blowing off Andrew with a promise to talk later at the dinner. She stopped off at a roadside stand on the way back and picked up two orders of fried shrimp and grits; she knew she would be much too nervous about her impending speech to actually eat at the event, but she'd no doubt be starving as soon as her bit was over.

When she arrived home, however, the house was empty. Zane had scrawled a note on the back of a take-out menu that said *Wedding rehearsal. Be back by 6.* She let out a long breath. Part of her, when she realized he wasn't here, had wondered if he'd changed his mind. But no, surely the previous night hadn't thrown him for the loop that it had her. He was a guy, for one thing, and a passionate kiss probably didn't mean as much to him as it did to her. For another, he still needed her more than she needed him—the wedding of an ex trumped an awards ceremony in the hierarchy of embarrassments.

She was just getting out of the shower, a fluffy bath towel wrapped around herself, when she heard the front door open. "Is that you, Zane?"

"Yeah, where are you?"

"Bathroom … don't come in!" She hid behind the door in case her warning had been too late. "I left you some food on the counter in case you want it."

"Thanks," he called back. "Are they not serving us dinner?" His voice was getting closer. He must be standing in the bedroom.

She flipped the privacy latch. "Yeah, but I'm going to be too nervous to eat."

"Ah. Understood. I'll wait for you in the living room then."

She waited for his receding footsteps before she took a breath, aware that she was flushed, her heart beating rapidly. She needed to get this out of her system before she made a total fool of herself. For heaven's sake, they'd shared one kiss—maybe two, depending on how you counted. Nothing else. Nothing to make her feel as nervous and giddy as a teenage girl on her first date.

She forced herself to take her time with her hair and makeup. For the first time since she'd been here, she wore her hair down, curling softly over her shoulders; her makeup was just slightly on the glamorous side of natural. Once she slipped into the black lace sheath dress and buckled up her dress sandals, she felt like herself again. A quick moment to transfer her essentials from her purse to a tiny satin clutch, and she was ready to go.

She walked out of the bedroom into the living room, where Zane stood looking out the window, his hands in the pockets of his dark gray suit. He turned, and Bailey caught her breath.

He looked … he looked … incredible. There was no other way to say it. He'd had his hair and his beard trimmed, both reading more European fashion model than Key West beach bum. The gray suit—custom, she remembered—fit him perfectly, emphasizing his broad shoulders and narrow waist, also reminding her just how up close and personal she'd gotten to the smooth, hard muscle hidden beneath layers of fabric. She realized she was staring, but all she could think to say was, "Wow."

He actually looked uncertain. "Is that a 'Wow, you clean up nice?' Or 'Wow, I thought you could manage to do better than that?'"

Bailey cleared her throat. "Definitely the first one."

His smile broke free, and it did strange, unexpected things to her insides. "Thank you. But I'm afraid you took my line. You look amazing."

Bailey looked down at herself, tempted to trot out the usual demurral, but then she caught his eye. "Thank you. I do."

He laughed, and like that, the tension was broken. At least the tension that came from wondering if they had ruined their friendly camaraderie.

The other tension was still there, thick beneath their words, humming over their skin. Zane held up a blue-and-gray striped tie. "What do you think? Tie or no tie?"

Bailey moved close enough to take the tie from his hand, then held it up to his collar. "No tie. Definitely."

"No tie it is." He tossed the scrap of silk onto a side table and offered her his arm. "Shall we?"

Bailey took his arm and let him escort her from the beach house and down the stairs—a practical decision considering how high and skinny her heels were. Once they were in the car and Bailey was making a U-turn in the drive, she said, "I imagine your lack of car is because you got to Islamorada by boat?"

"You are absolutely right." He hesitated. "Speaking of boats, I hope … I hope I wasn't out of line last night. That wasn't my intention."

So they were going to go straight there, were they? Bailey thought they were going to just pretend it hadn't happened, but she rather admired his willingness to face the subject head on. "No, I didn't feel you were out of line. As I recall, I kind of started it."

Zane considered that for a moment. "You're right. You did. I think maybe you owe *me* an apology."

"Hey!"

Zane dissolved into laughter. "Really, though, I don't want to make anything awkward. We're sharing a place until Sunday, we have two events to get through. I just want to make sure we're good."

Bailey dared a look away from the road. He looked sincere. Handsome and sexy, but sincere. Not helping. "Yeah. We're good."

A few minutes of silence passed before Bailey asked, "So, why the haircut and the beard trim?"

He shrugged. "Pretty sure Meredith expects me to show up at the wedding half-dressed and hung over, which is ridiculous considering neither of those two things have happened since she's known me. I figure the best revenge is to do everything right. She's her own worst enemy. She'll be waiting the whole time for the other shoe to drop."

So it wasn't for her. It was stupid for Bailey to have even thought it. Besides, why would he think she wanted him to clean up? She'd clearly not had any problem with him before.

She'd completely lost her mind.

Still, she didn't hate the heads that turned when they walked into the ballroom together several minutes later. She'd almost have anticipated that he'd be ill at ease, out of his element, but he seemed just as comfortable here in a suit as he'd been in a dive bar in shorts and flip-flops. She led him straight to the main table directly in front of the podium, which was marked with a printed *Reserved* sign.

Andrew was already sitting there, alone, and he rose as soon as he saw Bailey. "There you are! I was wondering if you'd decided to bail! I know how much you hate these things." He didn't wait for an answer before turning to Zane and offering his hand. "Hi, I'm Andrew Harris."

"Pleased to meet you. Zane Whitney."

Andrew kept hold of Zane's hand, his eyes narrowing as he studied him closely. "Zane Whitney. You're not …" He looked to Bailey, a smile spreading across his face. "You are, aren't you!" He looked around for someone with whom to share his newfound epiphany and settled on Carlos, who was still a table away. "Carlos, get over here. You won't believe who Bailey brought!"

Bailey watched the whole hubbub, baffled. Zane had said he'd been recognized, but only in the tech sector. Why on earth would Andrew be making such a big deal? To his credit, Zane looked neither ill at ease nor flattered—mostly, he just looked vaguely amused by the whole thing. Who the heck was this guy?

"Carlos, this is Zane Whitney. Founder of MarketMonkey."

Now Bailey thought the floor might drop beneath her feet. She cursed herself for not having Googled him last night when she had the chance—she'd been too distracted by the fact she'd kissed him to realize she'd made out with a tech billionaire. Okay, not quite a billionaire. But a millionaire many times over. He could have owned one of those yachts had he wanted to.

"Now I see why Bailey was being so cagey about her guest. You'll be lucky if you get out of here without being mobbed. Ninety-five percent of the people in this room owe their success to you."

Zane just smiled and extricated his hand from Andrew's so he could shake Carlos's. "You're kind to say so, but my app just aggregates the data. What you do with it is really up to you."

"So modest too." Andrew really was making a fool out of himself, fanboying all over Zane like he was a celebrity. "Honestly, I know your story, but I would love to hear it in your own words."

Zane looked at Bailey, as if asking for her permission.

She shrugged in reply.

He didn't immediately answer though. Instead, he snagged two glasses of champagne from a passing server, then pulled out her chair for her. She took both the flute and the chair. Secretly, she was just as interested in what he had to say as Andrew was—her boss might be effusive, but he was right about one thing. She wouldn't have done half as well as she had without Zane's app.

Once they were all settled and eyeing Zane expectantly, he took a sip of his champagne. "You know, of course, that I never intended to become an app developer. My major was actually in math and data analytics. After a couple of disastrous roommate choices, I decided there had to be a better way—online dating for roommates, so to speak. So I created RoommateMonkey, which let students put in their preferences, their study habits, and their sleep hours among other things, and they were matched up by compatibility. It turned out to be so popular that the school housing department actually bought the program from me."

He flashed a smile at the table, but his eyes landed on Bailey and lingered there. "For a pittance really. As I was looking for a place to buy with my profits as an investment, I realized that I had no way of knowing what was a good deal or not, if I would make any money on it. Real estate was suffering from a lack of data. So I started investigating if I could correlate all sorts of factors to market prices: local taxes, weather trends, the stock market, you name it. And when I was done, I was surprised to find that there were some clear trends that could predict with about 85 percent accuracy where a market was going. That's it really. You all use it. When I got the chance to sell it—for quite a bit more than I made on RoommateMonkey, let's be honest—it seemed like the right time to move on."

He made it seem so simple. And in a way, it was. There were agents who still didn't trust the data—when it was wrong that fifteen percent of the time, it was *really* wrong, and people had lost boatloads of money speculating in real estate based on the app's predictions. But for someone like Bailey, who had an instinct for her neighborhoods, it just reinforced what she already knew about pricing and timing. There was a reason she'd built a reputation in West Palm Beach for selling fast and high—her houses rarely sat on the market.

But ... Zane? That juggernaut of an app was all due to laid-back, funny, sexy Zane?

Carlos was in the middle of asking Zane if he used his own app for investment when a statuesque brunette holding a little girl by the hand approached the table. Andrew immediately rose and greeted the woman with a kiss on the cheek. "Everyone, this is Darlene. And this is her daughter, Kelly."

Bailey blinked. Kelly was a little girl? She was adorable, maybe about eight, in a frilly pink dress and missing one of her top teeth. She grinned at the people at the table and Bailey couldn't help but smile back.

Darlene shook everyone's hands, and when she got to Bailey, she didn't even blink. "It's so nice to finally meet you. Andrew's told me all about you."

Bailey blinked. "Thank you, I think? I'm afraid Andrew hasn't told me anything about you. How long have you two known each other?"

Darlene glanced questioningly at Andrew. "We met, what, six months ago? At that regional conference." She looked back to Bailey and smiled. "Anyway, thanks for making room for us. It was a bit last minute."

Andrew pulled out Kelly's chair first, then Darlene's, careful not to meet Bailey's eye. Six months. That meant either their relationship overlapped with his and Bailey's ... or he'd dumped her for this woman.

Inexplicably, that didn't make her feel worse. It made her feel better. Of course you didn't mess around with a woman who had a child. It was one of the cardinal rules of dating, and only the biggest tool on the planet would break it. Bailey was beginning to think that Andrew was only a moderate tool.

Conversation shifted over to Andrew's side of the table, and Zane took the opportunity to whisper in Bailey's ear. "So. Now you know. Are you mad at me for not telling you?"

Bailey turned her head, found they were only inches apart. Even in a room full of people, the urge to kiss him was so strong that she felt breathless. "No," she said finally. "I understand why you didn't tell me. You're practically a hero to this group."

"And to you?" His lips tipped up in a half-smile.

She lowered her voice and moved her lips to his ear. "Sorry to disappoint you, but you're just a beach bum with a boat to me."

Zane burst into laughter, drawing the attention of the rest of the table, but they were quickly distracted by the squeal of a microphone as their first speaker stepped up to the podium. "Welcome to the annual Constantine Richards awards dinner."

All eyes swiveled up to the stage for the company owner's opening remarks.

All except Bailey's. Her eyes were on Zane.

eight

OVERALL, THE DINNER WAS EVERY BIT AS BORING as Zane had expected it would be. First the owner of the company made his opening remarks and dumb jokes that elicited weak, dutiful laughter from the crowd. Then servers came out with the obligatory island seafood entree, which was not nearly as good as it should have been considering the location. He suspected they got their seafood frozen from some supplier rather than fresh off the docks. Then another speaker—a regional manager, he thought, followed by the individual brokers to present the awards for top sales in every region.

None of that mattered. Even if he had been interested or known any of these people, Bailey's presence beside him was far too distracting for him to have focused on anything else. Every time she moved, he caught the faint scent of tropical flowers that he could only guess was her shampoo or her perfume. Every once in a while, she'd glance at him in concern, as if worried he was bored out of his mind, and he reassured her with a smile. Once, he caught Andrew staring at them with an appraising look. He wasn't sure what that was about, especially since her boss had evidently moved on to someone else, but Zane couldn't resist draping his arm possessively over the back of her chair. From the shy smile Bailey shot him, she didn't mind.

Halfway through the dinner, however, the little girl started fidgeting in her seat, kicking her chair legs with a thump and garnering a warning look from her mom. She leaned her head on her hand, her expression clearly the childhood version of "somebody kill me now."

Zane darted a glance at the stage then bent his head toward the little girl. "Hey. I think you've got something in your ear."

She sat up straight and poked her finger into her ear. "Did I get it?" she whispered.

Zane shook his head. "No, let me get it for you." He reached over and when he took his hand away, a shiny quarter showed between his fingertips.

Her eyes lit up, then narrowed at him. "That wasn't in my ear. You had it in your hand."

Zane lifted his eyes to her mother, who was watching the proceedings with amusement. "Tough crowd."

"You'll have to do better than that," Darlene whispered with a smile. "She's hard to impress."

"Hmm." Zane sat back in his chair as the next broker went up to announce the winner of the Upper Midwest region's award then reached into his breast pocket for a deck of cards. Kelly sat up straight with anticipation. Quietly, he shuffled them in his lap, out of sight of the rest of the guests. He couldn't do a trick while someone was speaking, but he knew the mere anticipation of what he might do next was enough to keep the little girl occupied and out of trouble. Finally, he held out the deck and whispered, "Pick a card."

He was watching the stage when she pulled her card from the deck, but he waited for the applause before he had her cut the deck and replace the card back in it. Then he shuffled them and set them on the table. While the next speaker was moving up to the podium, he flipped them over and fanned them out. He tapped a six of hearts. "Is this your card?"

She grinned and shook her head.

"Hmm." He squinted at the cards and pulled out an ace of spades. "Is this your card?"

She shook her head.

He looked more closely. "You know. I really don't think your card is in here. Are you sure you put it back?"

She grinned her gap-toothed smile. "Yep."

Zane looked around then waved to a server who was refilling water glasses. "I'm sorry, ma'am, but could I just check something really quick?"

Her brow furrowed, but he took that as assent. He quickly dipped his fingertips into the pocket of her apron and drew out a three of clubs. "I have a feeling this might be your card."

Kelly gasped and turned the card over and over. "How did you do that?"

Zane shrugged. "Magic." He took the card from her hand, replaced it in the deck, then tucked the box back into his pocket. Only when he shifted back around to face the front did he catch Bailey's smile.

"How did you do that?" she whispered. But he had no time to answer—not that he would have—because Andrew rose from the table. It was Bailey's turn.

In an instant, her smile vanished, and she clutched at Zane's hand. But instead of entwining his fingers with hers, he lifted her hand to his lips and pressed a gentle kiss to the back of it. "Relax," he whispered. "You're going to be great."

"The award for the top performing associate in Florida goes to someone who should also receive the award for most promising rookie. When she came to us immediately after receiving her license, she quickly rose to the top three performers in the state. This year, she is number one in both total properties sold and in total revenue. Please help me in honoring our top Florida associate, Darlene Mitchell."

Bailey froze a couple of inches off her chair, in the process of standing to retrieve her award. She quickly flopped back down, a flush climbing from her neck into her cheeks, while Darlene rose gracefully and strode up the steps to the dais. She accepted the glass plaque with a smile and moved to the microphone.

Zane didn't hear anything that the woman said; he felt as stunned as Bailey looked. Then she shook herself and plastered a smile on her face, clapping as Darlene finished her speech. Was she really just going to sit here and pretend like she didn't care, like nothing had happened? What *had* happened? To Zane's understanding, there was no suspense in these awards. The numbers were the numbers. So what exactly was going on?

One thing he knew was that the misunderstanding had not been Bailey's, because when Andrew returned to the table, escorting Darlene, he wouldn't meet Bailey's eye … and she was trying.

Finally, she tossed her napkin on the table, picked up her clutch, and marched out of the ballroom.

Bailey couldn't sit there another minute. She grabbed her things and walked out of the ballroom with her back straight, aware of the heads that were turning in her direction, her fellow agents wondering what was happening.

That was a good question. What *had* happened? She'd had it in the bag. Andrew had told her that far and away she had the highest sales of anyone in the region. So how exactly had Darlene—a woman she hadn't even *heard* of, let alone worked with—managed to steal her award from under her nose? And even if that were possible, why hadn't anyone told her?

She ruffled her fingers through her hair as she paced the deserted lobby outside the ballroom, aware that she was stripping every last bit of curl from it. As if it mattered. There were no photos to pose for, no smiling for the camera while holding a glass trophy. For heaven's sake, she'd told *everyone*. Her parents. Her friends back home. She'd even posted it on Facebook. She'd been so proud of what she'd managed to accomplish in three short years as an agent at Constantine Richards that it hadn't even occurred to her that it was up in the air. Embarrassingly, she had note cards in her purse for her speech, which she'd mentally amended at the last minute to mention Zane, who after all, had played a pretty big part in her success.

Zane. She'd just left him sitting there with a bunch of strangers. But there was no way she was going back in there. She could text him or something. She wasn't facing that crowd again. Half of them had seen her rise to accept an award that wasn't even hers.

The door to the ballroom swished open, and Bailey turned, expecting to see Zane. But it wasn't Zane. It was Andrew.

"Bailey, I'm sorry." He approached her, hands extended as if in supplication.

"Andrew! What was that all about? What the heck happened? Did you just … lie to me?"

His eyes widened. "No. Not at all. It was … it was just a mistake and it wasn't cleared up until yesterday. That's why I needed the seat for Darlene and Kelly at the last minute. I just found out."

"So you knew when you talked to me yesterday, but you didn't tell me?"

Andrew looked away uncomfortably.

"Wow. I knew you were a coward, but that really takes the cake."

The insult seemed to cut through his discomfort. "Hey now …" But he apparently couldn't think of any way to defend himself.

Bailey crossed her arms and tapped her high-heeled sandal on the marble floor. "So, what happened exactly? Who is she anyway?"

He cleared his throat. "Panhandle."

"What?"

"Panhandle. You see, in the past, they've included the Florida panhandle in the gulf coast region, not Florida. Darlene is the top grossing agent in that region. But this year, they pulled it into our region with the rest of the state … they just forgot to tell the person tabulating everything until the last minute."

"So she beat me. Fair and square."

"Not by much. One property and a hundred thousand dollars."

Bailey blew out her breath. So it wasn't anything nefarious. Just a stupid accounting error. "So why wasn't she here already?"

Another throat-clearing. "Because she wouldn't have won Gulf Coast. The Louisiana guy had her outsold by a couple of million. New Orleans is a hot market."

All of a sudden, Bailey just felt defeated. It wasn't the award. Not really. It was the fact that she had worked so hard, that she was so sure she could go out on her own, that she was finally getting recognition among her peers for being a good agent and not just Andrew's girlfriend, that really burned her. No doubt all her colleagues in West Palm Beach were going to be whispering about this reversal of fortune. There would be more than a few people taking pleasure in her downfall. It just made her … tired.

"I'm really sorry, Bailey. I know the last few months have been hard on you. And I'm partially to blame for that. I never meant to—"

The door swung open again, drawing Bailey's attention, and this time it was Zane, looking a little disgruntled. At her? Because she'd left him there? How dare he? It wasn't as if this had been a real date.

But when Zane stopped at her side, it was Andrew on whom he focused. "I'm taking Bailey home now. You can say everything you have to say to her in the office on Monday."

Bailey let Zane take her arm and lead her away from a deflated Andrew. He waited until they were out the front doors to dip his head and whisper in her ear, "I'm sorry if that was presumptuous. You don't look too steady on your feet, and I figured you probably didn't want to give him the satisfaction."

Now that he mentioned it, she was feeling a little strange. The surge of adrenaline from when she thought she was going to have to go up and accept her award, followed by the immediate crash of disbelief, made her nerves feel like trampoline springs. "No," she murmured. "It's fine. I'm fine. Thank you."

The warm, humid air after the clammy air conditioning hit her skin and thawed a little of the shock. "I'd be mad, but it was all just a big mistake. An accounting error. He only just found out."

"And he couldn't be bothered to tell you ahead of time so you weren't blindsided?"

Bailey threw him a wry smile, feeling more like herself by the moment. "He's not exactly big on confrontation."

"I'll say." Zane blew out his breath in a gesture of frustration that endeared him to her even more. He was acting as if this was his disappointment, that he had been the victim of corporate ineptitude. Weirdly enough, that bit of empathy might be the nicest thing anyone had done for her in a while.

"Well, what do we do now?" she said, gesturing between the two of them. "We're all dressed up. I'll feel like a loser if I just go home and go to bed. What's there to do on a Friday night in Islamorada?"

"Depends on what you're up for. Listen to some music, dance out your frustrations, or drown your sorrows?"

She paused and glanced up at him. "Isn't there a place we can do all three?"

Zane grinned. "Now that you mention it ... I think there is."

nine

THE CABANA BAR was little more than a dive, but in Zane's opinion, that was a part of Islamorada's charm. All you really needed for a good time were some ocean breezes, live music, and copious amounts of alcohol.

Or so it seemed. Zane liked his Bahamian beers when he was down here, the occasional shot of whiskey to keep himself from doing something stupid that he'd regret, but he wasn't much of a drinker. And despite Bailey's insistence that she needed the biggest margarita known to man, so far he'd seen her consume no more than half a glass of champagne.

But tonight especially, what Bailey wanted, Bailey got. And that meant the Cabana Bar.

Zane had folded his suit jacket in the back of the car and rolled up his shirt sleeves, but Bailey couldn't do much about the lace cocktail dress she was wearing. Instead, she just knotted her hair on top of her head, secured it with a ballpoint pen she found in her purse, and kicked off her heels the minute they hit the sandy beach where the band was already in full swing. To his surprise, she hadn't resisted his proffered arm, clinging to it as they walked into the establishment and not letting go as they sidled up to the bar to order their drinks. That alone suggested she was more upset than she was willing to let on.

The bartender spotted them and moved their way. "What can I get you?"

"Biggest strawberry margarita you have," Bailey said immediately.

The bartender gave her a grin, which Zane interpreted to mean she didn't know what she was getting into. Then he turned to Zane. "And for you?"

"Just a Kalik." Something told him he needed his wits about him tonight.

Bailey hopped up onto the stool. "You know what really gets me? For a second, I was actually glad when I saw Darlene. I thought they were dating. I could understand why he'd dumped me if he had met a woman with a kid. It meant he actually did have some scruples in there somewhere. You don't cheat on a single mother."

"Well, technically, you don't cheat on any woman if you're a decent human being."

Bailey waved a hand. "True. But I didn't say he was a decent human being. Just that maybe he had a personal line he didn't cross. But no, even that wasn't true. All this time I've been wondering, what was it about me that made it so easy for him to cut me loose?"

The bartender set Zane's Bahamian beer in front of him and disappeared again. Zane took a drink before speaking. "Were you sleeping with him?"

She blinked. "I don't know if that is any of your business."

He shrugged. "I mean, it really isn't my business. But you wanted to know why he dumped you, so I asked if you were sleeping with him."

She cleared her throat, slightly uncomfortably. "No, I was not sleeping with him."

"Then there's your answer. He cut the girl who wasn't putting out. If he was dating other people at the same time he was seeing you, he was obviously just in it for the sex. No sex, no more Bailey."

Bailey gaped at him. "Are we in high school?"

"Guys like him? Yes. Perpetually in high school." He took another drink, surveying her from behind the bottle. For someone who was so accomplished and smart, she was still a little naive. It was actually refreshing. So many women were jaded, saw the worst in every man they came across. He supposed that was more a reflection on the men in their past than themselves, but somehow Bailey had avoided letting it poison her outlook on life. The southern belle vibe was apparently not an act.

Her answer was cut off by the arrival of her margarita, which wasn't so much served in a glass as in a stemmed fishbowl. Her eyes grew wide when she observed the volume of violently salmon-colored drink. "How on earth am I going to drink this?"

Zane peeled off a couple of bills and tossed them on the bar then picked up his beer. "Carefully. Come on, let's get a table."

He led her to a tall table where the patio met the beach, and she sighed as she dug her feet into the wet sand. "Those shoes were killing me."

"So why do you wear them?"

"Part of the image. Plus I'm only five one. I need a few inches of height to get taken seriously."

"Seems to me you could get taken seriously based on your performance and work ethic alone."

She shot him a wry glance and took a long drink of her margarita. "Now who's being naive?"

"I never called you naive."

"Yeah, but you were thinking it. I could see it on your face."

Seemed she could read him as well as he could read her. "So what now?"

She shrugged. "I finished my eight hours. I pick up my CEU certificates tomorrow. Submit it for my license renewal, then I enroll in the broker's program, just like before. Nothing's changed. It would just have been really nice to be able to claim I was the top-performing agent in my region." She took another drink and shot him a mischievous look. "I thought Andrew was going to ask you to sign his chest or something. I've never seen him fan-boy anyone so hard."

Zane grimaced at that image. "I thought for sure you would have Googled me. Were you mad that you got caught off guard?"

"Not really. And I would have Googled you, but I was a little distracted last night." She threw him a cheeky look before she went back for a third long draw from her fat straw.

"You know, I'd pace yourself. The margaritas are pretty strong here. There's probably enough tequila in that glass to drop a horse."

She waved a hand airily in dismissal. "Seriously, though, you're like a really big deal. You were in *Forbes* '30 Under 30,' weren't you?"

"I was. Does that change what you think of me?"

She studied him for a second. "No. But now that I know you're worth about seventy kajillion dollars, I'm absolutely going to let you pick up the tab."

"Seems fair. Bailey, I—"

"Ooh! I love this song! Come on!" Bailey grabbed his hand and dragged him toward the sandy, makeshift dance floor. The band—a four-piece cover band with drums, guitars, and bass—had just launched into the Key West classic, "Margaritaville." Judging from the slightly glassy look in her eyes, she was already feeling the effects of her own trip to Margaritaville.

But he let himself be pulled out onto the dance floor to dance to a song that wasn't really danceable, because in that moment, he knew she had him twisted around her little finger. Heck, he'd known it when he'd kissed her in the warm waters off the side of his boat; maybe sooner. What had started as a convenient arrangement had begun to turn into a genuine friendship. And the minute their lips met, he knew that he was not going to want to let her go at the end of the weekend.

But for now, he danced to "Margaritaville," and the song after and several songs after that. When they finally stumbled back to their table, sweaty and thirsty, their glasses were standing in pools of condensation. Bailey dove on hers like it was an oasis in the desert, the level of bright pink liquid sinking ever farther down with each draw.

"Uh, Bailey, I'm serious, you should probably take it easy on that. That's like, equivalent to four regular drinks right there."

"I'm fine." She stepped closer to him and smiled up at him. "I'm more than fine, actually."

The server chose that moment to stop and ask if he wanted another beer, but he waved her away. Right now, what was coursing through his veins was more potent than alcohol, and he'd have a hard enough time resisting it without additional help. "You," he said with a smile, "are already drunk."

"I am not," she said resolutely. "I never get drunk. I don't like to be drunk. It makes me flirtatious." She ran a hand up his arm, lingering over his biceps.

He smiled, despite himself. "You don't say."

"So, I'm definitely not drunk. I'm just here with you." She cocked her head. "Has anyone told you that you're really hot?"

He choked on the last remnants of his beer and wiped his mouth with the back of his hand. "Okay, you're definitely drunk."

"Nope. I've been thinking it ever since I saw you in my bathroom, shirtless. You should go shirtless more often. You look really good without a shirt. You work out, don't you?"

Zane heartily hoped that she wouldn't remember any of this in the morning, because if he knew Bailey even a little bit, she would be mortified that any of these words were coming out of her mouth. Which meant that *he* would be mortified, because it was about him. Though it stoked his ego more than a little to know she'd been thinking of him in that way.

"I think I'm going to kiss you now," she said, and she leaned in.

Except she misjudged, and her lips landed somewhere around his chin.

"All right, I think that's a sign that we're ready to go." He glanced over at the drink, which was two-thirds gone, and tried to calculate how much aspirin she'd need to take before bed so she didn't wake up with a hangover. It was … a lot.

"I'm not done with my drink!" she protested.

"Oh yes, you are. You have an early morning tomorrow, and I'm not going to be responsible for you missing it. Let's go."

She hopped off the stool and immediately her knees buckled. Her eyes went wide with alarm. "Zane? I think I'm a little drunk."

"You think?" He put an arm around her but quickly discovered that the height differential was going to make this walk out to the car particularly difficult. He looked around then said, "Want a piggyback ride?"

He expected her to scoff, but she just smiled widely and gestured for him to bend down.

Which is how he ended up with her legs wrapped around his waist, her heeled sandals dangling from her hands and smacking him in the chest with every step. Oh, she was not going to be happy with this one when she remembered it in the morning. *If* she remembered it in the morning.

She was quiet on the way back to the house, her eyes finally drifting closed when they got back to Upper Matecumbe. He thought she was asleep when he parked, but her eyes popped open when he opened the passenger door, preparing to carry her up the steps to the front door.

"Zane? Thanks for coming with me tonight. That would have been so much worse without you." Clearly, she was still feeling the effects of her gallon-sized margarita, but he also recognized the sincerity in her voice.

"You're welcome. Now, come on. Let's get you in bed."

She didn't protest while he carried her upstairs, straight through the living room, and into the bedroom. He peeled back the neatly made bed coverings and laid her gently on one side.

"Good night, Bailey," he whispered. He leaned down to kiss her on the forehead, turned off the lamp, and crept out of the room, leaving her alone where she belonged.

ten

IF DEATH COULD FEEL LIKE SOMETHING, this is what it would feel like.

Bailey rolled over on her down pillow, the simple movement setting off a pounding in her head. This was why she didn't drink … the nausea, the headache, the big blank spots in her memory. Especially that last one. She had the nagging feeling that she had said or done something that, were she to actually remember it, she would seriously regret.

In one motion, she sat up and threw back her covers, then groaned as the room joined her head in a banging-spinning combination. When she could see straight again, she looked down at herself and froze. She was still wearing the dress from last night, the lace twisted around her body, the hem hiked up to her thighs. She didn't remember even coming home last night, but surely she couldn't have drunk enough to climb into bed fully clothed in her $300 cocktail dress.

Then again, she clearly remembered a glass the size of a punch bowl.

She groaned, but the effort just started another round of pounding in her head. Gingerly, she unzipped the dress and shimmied out of it then slipped on her discarded shorts and T-shirts. She was feeling only marginally steadier when she made her way haltingly into the great room.

Zane sat at the table, drinking a cup of coffee and flipping through the morning's newspaper. He glanced up. "Morning, Sleeping Beauty. How you feeling?"

"Awful," she mumbled. "What time is it?"

"About ten."

"What?" Bailey stiffened in alarm and then clutched her hands to her head at the new wave of pounding. "What?" she repeated more quietly. "Why didn't you wake me up?"

"You said you'd already completed your hours, so I thought it was worth letting you sleep."

"But I have to get my certificates! Without proof …"

"Shh," he said gently. "They're right here. I ran over and got them for you this morning." He nudged a manila envelope across the table toward her, where she gingerly lowered herself into a chair.

"They let you take them?"

He had the grace to look abashed. "I had to introduce myself, and then she remembered hearing that I was there with someone so …" He cleared his throat. "The conference staff might think we're together now."

"There are worse things," she said wryly, but even that much effort made her head ache. She touched her forehead. "What was—"

"In that margarita? My guess would be half a bottle of Cuervo. I take it you don't feel like eggs for breakfast?"

Her stomach churned in response.

He smiled sympathetically. "Then my handy-dandy hangover cure it is. Hold tight."

There was little else she could do but hold tight. Why, oh why, hadn't she heeded his words about the margarita? She'd known it was big, but she hadn't quite anticipated it being that strong. It was so sweet and fruity she hadn't even been able to taste the alcohol. Which, she supposed, was kind of the point. But she hadn't paid attention, maybe even wanted to blur the sharp edges a bit, and now she was paying the price.

Zane rummaged around the kitchen for a minute then came back with a juice glass filled with dark red liquid. He pushed it across the table to her.

"What is this?"

"Hair of the dog, what else?"

She pushed it away. "A Bloody Mary? I'm really not sure more alcohol is the solution right now."

"Relax. It's a Virgin Mary. Well, technically, it's a glass of V8 with a shot of liquid vitamins. You could just do the vitamins, but the juice at least hides the taste."

Tentatively, Bailey took a sip. It was awful, but it was hard to tell whether it was the vitamins or the tomato juice that made it taste bad. She forced herself to continue to drink it, and within a few minutes, she had to admit she did feel slightly better. Zane was still flipping through the newspaper casually, pausing every once in a while to take a sip of coffee. Evidently, she was the only one who had overdone it last night. She remembered him drinking beer, though for all she knew, it was just the single bottle. She had the distinct recollection of dancing with him, and unless her memory was playing tricks on her, he was actually pretty good.

It took her most of the glass to summon up the nerve to ask, "Did I say … anything last night? Or do anything … that I should be aware of?"

Now he looked up, his eyes sparkling. "What kind of things?"

She had the vague recollection of feeling him up at the table, but she wasn't sure if that was a memory or just the recurring fantasy she'd had since she met him. "Um, I don't know …"

Zane turned the page, his lips twitching. "Not really. But in answer to your question, yes, I do work out."

That was all it took. The memory of her drunk flirting came rushing back. She winced and buried her face in her hands. "Ah, yes. I did ask you that." Well, there was no use denying it. Drunk Bailey had said everything that Sober Bailey had on her mind. "In my defense, you are hot."

He didn't even look up from his paper, though she could still see a hint of a smile as he raised his mug in a toast. "Right back atcha."

Bless him. He wasn't going to make a big deal out of it. It sounded like she'd gotten a little flirtatious and a lot sloppy, and he'd driven her home. She was lucky she hadn't been with a different man or things could have turned out differently. She shuddered. Another reason she usually didn't drink.

Margaritas were officially off the menu, at least at the Cabana Bar.

She took another sip. Once she'd finished the entire drink, she felt less nauseous and the headache had thankfully turned down a notch. She cleared her throat. "So, what's the plan for today?"

He folded the paper and finally looked at her. She realized he hadn't been ignoring her, but rather he'd been giving her a chance to get herself together. "I have some things to do this morning. But I'll be back around four. The wedding starts at six, so we should probably leave here about five just to be safe."

"I'll be ready. Is the one I wore last night okay?"

He hesitated. "You might want to check it. I thought I heard a rip. During the … piggy back ride."

She groaned. Guess she would be shopping while he was gone, then. "Anything I need to know? Is it Hawaiian print only? Black tie?"

He cringed. "Black or white."

She stared at him. "I was joking."

"Meredith is not joking. I didn't mention it because you already had a black dress."

"Wow. A black and white wedding in Florida. At least she can't complain if guests wear white …" The more she heard about his ex, the more she wondered what they had ever seen in each other. Zane seemed like the least picky person on the planet. Though she was beginning to wonder if that was just a recent avocation. You didn't build a company the size of MarketMonkey by not having at least a little type-A in you. Maybe that's why they'd broken up—once he'd sold his company, he'd become a totally different person. Relationships had failed over a lot less.

Bailey was still considering climbing back in bed for a couple of hours when Zane left. She barely noticed, though part of her did register that he looked unusually nice compared to his usual daytime apparel of cargo shorts and surf shop tee. But it wasn't her business to ask, nor was it within her current capabilities to form the question, so she instead focused on finding a couple of pain relievers in her purse and washed them down with an entire glass of water.

After a long hot shower, she felt considerably better—Zane's hangover cure really did work—but she still put minimal effort into her hair, makeup, and clothes, knowing that she'd just have to do it all over again in a few hours when she got ready for the wedding. She prayed that she'd be recovered by then. Zane had held up his end of the bargain, and she would have to be at 100 percent to return the favor. Even if last night hadn't turned out the way she'd expected, he'd done everything she could have asked of him and more. The recollection of him entertaining Darlene's daughter with card tricks made her smile, even though it quickly slid away when she thought about Darlene herself.

But that was just petty. It wasn't the woman's fault that an accounting error had pulled away the award Bailey was counting on to help her launch her own brokerage. She was still one of the top agents in West Palm Beach, and her 4.9-star Google rating was more likely to gain her clients than some random award that no one outside her industry—heck, no one outside her company—actually cared about.

It was just, if she were being truthful, she wanted that moment in the spotlight, to prove that she actually deserved to be there, that Andrew hadn't just hired her because she was a pretty face and her photo looked good on a bus bench. And if she could prove that, maybe she could convince herself that she had half a shot at succeeding with her own brokerage.

And there she had it—all her worries and insecurities laid bare, if only to herself. She was only five years into this career, and if she really stopped to think about it, a certain part of her wasn't sure that she had it in her.

But her self-doubt would have to wait.

She held her breath while she examined the black lace dress for the source of the reported ripping sound—and found a four-inch section where the skirt had torn up the back slit. It would be reparable, if she had a needle and thread handy, which she didn't. She'd have to go in search of a pharmacy or big-box store.

Though … if she were going to leave the house anyway, she might as well see if she could find something more suitable for a beach wedding than a lace cocktail dress. She had time to kill after all, and worst-case scenario, she'd find black thread and fix what she already had.

Bailey wasn't that familiar with Islamorada, but she did recall seeing a cluster of pastel-colored boutiques off the Overseas Highway on one of her trips up and down the village. She set off for the shops like a slightly achy conquistador, determined to return with treasure.

It was easier said than done, though. Apparently, those stores were mainly island gift shops that sold straw hats and gaily printed sarongs but nothing sophisticated enough or white enough for Meredith's monochromatic vision. But one shop owner sent her to another shop; the owner of that shop sent her to another; and so on, until Bailey found herself standing in front of a small blue cottage called Del Mar Designs, tucked inconspicuously between a seafood restaurant and a paddleboard rental.

Mentally crossing her fingers that this would be the last stop, Bailey pushed the door open amid the tinkling of brass bells, cool air washing over her.

She instantly knew she was in the right place. Driftwood floors, warm wood hangers, and a shell chandelier set off rack after rack of beautiful, elegant, and most importantly, island-appropriate clothes. Soft Calypso music floated from behind the counter, where a pretty middle-aged woman was tapping away on her computer.

She looked up as Bailey entered and sent her a welcoming smile. "Afternoon. Make yourself at home and let me know if you need anything." Her voice was laced with a Bahamian accent.

Bailey wandered through the racks, fingers brushing over garments as she passed, pulling the occasional dress out to hold up against herself to gauge the length. It was a typical problem being petite—few things seemed to fit her off the rack, and she kept a local West Palm Beach seamstress in business with all the hemming. And then her eyes landed on a white dress hanging by itself on the back of the single dressing cubicle's door. She hurried over to it and checked the tag. What were the chances? It was actually her size.

"Excuse me?" She held up the dress so the proprietor could see it from the front. "Is this for sale?"

"Last one," the woman said with a smile. "It's been my most popular design."

Once Bailey stepped into the dress and did up the side zipper, she could see why. It was made from layers of white cotton, pin-tucked through the fitted bodice and cascading in layers through the skirt. Though it was clearly designed to hit at the knee on someone taller, the high-low hem drifted from mid-calf in the front to just above her ankles in the back.

She looked like—she felt like—some sort of Caribbean Cinderella. The dress was so pretty and simple she could almost imagine it as a beach wedding dress. That alone was enough to give her pause—the last thing she wanted was to be mistaken for the bride—but then again, that was Meredith's fault for insisting on black and white. Who did that? And in the Keys of all places?

A knock sounded at the cubicle's door as she was admiring her reflection like a giddy schoolgirl. "How is it?"

Bailey unlatched the door. She took one last glimpse of herself and smiled. "It's perfect. I'll take it."

eleven

ZANE FELT VAGUELY like he was doing something wrong as he left Bailey nursing her hangover headache at the table and went down to the black Mercedes idling just beyond the gate. He pulled open the passenger door and plopped into the leather seat, frigid conditioned air sliding over him.

"I thought for a second you'd changed your mind." Andrew Harris threw the car into a quick U-turn and sped off down the road, casting the occasional appraising glance Zane's way.

"I almost did. You didn't give me very much to go on over the phone."

"Sorry about that. It's just easier to lay out the whole thing in person. What did Bailey say when she heard you were meeting me?"

"I didn't mention it. After all, I have no idea what you want from me." He flicked a wry smile in Andrew's direction to soften his word's sharp edges, though those sharp edges were intentional. He already didn't like the guy, though it was difficult to say how much his opinion was being colored by Bailey's experiences. Possibly quite a bit, given that even being in this car felt like a betrayal.

As if he could follow the direction of Zane's thoughts, Andrew shot him a wry smile. "Probably a wise idea. I'm not her favorite person at the moment."

"You said it, not me." He was beginning to regret having answered his phone this morning while Bailey was sleeping off last night's margarita, let alone giving his business card to the broker before he'd left the table. He'd been so anxious to get to Bailey that he'd just handed it over when Andrew had asked, and then the broker had beat him to her anyway.

"It really was an unfortunate situation. She didn't expect to have any competition, and I don't blame her. Bailey's always working all the angles."

Zane stared at Andrew. "Surely you're not blaming her for expecting some loyalty."

He blinked. "It was just business. I wasn't the one who made the decision."

"Wait … what exactly are you talking about?"

"The award!" Andrew frowned. "What are *you* talking about?"

"Your relationship."

"I wouldn't exactly call it a relationship," Andrew said uncomfortably. "It was … convenience. For both of us."

"I wouldn't call Bailey a convenience." That implied something you could take for granted, drop when you wanted, and pick up where you left off. Zane was hard pressed to imagine how any man could get close to her and not have her on his mind constantly. That was anything but convenient.

But Andrew took the comment an entirely different way. He let out a guffaw and slapped Zane's shoulder. "You're right about that. She's high-maintenance, but she's gorgeous so you can't help but overlook it."

Zane now officially hated Andrew Harris.

But Andrew seemed completely oblivious to his faux pas, and while Zane was marveling at the other man's utter lack of self-awareness, he didn't notice their destination until they stopped. The valet stand at Plantation Key Resort. What were the chances?

The similarities intensified as they walked inside and Andrew headed for the Bay Club Restaurant where he'd met Tony and Meredith two days ago. The same maître d' showed them to their table, and he thought the server who filled their water glasses might be the same as well. Déjà vu, and not in a good way. Zane was already thinking this would be more painful than seeing his ex, and he didn't even know what Andrew wanted yet.

He managed to keep his curiosity to himself until after they ordered—he did not choose the seafood pasta again—but finally he ran out of patience. "Tell me, Andrew, what's on your mind?"

Andrew folded his napkin on his lap. "What I'm about to tell you is confidential. It hasn't been made public yet."

"Understood."

"I'm leaving Constantine Richards and going out on my own. But I'm not thinking small this time, sticking with West Palm Beach. I'm thinking all of Florida. All of the Southeast eventually."

"Ambitious," Zane said blandly. He didn't really know enough about the brokerage side of real estate to know if that was a logical move or if the man was overreaching. "And you think I might be able to help you?"

"The key to being a successful broker is not just favorable commission splits. In order to recruit and retain top talent, I have to offer something of value that no one else can. To that end, I want to create an entire … online environment, for lack of a better word. Onboarding for new hires. HR resources. Access to digital files. Ways to communicate with lenders and appraisers. Web-based continuing education. And of course, real time market analytics for our region. All on one platform, easily accessible by desktop or app."

He couldn't help but be impressed. The guy might be a blowhard, but he had a vision. Zane had talked to enough real estate agents in his time building MarketMonkey to know that what Andrew had laid out was exactly what top agents would want in a brokerage. "What you're suggesting doesn't come cheap. We're talking in the realm of hundreds of thousands of dollars, if not more. That's whether it's from me or someone else. Are you prepared to make that kind of investment up front?"

Andrew cleared his throat. "Not exactly. But hear me out. Typically, agents pay a monthly fee to the broker. It covers overhead—office space, supplies, and so on. I would be willing to pay the better part of that amount as a license fee to you for use of the software. Technically, you would own it, though you'd give us exclusivity for a period of time not yet determined. Then for every agent I sign up, you get a monthly fee. I'm motivated to recruit only the highest performing agents; you're motivated to be flexible and make continuous improvements." Andrew took a long drink, giving Zane time to digest what he'd just said. "What do you think?"

He thought he may have underestimated Andrew—as much as he disliked the man personally, he had big ideas and just enough hubris to make it work. He cleared his throat. "I wouldn't do it as a straight license deal, nor would any developer capable of pulling this off. You'd pay up front. Just maybe not as much as you would without it."

"So you'll consider it?"

"I'd need to know more about your requirements. There's some non-compete language involving MarketMonkey that I'd need to get around."

Andrew smiled as if he knew Zane was tempted. "So you'll think about it then?"

"I … will consider the possibility."

Andrew broke into a grin and pumped Zane's hand with glee. "Fantastic. I knew you wouldn't be able to ignore the challenge. But you agree—not a word to anyone about this. It's going to take me six months to a year to make the move, extract myself from Constantine Richards. If my agents get a whiff of this ahead of time, they'll jump ship like rats fleeing the *Titanic*. And if I don't have my share of their commissions, I won't be able to keep the lights on. I have to be able to offer them an alternative to finding another broker before I go public. And I need to have the framework to entice them."

Zane's heart sank as he realized what Andrew was saying. He'd been feeling like he was betraying Bailey with his presence, when really it was much worse. He couldn't even give her a sneak peek of what was coming. He knew how hurt she'd be if she learned he'd known about Andrew's plans and hadn't given her a heads up.

She'll already be off on her own when this happens, he reasoned. She'd already have her own brokerage, be recruiting her own agents …

And she'd be in direct competition with her ex-boyfriend/ex-boss who was stacking the deck to make sure he caught all of the quality agents in Florida … because Andrew had something only he could provide. Which was something only Zane could provide.

All the way home, a sick feeling churned in Zane's gut. He felt like the worst sort of sneak. He tried to reason away the feelings—after all, he didn't owe Bailey anything. They were two strangers who had met by chance. Their "relationship" was merely playacting for their respective exes. When this weekend was over, they would never see each other again.

But even as he thought it, he knew it wasn't the truth. He liked Bailey, enjoyed her company. He was attracted to her, yes, but he actually appreciated her as a person: the way she wore her thoughts on her face, her sarcasm, how she looked when she was trying to lay down the law …

all five foot one of her. Already, he was mentally mapping the distance between Miami and West Palm Beach. And if he were honest, he'd started to consider whether property in West Palm Beach wouldn't be just as good an investment as Islamorada.

But none of that actually solved his problem. It merely made it more complicated.

He was relieved to find the house empty when he let himself in—he wasn't sure what might come out of his mouth if Bailey asked him point blank what he'd done today. He had to tell her; it was the only right thing to do. But he had to admit he was intrigued by Andrew's project. It would be a fun challenge in a year that had been rather short on challenges. And if he did take the job, didn't that obligate him to some sort of confidentiality?

He wasn't going to solve that issue in an empty house, so he changed into his swim trunks and went to the storage unit on the ground floor, where he retrieved one of the paddleboards leaning up against the wall. The tide was still low, the water relatively still, and as he climbed onto the board and began to propel himself away from the shore with the long paddle, he mulled the other question that had been nagging him. How did he broach the subject of what happened after they said goodbye on Saturday?

He'd thought Bailey might feel the same level of interest, but she'd been pretty straightforward with him since their kiss the other night. Sure, she'd flirted at the bar, but he knew not to read too much into alcohol-fueled behavior. Some women just got flirty when they drank and didn't remember a bit of it later. He didn't consider his ego fragile, but what guy really wanted to put himself out there only to find out the interest had been one-sided?

He'd just have to take that risk, he decided. The alternative was walking away from her tomorrow with no chance of seeing her again, and that was the one outcome that was unacceptable. If she laughed in his face—or more likely, let him down easily—at least he would know. He could move on. And if she responded the way he hoped she would ...

He realized he was smiling as he paddled parallel to the shore, absorbing the rock of the waves with his legs. He'd soak in the warmth of the sun and the freshness of the salt breeze for a little longer then he'd go in and get ready so Bailey could have the bathroom.

Somewhere, his dread over the wedding had shifted to anticipation. He'd do his almost best man duties, stand up with Tony, give the toast. But as far as he was concerned, this night was just an excuse to spend time with Bailey, dance with her, and if he played his cards right, kiss her again. And then he'd bring up the idea of seeing each other when they were back on the mainland. Miami and West Palm Beach weren't exactly in the same zip code, but he wasn't going to let something as insignificant as an hour's drive keep him away from her if she was willing to give him a shot.

For the first time since he'd sold his company, after almost two years of drifting, it felt like things were finally coming together.

twelve

THE HOUSE WAS EMPTY when Bailey returned, but the clothes that Zane had been wearing this morning were neatly folded over the back of the sofa, so she knew he had to be around somewhere. Fair enough. She wanted to get ready early so they wouldn't be late—she wasn't going to give Meredith any reason to dislike her or be critical of Zane. Why she cared so much about Zane's ex when she was marrying another man, Bailey couldn't say … but she knew without a doubt she would be on display. Which was why she'd spent so much time and effort tracking down the dress and shoes and jewelry.

But even as she thought it, she knew it was a lie. She'd loved the sharp spark of interest she'd seen in Zane's eyes when she'd emerged from the bedroom in the skinny black cocktail dress, a sudden vibration of tension like he was barely keeping himself from approaching and putting his hands all over her. She wanted to see that look again. Heck, if it weren't for her headache this morning, she'd probably have been disappointed they'd wasted the evening instead of picking back up where they'd left off. Now that the annoying throbbing in her head was gone, she was replaying their kiss in her mind. On repeat.

Somewhere, the switch had flipped in her head from the idea that Zane was to be resisted as an unwelcome temptation to a sudden panic that this was coming to an end without anything being decided. Were they really going to part ways tomorrow with a handshake and vague well-wishes? Were they going to ignore the electricity that crackled between them when they touched, write it off as an impulse they could have acted on but chose not to?

Because maybe she was fooling herself—God knew it wouldn't be the first time—but she thought their connection was more than physical. She'd never found it so easy to talk to a man before, about everything and nothing. He made her feel like she could say anything she thought without judgment. Express her hopes and dreams and get validation instead of discouragement. He talked like an English major sometimes, but he also kind of thought like one. All the disparate parts—the entrepreneur, the analyst, the adventurer, the empath—came together into a whole that Bailey couldn't deny she really, really liked.

Tonight she would tell him, she decided as she climbed in the shower. Even if it made her look silly. Even if it turned out that he was like this to everyone, that she wasn't actually special. She could take the disappointment, the embarrassment. What she couldn't take was the idea of walking away from him and always wondering what might have been if she'd only had the courage to act.

If honesty really was her highest value, then she had no choice but to tell him how she felt.

She was wrapped in a towel, blow-drying her hair when a sharp rap came at the door. "Bailey?" Zane's voice called. "Are you almost done? It's after four."

She glanced at her watch, abandoned on the counter, and grimaced. How had it already gotten so late? "Sorry! Give me two minutes!" She flipped off the blow dryer, then looked around for her clothes. Which were definitely not in the bathroom.

She weighed the pros and cons to actually asking him to retrieve the clothes laid out on the bed, but that would require him retrieving her bra and panties as well. And she was not prancing out there in a bathroom towel that would barely cover her boobs and her nether regions at the same time.

"Okay, I'm coming out, but you have to close your eyes."

A deep laugh. "Close my eyes?"

"That's what I said."

"Okay, okay, they're closed."

Bailey clutched her hair dryer, curling iron, and her makeup case to her chest and cracked the door. Sure enough, Zane was standing with his back to her, one hand clapped over his eyes. Shirtless again—and his back was just as nice as his front. She tiptoed past him to the louvered closet.

"Okay, you can go in now."

Amusement tinged his voice. "Bailey? Are you actually in the closet?"

"I won't be if you'd just go in the bathroom."

"Wait … are you naked in the closet?"

"Not quite," she squeaked. "Will you just go please?"

His laugh rumbled, deep in his chest. "What if I just hang out—"

"Go!" she practically shrieked.

"Okay, fine." His laughter faded and the bathroom door clicked shut, but she still poked her head out to check that he wasn't just messing with her. She let out a sigh of relief and went for her underwear and ubiquitous shorts-tee ensemble. But she was smiling.

When he came back out twenty minutes later, he was still shirtless—heaven help her—but at least wearing his dress pants, a towel draped around his neck. "Can I borrow the blow dryer?"

"Uh, yeah. Here." She handed it over, trying to keep her gaze from lingering on skin, but he paused.

"Looks like we've come full circle, haven't we?" he said with a grin.

She returned the smile. "Hard to believe that was only three days ago, isn't it?"

"It is. Bailey—"

"Talk later." Bailey pointed to her watch. "It's four-forty. We have twenty minutes to get out the door, and I haven't even finished my makeup."

"Leave it," he said with a grin. "The bride will be mad if you look better than her."

She rolled her eyes and waved him away, but in another couple minutes, she thought Meredith might be unhappy anyway, because the ensemble read more than a little bridal. The white dress was beautiful. She'd paired it with a pair of white canvas espadrilles, their satin laces wrapping her ankles like a ballerina's ribbons, and a delicate silver necklace with tiny paper-thin capiz charms. She was just fussing with the individual waves in her hair when Zane stepped out and whistled.

"Wow. You look…wow."

"Is that a 'Wow, you clean up nicely' or a 'Wow, is that the best you can do'?" She paraphrased his previous words with a smile.

"It's a 'Wow, I can't believe I'm the lucky man who gets to spend the evening with you.'" Frank appreciation glimmered in his eyes, and he moved toward her, his intentions clear.

"Oh no you don't," she teased, though her heart was beating a rapid tattoo in her chest. "I just put on my lipstick."

"Don't care." He caught her around the waist in a possessive grasp she didn't really resist. But instead of moving in for the kiss, he just pressed his lips, feather-light, against the side of her neck. The touch made her shiver.

He stepped back, and she knew he hadn't missed her reaction. She couldn't even pretend—she still felt breathless. If she'd thought there was any question of his interest, the way he was looking at her now left no doubts.

She cleared her throat. "Do you need help with your tie? I assume there's a tie."

"Right." He looked around and landed on his suitcase then retrieved a length of tone-on-tone striped white silk. "This is it."

Bailey took the tie and looped it around his neck, her fingers brushing against slightly damp skin as she turned up his collar. It reminded her again of those heady moments in the water, wrapped around each other, and she had to take a steadying breath.

"If tying a tie makes you so nervous, I can do it myself," he teased, and just like that, they were back to their teasing, chummy, slightly flirtatious tone of the past days.

"Funny. Now hold still so I don't accidentally strangle you." She carefully avoided his gaze while she tied a full Windsor knot and smoothed the tie flat against his chest. "You look very nice," she said primly. Then she caught his eye, her lips twitching. "And to think I initially thought you might be homeless!"

"Hey!" he protested, but there wasn't much heat behind it.

"Okay, now we really have to run." She gathered the bare minimum she would need that evening—keys, lipstick, driver's license—and shoved them into the tiny straw clutch she'd purchased earlier that day. She hesitated and removed the keys, dropping them into his hand. "You drive."

"Okay then. Let's get this wedding over with so we can have some fun, why don't we?"

Bailey smiled. "Lead the way."

thirteen

Zane was counting down the minutes. Once, he would have done that because he couldn't wait to get the night over with. Now, he simply wanted to discharge his duty to the bride and groom so he could get on with things. He might have to stand up with Tony and give a toast, but the rest of the night was for him and Bailey.

Who looked absolutely stunning. He repented of his first impression that she was just cute—though to be fair, she had been dressed like a college girl. Now, he thought she was beautiful. Stunning. Likely to steal the spotlight from the bride, which he couldn't manage to feel bad about. Not when he was the one who got to spend the night in her company.

His sudden impulse to rapturous devotion was perhaps his first inclination he was done for.

He'd keep that to himself, however. Because despite her involuntary reaction to his brief kiss, she still hadn't given him any indication she thought of him as anything more than a convenient date.

He drove them to the resort, and they both fell quiet, though it was a companionable sort of silence. Comfortable. Unfortunately, that gave him time to think about Andrew's proposal and what his obligations to Bailey were. Maybe he was overthinking it. She was a businesswoman: she would understand that you didn't need to like or respect your clients. Surely she'd negotiated houses for people she wouldn't put on her Christmas card list. But he also remembered her slightly forlorn, wholly vulnerable look when she'd wondered why Andrew had cut her loose. That seemed to say her feelings about the man were beyond reason.

Later, he told himself. First, he'd see how she reacted to the idea of them seeing each other back on the mainland. If she was as enthusiastic about the idea as he hoped she'd be, he'd tell her everything. He didn't believe in starting a relationship with secrets. But if she wanted to part tomorrow as acquaintances, then he had no obligation to tell her. She'd be out on her own long before Andrew was ready to launch anyway. It would be him having to compete with her. If she wanted to hire Zane to do something similar, then she could.

It was too bad that it all felt like a bunch of justifications to ease his conscience.

They pulled up to the valet in her car, Zane smiling slightly at the recollection of handing over his bicycle the previous day. He met Bailey at the curb and offered his arm. She took it with a weak smile. Was she nervous? What did she have to be nervous about?

Too late he caught sight of Tony zipping across the lobby, wearing a harried expression, and remembered he was supposed to have arrived early.

"Where have you been? We've been waiting on you for pictures for half an hour!" Tony finally noticed Bailey, his whole demeanor changing. "Hello, you must be Bailey. Pleasure to meet you." He smiled and shook her hand briefly. "I'm afraid I have to borrow him for a bit. The bar is over there, though, if you want to grab a drink …"

Zane could swear that, for a moment, she turned an unhealthy shade of green. He grinned as he leaned close on the pretense of kissing her cheek and then whispered, "If you can devise a way to smuggle one in for me, I'll be your slave."

Bailey's eyes flashed amusement. "I'll see what I can do."

Zane reluctantly left her in the lobby, practically dragged away by Tony. Once they were out of earshot, Tony said, "I heard that." Before he could apologize, Tony reached into his suit jacket and withdrew a leather and silver flask. "Gift from Mer's dad."

Zane barked out a laugh then felt guilty about his amusement. Meredith wasn't that bad … she was just easily stressed. And what could be more stressful than a wedding? He waved off Tony's flask and tried to look contrite. "Sorry I'm late. I forgot about the pictures." He wasn't sure he'd actually been told what time to get there, but better he take the blame for it regardless.

The photographer was waiting for them on the beach near where the chairs and the gazebo for the ceremony were located, the broad expanse of blue behind them the perfect backdrop. Meanwhile, guests began to meander over to the chairs, most of them with drinks in hand. Zane chuckled to himself. That wouldn't fly in a church yet somehow felt perfectly appropriate in Islamorada. He tried to focus on the photographer's directions to Tony and the cluster of groomsmen, but then Bailey appeared, drawing attention like a beacon. He saw the eyes of the male guests follow her as she walked down the center aisle and chose a seat somewhere in the middle. It wasn't just him, then. He was surprised by the sudden surge of protectiveness. Or was it possessiveness?

"Zane," the photographer said, his voice holding a tinge of exasperation.

He managed to stay focused for the rest of the photos then followed Tony to the front of the assemblage to take their places while the cellist warmed up, preparing for the processional. Zane leaned around the best man to whisper to Tony, "You ready for all this?"

He half-expected Tony to make a flippant reply, but instead he just smiled calmly. "I've been ready for this my whole life."

And that's when Zane realized that Meredith and Tony were truly in love. He'd been skeptical because of the speed of the engagement—Meredith wasn't one to leap without considering all the angles—but Zane had only ever seen them together when she was irritated with him. The look on Tony's face said it all—when you knew, you knew.

Three days ago, he would have said that was crazy. Magical thinking. Real life didn't work that way. But now?

He found Bailey in the audience and realized she was already watching him. He returned her smile. No, he was definitely going to do everything in his power to convince her to see him when they returned to the mainland.

The cellist paused, then struck up a classical piece Zane didn't recognize. Slowly, a procession of bridesmaids in floaty black sundresses emerged from the building and made their way to the assemblage, then down the aisle. And then, finally, came the bride.

Meredith looked beautiful. Even Zane had to admit that. She wore a flowing white gown, her dark hair falling in waves over her bare shoulders, a crown of white flowers on her head instead of a veil. She looked every inch a bride, and there was a time when he would have given almost anything to be the one toward whom she was walking.

But now? All he felt was a vague sense of relief that chapter of his life was officially over. He glanced at Tony, who was watching his bride with a rapt expression, and smiled. Everything was as it should be.

Zane barely listened to the vows—he didn't have any responsibilities here—then joined his assigned bridesmaid to walk back down the aisle. He caught Bailey's eye, and she surreptitiously passed him a cocktail she was hiding in the empty seat beside her. He laughed and hid it behind his back from the photographer.

"Good idea," his bridesmaid said. He couldn't recall her name, even though he'd met her at the rehearsal last night. Melissa, maybe? Melinda? "I could use one myself. Meredith was on a tear."

Maybe she had been earlier, but now that the wedding had gone off without a hitch, Meredith seemed blissfully happy and relaxed. After the receiving line, they gathered for more photos of the entire wedding party then were finally released while the photographer snapped the bride and groom together. Zane found Bailey on the patio where the cocktail hour was being held.

"I'm all yours," he said with a smile. "I'm sorry I had to bail on you. I completely forgot about the photos."

"It's fine. I chatted with some strangers at the bar for a while. Declined an invitation to go sailing on some guy's yacht."

"It's the dress. That dress says you belong on a yacht."

She laughed. "Well, I told him I had a date with a handsome surfer tonight."

"In that case, I guess I should step aside."

"Cute. Is that a ploy to get me to reinforce that gigantic ego?"

"Hey! Don't mistake confidence for ego—"

He would have said more, but just then a woman in a hotel uniform tapped a glass to get everyone's attention. "Dinner is being served in the Bayview Room. Please follow me."

Bridezilla or not, Meredith had style. For the next hour, they were treated to a plated three-course meal that was better than anything Zane had ever eaten at a wedding. The bride and groom had their own cozy table for two in front of the windows, the ocean spread out behind them, leaving their attendants and their dates to sit at two larger round tables on either side. Bailey immediately struck up a conversation with Zane's bridesmaid—whose name he finally remembered was Milla—and her husband, a smooth-pated marathoner named Jacques.

"I did a half-marathon in college," Bailey was telling them enthusiastically, "but I thought I might die before I crossed the finish line. I can't imagine doing a full."

"I didn't know that," Zane murmured in her ear.

"Well, why should you?" she threw back with a smile then nudged him to show that she was just kidding.

Jacques plowed on as if the exchange had never occurred. "It's not that much harder. You just structure your training differently. If you can do a half, you can do a full."

Bailey looked unconvinced, but she asked to hear more, so Zane turned to another of Tony's groomsmen, Lee, seated across from him. They'd gone to college together, but he'd always been more of Tony's friend than his. "What have you been up to? I haven't seen you in years."

"Got married." Lee slung an arm around the woman seated beside him and smiled. "You're the last holdout."

"Well …" Zane began, and Lee cringed, realizing what he'd just said. There probably wasn't a person in the room, or at least in the wedding party, that didn't know Zane was Meredith's ex.

In what might have been the perfect—or worst—timing ever, a woman Zane recognized as the wedding planner appeared at their table and crouched beside Zane. "It's time for the toasts. The bride said you're giving the first one?"

He was tempted to pretend he had no idea what she was talking about, but Meredith would murder him, and besides, it would be a shame to waste all the embarrassing stories he'd saved up about Tony's college antics. So, Zane rose and tapped his water glass several times with his spoon until the hum of conversation died and all eyes turned expectantly toward him.

"If there's one thing you need to know about Tony," he began, "it's that he's the most fearless person you'll ever meet. That's the only way to explain the reason he chose—"

Meredith's eyes flashed with sudden apprehension, and he smiled.

"—me to give the first toast. Most of you know him as the super-responsible, conservative finance guy. I, however, know him as the guy who crashed the Kappa Alpha Theta sorority's Karaoke Night and won with his rendition of Abba's 'Dancing Queen.'"

Laughter rippled through the room, and Tony pretended to be embarrassed, though Zane knew full well he was still incredibly proud of the choreography—as well as the plaid skirt and blonde wig—that had won him the karaoke title. The rest of his stories were equally as goofy, showing Tony in a slightly embarrassing but still lovable light; he left the truly humiliating ones in the recesses of his memory where they belonged. From the laughter around him and the amusement on the bride's and groom's faces, he knew he'd chosen well. Then as his time concluded, his tone sobered.

"Honestly, when I'd heard that Meredith and Tony were getting married, I was taken aback. Meredith isn't one to make hasty decisions, and Tony isn't the kind of guy Mer would make hasty decisions *with*."

Meredith stuck out her tongue at him, but there was a softness in her eyes that said she wasn't mad at the way the speech had gone. He gave her a smile and a little nod.

"But looking at them now, I think they've figured out what marriage is supposed to be about. Not finding someone who is perfect, because who is? But rather, finding someone who appreciates your strengths and bolsters your weaknesses. Someone who takes you as you are and loves you *for* your flaws instead of despite them. Because without our flaws and past failures, we wouldn't recognize what's true and real when it comes along."

He raised his champagne glass to the happy couple. "To Tony and Meredith. May you have a lifetime of perfect happiness together."

Glasses were raised and clinked together, and Zane sank into his chair with a relieved smile. Bailey leaned over to him and whispered, "Well done."

He reached for her hand and squeezed it briefly while Meredith's maid of honor rose to give her speech.

Fortunately, the rest of the toasts went quickly, and the DJ's voice boomed out through the speakers. "Now we are going to kick off the dancing with the first dance between the bride and groom!"

The newly married couple took the floor to John Legend's "All of Me," swirling around the dance floor in a smooth way that made Zane think they'd taken ballroom dancing lessons prior to the wedding. No way

Meredith would have left this all-important first dance to chance.

Finally, the music changed to something more upbeat. Apparently, they were dispensing with all the other traditional dances, because Tony made an oversized gesture that was obviously meant to bring the guests onto the dance floor.

Bailey smiled and rose, holding out a hand. "Dance with me."

After a moment's hesitation, he took her hand, then led her out onto the floor.

Somehow he'd expected her to be more inhibited without a giant margarita in hand, but if anything, she was even more exuberant stone-cold sober. And when the music turned to a song made famous by the movie *Pulp Fiction*, she had no problem busting out some dance moves that even John Travolta would have been proud of.

Zane threw his head back and laughed. Just when he thought he had her figured out, she managed to surprise him.

And then, once more, the DJ put on a slow dance, and she let him reel her into his arms. She smiled up at him. "How's this?"

"Having you two inches away from me? This is great."

She laughed. "I mean, this." She made a vague gesture around the room. "Did you mean what you said in the toast?"

She wanted him to talk about his feelings, but it didn't bother him. "Yes, I meant what I said. In a weird way, they complement each other. I wish them all the best."

"That's very mature."

"Easy to be mature when I'm with the prettiest and most interesting woman here." He spun her around and dipped her backward, and she laughed again. He'd been dreading this day for so long, yet now there was nothing but a light feeling in his chest.

"Bailey—"

"Do you want to take a walk?" She nodded toward the French doors, beyond which a spectacular sun was dropping below the surface of the water, shading the sky from pink to blue-gray.

"Sure." He let her lead him off the dance floor and onto the patio, glad that he had a few more seconds to consider his words. This was their last night together.

He had to get this right.

fourteen

BAILEY SAW THE EXACT MOMENT that Zane's mind shifted away from the fun they were having on the dance floor to something more serious and searching. She sensed they were both feeling the rapid ticking of the clock on their time together, the need to talk about what would—or what wouldn't—come next. But there were far too many ears tilted in their direction on the dance floor. A bridesmaid who, from the resemblance, had to be related to Meredith, had been giving them searching looks ever since the slow dance started, and Meredith was only two couples away, wrapped around Tony and looking blissfully in love. Whatever they had to say, it should be done out of earshot of his ex and her family, especially if Zane and Bailey were still making believe they were an item.

But it didn't feel like make-believe as they held hands to leave the ballroom and worked their way down to the sandy shore, a stiff ocean wind stirring her dress around her legs, ruffling their hair. Bailey untied her espadrilles and draped them in her free hand, feeling the residual warmth of the sand on her feet. For only being a couple of hours away from home, it suddenly felt like the last day of a vacation she was sorry to see end.

She could tell he was trying to decide how to broach the subject—or at least she hoped he was—so she decided to go easy on him. "So, we go home tomorrow. What happens then?"

He stopped and glanced at her, a smile playing on his lips. "That all depends on you."

"On me?"

"On you. Because I think you can tell already that I'm crazy about you. We've only known each other for a few days, but I'm not ready to let you go."

The words sent a surge of pleasure through her, warming her cheeks. "Me neither. I've had more fun with you since we got here than …" She shook her head. "Let's just say it's been a long time."

"Maybe that's just proof that you need to get out more."

"That's the thing, though. I've dated, I've met people, but work has always come first. You're the first person who's made me wonder if I have my priorities out of order."

He tugged her around so she was facing him, sending her shoes tumbling to the sand. "That's because you are seduced by this glamorous homeless beach gypsy lifestyle I seem to lead."

She grinned up at him. "What if I am?"

"At some point, I probably should do something else with my life. I'm pretty young to call it quits on gainful employment."

"Do what you want, Zane. I know I've teased you, I know Meredith had opinions on your early retirement, but you worked hard for that opportunity. If you just want to surf, surf. If you want to form another company, do that. But make sure you do it because *you* want to do it, not because you don't want to deal with everyone else's opinions."

He pulled her a little closer. "You know this was supposed to be me telling you that I wasn't ready to let you go, not you giving me advice on my life choices."

She could feel the warmth of his hand spread across her back in the rapidly cooling evening, and it made it a little hard to concentrate. She smiled up at him. "I'm just making sure you realize what you're asking. I'm not a woman who holds back her opinions."

Zane chuckled. "Oh, I've figured that out already."

"Have you now?"

He nodded slowly. "It's one of the things I like about you."

"Oh, really. And what else do you like about me?"

"Hmm." He pretended to think. "Well, for one, I like this freckle right here on your shoulder." He pushed aside the strap of her dress a fraction of an inch then brushed his lips over the spot, sending a shiver through her. He met her eyes with a knowing smile. "I also like this little curve right here …" He pressed his lips again to the spot where her jaw met her neck just below her ear, and she could swear her knees went a little weak. "And I love the way that I can see in your expression that you wish I would just stop teasing you and kiss you already."

"You've got that part right," she murmured.

He didn't keep her waiting any longer. If their first kiss had been accidental, a product of the moment, this one was deliberate but gentle, a conversation, a question answered. Bailey slid her hands up his chest, giving in to the moment, letting herself be washed away in the sudden feeling of rightness. It was as if meeting him this weekend, kissing him on the beach, had always been in the cards. She'd just been wandering aimlessly until this moment. He slid his fingers into her hair, tilting her chin to deepen the kiss, and she let out a little moan of need, her fingers tightening in the fabric of his shirt.

The sharp bark of a dog nearby brought Bailey back to her senses, and she jerked back from Zane, flushed when she realized she was engaged in a heated clinch only steps away from his ex's wedding. She let out a shaky laugh and brushed her hair away from her flushed face. She couldn't remember the last time a man had made her forget about everything when she was with him. No nagging work tasks, no self-consciousness. It was like the minute he kissed her, it sucked all the air out of the room, stretching time, putting her in a bubble the outside world couldn't touch. And maybe she could chalk that up to chemistry or hormones or something equally scientific and unromantic, but there was a little kernel deep inside that hoped it meant something more.

Zane chuckled and leaned toward her again, but this time he only kissed the tip of her nose. "Does that mean you're willing to see me again when we get back to the mainland?"

"Yes. We're only, what … an hour away from each other?"

"An hour and seven minutes from my house to your office."

Bailey laughed. "You already mapped it? That sounds like something I would do. I'm already rubbing off on you."

"Do you see me complaining?"

"Not one bit." She stretched up to kiss him again, which he obliged, all too briefly.

"Do you have to go back home right away tomorrow?"

"No. Why?"

"I was thinking … maybe you'd like to go out on the boat tomorrow?

Do some snorkeling? There are some great spots off Key Largo or Big Pine Key we could visit."

She had no idea why, but this, more than anything they'd done so far, sounded like a proper date. "That sounds like fun. Why not?"

By silent agreement, they turned around and began to make their way back to the resort, where light, laughter, and disco music poured out from the ballroom's open French doors. Some of the guests had already trickled out, but the party was still going strong, with a laughing, quite possibly drunk Tony doing his version of "Saturday Night Fever" in the middle of the dance floor. His bride was nearly doubled over in hysterics at his antics.

Zane and Bailey found seats at an empty table, where he tossed his phone on the table, shrugged off his coat again, and rolled up his wrinkled sleeves. He watched Tony and Meredith in amusement for a minute then looked back to Bailey. "I'm going to grab a drink from the bar. You want anything?"

"Just soda water. I'm still detoxing from that margarita." She leaned over conspiratorially. "Please tell me I didn't look like that when I was dancing last night."

"Okay, I won't tell you." Zane ducked out of reach of her swipe as he stood and then headed for the reception area adjacent to the ballroom where the bar was located.

The music shifted to something from this decade, and Bailey leaned back in her chair, practically glowing with happiness. Or maybe it was just leftover adrenaline. She had to hand it to him, the man could kiss. But why should she be surprised? From what she'd learned of him, it seemed that he did everything well.

She was so lost in thought that she nearly jumped when Meredith flopped down in the chair beside her, flushed and sweaty, her flower crown slightly askew. "Hey."

Bailey blinked. "Hi."

Meredith looked her over and held out her hand. "I'm Meredith, by the way."

Bailey chuckled. "I kind of guessed that. Congratulations. It was a beautiful wedding. I'm Bailey."

"I guessed that as well. Though," she said with a wry smile, "for a while I wasn't sure if you actually existed."

"Oh? Why is that?"

Meredith shrugged. "Because Zane has a habit of seeing things in the rosiest possible light. I mean, don't get me wrong, it's an admirable character trait. It just doesn't always prove out."

Bailey wasn't quite sure what to say to that. She supposed she could see that about him—after all, this whole date exchange had been his mad idea—but Meredith spoke with the weight of experience. She'd known him for four years. Bailey had hardly known him for four days.

"So what do you do?" Meredith asked.

"I'm a real estate agent. I'm getting my broker's license." Bailey didn't know why she added that last part. She didn't care what Zane's ex thought about her.

Scratch that. She didn't *want* to care what Zane's ex thought about her.

But Meredith just nodded. "So maybe you would understand him, that whole entrepreneurial thing. I have to admit, the uncertainty of the start-up life was not for me. And the hours. They used to make me crazy." She threw Bailey a wry glance. "And that's coming from a lawyer."

"What kind of law do you practice?"

"Intellectual property."

"Sounds interesting."

"It can be. Sometimes it can be dead dull. But it's predictable, and that's what I like about it."

Bailey sensed that Meredith was trying to say something without saying it directly. Was she trying to warn her off Zane? Or was she trying to ascertain if Bailey was a good match for him? She'd thought she'd understood the status of his relationship with his ex, but now she wasn't so sure.

She knew that she should let it lie, that she should smile and say vague things until Meredith went away. But she couldn't seem to help herself. "Zane seems to think you and Tony disapprove of his early retirement plans."

"Does he now?" She shifted in her chair in a rustle of chiffon, that calculating look surfacing again. "I wouldn't say I disapprove. More like … disbelieve."

"Oh? And why is that?"

"He has these … fallow periods. Where he's overwhelmed with his life and he just wants to get away from it. I call that Zen Zane. But eventually, he can't resist the pull of the work. He likes inventing. He likes tinkering." She looked at Bailey significantly. "He likes a challenge. If you've only known him since his Key West fishing boat phase, just be prepared. Eventually he'll find a project that strikes his fancy, and he'll be back to spending eighteen hours a day at the computer."

Bailey would be tempted to think that Meredith was just trying to scare her off, but she'd seen how she looked at her new husband. Whatever her motivation, it wasn't jealousy. And Bailey's instincts told her that the woman was being honest. Trying to be helpful even.

"I'll keep that in mind," Bailey said. "I can be a bit of a workaholic myself, so—"

Her sentence was cut off by the shrill ring of Zane's phone as the screen lit up in front of them.

Meredith looked at her knowingly. "So it begins. I knew when I saw him taking a business meeting before the wedding that he had something in the works."

"Business meeting?"

Meredith frowned. "He didn't tell you? He was here earlier today. Meeting with some guy. We happened to be passing by as they left. I don't know what they were talking about, but it was some sort of business deal."

The phone continued to ring, making it difficult to focus on what Meredith was telling her. Zane. Was here. Doing some sort of business deal. Why hadn't he told her? Was that what he was trying to get at when they'd talked on the beach? She'd assumed he'd been worried about what she thought about him staying retired. Had he been talking about going back to work instead?

"No," she said faintly, "He didn't mention it."

Meredith shrugged. "Well, he tends to be close-lipped until the ink is dry. Doesn't like to jinx things or something." She pushed herself to her feet. "It's good to meet you, Bailey. I'm glad he's found someone nice."

Bailey watched Meredith go, confused, uncertain of what had just happened. Only a few seconds later, Zane appeared with two glasses, one of which he set in front of her. "What was that all about?"

"I'm not sure, exactly." Bailey nodded toward his phone. "You just missed a call."

But as Zane reached for it, her eyes landed on the blue band across the screen that indicated a missed call. She felt the blood slowly leave her face as she read the contact name. "Zane? Why is Andrew Harris calling you?"

And from the suddenly guilty look in Zane's eye, Bailey thought that maybe Meredith had been trying to warn her after all.

fifteen

ZANE STRUGGLED FOR AN EXPLANATION that would make that shocked, slightly hurt expression disappear from Bailey's face.

"Why is Andrew Harris calling your cell phone?" she repeated. Then understanding flashed across her face. "He's the one you met here this afternoon, wasn't he?"

How on earth did she know about that? He cleared his throat, knowing he was only killing time so he could think. "Who told you?"

"Meredith, of course. She saw you, though you obviously didn't see her. *Why* were you having a business meeting with my boss?"

There was no way forward but with the truth. And honestly, the truth wasn't that bad. It was all the other things he couldn't tell her that were eating at him. "He's interested in hiring me."

"For what?"

"I really can't say anything about it, other than what you'd guess … it's obviously software, data analytics, that sort of thing. He asked me not to say anything to anyone else, and I take client confidentiality seriously."

"Okay. Then why didn't you mention that you were meeting him?"

"Come on, Bailey. You can't tell me you'd actually have been fine with it." He knew he'd made a mistake the minute the words left his lips, the tone placating. He hadn't meant to sound condescending, but from the sudden furious shift in her expression, he saw that was how it had landed.

"I don't know," she said in a stiff voice. "I hadn't really thought about it, to be honest. Because you didn't give me the opportunity."

He rubbed his temples. "I'm sorry, Bailey. I thought … I was waiting to see if you and I were going to … you know, make a go of it when we got back home. I figured if you didn't want to see me again, I didn't really have any obligation …"

"Obligation?" Bailey's eyebrows climbed toward her hairline.

He cringed inwardly. "Okay, so obligation is the wrong word. I just meant …"

Bailey stared as if she'd never seen him before. "What I can't figure out is what's so bad that you thought you had to hide it from me. Do you really think I'm so unreasonable that I wouldn't understand you might consider doing some work for an interested party, regardless of whether he's my boss or ex or whatever part of that scenario is bothering you? Have I ever given you reason to think I was that person?"

"No," he said quietly. "Of course you haven't. It's just that …"

She stared at him, waiting. He opened his mouth to tell her what Andrew had said, that he was leaving Constantine Richards, opening his own brokerage, bucking to be her next big competitor. But he found he couldn't. It felt wrong not to tell her, but it felt equally wrong to turn around and spill what he'd been expressly asked not to share. While he was fumbling for what to say, she sighed and rose from her chair, keys in hand.

"I think I'm going to go home now. Do you want a ride?"

It was like a switch had flipped off. Whereas her expression had been sparkling with excitement just minutes ago, now she looked tired, defeated. Not angry—he probably could have handled angry. But disappointed. That was more than he could bear to see, especially when he knew that it was him and his bumbling that had put it there.

"No, I think I might hang out a bit longer. I'll take a taxi back."

She nodded and paused, her mouth opening like she was going to say something. But apparently, she had no more idea what to say than he did, because she closed her mouth firmly, gave him a terse nod, and walked away.

And instinctively, depressingly, he knew that this would probably be the last time he ever saw her.

Bailey retrieved her car from the valet, her elation from only minutes ago vanishing. Maybe walking out of the wedding was a little dramatic, but she needed to think, away from his handsome face, his pleading, hurt look.

It wasn't that Zane had done anything wrong. It wasn't like they were in a relationship where he was obligated to share every moment of his day, his future intentions to do business with a man she couldn't stand. Even if they had been, she considered herself a reasonable woman. She had an idea of what he charged for his services; was she really going to demand he turn down a paying job just because she didn't like the guy?

It was the fact that four days into their acquaintance, Zane thought he had to manage her. That she was going to react badly, that he had to hide things from her. An omission because it didn't occur to him that it might matter to her? That, she could live with. A drawn-out thought process over her likely-unreasonable reactions and his … obligations … to her? That was something else entirely. It seemed to indicate a different kind of relationship than she'd ever wanted for herself—one that involved drama and managed expectations, tiptoeing on eggshells. He didn't know her at all if he thought that was what she wanted.

And that was the problem. They didn't actually know each other at all. This arrangement had created a weird, compressed courtship, thrust together into the same house, pretending an intimacy they didn't possess for the sake of their friends and business associates. They'd shared a steamy kiss, seduced by the magic of still waters and a midnight swim, then another in the wake of a wedding and a stunning Florida sunset. She'd never considered herself to be overly romantic, but she'd let herself get swept away all the same.

But when she was truly honest with herself, she had to admit that Zane was the last person she would have given a second look in West Palm Beach. His nomadic lifestyle, by his own admission, made meaningful connections difficult. The same things that drew her to him—his spontaneity, his slightly offbeat way of looking at the world— were the traits that would make a real relationship impossible. The person she'd been in these four days in the Florida Keys was an idealized, vacation version of herself—a woman who went out on boats with strangers, drank too much and danced with abandon, bought fabulous, expensive dresses that made her look and feel like an island Cinderella.

The real Bailey spent her days in a grind of house showings, marketing, and studying for her next exam, repeated each day with minimal variation. She couldn't just shut down on random weekends—prime house showing times—because her boyfriend wanted to motor to the Caribbean.

Maybe that's not the real him either, her subconscious whispered as she drove down the Overseas Highway back to their rental. *Meredith did try to warn me that he was a workaholic.* But what Meredith considered workaholism was Bailey's life. She'd had a problem with the fact that Zane swiveled between the driven entrepreneur and the free-spirited surfer with the ease of flipping a light switch.

All this time, she had been thinking that Meredith had left Zane because she was the wrong woman for him, but Bailey was far more like his ex than either of them wanted to believe. Zane was the wrong man for both of them.

By the time she got back to the house, Bailey had made up her mind. It was better that they face the facts and end this here and now. They'd had several fun days together, and that would have to be enough. It would be easy to explain to everyone later that they'd broken up. Easier than explaining the reality—that it had been a convenient arrangement for a few days that had accidentally gotten entangled with real feelings. Or the beginnings of real feelings at least. The fact that she'd actually thought their intense, sudden attraction was a product of anything but circumstance showed how swept up in the charade she'd let herself become.

Bailey let herself into the house, walked to the bedroom, and changed out of the dress into shorts and a T-shirt. In the bathroom, she removed her makeup, leaving her skin scrubbed pink and raw. This was the actual Bailey, the one who had defied her parents' expectations that she find a husband while still in college, settle down, and have some kids. The Bailey who had decided to make her own way in the world, build a business from scratch away from her sweet but overbearing family's influence in Georgia. The one who knew she was going to have to work harder than any man to get ahead, to prove that she wasn't some southern peach beauty queen whose sole talent was making sweet tea.

That woman told herself she'd been mad to think that she had the time or the inclination for a relationship with a stranger, no matter how handsome or charming or affecting.

It took a surprisingly short time to pack up her clothes and toiletries into her single roller case, even considering it took her three tries to fold the dress before she gave up and put it back on a hanger. It could ride home draped over her backseat. A reminder of how easily she had almost gotten derailed from everything she'd worked for.

She was in bed but still awake hours later when she heard the front door open and close, the soft, stumbling sounds from the front room saying that Zane was trying to be quiet but failing. Probably a little drunk. Another reason it was better that they ended this now. Her massive margarita had been an aberration and not the norm … maybe it wasn't the same for him.

But she also knew she was just trying to justify a conclusion that didn't sit nearly as comfortably as she wished it would. She lay awake for a long time after the noises beyond her door ceased, and when she woke up shortly after dawn, feeling raw and exhausted, Zane and all his things were gone.

sixteen

It was almost shocking how quickly Bailey's life went back to normal. She left the rental house as the sun was still rising over Islamorada, driving back up the Overseas Highway through the chain of keys until she hit the mainland, with the crush of mad traffic that characterized Miami. A little over an hour later, she was pulling into her Florida-style cottage in West Palm Beach, feeling as if she had just returned from the surface of the moon, not an island sixty miles away.

Less than two hours later, freshly showered and wearing a pair of jeans and a cute chiffon blouse, she was answering calls and work emails at the desk in her home office as if she had never left. Only the beautiful white cotton gauze dress on the back of her bedroom door proved that the last four days had been anything but a fever dream.

The week went pretty much as she could have predicted, after four days away—a crush of urgent tasks regarding two house closings, including a buyer who was making unreasonable demands for repairs (Bailey explained patiently that a seller wasn't required to change the carpet just because the color clashed with the buyer's sofa) and a different seller that refused to make any repairs at all, despite demanding that Bailey get top dollar for his property. There was a new listing to photograph, stage, and put up on MLS, and a closing to attend—her favorite moment was always when the keys were handed over; it was practically the only time in the real estate process when both parties were happy, however temporarily. She took the bright new agent in the office out to lunch and gave him tips about how to build his business from the ground up. It wasn't merely from the goodness of her heart; she'd already decided she wanted to poach him for her own brokerage. If she could help him achieve some early success, there would be no doubt he would go with her.

If she kept herself busier than usual, no one could blame her; after all, everything she'd worked for was on the line. She'd immediately renewed her license and enrolled in the broker's program, which started at the beginning of next month. There was little time to waste.

But on the rare off-hours, when she took a glass of wine or a mineral water out to the Florida room and watched the boats pass on the small canal that backed her house, she knew she wasn't being completely honest with herself.

She missed Zane.

It was insane. She'd known him a mere four days, but he'd brought so much color to that short time that his absence had her feeling as if she was living life through a dim filter. The quiet she'd craved when she bought this small house, fit for a busy single woman, now felt oppressive. Lonely. It only took seeing a happy couple walking through Rosemary Square, his hand in her back pocket, her arm around his waist, to strike a pang of longing into her heart. She had pulled out her phone more than once to dial Zane's number, but something kept her from pressing *Call*.

Self-preservation, she told herself, but deep down she knew the real reason. *Fear*.

Fear that she'd walked away from something that might have been real and good. Fear that even if she contacted him, he'd sneer at her because of the way she'd left him unceremoniously the night of the wedding— even though she was pretty sure that his good-natured face was incapable of twisting into a sneer. Fear that should she commit herself to this, he'd turn around and leave her as cruelly and inexplicably as Andrew had. Because the tiny spike of insecurity that he'd driven into her heart would become a chasm if she let Zane in.

It was a different kind of fear that had her picking up the phone a few days later, though: news of an unusual late-coming tropical storm heading straight for southern Florida and the Caribbean. She had the vague premonition that he hadn't gone straight home to Miami, but had taken his boat out to one of the islands instead. Apparently, she'd learned enough about him to guess that his solution for a slightly bruised heart would be sand, sun, and saltwater.

But the phone simply rang twice and went straight to voicemail. She bit her lip as the tone sounded, then hung up before she could leave a message. What was she going to say anyway? *Just checking to make sure you're not dead or stupid enough to boat through a tropical storm. Okay, see ya never.*

At least Andrew was a distraction, if not a welcome one. Whereas he had formerly been a ghost around the office, doing little but hovering, drinking coffee, and occasionally updating the sales board outside the conference room, now something had lit a fire under his butt. What he did not do was spend any more time in Bailey's presence than absolutely necessary. If she didn't know better, he looked a little guilty. Fine with her. She didn't know what he'd done that would make him look like that, but by her count, she had only three more months before she gave her notice. She was already working on the articles of incorporation for her new business, to be filed the day her broker's license came through.

It was only when Andrew took a listing of his own—the first in longer than she could remember, and in Miami, inexplicably—that she began to understand. As she clicked through the photos of a beautiful Spanish-style bungalow in Coconut Grove, a growing sense of recognition built in her chest. It was confirmed when she got to the last picture in the gallery, of the house's deepwater dock ... and beside it, a very familiar thirty-two-foot boat. She knew the truth even before she zoomed in to see the name painted on the hull: *Celestine.*

Bailey sat back in her leather chair and pressed her fingertips to her temples. Why was Andrew listing Zane's house in Miami for sale? And why, if he'd wanted to sell, had Zane not contacted her directly?

But she knew the answer before the thought even fully formed in her mind. Because he'd decided, just as she had, that they were better off pretending like Islamorada had never happened. And if Andrew and Zane were working together, of course he would think to offer the listing to him first.

That didn't stop Bailey from sweeping into Andrew's office with the flyer, fresh off the office printer, in one hand. She slapped it down on the desk in front of him. "This is Zane Whitney's house."

Andrew didn't deny it. Instead he gestured to a chair across from his desk. "Sit down. Actually, close the door first. I need to talk to you."

She did as he asked and sat, perched primly on the edge of her seat, her heart already pounding as she anticipated his placatory speech on why her ex—whatever he was—had come to him and not her.

Instead, he said, "I'm leaving Constantine Richards to start my own brokerage."

Bailey blinked. "What?"

"Everything's in the works. I've already given my notice to the Florida franchise owner, but things won't be finalized until April."

Exactly when Bailey intended to leave to start her own brokerage. She opened her mouth, and he held up a hand. "I know very well what your plans are, and I think you could be successful at it. But there's an alternative." He took a deep breath. "You could come work with me as my partner."

Now she was really stunned. "I don't understand. You … you want me to be the co-owner of the new brokerage?"

"Hear me out. I know I haven't always been the best boss, but you are without a doubt the best agent I've ever worked with. I have no concerns that you will be equally successful out on your own. But I have a secret weapon. I've got Zane Whitney developing an entire software suite for me, to do everything from onboarding new agents to automating appraisals to a new version of MarketMonkey—with some notable changes, of course, to get around Zane's noncompete. And between you and me, even your stellar track record won't be able to sway agents to sign with you instead of me."

She gaped. Her brain had stopped processing information once she heard Zane's name. "That was what the meeting in Islamorada was about."

He nodded.

"And now you want me to work with you."

He shifted uncomfortably, and she drilled him with a look. "What?"

He cleared his throat. "It was kind of one of Zane's conditions."

Now she was really confused. "I don't understand."

"Before he started work for me, he said I had to tell you about my plans to leave and start my own brokerage … and give you the option to join if you wanted to."

She had no idea how to react to that. "He said you had to take me on as a partner?"

"It wasn't much of an ask, to be honest. I know I was a jerk to you,

Bailey … and pretty much every other woman I've been with over the last couple of years. But you can't deny that we could be incredibly successful together. I've got the money for the technology, and the agents here love you. As soon as you started talking about your broker's license, the whispers began. It's a benefit to me if I can get you on board and a benefit to you because you'll have access to technology that you wouldn't be able to afford otherwise." She opened her mouth, but he held up a hand. "Think about it."

Bailey just stared at him, wide-eyed, and nodded. And then she asked the single question that could bubble through her muddled thoughts. "Why did Zane make that a condition?"

"I'd thought that would be obvious."

She blinked at him. "Spell it out for me."

"He's crazy about you, Bailey." Andrew smiled faintly. "And I honestly can't blame him, even if I figured it out myself a little too late. I put him in a bad position back in Islamorada. I insisted that he couldn't tell anyone about my plans to leave Constantine Richards, including you. I didn't even want him to tell anyone that we were meeting, because I couldn't risk my plans getting out too early. But it never sat right with him. So he said he wouldn't start until I'd told you everything and given you a choice of what you wanted to do."

The revelation left her reeling. So that's why he'd acted so odd. Not because he'd been trying to keep her from knowing about his work for Andrew, but because he knew that her boss was soon to become her biggest competitor, and he couldn't warn her about it. "Why is he putting his house on the market then?"

Andrew gave her a sideways smile. "You would have to ask him that yourself. He's still a client, and I don't feel right sharing that for him. You should go talk to him."

Bailey whipped out her phone to check the time. "With Miami traffic …"

"Oh, he's not in Miami. He's in West Palm Beach."

"What?"

Andrew pulled a business card out of his jacket pocket and handed it to her. It was heavy, glossy, with a modern looking font: *Whitney Software Consulting*. And it had an address of a business park only about twenty minutes from her office. Bailey rose to her feet of her own accord and turned toward the door.

"Bailey?"

She stopped and turned, blinking. She'd already forgotten Andrew was there.

"I could really use an answer soon. About the partnership," he added when she looked at him blankly. "Take some time. But not too much time, if you know what I'm saying."

Bailey gave him a terse nod, but her mind wasn't on the offer. It was on Zane, who apparently had been twenty minutes from her this entire time. He had some things to explain to her.

And she had some apologies to make.

Zane considered himself a risk-taker, even if his risks had always panned out. He'd dropped out of his master's program at Stanford to start a company that, admittedly, sounded a little crazy. He regularly surfed the most dangerous spots in the world, scuba dived the depths of Belize's Blue Hole, took to some of the most unpredictable seas in the Northern Hemisphere with a mere thirty-two feet of fiberglass separating him and the power of nature.

But trusting his future to a man like Andrew Harris surely had to be the dumbest, riskiest thing he'd ever done.

Over the past three weeks, though, he'd realized that the man was both smarter and savvier that he let on. He'd just lost his way a little. He was sharp, he had great business sense, and he was no doubt going to be wildly successful, especially with Zane's help.

But when it came to women, he was a little sketchy.

Still, Zane had made it clear that he wasn't starting a single line of code on the project he was jokingly calling BrokerageZoo (because it contained a version of MarketMonkey and more significantly, because he still thought Andrew was a bit of a horse's behind) until he came clean with Bailey and told her everything. It had been three weeks, and he had stopped jumping every time his phone beeped or buzzed. Except for that one call that he'd missed from Bailey when he'd had intermittent cell service on his boat, she hadn't contacted him, and he knew he couldn't explain until Andrew had talked to her. He had begun to think that maybe Andrew would never get around to it.

He should have never trusted his romantic prospects to a man who'd messed up his own love life so badly.

It wasn't as if Zane didn't have enough to keep himself occupied. He'd spent the last few weeks doing the boring, mundane work of starting a new business: filing for his licenses, incorporating his one-person business for tax purposes, renting a tiny office space in an unpopular building on the edge of West Palm Beach. (He'd learned long ago that working in close proximity to his boat and his refrigerator was not good for his productivity or his waistline.) And now that all that was done, he'd taken the final step of listing his house in Miami for sale.

A very large part of him knew this could all be for nothing.

And then came a knock on the office suite's main door.

Zane stood from where he'd been working on his business's new website, frowning slightly as he went to the door. He flipped the lock and opened it … and found himself looking directly at Bailey Jensen.

"Hi," she said shyly. "Can I come in?"

He stood aside for her to enter and then let the door fall closed behind her.

"Nice place," she said vaguely, looking around.

He followed her gaze, took in the dingy gray walls and the generic office furniture, and let out a little laugh. "No, it's not. But it's quiet."

She stopped and looked at him now, really looked at him, confusion written over her face. "What are you doing here?"

"I live here."

"In this office?"

He chuckled. "No. In West Palm Beach. I've rented a place while I wait for my house in Miami to sell." He cringed a little. "Sorry about not listing with you. I thought it might be a bit awkward."

"Business is business," she said, but it had the sound of a platitude rather than anything she actually believed. "Andrew told me everything."

Zane heaved a sigh of relief. "Then you understand why I couldn't tell you any more. I'm so sorry, Bailey. I wanted to. I just felt like I was stuck in … an ethical dilemma. I gave my word, and I take that seriously, even when it involves someone I … care about."

She just stared at him, and he realized with a painful throb of his heart that he was messing this up again, just as badly as he had the night of the wedding. Why was it he could give a TED Talk without a hitch, but when it came to talking about his feelings, he clammed up like a moron?

Bailey broke into a smile, and he realized he'd said that last part aloud. "Because at the end of the day, you don't go home to a bunch of people from a TED Talk?"

The uncertainty and nervousness melted away. "Bailey, I was an idiot. I'm sorry. I just didn't know how …"

She waved a hand. "I didn't make it easy for you. I didn't really let you explain. I was scared of getting derailed from my plans, because you were so not what I was looking for at the time, and it was like everything I worked for didn't matter when I was with you …"

"And here I thought it was because of what Meredith told you."

She blinked in surprise. "What?"

"I talked to Mer later that night. She told me that she'd spoken out of turn. She hadn't really meant to scare you off. She just wanted you to know that what you were getting of me from a weekend in the Keys isn't the real me. Or, at least the whole me."

"I don't understand."

"The fact is, Bailey, I'm both. I can disappear for weeks at a time into a project, barely coming home to sleep. And I can just as easily disappear to the islands on my boat and not think about work the entire time. And then I repeat the process. It's how my brain works. It's kind of all or nothing for me. For someone like Meredith or you, I know that can be difficult to deal with."

"You know, Zane, it's not exactly like I hold typical hours myself. I haven't been home before ten o'clock any night this week, and I worked through the entire last weekend."

He bowed his head. "I realize that. But I also realize that it was my fault that things fell apart with Meredith." He held up a hand at her alarmed expression. "I don't want to get back with her, not that I could now. I realized at the wedding that she and I were a mismatch. Oddly, Tony and Mer really do fit together. He's dependable, if a little dopey at times, and I think Meredith likes that. She likes having someone to take care of when she comes home. I was always a little too independent for her taste, I think.

"But I never put our time together first. I was always so consumed with running a business and my responsibilities to my employees that she only got what was left. And if we … that is, if you were willing to give me a chance … I needed to be able to prove to you that I could put you first."

A smile had begun to form at the corner of Bailey's mouth. "And that was what all this is about? Moving to West Palm Beach? Starting this business?"

He nodded. "I'm doing things differently. I'm consulting this time … all I'm doing is building stuff for other people to use. When I'm done, I'm done. And I'm smart enough this time to build in days off and Monday lunches and evenings at home in my schedule." He swallowed. "We're both busy people. I didn't want us to have to meet for dinner halfway between here and Miami. I wanted to be close enough to come over if you had a rough day or a free hour or five minutes for a really good kiss."

The smile broke free for real. "You moved here so you could kiss me for five minutes."

He swallowed. "As often as you'll let me."

The smile widened to impossible dimensions, and then he saw it no more, because she threw her arms around his neck and kissed him. He didn't hesitate to draw her against him, burying one hand in her hair and mussing her braid beyond fixing, pouring every last bit of sincerity into the touch so she would understand what he was so imperfectly trying to say.

"Yes," she said.

"Yes what?" He didn't remember asking a question, though right now he was having a hard time thinking at all.

"Yes to whatever you're asking. Yes to giving this a shot. Yes to Monday lunches and evenings at home in front of the TV and weekends on the boat." She smiled a little shyly now. "Yes to us."

He pulled her close and kissed her again, more briefly this time, then smiled. "I've never really believed in love at first sight. Maybe I just lacked imagination. Or faith. Sometimes, when you know … you just know."

She smiled again. "You sound like an English major."

"Only with you," he said. "You bring out the romantic in me."

And he kissed her again, slow and long and deep, so she would know he was telling the truth.

epilogue

One year later

"I JUST NEED TO RUN into the office to check on something. I promise I won't be long."

Zane smiled at Bailey from the driver's seat of his car. He'd already shifted from his usual work wardrobe of jeans and a band T-shirt to full-on island wear—a funky shirt printed with flamingos, cargo shorts, and the flip-flops that she'd tried and failed repeatedly to make him get rid of. She reached for the door handle then impulsively leaned back toward him to steal a kiss. "I love you."

"I love you. And I will still love you when your quick trip into the office turns into forty-five minutes of putting out last-minute fires."

Bailey grinned at him. "You know me too well. What can I say? I'm the boss."

"That you are."

Bailey climbed out of the car, the sound of passing traffic on the nearby Overseas Highway blotting out the rumble of Zane's car's engine, then strode into the tiny beach cottage that served as her office on Islamorada.

Bailey and Zane had tried the arrangement in West Palm Beach. They really had. He'd stuck to his vow of only taking on consulting projects that would allow him to spend Monday afternoons and weekday evenings and random five-minute kissing intervals with Bailey. Not surprisingly, after six months, he was turning down clients because his work hours were spoken for, and he wasn't willing to devote himself to a company with multiple employees again.

Bailey had accepted Andrew's offer and joined him at the new brokerage as a full partner. They divided the work according to their strengths: besides their own listings, she worked on agent development and continuing education, while Andrew dealt with marketing and various business concerns. He'd been right—once they'd settled their differences, they worked remarkably well together. Their first quarter revenue was more money than Bailey thought she'd ever see in her life.

And within six months, she realized she'd never been so miserable.

Zane might have been available for all those things, but Bailey was never around to eat with, watch TV with, and kiss. The brokerage absorbed every waking hour; agents called her with problems at home, and she'd already had to let one agent go because of contract irregularities. It was one thing to be her own boss, but she hadn't quite realized how much she would dislike being someone else's. When she shared this conclusion with Zane, he'd smiled ruefully at her—it was the same conclusion he'd come to more than two years earlier.

It wasn't until they found themselves taking off every Wednesday afternoon to motor to Key Largo or Key West or Islamorada that she realized what she really wanted. So she'd plugged coordinates into his GPS/chart finder (yes, she'd finally figured out how to use all the complicated hardware on the boat), and she'd taken them to the hurricane-damaged house on the canal that Zane had showed her on their first night together.

"It's still on the market," she'd said. "I think we should buy it."

He looked at her. "What are you saying?"

She'd worked the diamond ring around her third finger, as if it had the answer. "You can do your work remotely from anywhere. And it's only about an hour from the mainland." She smiled up at him. "If we start now, we could probably be finished before the wedding."

And to Zane's credit, even though he'd been hinting around the idea for more than three months, he'd just smiled and said, "I think that's an excellent idea."

Which was how they were here, full-time residents of Islamorada and proud owners of two small businesses. Zane was working out of his apartment while the finishing touches were put on their new home. Bailey had rented the commercial space on the main drag of Upper Matecumbe and hired an assistant to watch the phones and help her with everything and anything. To say that real estate was different in the Keys was like saying there was culture shock when moving to Mars, but fortunately Brianna was a Keys native with real estate experience, and she navigated the often-odd intricacies of the island in a way Bailey never could.

"Hey, Brianna," Bailey said as she breezed through the front door. "We're off to the hotel now. I just wanted to check to make sure we finished up the—"

"Daniels listing? Done." Brianna gave Bailey a reproving look. "You're getting married tomorrow, Bailey. I've got this under control. Go."

"And can you drop by and make sure that the painters have finished—"

"Already on my list," Brianna said, holding up her notepad. She smiled. "Go marry that delicious nerd. I'll make sure the house is ready to move into by the time you get back from your honeymoon. I will even send you pictures if you promise that you will not call me about work for the next two weeks."

"Yes, ma'am," Bailey said with a smile. "What would I do without you?"

"God only knows," Brianna returned dryly. "Work yourself to death, probably. Did I mention that delicious nerd of yours? Go."

Bailey chuckled, gave her bossy assistant a little wave, and returned to the car where Zane conspicuously clicked his watch. "One minute and forty seconds," he said approvingly. "That might be a record."

"Well, Brianna threw me out of the office, so …"

"Have I mentioned how much I like Brianna?" Zane leaned across the seat to kiss her, long and slow, and she knew she must have a dreamy look on her face when he pulled away.

"I love you," she said again. She couldn't keep herself from saying it, over and over.

He smiled. "I love you, too. I'm so glad you said yes to us."

Bailey reached for his hand and squeezed it, filled with a happiness that once, she could never have even imagined.

"Every day and always."

About the Author

Carla Laureano could never decide what she wanted to be when she grew up, so she decided to become a novelist–and she must be kinda okay at it because she's won two RWA RITA® Awards. When she's not writing, she can be found cooking and trying to read through her TBR shelf, which she estimates will be finished in 2054. She currently lives in Denver, Colorado with her husband, two teen sons, and an opinionated cat named Willow.